THE COUNTRY HOUSE
LONDON PREP: BOOK 6

THE COUNTRY HOUSE
LONDON PREP: BOOK 6

JILLIAN DODD

Editor: Jovana Shirley, Unforeseen Editing

Jillian Dodd Inc.
Madeira Beach, FL

Jillian Dodd, The Keatyn Chronicles, and Spy Girl are Registered Trademarks of Jillian Dodd Inc.

ISBN: 978-1-953071-72-9

SATURDAY, OCTOBER 19TH
Cheers to that.
1:30PM

"CAN YOU PASS the crisps?" Harry asks, bumping his shoulder against mine.

I dig through the tote bag full of food that Helen sent with us, finding a bag of crisps already opened. Its top is rolled down and clipped closed. Helen must have grabbed it from the pantry before putting it straight in the bag for us.

"Yeah, sure." I pull out the crisps and hand them to Harry.

"Your mum's the best," Harry says to Noah as he dips his hand into the bag. A second later, he's inhaling a mouthful, crunching away.

"We should have just eaten at the house first," Noah responds. His focus is on Harry, who's now licking salt off his fingers.

"We needed to get on the road," Mohammad disagrees as I start passing out the packed lunch.

There's a juice box for each of us, leftover roast beef sandwiches, the bag of crisps, carrot sticks, and a handful of granola bars.

I give everyone a juice box and sandwich and keep the bag of carrot sticks in my lap.

"Are there any sweets?" Mohammad asks as he stabs the

straw into his apple juice.

I check the bag again but find it empty.

"Nope," I reply, biting into a carrot stick. "But there are granola bars for later."

"Not exactly candy, but at least she didn't forget Noah's granola bars." Mohammad frowns.

"They're for everyone," Noah says in between bites of his sandwich.

"They're for you," Mohammad disagrees. "Helen knew no one would want to be stuck in a car with you when you're hungry—that's why she packed them."

"She packed them because Noah's picky," Harry disagrees. He's digging around in his coat pocket, obviously looking for something. His juice box and sandwich lie unopened on the seat next to him.

Noah rolls his eyes. "I'm not picky."

"It's true," Harry replies.

I take another bite of my carrot stick and watch Harry move to his other pocket, searching through it.

His eyes immediately light up. "I found them."

"Found what?" Noah asks, looking up from his sandwich.

"Candies," Harry says, holding out a handful of un-wrapped candy that apparently came from his pocket.

I try not to gag.

"Mate, that's disgusting," Noah says, shaking his head.

"I pocketed some at the house," Harry replies with a shrug before popping a piece into his mouth.

"Oh, yes, please!" Mohammad says excitedly. He leans toward Harry and grabs a piece of candy from his hand.

I watch in horror as he deposits it into his mouth. He didn't even wipe it off. Or blow on it in the hopes of cleaning it. *No.* He just popped it right into his mouth.

"Mohammad, that's gross!" I say, immediately losing my

appetite.

"It's just candy," he replies.

"You're missing the point. It's candy that came from *Harry's pocket.*" I flare my eyes at him. "A pocket that's probably full of lint. And dirt. And who knows what else?"

I look over to Noah, wondering if he's going to chime in, but he's halfway through his sandwich and not paying us any attention.

"If you're worried about germs, don't be," Harry says, pulling a flask out of his jacket pocket. "This will kill anything." He brings the flask to his lips and takes a swig before handing it to Mohammad.

Mohammad accepts it and does the same as they both finish off the candy.

I look out the window and try to ignore them. We're getting close to the outskirts of London, and I watch as we pass through an unfamiliar neighborhood.

"Are you ready to get out of the city?" Mohammad asks me.

"I've never actually been outside of London, so it's pretty exciting," I say with a smile, looking forward to seeing more of England.

"It's nice. The fresh air. Open spaces," Noah adds.

"And no parents!" Mohammad reminds.

"Cheers to that," Harry says, taking another swig from his flask before dropping his hand back into the bag of crisps.

"So, do we have any other plans for the weekend, besides shooting and that dinner thing?" I ask Harry, eager to get the weekend started.

"We can do whatever we want. I've got a few ideas though, and of course, the staff knows about our arrival," Harry says.

"The staff?" I ask.

"Mum rung ahead, obviously, so we will get the proper greeting. A full tour. Champagne on the terrace. Those delicious mini sandwiches," Harry says, pinching his forefinger and thumb together, pretending to hold one. "Then a quick lawn game to ease us into dinner and drinks."

"Wow, fancy," I say with a grin.

"As expected." Harry grins back at me. "But we'll get time to relax. The staff is around only as much as we want them to be."

"I don't care as long as we get a chance to play some FIFA," Noah says.

"Absolutely," Harry says. "Then, tomorrow, the real fun begins."

"What do you have in mind?" Mohammad asks, rubbing his hands together.

"Shooting in the morning," Harry states.

"Should I be concerned about this whole *shooting* thing?" I ask, looking between the three of them.

"Don't worry. They're just clay pigeons," Noah informs.

"There's nothing to fear," Harry agrees, waving off my concern. "There will be a professional with us the entire time. It's a blinding time."

"Like that will stop you," Mohammad scoffs. "I clearly remember you almost shooting me once."

I snap my head in Mohammad's direction.

"What?" I ask.

Because he has to be joking … *right?*

"It wasn't my fault; it was the vodka," Harry disagrees. "I thought you were the target. And anyway, I was thirteen and smashed."

"You went shooting drunk?" I ask, growing more and more convinced that I should probably—*no, definitely*—sit tomorrow out.

"One too many Bloody Marys," Noah explains.

"Exactly. It was a simple miscalculation," Harry agrees.

"That's dangerous!" I scold.

"It was hilarious. You should have seen Mohammad run. It took us the rest of the morning to find him." Harry laughs.

"Weren't there any adults with you?" I ask. "Didn't you get in trouble?"

"It was just Noah and me at the time. You usually have someone with you, but we cut him loose. Wanted to venture out on our own," Harry explains, almost sounding fond of the memory.

"Which was a terrible idea!" Mohammad says, crossing his arms over his chest.

Apparently, he hasn't gotten over being shot at.

And honestly, I don't blame him.

I switch my attention to Noah, who's concealing his laugh behind his hand.

"Noah! You allowed him to do that?" I say, pointing to Harry, who doesn't at all seem concerned. If anything, he seems amused.

"Don't blame me!" Noah says. "Harry wasn't the only one who had unknowingly consumed booze at the family brunch. I'd thought I was drinking tomato juice."

There's a sparkle in Noah's eye, and I can't tell if he's telling the truth or lying.

"Well, the booze didn't do anything to ease my pain! I was terrified," Mohammad says, his eyes going wide.

"*We know*," Harry and Noah say at the same time.

"We found him hiding behind a tree," Harry explains.

"Made us dump all the ammunition before he'd come out and go back to the house with us," Noah finishes.

"Which was a smart decision," I reply, giving him props.

"Once he came out, he was fine though. We went home,

made him take a hot shower, and then put him to bed," Noah says.

"Aww, Mohammad," I say, reaching for his hand and giving it a squeeze.

He gives me a quick smile, but it's quickly gone.

"It was traumatic, not funny, and I don't want to talk about it anymore," Mohammad says, ending the conversation.

I glance at Harry, half-expecting him to keep poking fun at Mohammad.

But he doesn't.

"Fine, back to the plans for the weekend," Harry continues, not missing a beat. "Apart from shooting tomorrow and dinner Tuesday, we can do whatever we'd like. There's a village not far from the house. A pub to spend the day hidden in."

"I've got to keep up on my workouts," Noah says.

He's finished his juice and sandwich, and I watch as he places the empty wrappers into the grocery bag before pulling out one of the granola bars.

Mohammad looks between the granola bar and Noah, giving him a pointed look that I wouldn't want to be on the receiving end of. But it doesn't seem to faze Noah.

"You're allowed a break," Harry disagrees.

"Coach doesn't think so," Noah says, biting into the granola bar.

Harry starts on his sandwich, speaking as he chews. "Please, you carried the match this morning. I don't think he's going to hassle you."

Pride flashes across Noah's face, tinting his cheeks pink.

"Today, we played a solid game," Noah agrees. "But the match last week … it wasn't a shining moment for me."

"It really wasn't," Mohammad says, his face souring at the memory of how bad Noah played.

I flare my eyes at him and tap him with my elbow.

"Mohammad's right. It was a shit game. Anyway, I know Coach was happy about our win today. I'm just hoping that he doesn't think it was a fluke."

"Well, I guess football is on the agenda as well," Harry says to me.

I bite into another carrot stick as I think. "We can make it fun then. Maybe I could be the coach, make you guys run sprints!"

"Hell no," Mohammad replies adamantly.

"You going to whip us into shape?" Harry laughs, not taking me seriously.

"I'm serious!" I swat my hand in the air and turn to Noah. "What do you think?"

"I think that sounds like a terrible idea. If anyone should lead us through a practice, it's me."

I roll my eyes at him. "No fun."

"Whatever. As long as I'm not sprinting, I'm happy to be out of the house. And school." Mohammad sings, "Freedom at last!"

He takes the flask from Harry and is downing some of the alcohol when his phone rings.

"How the fuck ..." he says, staring at his phone.

"What?" I ask.

But Mohammad doesn't say anything before answering.

"Hello?" he says timidly into the phone, his face going white.

I share a glance with Harry and Noah, who both look confused.

And concerned.

"Yes, I know," he says under his breath, handing Harry back the flask. He rolls his eyes, the phone staying up at his ear. "What?! Are you serious?!" His eyes go wide as his mouth falls open.

I lean in closer so I can hear and immediately connect the dots.

It's his mom.

"I'm sorry," he mutters, looking annoyed. "Yes, I'll send you a picture when it's done. All right, all right. Love you too."

Mohammad hangs up and lets out a loud moan as he brings his hands up to cover his eyes. His hands shift, and he moves them, running his fingers back through his hair.

"Ugh, what bullshit," he groans.

"It was his mom," I say to Harry and Noah, who both still look confused.

"What did she say?" Noah asks.

"Apparently, Mum reached out to my professors to see how I'm doing in my courses, and she wasn't thrilled to find out that I'm doing shit in History."

"That's not a surprise," Harry chimes in.

"And now, she's forcing me to do extra-credit homework over break," Mohammad huffs.

"Bollocks. You're on break," Harry says.

"Exactly! But Mum said if I came back and didn't have it done, she'd basically murder me." Mohammad rolls his eyes. "She's even making me send a photo as proof."

"Well, I guess you'd better get it done then," Noah states.

Mohammad hangs his head.

I rub a circle on his back with my palm.

"I don't even know where to start," he finally admits.

"Do you have trouble in History?" I ask.

"No."

"Then, what's the problem?" I ask while keeping my hand on his back.

"His problem is that he gets distracted," Noah cuts in.

I turn to Noah. "By what?"

"I just don't pay attention in class," Mohammad says.

"I don't pay attention in class either," Harry adds, patting Mohammad on the knee.

"Because you're bored?" I ask them.

"Because I have both Olivia and Sarah in my class! There's way too much hotness in that room," Mohammad says. "Mum should understand that. It's a miracle I'm not failing."

"Maybe you need to take a little accountability for your actions. You can't blame someone else for distracting you," I try to tell him.

"Ah, leave the bloke alone. He's having a rough time. *Women*—they really do scramble your brain," Harry agrees.

"They do," Mohammad fires back.

"Anyway, I'll help you." Harry says it nonchalantly, but it captures everyone's attention anyway.

Because Harry? Helping Mohammad? In History?

"I thought the only thing you noticed in History was Miss Gunters?" Noah teases, causing both Mohammad and me to laugh.

"Way to pour salt in my wound," Harry says, looking offended. "And as a way to spite Miss Gunters, I've started paying attention in class."

"So, to spite her, you're going to start doing well?" Noah asks, trying to keep up.

"Exactly. She was always calling me out before, and I think she liked that I didn't know the answers. But now that she's got herself a lover, I'm going to show her I can't be her little toy anymore. So, every time she calls on me, expecting me not to know, I know," Harry says proudly.

"Good for you, mate," Noah says, a genuine smile forming on his lips.

"Thank you." Harry smiles back.

"Well, shit, I'll take all the help I can get," Mohammad says to Harry before they fist-bump.

"Have you thought about changing classes next term?" Noah asks me.

"I've thought a bit about it, but I haven't decided," I reply. "I might do French instead of Latin."

"And you're telling me this now?!" Mohammad says. And it's clear he's about to have a crisis.

"I didn't say I was switching for sure. I'm just thinking about it."

"Well, don't. I need you in Latin," Mohammad says, causing me to smile.

"We do make a good team," I agree.

"We do."

"What about Statistics? You're not the biggest fan of the course," Noah says, looking at me through his thick lashes.

And I suddenly understand what he's getting at.

He wants to know if I'm going to stay in Stats.

With him.

"I'll stay in Stats," I tell him, my heart pounding in my chest.

"I think that's a good idea," Noah replies. His hand grazes mine as he reaches into the bag, pulling out another granola bar. He must be hungry after his match this morning.

I try to focus on Mohammad.

And Harry.

But all I can seem to do is watch Noah looking at me while he eats.

Where to find me.
3:00PM

THICK TREES LINE a long, extended gravel driveway. Noah rolls down the window, and I look out as we approach an enormous Georgian home.

"We're here," Harry says, barely glancing outside.

"Harry, this is beautiful." I suck in a breath of fresh air, the beauty of the house settling in as we drive closer and closer to it.

Windows punctuate the entire front of the two-story house, and meticulously cut grass is all that separates the house from the circular driveway. We roll to a stop in the car.

"It's an eighteenth-century manor house my parents renovated and had modernized," Harry informs.

The fact seems second nature to him, like he's had to tell numerous other guests the same piece of information. Only a beat later, a woman and man walk out the front door, and the car door is opened.

We didn't have time to pack up any of our snacks or collect our phones, so we all scramble to gather our stuff and toss them into the bag before we get out.

Harry's feet are the first to hit the ground.

"Afternoon, Muriel," he says.

Noah's out next, followed by me and then Mohammad.

"Good to see you, Harry," she says in a firm voice. Her hair is pulled back in a sleek bun that matches her light-gray two-piece suit.

"You as well. Everyone, this is Muriel," Harry says. "Muriel, you know Mohammad and Noah. And this is Mallory."

Muriel's gaze moves from Mohammad and Noah to me. She smiles, then extends out her hand.

"Nice to meet you," I say, shaking it.

"Lovely to meet you," she replies.

"Muriel is the house manager," Harry explains.

I nod but don't say anything.

"Let's get you all inside and settled," Muriel says, motioning for us to move inside.

I glance over my shoulder, seeing that our luggage is already being unloaded.

When I turn back, I catch Muriel watching me.

"Your luggage will be taken to your rooms and your bags unpacked," Muriel says. "In the meantime, how about a tour of the house for Mallory?"

Harry turns to me. "Do you want the tour?"

"I don't mind."

"A quick one," Harry says back to Muriel.

"Of course. Champagne?" she asks, motioning to the entryway table. There are four glasses of champagne on it, one for each of us.

"Thank you," Harry says. He walks to the table, picks up two glasses, and hands them to me and Noah before getting his and Mohammad's.

I take a sip and look around. The entryway is beautiful. It's more of a hall than a room, and the parquet floor stands out against the dark blue walls. White trim frames the ceiling and every doorway. Large pots of plants make the room feel full, and with the sunshine streaming in, I can't help but smile.

Because Harry's house is beautiful.

And I'm with three of my best friends.

"There are just a few things I'd like to go over with you, Harry. As usual, we've got the driver on call for you if you need a lift into the village."

"Great," Harry says, sipping his champagne.

"We're a fully staffed house," she says more to me than Harry. "With a cook, two maids, a butler, and the gardener. But if you have any requests, please come to me, and I'll make sure you have everything you need."

I glance at Noah and Mohammad and see that neither of them is paying any attention to her. Mohammad's drinking his champagne and looking at one of the paintings. Noah's looking out the window, watching as the rest of our luggage is unloaded.

Muriel claps, grabbing all of our attention.

"Now, the house is two main floors with the grounds and gardens outside. There are shaded terraces and many spots for you to explore," she explains.

She motions for us to follow her into a room off the left of the entryway. Everything is painted in dark rich tones of navy, green, and grey. It reminds me of the Ralph Lauren showroom in New York. Everything is moody and sleek, making the giant rooms feel more intimate.

"This is the breakfast room and morning room," she says, leading us quickly through two rooms.

At her pace, I barely have a chance to look at anything that's in them. I notice a wooden table, a large marble fireplace, and lots and lots of chairs.

"On the main floor, there's also the drawing room, living room, mudroom, cloakroom, kitchen, cellar, the library, and the main bedroom."

Muriel moves swiftly into the drawing room, which has multiple seating areas and a large table in the center. Every room we move through features open fireplaces, sculptures, beautiful lighting, large portraits, and big ferns. It's easy to tell it's been renovated even though the decorating has a slight

Victorian feel.

We follow her into a bedroom next.

"Harry, we've put you in the main bedroom," Muriel says.

I look around the room, finding it bright and airy. The walls are lighter than the rest of the house—a pretty grayish-blue. Black furniture fills the room along with a four-poster bed with spindles that rise almost to the ceiling. White bedding makes it look cozy and luxurious at the same time.

I'm not sure what I expected. I thought Harry's country house would be cold, like his parents.

But this doesn't feel like a place that people use to show off their wealth.

It feels like a home.

From the placement of chairs to the partially burned candles and all the books lining the shelves, it's obviously been lived in.

Or at least, it appears to be.

Harry walks to French doors that lead out onto its own patio. The sun is shining as he unlocks the doors and pops his head outside.

He instantly smiles.

"What a day," he says, stepping back inside and closing the doors.

"Lovely weather," Muriel agrees. "Once we finish the tour, I'll leave you to the terrace."

Harry and Muriel are the first out of the bedroom. Mohammad, Noah, and I follow behind.

"What's through there?" I ask, pointing to a hallway we haven't been down.

"The kitchen," Noah says in my ear.

"And the cellar," Mohammad adds.

"Cellar?" I question.

"Wine cellar," Mohammad clarifies, shooting me a wink.

I laugh.

"Do you three usually sneak wine when you're here?" I whisper to Noah.

Mohammad overhears and says, "We might have nicked a few bottles before."

"Now, Harry has full access though," Noah chimes in.

I look from Noah to Harry. He's walking beside Muriel, his normally long strides reduced to match her slow, steady pace. And I think it's finally hitting me that all of this is going to be his one day.

He really is the heir to an empire.

And I can see why he'd be scared to give this all up.

"Your rooms are upstairs," Muriel says, leading us back to the main entrance hall and to a wide staircase. "There are three bedrooms with en suite bathrooms and dressing rooms made up for you."

We follow her upstairs and then enter one big hallway with one door after another. Quickly, she shows Noah and Mohammad into their rooms.

"I'll show Mallory to her room," Harry calls out to Muriel.

He takes my elbow and guides me just down the hallway, to the room next to Noah's. With the amount of space between them, I know that the rooms must be big.

"This is my usual room, but I thought for this trip, you would like it," Harry says, ushering me through the door.

I step inside, immediately taken aback.

"It's been coined the Asian room," Harry says in my ear.

I scan the room, seeing that the name *definitely* fits the decor. Everything is black and red. The same four-poster bed that was downstairs has a matching sister in this room.

Red striped wallpaper coordinates with the red-and-white

bedding and rugs.

"Harry, this is amazing," I say, my mouth sliding open.

"Everything in this room was brought back from Shanghai," Harry replies. "But that's not even the best part."

He motions for me to follow him, and quickly, we're standing in the bathroom.

"Holy shit," I mumble, doing a full three-sixty spin.

The same rugs cover the entire floor, and thick velvet curtains sit opposite a large black bathtub. Two Asian-style chandeliers give the room a warm glow.

"Thought you'd like it." Harry smiles.

"Like it? I love it! Harry, this is so cool."

"My parents do have good taste," Harry replies. "Well, good *decorators*."

"I can't believe this is your house. It looks like something you'd see in *Architectural Digest*."

"The bath isn't half bad," Harry replies with a playful smirk.

"Not half bad," I repeat, my eyes scanning over everything again. But then I'm reminded of what Harry just said. "Wait, this is usually your room?"

Harry leans back against the freestanding marble sink. "Normally, yes."

I furrow my brows. "Then, why am I in it?" I ask.

Harry's blue eyes find mine. "Usually, I'm with my parents on these trips, so I never have the chance to sleep in the main bedroom. If you think this washroom is crazy, you should come down and check out the shower in mine. It's got three showerheads!"

Harry's words are lighthearted, but I can tell there's something else going on.

"So, you gave it up for the shower?" I ask, trying to figure out how much of this is just a joke to him.

"That might not be the whole truth," Harry says, pushing off the counter. "I didn't want a constant reminder of what was to come."

I walk over to him, placing my hand on his shoulder. "Your trip to Shanghai?"

He nods.

"So, I figured it'd be best to avoid any pitiful nights by sleeping in a different room. Besides, it cheers me up, knowing that you'll be sleeping in my bed," he says, pinching my chin.

A grin is back on his face, and I can tell his mood has already lightened.

"I'm not sleeping in *your* bed. I'm just sleeping in *a* bed. There's a big difference," I point out.

"Of course. But if you ever get lonely, you know where to find me." Harry shoots me a wink before grabbing my hand. "Come on. I have a surprise."

As we walk out of the bedroom, I see the same man who unloaded the car bringing my suitcases into the room.

Harry weaves us around him and into the hallway, where we find Noah and Mohammad with Muriel.

"Let's head out to the terrace," Harry says, looking between the boys. "Have a fag and relax while everything gets unpacked."

"Sounds good," Mohammad replies.

I wait for Noah to agree, glancing over at him. It's not until then that I notice his eyes aren't even on Harry.

They're on his hand.

Well, *our* hands.

Linked together.

I immediately want to loosen my grip and drop Harry's hand, but I don't. If anything, that will bring more attention to the harmlessness of it.

Noah's gaze flicks up to us, and quickly, coloring comes back to his cheeks as he smiles at Harry.

"Let's go," Noah agrees.

Harry drops my hand as we walk back down the stairs and out the heavy French doors.

The sun is out in full force, and I tilt my chin up toward it. It's bright and warm.

"No way!" Mohammad says, excitement in his voice.

I follow his gaze to a large wooden table. It's situated underneath an open black umbrella with a rich wooden stand. Benches with neutral cushions are on either side of it, and the table is filled with food and drinks.

"You had this all set up for us?" I turn, asking Harry.

"It's what we traditionally do when guests arrive. If the weather's shit, we have tea and sandwiches inside, but since it's so nice …" Harry says.

"We've arranged everything per your request," Muriel says, suddenly at Harry's side.

"Thank you." Harry surprises me when he takes her hand in his, giving it a warm squeeze.

Muriel smiles.

"Gerald is just putting your cases away, and then he will be out. Please let him know if you need anything, and don't hesitate to come find me," Muriel says, addressing all of us.

"Thanks, Muriel," Mohammad says, already shoving a sandwich into his mouth.

"Thank you," I say before she goes back inside.

Once she's gone, I take the time to look around. The terrace reminds me of something you'd find outside an Italian villa. The grounds are gravel, and tall, uniform hedges give the space an enclosed feel. I walk around the corner, looking out into a wide green yard.

"The gardens are on the other side of the property," Noah

says, coming up next to me.

"It's gorgeous here."

"It's great in the summer, although we usually visit for Christmas," Noah explains.

"If I were Harry, I'd want to be here every summer."

"I think Harry would rather be where his parents aren't." He places his hand on my shoulder and smiles at me.

"Come on," I say, lacing my arm through his and leading us back to the table.

Mohammad's already seated and making a plate for himself. Harry's next to him, sipping on a fresh glass of champagne.

"What do we have here?" I ask, looking at the spread of food.

"Champagne, fruit water, soda," Mohammad says, pointing to a bottle chilling in a silver bucket of ice and a glass pitcher next to another bucket of ice, which is filled with glass Coke bottles.

"I requested sandwiches and crisps," Harry says, nodding toward the table. "And cookies. Shit of substance."

Noah suppresses a laugh.

"Looks great," Noah says, picking up a cookie and examining it.

"Tastes great too," Mohammad says, loading two sandwiches and two cookies onto a plate.

"Let's move the benches, so they're in the sun," Harry says, setting his glass of champagne down on the table.

Mohammad sets down his plate, and they both lift up a bench, moving it out from underneath the umbrella.

"Want to move the other one with me?" I ask Noah.

He looks at the bench and then to me with a smile. "Sure," he replies.

I go to one end, and he goes to the other. We pick it up at

the same time before the butler rushes out of the house, saying, "Let me."

"That's all right, Gerald," Harry cuts in, joining me and Noah, champagne in hand. "We decided last minute to get some sun."

"Of course," Gerald replies. "Is there anything else I can get you?"

"Not yet," Harry says. "But thank you, Gerald."

"I'll bring over some tables for your drinks," Gerald says anyway.

Harry nods, then plops down onto the bench, crossing his outstretched legs in front of him. Mohammad joins him on the bench, his plate in hand.

"Want a drink?" Noah asks me as I sit down too.

"A water would be great," I reply as Gerald brings over two wooden tables for us to set our drinks on.

"I'd be happy to get that for you. Would you like me to make you up a plate as well?" Gerald asks.

"Just a water for now," I say. "But thank you."

"My pleasure."

"Gerald, don't listen to her. Make her up a plate and bring her a glass of champagne too," Harry calls out.

Gerald smiles bashfully.

"I want to toast," Harry explains.

"Well then, I'd better get a glass too," Noah says, moving to get up.

But Mohammad beats him to it.

"I'll get it," he says, springing up as Gerald comes over to me, tray in hand.

He sets down the water and plate, then gives me a flute of champagne.

"Thanks." I smile as Mohammad rejoins us, two glasses of champagne in hand.

He gives one to Noah before sitting back down next to Harry.

"Cheers to the start of a cracking weekend," Harry says, holding his glass up in a toasting position.

"Cheers," we all say, clinking glasses.

I lean my head back, letting the sun warm my face. "This is perfect," I say dreamily.

"It's very unusual weather," Noah comments.

"We never get this nice of weather this late in the year," Mohammad agrees.

"Beats playing a match in the rain," Noah says, taking a sip of champagne.

"Aren't you used to it by now though? It seems like it's always raining in London," I ask.

"Used to it, yeah. But that doesn't mean I like it," Noah answers.

"Obviously, he prefers the dry weather. Did you see him today?" Mohammad says, his eyes glazing over.

"Today was all right," Noah says humbly.

"Today was insane," Mohammad disagrees. "What happened out there? Where did that come from?"

"What he means to ask is, can you do it again?" Harry teases, lighting up a cigarette.

"It was just a good day." Noah shrugs.

"Good day?" Mohammad gapes, his mouth falling open.

Noah rolls his eyes and looks at me like he wants me to agree with him.

"I'm siding with Mohammad on this one. I think you're selling yourself short." I give his shoulder a nudge.

He shouldn't be so bashful about it. He did great.

And he deserves to celebrate it.

"It's not a big deal." Noah flushes.

"It's not a big deal? It's a *huge* deal. If you keep that up, every girl in school is going to want you," Harry chimes in.

"And then they're going to want me," Mohammad says triumphantly.

"And what about your dear Naomi?" I ask, pointing out his obvious overlook.

"Any status elevation at school that benefits me will, in turn, benefit her. So, I think she'll be pleased," Mohammad counters.

"I'm glad you're finding a way to use my good match to your benefit," Noah says with a chuckle.

"*Phenomenal* match," Mohammad corrects with a grin.

Noah rolls his eyes, but I can tell he's happy about the compliment.

"At least you got confirmation that your ridiculous exercise regimen is paying off," Harry says, inhaling his cigarette. "Otherwise, that would have been a letdown."

Noah laughs. "That's true."

I pick up one of the tea sandwiches and offer it to Noah. He takes it happily.

"You should eat too," Noah tells me.

"I'm pretty full from our lunch in the car."

"At least have a cookie," Noah insists.

He picks one up and gives it to me. His hand grazes my fingers as I accept. My face flushes, and I quickly look away from him. I take a bite of the cookie, washing it down with the champagne as I try to focus on something other than Noah.

And how close he is sitting next to me.

I bring my eyes to Harry.

He's leaning back, taking in the sunshine, his cigarette hanging between his lips. His collar is popped, and his champagne is still in hand.

My mind shifts back to the tour.

To what Harry said in the bedroom about Shanghai.

And all I can think is that I don't want him to go.

"Harry, do you want to talk about your trip?" I ask. Because I don't want to dance around his feelings. Or his reality.

He keeps his head back, not moving to look up at me. "Nope. I'm going to ignore the fact that I have to return home in a few days and then leave with my parents."

"Maybe you should stay here."

"It's not a bad idea," Harry agrees.

"You have to go though," Noah cuts in.

"Does he?" Mohammad asks boldly.

"What do you think? Would country life suit me?" Harry asks, sitting up and looking between the three of us.

"You'd get bored," Noah answers.

"Get bored? This place is great. He has a full staff. No parents and fuck all to do," Mohammad says.

"I agree." Harry clinks his glass against Mohammad's. "I'll take up a sport."

"Or learn to live off the land," Mohammad rings out.

"Harry lives on an estate," Noah says, bringing them both back down to reality.

"You're just upset at the thought of me leaving London. But you could visit. And I'd learn a trade. Maybe I could build something," Harry offers.

"Or you could stick to making my life less boring and stay in London," Noah says.

"Do you think your life's boring?" I ask, moving my gaze to Noah.

"He means less fun," Harry answers. "Anyway, Noah's right. London suits me."

"What do you think suits me?" Mohammad asks, tearing into another sandwich.

"You know, I could see you liking it out in California," I

say.

"Mum would be too thrilled if I went to the States for university," Mohammad replies.

"I thought when you tried to talk her into letting you go before, it didn't go well?" Noah asks.

"That's because I wanted to run wild in the hills of LA. Cruise down the highway in a convertible. Not shack up with engineering textbooks at some technology school like she wants," Mohammad says.

"Ah," Noah replies, finally understanding.

"Exactly. I guess I could always get into uni there and then drop out. Make my millions through matchmaking but for high-end clientele."

"Interesting. You think people in the States need you?" Noah asks, raising his eyebrows.

"I think everyone could use a little Mohammad. I have a lot to offer. I could call my business ..." Mohammad taps his chin as he thinks. Suddenly, his eyes light up, and I know he's got it. "*Mohammad Matched.*"

"Fucking brilliant name," Harry says.

"Thank you." Mohammad beams.

"Maybe you should consider basing it here instead. Then, we can all be together," I say, suddenly thinking about college.

"Well, not all of us," Harry says, his gaze shifting away.

Noah looks at him and frowns.

"Eventually, we will all be back here together." Noah reaches over and pats Harry reassuringly on the shoulder.

As Harry looks toward Noah, his expression visibly lightens.

"It's a plan," Harry agrees, cupping Noah's forearm in his hand in a quick embrace.

My phone buzzes in my pocket, capturing my attention. I pull it out, seeing an email pop up in my inbox. I scan the subject line, my eyes flying wide open. I look up to the boys with growing excitement.

"I just got an email back from a headmaster!" I screech.

"You mean from Mr. Compton?" Harry asks, his brows weaving together.

"Wait, seriously?" Mohammad asks.

"Let me see." Noah grabs my phone out of my hand.

"I haven't even read it yet," I say, trying to take it back.

But Noah ignores me. His full focus is on my phone. "You sent this?" he asks, looking up at me with wide eyes.

"Sent what?" I ask.

"The first email," Noah says, showing me that he scrolled back to see my initial outreach email. It's when I didn't want to stay at Kensington and tried to contact other headmasters.

"Oh my God, you literally rubbed his nose in the fact that he had a shit debate team." Noah gapes at the phone.

I try to take it from him again but fail.

"I was desperate! And obviously, it worked." I smirk. "Headmaster Compton even got calls."

"Could you imagine if you weren't at school with us anymore?" Harry says, looking struck.

Mohammad steals my phone from Noah.

"It's a good letter. I can see why they're interested," Mohammad says sweetly.

I grin at him. "Thanks."

"So, what was his response?" Harry asks.

I finally get my phone back, scan the email, then say, "Apparently, he contacted Headmaster Compton this week and heard I was staying enrolled. But he told me to keep him posted if I ever decide to switch schools."

"Only you would somehow find a way to have a headmaster wanting you to transfer," Noah says, looking an odd combination of impressed and concerned.

"Usually, you or your family has to have an interview, depending on if you transfer or grow up in the school," Harry adds.

"Did you have to interview?" I ask Harry.

"I'm a Brooks," he scoffs.

"What about you two?" I glance between Noah and Mohammad.

"We've both been at Kensington since we were young," Noah answers.

"Aww. I can so picture you two as little kids. Noah running around with a football. Mohammad chasing after girls."

"And what about me?" Harry asks.

"Well, you're easy. You probably loved playtime, pretending to be a king or something." I laugh, imagining Harry as a child.

Harry lets out a sharp laugh, and I know I'm right.

"What about you? What were you like as a kid?" Mohammad asks me.

"I was too serious as a child to care for games," I try to say with a straight face.

"No way," Mohammad says, raising an eyebrow in question, causing me to laugh.

"I don't know. We traveled. I always enjoyed that. Anna and I have been friends since we were kids. She always liked making bucket lists over summers and wanted us to date guys who were friends. We used to go get takeout and watch movies, and sometimes, my parents would let us hang out in the park after school. When we were younger, my mom would go with us, but she'd give us our space."

"Well, I haven't heard of a more wholesome childhood," Harry says.

"I guess it was."

"It sounds nice. Nothing like my childhood," Mohammad says, a look of terror flashing across his face.

"Was your childhood *so* bad?" I tease.

"*Yes*, it was. Actually, for a while there, it was great. I was the one and only. And then my parents kept on making babies, and slowly but surely, the house became dominated by women. Figures," Mohammad huffs.

"Maybe that's how you learned so much about women though," I offer. "Aren't you always saying that you're a ladies' man?"

"Trust me, the only thing my sisters have taught me about is patience. You can't learn anything about wooing a woman from your siblings."

"What?" I laugh. "I think that's totally not true."

"You're an only child," Mohammad points out. "You wouldn't know."

I glance at Noah and nod my head toward Mohammad while flaring my eyes, urging him to help me out a little.

A smile envelops his face. He must get the hint.

"I think what Mallory is saying is that, while you might not get dating advice from your sisters, you do learn a lot about women from living in a house full of them."

Mohammad furrows his brows, contemplating that. "I might have picked up a few tricks here and there."

"Exactly!" I nod, smiling that I was right.

"So, what exactly have you learned?" Harry asks with interest.

Mohammad's eyebrows shoot up. "Well, generally, if tears are involved, hot chocolate usually solves the problem. If you need a little peace and quiet, never try hiding to get it. Because women see it as a game and they'll always find you."

I laugh, imagining Mohammad trying to hide from his sisters.

"What do you do then?" Noah asks seriously.

"I hide in plain sight. I go into the kitchen and pretend I'm making something healthy, like steamed carrots. They can't run away fast enough." Mohammad grins.

"Genius," Harry says in praise.

I just roll my eyes.

"I can never hide from Mia," Noah chimes in. "She's always barging into my room."

I look in his direction, my cheeks immediately flushing. Noah catches my gaze, a hint of a smile on his lips.

Because last time Mia barged into his room, he was about to kiss me!

"You're not alone," Mohammad says, raising his glass of champagne at Noah.

"Luckily, I'll be moving into my house soon, and we can hang out there without disturbance. My parents are always out," I say, trying to change the subject.

"Shit, you haven't even told us about your house yet," Harry says, his eyes softening. "I'm sorry I pulled you away from your viewing early."

"That's all right. I got the full tour."

"So? What is it like?" Mohammad asks, sitting up eagerly.

"It's beautiful. It overlooks the river and has the coolest glass-enclosed balcony. It's more industrial than I expected from my parents. The ceilings are tall, and the kitchen is open to the living and dining space. There's the main bedroom and then two bedrooms upstairs."

"Do you think you'll feel at home there?" Noah asks.

"Honestly, yeah. It will be nice to have my own bedroom again. There are huge wall-to-wall windows in almost every room. And in my bedroom, I have a pretty window seat," I explain.

"Think we'll hang out at your house much?" Harry asks with interest.

"Honestly, I don't know. Usually, I have the house to myself, so we should be able to. But I'm sure it will be a madhouse for a while, with moving in and decorating. Although my mom already has a designer, so knowing her, it will be done quickly."

"Will you redecorate your room?" Noah asks, sipping his champagne.

Harry gets up and fills a plate with sandwiches and cookies. Gerald looks frightened at the fact that Harry is actually filling his own plate and rushes to his side. After a second, Gerald picks up the champagne, coming over to refill our glasses.

"I'm not sure," I say, momentarily distracted. "My room was silver and cream in New York. Really modern, so it would go with this apartment. I guess I'll just have to see what my mom wants to do. It would be fun to change things a bit."

"I hate decorating," Harry says, handing both Noah and Mohammad some of the sandwiches.

"Do you *have* to decorate?" Mohammad asks.

Harry shrugs. "No, I suppose not. But I hate the idea of it. That's why I find it nice that we've kept our house in London for so long."

"Has your room always been the same?" I ask.

"More or less." Harry nods.

"What would you want this time, if you redecorate?" Noah asks me.

I take a sip of my champagne, thinking. "Maybe something a little darker to make it cozy. The walls are this pale pink. It's pretty, and I love the window and all the light it lets in. But it also overlooks the city, and it sort of feels bright but empty, you know?"

"You made that picture in art for your room, right? The one with the gold and purple in it? Maybe you could have your mum decorate around that," Noah offers.

Mohammad looks over at him, raising his eyebrows.

Noah looks back at Mohammad and shrugs. "What? It's just an idea."

My lips pull into a smile. "It's a really good idea actually. Maybe I'll talk to my mom about it."

My mind shifts to what I want my room to look like. I know I'd want to have space for photos. I have pictures with Anna. The photo of Harry and me. Noah's family. I have books from home and the painting I made in art.

And then there's Noah's collage.

Maybe I could convince my mom to let me have a bulletin board. Somewhere to display all of that.

"I can't wait to show you guys. There's actually a pool table there," I say, thinking about the apartment.

"Sweet! It will be the Boys' Club 2.0!" Mohammad says excitedly.

"At least if I need somewhere to escape to, I know where to go," Harry says.

"You mean, besides any of your other houses, my house, or Mohammad's." Noah chuckles.

"You forgot the club." Harry smirks. "And, yes, other than that."

"Once your parents get here, I'll suggest to my mum that they all go out for dinner," Mohammad says. "Then, we can chill at your place."

I smile at Mohammad. "I'm sure they'd love that."

"Then, we will have your house to ourselves and can party!" Mohammad goes on, causing Harry to burst out in laughter.

"Like we don't already party," I tell him.

Harry laughs as Gerald brings over the tray of cookies, offering us more. I happily take one, washing it down with the rest of my champagne. Harry inhales two sandwiches as Noah picks at another cookie.

"If I have any more food, I might burst," Harry says, standing up. He extends his arms out over his head in a slow, catlike stretch.

"I love coming to your house," Mohammad says in a daze. His head falls back, an easy smile on his lips. "There's always food. And booze."

"And even sunshine today," Noah adds, looking up at the sky.

"I think we should stay outside then. Enjoy the day," Harry says.

"I agree," Noah replies.

"What do you want to do?" Mohammad asks, looking lazily in Harry's direction.

"I had them set up croquet. Let's take our drinks and go play," Harry suggests.

"No way!" Mohammad says, excitedly jumping up.

Harry leads us from the terrace around to the lawn.

"Harry, you had them set up the net?" Noah asks, his eyes going to the soccer goal at the far end of the lawn.

"I figured you'd want to practice," Harry says like it's no big deal.

But I know to Noah, it is.

Noah looks back at it, a wide smile settling on his face. "Mate, thank you," Noah says, pulling Harry into a hug.

Harry's face flushes at the attention, but he hugs Noah back.

"This is awesome," Mohammad says, taking in the croquet setup.

There are lawn chairs looking out at the grass with thick pillows resting on them. He flails himself onto one, spreading his body out in a dramatic lounge. I laugh as I watch him.

"Do you know how to play?" Noah asks me.

I look out at the lawn. "I think I get the gist. There are balls, things to hit the balls with, and mini goals to go through, right?"

Noah chuckles. "Basically, yeah. This is your mallet," he says, picking up a wooden stick that looks like an oversize judge's gavel.

He hands it to me, and I practice by gently swinging it back and forth in front of me, getting a feel for it. Noah watches me intensely.

"And I hit the ball and send it through the hoops, right?" I ask.

"Exactly, but there are more rules than that."

Which means that Noah's about to explain them all.

In depth.

I rest my mallet on the ground, knowing I'm going to be here for a while.

"We don't need to play by the rules," Mohammad calls out to us.

I look up, seeing him holding a mallet in one hand, his champagne glass in the other.

Noah ignores him.

"Of course we have to play by the rules," Noah says more to himself than to anyone else. "Anyway, why don't you take a few practice shots?"

Noah's hand grazes mine as he helps me.

"Thanks." I flush.

"Course. You'll do great," Noah says approvingly.

I hit one of the balls, sending it flying across the grass.

"Oh shit," Noah mutters.

"You should yell *fore* with that swing!" Mohammad says with a laugh, running over to us.

"At least we know she's got some fucking power," Harry

adds in.

"I think you might need to be a bit gentler," Noah says in a sultry voice.

I flick my gaze over to him before refocusing on another ball. When I pull back the mallet, I do it slowly before gently tapping the ball, causing it to barely move.

"Maybe a bit more force," Mohammad says.

I walk and hit it again. This time, I send it across the grass at a good medium speed. I do it a few more times, trying to get a feel for it.

"Nice one," Noah says when I make it through a hoop. "I think you've got it."

I grin, spinning around to face Harry and Mohammad.

"Noah says I'm ready," I tell them, excited to play.

But neither Harry nor Mohammad is watching me. Gerald is refilling the champagne glasses in their hands.

When he's done, Harry walks over to us, a glass in each hand.

"Look, there are only two rules you need to follow when playing croquet," Harry says. "Firstly, you never, *ever* play without a drink in your hand. And secondly, you want to try and get the ball through the hoop. However, if the hoop starts to move too much on you *because of too much alcohol,* getting somewhere close enough to it will do."

Noah laughs, his head falling back as he does.

"Are those your rules?" Noah asks Harry.

"Those are it," Harry confirms with a naughty grin. He hands me one of the champagne glasses.

"Those basically negate the real rules," Noah says, looking at me. "You really should hold the mallet with both hands to keep it steady. The object of the game is to advance the balls around the lawn by hitting them with your mallet. You'll score a point for each hoop made in the correct order and direction. And if you can't put it through the hoop, hit your opponent's ball out of the way, which is fun too."

"And we're off!" Mohammad calls out, hitting the first ball.

Noah laughs, walking over toward him, leaving me and Harry alone.

"So, how did your talk go with Helen and Gene?" I ask.

"What, this morning?"

"Yeah. She told us at breakfast they wanted to wait for you to talk about the party before Noah's match."

Harry nods. "They just wanted to see where my head was at."

"And where is your head at?" I ask, looking up at him.

"Here," he replies, moving closer to me. His blue eyes look clear and certain. Like he actually means what he says.

I smile. "I'm glad."

"I'm glad too. They just wanted to make sure I was all right. Offered to let me stay at their house." Harry shifts, hitting the ball, pushing it right through the hoop. "Even suggested they ring my parents to see if I could stay with them instead of going to Shanghai."

"Really?" I ask, the word happily slipping off my tongue.

"I had to tell them no. But it was a nice thought," Harry answers.

"It is nice they offered," I agree. "I wish you'd consider taking them up on it."

Harry glances away, his forehead creasing. "The question was only a courtesy. It was a gesture. I knew—and they knew—that I would never be able to get out of it. Anyway, it's only a few days, and then I'll be back."

"I can't believe you're bailing on me just when I need you," I say, swinging the mallet back and hitting the ball.

"Just when you need me?" Harry laughs, but I can tell I've

piqued his interest.

"Yep. My parents are getting here. I'm moving. And I'm somehow supposed to manage those two in your absence," I say, glancing over to Mohammad and Noah.

Mohammad's lying down on the grass, letting Noah hit the ball off him with the mallet, like he's taking a chip shot with a golf club.

Harry laughs again, the corners of his eyes creasing as he smiles.

"They'll manage without me," he replies. "But if you want, I'll ring you when I'm there. You can tell me about the house. Keep me up to date on what those two get up to while I'm gone."

"Promise you'll call?" I ask seriously.

"Of course."

"Good."

I move out of the way, letting Harry take a shot, and he sends it through the wicket easily.

"And I need lots of pictures. I'm pretty jealous you get to go to Shanghai. I mean, your family issues aside, you have to make the most out of your time in the city."

"I'll send photos, but I'm not sure I'll get much time to explore. I'll do my best though. Just prepare for boring photos."

"You can send me the play-by-play." I laugh. "Waking up. Your breakfast. Your car ride to the office. Hopefully, a few from sightseeing after your meetings. A cocktail or two."

"You're not as concerned with photos of Shanghai as you are with photos of me," Harry says playfully. He shifts past me, hitting the ball. "Worried I'll get myself into trouble?"

A laugh escapes my lips, and I cover my mouth with my hand. Harry looks up at me, his eyes sparkling.

"I have no doubt you'll get into trouble if you want to," I

35

say, shaking my head. "But no. I was just thinking that I love the city. And I'm going to miss you."

"I'll send photos then. Some of the city. Some of me." Harry smirks, and I quickly understand what he's getting out.

"Appropriate ones only," I say, trying to sound stern.

"How about, I'll send whatever photos I want, and you can be the judge of which ones are *appropriate*?" Harry says smoothly.

I take in a breath, surprised by Harry's words.

"Although it might be good for you to miss me," Harry says, reflecting. "Maybe I'll get a warm welcome home if I make you go cold turkey without me for a bit."

My mouth falls open. I'm shocked that he'd consider that.

"You wouldn't ..." I say seriously, growing nervous. Because if I didn't hear from Harry while he was gone, well, I think I'd panic. I need to know that he's okay. That he's doing all right. And I need him to know that we're here for him, waiting for him to get back.

That he has us to come home to.

"Would it work?" Harry asks, sounding too amused.

"No!" I laugh, giving him a shove. "It wouldn't. And I would be upset if you didn't message me and let me know how things were going. So, if you want a warm welcome home, you'd better message me."

Harry's face softens, his smile growing. "All right, I promise I'll message."

"Good," I say, shaking off my previous panic.

"Now, let's see that swing of yours," Harry says, motioning for me to hit the ball.

More champagne.
4:00PM

"DO YOU WANT to grab another sandwich?" Mohammad asks me and Harry later, his mallet swinging lazily at his side.

"Another? I'm not sure I can handle any more food."

Mohammad rolls his eyes before glancing over his shoulder at Noah.

"Then another drink," he says before wrapping his arm around me.

A second later, he's leading me off the lawn toward two lawn chairs. I glance over my shoulder at Harry, raising my eyebrows at him.

Because what is going on?

Harry shrugs in return before turning his attention to Noah.

"I'll make us a plate," Mohammad offers as I take a seat.

I nod and watch as he walks toward the terrace. I lean back in the chair, letting my face tilt up toward the sun. It feels amazing on my skin. The guys were right; we couldn't have asked for a more beautiful day.

I close my eyes and smile.

"Got you some more champagne," Mohammad says.

I peek over at him as he sits down next to me. He's got champagne for me and a plate filled with sandwiches for him.

"Thanks." I take the champagne flute and have a drink before setting it down on the arm of the chair.

Harry and I finished off our last glass well before our game was over.

Mohammad is studying Harry and Noah as he eats. Finally, he says, "So?"

"So what?" I repeat, not sure what he's asking.

"You said you wanted to tell me about yesterday. About this morning."

I look at him, finally understanding.

He wants to know what's going on with me and Noah.

"I don't know where to start," I say, thinking over the past twenty-four hours. "So much has happened."

I glance out at the lawn, watching Noah and Harry talk as they play. Harry leans forward, hitting the ball backward through his legs. Noah watches, looking amused.

"What changed things?" Mohammad asks, taking another bite of his sandwich.

I press my lips together and let my eyes slide shut. Yesterday flashes through my mind. How unsettled I felt about everything.

And then finding Noah's poem.

"Noah's birthday present to me," I answer, turning to look at Mohammad.

"Birthday present?" Mohammad's brows pull together with his question.

"Yeah. He gave me his sweatpants on my birthday."

"Wait ... are you telling me that Noah finally won you over by gifting you joggers? Joggers!" Mohammad's eyes widen in disbelief.

"What? No!" I laugh. "You have to let me finish."

Mohammad's chest deflates as he leans back in his chair, relaxing. He extends out his hand, urging me on.

"When Noah gave me the sweats, it wasn't only about the sweats. He put a poem he wrote about me in the pocket. And I didn't find it until yesterday. I didn't even read it until after school."

"He wrote you a poem?"

"Yeah." I nod. Butterflies form in my stomach. "It was

about a storm. *About me.* About how I came rolling into his life unexpectedly. About how I made him feel. He didn't know whether to love me or hate me for it."

Mohammad narrows his eyes, his forehead creasing.

I continue, "He called me his dear raging storm. He told me, through his poem, how he felt. That he was scared and overwhelmed, just like I was."

"Fuck, he's good." Mohammad shakes his head once.

"Yeah."

I pick up the champagne, taking another drink.

We both look at Noah. I watch his chestnut hair bounce as he chases after Harry, who has stolen Noah's mallet. Mohammad and I share a glance, both smiling.

"It makes sense though. You can't beat Harry out with charm," Mohammad says.

"It's not a competition."

"Maybe not. But guys think strategically. Noah knows Harry's strength. He wouldn't try and win you over with moves alone," Mohammad argues.

"But that's the thing … Noah *does* have moves. And the more time I spend with him, the more I realize that I have no control. I have no countermoves."

Mohammad grins at me.

"Get to experience a few of them this morning?" he says, waggling his eyebrows.

I roll my eyes in response, but I can't help the grin that forms on my face.

"You're right though. Noah's got game," Mohammad continues, stealing the champagne from my hand, taking a swig.

I swat at his hand, but he pulls the glass away from me, handing me his half-eaten sandwich instead. I frown at him but take the sandwich.

"So, after you read the poem, what happened?"

"After I read the poem, I was in shock. I read it over and over. Walked all the way back to the hotel in a daze. And then I just, somehow, ended up at Noah's."

"Whoa," Mohammad says.

"I know! I'm not even spontaneous, but I just couldn't help myself," I say excitedly. Because it was a pretty big moment for me.

"Then, what happened?"

"Noah opened the door, and all I wanted to do was kiss him. But then Mia was there, and it kind of ruined the moment. We ended up in the kitchen, and Mia was going on and on, so I finally blurted out that I read it."

"Oh shit. Was he surprised?"

"He definitely seemed like it. We went up to his room and basically talked through everything. I told him how I felt. He told me that things were different now. That he couldn't just be my friend. We decided to give this *us thing* a shot. And then we kissed."

Mohammad's eyes go wide. "No."

"Yes."

"No!" Mohammad says again, looking struck.

"No?" I repeat, completely confused.

"That's mad. How was it?" Mohammad asks, taking another drink of my champagne.

"Honestly, it was hot," I admit.

"I'm going to need my own glass for this." Mohammad stands up and finishes off *my* glass of champagne before running off to the terrace.

"What's his deal?" Harry calls out to me.

I shrug my shoulders and hold up my hands in response. Because who knows what Mohammad's deal is. I already told him this morning about Noah and me, but even now, he seems shocked by every sentence that comes out of my mouth. But it also kind of makes it fun that I have someone to gush to about it. Usually, Anna and I would meet up and talk about these things, but with her not here, it's different.

"Okay," Mohammad says, plopping back down into his chair. He hands me a fresh drink, keeping the other in his hand. "Go."

I laugh and shake my head at him.

"Well, we were talking on Noah's bed. And finally, I thought we were going to kiss. We came so close to doing it when Mia walked in. She pretty much dragged me out of the room, wanting attention."

"Shit. And Noah let that happen?" Mohammad is practically giddy.

"We didn't really have a choice. Anyway, I went to the bathroom after a while, and Noah met me in there. And that's where we finally kissed."

Mohammad's forehead creases. "And that was hot?" He looks freaked out that our first kiss was in the bathroom.

"So hot. It was … amazing. It was more than I ever could have imagined. I know we kissed in the lunchroom, but it was different. This time, it was just us. He pinned me against the counter," I say, my cheeks flushing.

"Damn. You got tongue, didn't you?"

"Oh yeah." I grin.

"Too much information," Mohammad says, a shiver running through him like the idea of Noah and me kissing freaks him out.

"You're the one who asked!" I laugh at Mohammad, but quickly, my eyes slip shut as I remember kissing Noah. The way he made me feel.

"That's true. Then, what happened?" Mohammad asks with interest.

"Are you sure you can handle knowing more?" I raise my eyebrows at him in question.

He rolls his eyes but urges me to go on. I take a gulp of champagne before continuing.

"Well, after we kissed, that's when I had to go see the apartment. And then Harry messaged me, upset. I rushed back to the Bvlgari, and when I saw his duffel, I instantly freaked. I thought something major had happened. But then he told me he wanted us to go away, and about the trip. So, I spent the rest of the night packing."

"I'm not surprised Noah was the one to finally do it," Mohammad reflects.

"What do you mean, you're not surprised?" I snap my head in his direction, weaving my brows together.

"He said you'd never make a move."

My mouth slides open in shock. "Noah said that? Noah is the one who would never make a move!"

I've gone as far as begging him to kiss me, and he would never give in. But now, he has the audacity to say that I was the one who wasn't going to make a move.

The nerve!

"Whoa, chill out, Miss America. The moves were done, and you got your kiss."

"You mean, Noah got his kiss," I correct, feeling a little annoyed.

Mohammad gives me a stern, serious look before I roll my eyes.

"Fine," I say, giving in. "Regardless of who initiated the kiss, you're right. We did have our first kiss yesterday. And a lot more of them this morning."

I can't help but smile, thinking about kissing Noah in his bedroom. On the sidewalk. I think I could pretty much kiss Noah anywhere. My face grows flush at the prospect.

"Okay, okay," Mohammad says, pinching his face in. "I get the point. But what about this weekend?"

"What about this weekend?"

"Is it just a chance for you two to, you know, shag?" Mohammad whispers.

I pull my head back in surprise.

"What? Of course not." I shake my head. "Harry was the one who asked me to be here. It's not like Noah and I somehow planned a weekend away right after things with us changed. It's a time for us all to be together. To support Harry before his trip."

Mohammad's gaze moves out to the boys for a brief moment before he looks back at me. "And then?"

And then?

I swallow, thinking about what is going to happen after this weekend. About what Noah and I have talked about.

"And then Noah and I are going to see what exactly we have," I answer.

Mohammad grins. "Oh shit. That sounds hot."

"I'm being serious." I roll my eyes.

"I am too. Maybe I need to tell Naomi that I'm ready to figure out exactly what we could have together. Be poetic and shit."

"And shit …" I laugh.

"I know someone who could give me pointers," Mohammad says, like he's seriously contemplating it.

"Honestly, I'd take them."

"Noted," Mohammad says, taking another swig of his champagne.

"Are you two ready to go in? I'm fucking beat," Harry says, running up to us in our lawn chairs.

Noah follows behind, a wide smile on his face.

"You're not beat. You just *got* beat," Mohammad corrects,

looking between them.

"Oh, is the game over?" I ask, realizing that since Mohammad and I have been talking, I haven't really paid attention.

"I didn't *get* beat. We weren't keeping score," Harry says, grabbing Mohammad's champagne glass and downing what's left. "And I'm ready for some Xbox."

A little tipsy.
5:00PM

HARRY LEADS US to a living room with a big-screen TV and a comfy sofa. The room isn't decorated as much as the rest of the house, but it's still beautiful. A rich leather sofa and two low-slung chairs are situated to face the television. Harry draws the curtains closed.

"Noah, want to pick a game?" he asks. "I'm going to go change."

"Yeah," Noah replies, turning on the television and grabbing a controller.

Mohammad falls sideways onto the couch and pulls out his phone as Harry leaves to change.

"Someone's upset," Mohammad says when Harry's gone.

"He's a little salty he lost," Noah agrees, sitting down next to Mohammad.

I move to sit next to Noah but stop myself, deciding to leave that space for Harry. I plop down into one of the low-slung chairs instead.

"Salty *and* dramatic." I laugh. "But that's Harry."

"He'll be fine," Noah says, pulling up a game for them to play.

When Harry gets back, he's changed out of his clothes and into a robe.

But instead of having it tied at the waist, it's hanging open, revealing his underwear and lack of a shirt.

He looks like a hot mess.

"What a look." I laugh, noticing his pack of cigarettes sticking out of his pocket.

"Wanted to be comfortable," he says, shooting me a wink.

Apparently, his mood's lifted.

"I think in that outfit, you were just hoping to distract Noah," I say, teasing them.

"I've got laser focus," Noah replies, handing Harry a controller. "If Harry wins, we will be on even ground."

"And I will win," Harry says, bumping his shoulder against Noah's.

They start the game, and I pay attention as they get into it.

But after a while, it just gets boring.

Someone messes up; they yell.

Someone wins; they cheer.

Mohammad proceeds to ignore them, his gaze on his phone.

I pull out my own phone, clicking on random apps. But there's nothing new in the world and nothing interesting going on to distract me.

"This is boring," I mumble, sliding down in my chair.

Harry glances in my direction.

"Why don't you go get settled? Take a bath before drinks and dinner," he suggests.

"Shit, maybe I should," Mohammad says, perking up with interest.

"I think he was talking to Mallory." Noah laughs.

"What time are drinks at?" I ask, glancing at the time. It's just a little past five.

"Muriel's arranged for drinks at half past seven," Harry says.

"I'll watch you play for a bit longer, then go call my dad," I decide. "One of the conditions to me coming here was that I'd call and check in every day."

"Really?" Noah asks, pausing the game.

"He would have given in either way," Harry says, glancing over his shoulder and giving me a wink. "I can talk anyone into just about anything."

"What do you mean?" Mohammad asks.

"My dad spoke with Harry," I say, reminding them.

Harry told them this morning, but it was right before we left, and a lot was going on.

"Oh?" Mohammad questions.

"He was just worried. Made me promise to keep her safe. Be a gentleman."

"If that's even possible," I reply, sticking out my tongue at Harry.

"Shit, was it awkward?" Mohammad asks.

"Nah. He actually sounded pretty cool. I told him we could meet at the club for a celebratory drink when he arrives," Harry says.

"You make it sound like you have a date with my dad."

"A date with Mr. America! How delightful." Harry laughs.

Noah looks at me in question.

"I'm more excited to meet your mum," Mohammad cuts in. "I think we'll get along famously."

"That's only because you want to go shopping with her," I reply, raising an eyebrow at him.

"She's offering to restock your closet. You should be thrilled," Mohammad says.

"We wear uniforms. I don't need new clothes," I mumble.

"Between me and Mohammad, your parents' attention is going to be kept busy," Harry interjects.

"I don't know what your fascination with my dad is." I shake my head at him.

"I respect how strict he is with you," Harry says.

"Not strict enough to tell me I couldn't come," I point out.

Harry waves off my comment. "Either way, it's a good thing. It's clear he cares about you."

"Yeah, but he gave me the *be safe* speech too. He wasn't sure me coming on a *boys' trip* was a good idea, especially without parents." I roll my eyes. "Although his speech wasn't nearly as bad as Helen's. Hers was on a different level of embarrassment."

I flare my eyes, remembering how freaked out Helen was when she found out that Noah and I were more than friends.

But as soon as the words are out of my mouth, I instantly regret them.

Because Harry and Mohammad don't know about the conversation I had with her.

And Harry still doesn't know that there's anything going on between Noah and me.

At least, not officially.

Harry lifts his head in interest, his blue eyes finding mine. "What do you mean?"

I open my mouth, but nothing comes out. I don't know what to say. Or how to spin this.

"She's talking about the speech my mum gave us before we left," Noah says, cutting in.

I look over to Noah. When I meet his eyes, he gives me a subtle nod.

"Exactly. I didn't think she'd be serious about going over

rules with us," I add. "I guess she's just worried we all might have too much fun without parental supervision."

"Well, I know that I plan to." Harry laughs.

Noah laughs with him, shaking his head.

"I don't know why she bothered. We're going to do what we want anyway," Noah says.

"You'd break your mom's rules?" I ask, butterflies erupting in my stomach.

"I wouldn't *break* them outright," Noah says.

Does that mean he's considering breaking the no sex rule?

"Of course he wouldn't," Harry cuts in. "And anyway, Helen just cares about us. That's all her rules and guidelines are about."

"That's true. Although you'd think she'd talk to me about them in private," Noah replies, clearly annoyed.

"Mums are like that. They preach about boundaries, but when it comes to their kids and their friends, they have none," Mohammad agrees.

"I don't know ... I think Harry's right. Helen is just concerned. Besides, I think we have a bond." I smile.

Helen is like a second mom to me. And I know she feels responsible for Harry and Mohammad too.

It's just who she is.

"Let's be honest here. If Helen fancies any of us the most, it has to be me," Harry says, placing his hand on his chest. His smug expression causes Noah to laugh.

"Between you two, it's a wonder I get any attention at home." Noah shakes his head as he looks between me and Harry. He bites down on his lip, and I know he's trying to conceal a smile.

"You're the lucky one though. You get Helen as a mum," Harry points out.

"She considers you her son too, you know," Noah says

seriously.

"Well, hopefully, she doesn't think the same about me," Mohammad says.

"What do you mean?" I question, looking at Mohammad.

"The *last* thing I need is another mum in my life," Mohammad replies, causing both Noah and me to laugh.

Harry smiles at Mohammad, but a second later, his attention is back on the paused game. He grabs the controller, hitting play. I rest my head on the back of the chair as they start a new game. I try to get comfortable. My legs want to be outstretched, but then my neck will end up in a funny angle. I sit in the chair, growing annoyed.

Mohammad is seated upright on the couch, watching, engrossed as Noah and Harry play now. I try to focus on their game, but my eyes quickly grow tired. I huff in annoyance.

Noah looks over his shoulder at me. "All right over there?"

"I'm uncomfortable." I try not to pout, but it feels like it's been the longest day of my life.

Plus, I'm a little tipsy.

"You're tired," Noah says.

"I'm not tired," I say back. But my lips officially betray me when I start to yawn.

"You need to rest. Do you want to go take a nap?" Noah asks. He quickly pauses the game, causing Harry to erupt into a cry.

"Fucking hell, I was on a roll," Harry says, throwing his hands into the air.

"You'll still be winning when we start again," Noah says to Harry, but he keeps his focus on me.

"If you're taking a break, then so am I," Harry says, standing up. "I'm going out for a fag." He pulls the cigarette box out of his robe and nods to us before heading outside.

"Do you want me to walk you to your room?" Noah asks me.

"That seems a little much," Mohammad comments. His head is down in his phone now, and he doesn't look up at us.

Noah ignores him and looks at me in question.

"You don't need to do that."

"We won't have a good trip if you aren't feeling well," he says.

"But I want to be with you guys."

"Then, let's get you tucked in on the couch," Noah insists.

He strides over to me and pulls me up off the chair. A second later, he's pushing me down onto the couch and covering me with a blanket. It's long enough that I can lie down fully while still giving Mohammad room to sit.

Noah squats down, his face close to mine. "Better?"

I pull the blanket up under my chin and nod at him. "Thanks, Noah."

"Anytime." He smiles, shooting me a subtle wink as Harry joins us, smelling like smoke.

"You look like a burrito," Harry says, running his hand down over my hair before sitting on the floor.

Noah does the same. I watch as they unpause the game, but the heavy blanket makes me even more tired, and I let my eyes slip shut.

We had plans.
5:45PM

MY PHONE BUZZES, waking me up. I fumble to find it, grasping for it under the heaps of blanket. When my hand connects to it, I hold it up in front of my face and peek my eyes open to see who's calling.

Naomi's name flashes across the screen.

I answer without a thought and bring the phone to my ear.

"Mohammad's out of town," she states. And from the sound of her voice, she is *definitely* not happy about it.

I pinch the top of my nose, already knowing this conversation is going to go badly.

"I know. I'm with him."

There's a pause. I wait for her response, but there isn't one.

"Naomi?" I dare to ask.

"Seriously?" she barks out.

I chew on my lip, realizing I probably should have messaged her last night. "Yeah. Naomi, please don't be mad," I start, but she cuts me off.

"Mad? I'm not mad. I just … I thought we had plans. And now, you're gone?" she says, *clearly* mad.

"I know we did. I should have messaged you sooner, but I'll be back on Tuesday, and we'll have all next week to hang out. And with my parents arriving, I'll probably need somewhere to hide out during the move. I was hoping I could come over while my mom gets us settled," I say, hoping it distracts her from being upset.

"Won't they want your help?"

"Honestly, no. It's best to just leave my mom with the movers and designer for a few days."

"Of course you can come over," she chirps. "We can do a girls' night again. But that still doesn't answer the question of where you and Mohammad are."

It's not until she asks where we are that I scoot myself up to a seated position, looking at Mohammad. His eyes are the size of saucers. He's listening to my side of the conversation, his head tilted in confusion.

"We're at Harry's," I answer.

"I don't get it. Don't you want to be friends?" Naomi says, obviously annoyed.

My stomach flips at her question. I didn't expect for her to be so upset. "Of course I do."

"Then, why wasn't I invited? Because of Olivia? It's all just shit."

"What is?"

"This whole situation, Mallory. I thought we were over it, but apparently not."

"Naomi, honestly, I think you're just reading into it. Harry wanted to get away because of something with his family. That's all it was. This wasn't a planned-out trip or anything like that. It was a last-minute decision," I say, trying to explain myself. Not that I really need to. Because it's not my house.

It's Harry's.

And he decided who to invite.

But I know that Naomi is just upset that Mohammad is gone for the weekend. And it wasn't the best of me to leave when I had plans with her. But Harry comes first.

"This is why breakups are ridiculous. They cause the entire friend group to split up. Since Olivia and Harry broke up, he doesn't invite us to stuff like this anymore. And I find it rude. We've all been friends for years."

I chew on my lip, not sure what to say. Or how to even respond.

"Look, I know that if this was just a party, you'd be here," I say, trying to convince her. "You aren't missing out on anything, except watching the guys play Xbox."

"And you don't have other plans?" Naomi asks, sounding

a little less worked up.

"Nothing exciting. Noah has to work out for football, Mohammad has homework to do, and Harry ... well, he's currently sitting in a bathrobe and his underwear in front of the TV."

Naomi laughs, and it settles my stomach. I glance at Mohammad, whose mouth is hanging open. I avoid his eyes, and immediately find both Harry and Noah staring at me. They've paused the game, and they're fully turned around, listening in on my conversation.

I wave my hand in the air, wanting them to get back to their game.

But neither of them makes a move.

I stand up, needing a little privacy. As I do, Mohammad stands with me. He holds out his hands, palms facing up, looking concerned. I put up my finger, wanting him to give me a minute.

"That sounds ... terrible," Naomi finally says.

I move around the couch and out of the room, walking down the hallway until I can find somewhere private for us to talk.

"It's *something* all right." I laugh with her. "I was thinking about the party Thursday night ... you and Mohammad looked pretty comfortable together. He said you two kissed."

"Oh, *we kissed*," Naomi says. And I can hear her smiling through the phone.

"Aw, Naomi! That's great. Are you feeling happy about everything?" I ask.

Noah's gone on and on about letting them figure out their feelings for themselves, and I'm happy that they finally are. Naomi and Mohammad would make a great couple.

"I was excited—thrilled really. I normally don't pull boys into rooms to snog them, but Mohammad was looking so good—"

"Ew, okay," I say, cutting her off. "I don't need all the details."

Naomi laughs again.

"That's why I've been hurt. I thought since Harry invited me Thursday, things would go back to the way they used to be. Obviously, with you now included."

"Trust me, Mohammad can't wait to get back to see you. I know he likes you," I tell her.

"Maybe a little distance will do us some good," Naomi reflects.

"Are you not sure you want to date him anymore?" I ask, instantly growing worried.

"Of course not. Don't they say distance makes the heart grow fonder?"

I smile, relief flooding through me.

"Can I tell you something?" I say without thinking.

"What is it?"

"I think you were right."

"About?"

"About Noah," I say, tapping my finger. "And me."

"No way!" she says, a mix of surprise and excitement in her voice.

"Yep," I respond, thinking of Noah.

"Tell me all the details!" she squeals into the phone.

"When I know exactly what it means, I promise I will."

"And until then? What are you now?" And her question makes me nervous.

What are Noah and I?

"I don't know. But I do know that we're something, that we have something. It's just taken me time to realize that you were right. And even once I knew how I felt, the timing never seemed right until … recently."

"I knew it!" Naomi says triumphantly.

"Naomi, can this stay between us?"

"You don't want me to tell Olivia, do you?"

I let out a sigh. "I just need time to figure everything out. And once I do, there are people who need to hear about it first, from me," I explain, hoping that she'll understand. Because Harry and Noah need to talk about things. And as much as I want to trust her, I almost immediately regret telling her.

Because I know she's close with Olivia.

"I'll keep this between us. But only as long as you don't tell Mohammad about my freak-out. Deal?"

"Deal," I say. "But, Naomi, you know Mohammad's going to ask about you. He knows we're on the phone right now."

"Good. Tell him that I rang because I missed you and that I'm going out this weekend and I was asking for an outfit suggestion."

I raise my eyebrows, impressed. "You want to make him jealous?"

"I don't know if I'd use the word jealous," she says non-committally. "I just want him thinking about me."

"Trust me, that news will drive him crazy."

Naomi laughs.

"I'll message you later with how he takes the news. Sound good?" I ask her.

"Perfect," she replies. "Speak to you later."

"Bye," I say, ending the call.

I grasp on to my phone, holding it near my chest. And I think it finally hits me that I told someone other than Mohammad about Noah. Well, maybe not *told* her about us. But I at least hinted at the fact that she was right. That there are feelings between us.

I smile to myself, thinking of Noah, and quickly make my way back down the hallway and into the living room.

"Was that Naomi? What did she say?" Mohammad is rattling off questions before I'm barely in the room.

"She's mad that we left without telling her or inviting her. She's going out this weekend, and she's going to look hot," I say, getting straight to the point.

"Oh fuck," Mohammad says, pushing his hands back through his hair.

"Yep," I reply. "It's not good."

"I need to go into recovery mode," he says, his eyes moving a million miles a minute as he thinks.

"It's good she's upset. It means she cares," Harry chimes in.

"He's not wrong," Noah agrees.

"That doesn't change the fact that she's upset though," I reply.

"What do I do?" Mohammad asks me.

"Honestly, give her a little time. She's upset, but at the same time, she didn't want me to tell you she's upset. Think she wants to come off like it doesn't affect her," I explain.

"But it does, obviously," Noah says.

"Yeah," I agree. "Why don't you call her later? Tell her I mentioned that she and I talked and you've been thinking about her all day. It will mean more than a text."

"You don't think a call is too much?" Mohammad asks.

"If you want a chance with her, I think it's necessary."

"Well, fuck," Mohammad says, looking defeated.

"Don't worry about it, mate," Harry says, pausing the game. "She wants you."

"She does," I add in, agreeing. Because I don't want to see Mohammad upset.

I know he likes her. And it's obvious they both like one

another.

"Why don't you take my place?" Noah says, handing Mohammad the controller.

They switch spots as Harry starts a new game.

"I think I'm going to give Anna a call."

"Your best friend from home, right?" Noah asks.

"Yeah. I want to tell her about the apartment. And I think she's going to come visit soon," I say, excitement growing within me.

"Nice." Noah smiles.

"We can show her around London," Mohammad adds.

"You'd do that?" I ask in surprise.

"She's your best friend, Miss America. Of course we will," Mohammad answers.

My heart feels like it's going to crack open with Mohammad's words. I immediately crouch down next to him, pulling him into a hug.

"Whoa," he says, holding his hands up in the air, not hugging me back. "I wasn't trying to be sweet. I was just stating the obvious. She's your friend, so we will show her a good time."

Both Noah and Harry laugh.

I choose to ignore Mohammad's attempt to downplay his kindness, squeezing him tighter instead.

"Either way, I appreciate it." I pull back from Mohammad and sit down next to him. "When I found out I was staying in London, knowing I wouldn't be with Anna day-to-day was one of the hardest parts. Of course, I didn't know how I would fix things between us, but I also could barely stomach not going back home. Not getting to say good-bye to my favorite places, my room. It all felt so sudden. Like the rug was pulled out from under me."

"I know the feeling," Harry says solemnly.

"It's the worst when you feel like your life is spinning out of control," I say.

"Thinking you're in control is the problem," Noah offers.

"Of course you're in control of your life," Mohammad counters, looking at Noah like he's lost his mind.

"To some extent, we are," Harry interjects. "But Noah's right; most of life is out of our control. That's why we have to placate ourselves with good times and alcohol—to forget that we aren't in control of shit." He says the words seriously, but I can see the hint of sarcasm on his face.

"Not the healthiest approach," I tease, raising my eyebrows at Harry.

"Maybe not, but it is fun." He gives us a devious grin, causing everyone to let out a laugh.

"Either way, Anna will have fun when she visits. At least that much is in your control," Noah says, bringing us back on topic.

"That's true. All right, I'll be back in a bit." I get up from the floor and pull up Anna's number on my phone.

Harry turns the game on as I walk out into the hallway and bring the phone up to my ear.

"Mallory!" Anna exclaims, answering.

"Hey." I can't help but smile into the phone. "How are you? Is it a good time to talk?"

"It's perfect. I miss you," Anna says wistfully.

"I miss you too. I wanted to catch up and talk about when you can visit."

"After you suggested Thanksgiving, I talked to my parents about it," she says.

"What did they think?" I ask, nervously biting my lip.

"They said I could absolutely come!" she squeals into the phone. "I've been so upset since I found out you weren't coming back to New York. I even tried to convince my mom to let me do an exchange in London, so we could be together."

"Really?" I laugh, happy about her excitement. "What did she say?"

Anna huffs, "She said she didn't think she'd be able to handle me being away from home. It was pretty pathetic."

I smile, knowing that the more likely case is that her mom doesn't think Anna could handle being away from home. She's never been that independent. She loves new experiences but within the parameters of things she knows. She tends to frequent the same parts of the city and hang with people within the same friend group.

"I can't blame her for wanting to keep you there," I say.

"But they did agree to let me visit over Thanksgiving! All I have to do now is book my flight," she tells me excitedly.

Relief quickly floods through me at the prospect of having Anna with me.

"I can't wait, Anna, honestly. I'm not going to get a break since it's not a holiday here, but I'm sure you won't have any trouble finding stuff to do in the city. And the second I'm out of class, we can explore together. I want to show you some of my favorite restaurants. We can walk through Hyde Park. You'll love all the ducks."

"And I can't wait to tell all the girls that while they're stuck home, watching their cooks stuff turkeys, I'll be visiting my best friend in London for the holiday," Anna gushes.

"It will be great. You can meet everyone and see the new apartment. I just went and saw it yesterday."

"What did you think?" she asks enthusiastically.

"It's gorgeous. Not at all what I expected. There's nothing really understated about it, and it's pretty modern."

"Wow," Anna says, dreamy. "I'm so jealous. Your mom already told me that you were going to fully redo your room."

"When did she tell you that?" I ask with surprise.

"Shit, I forgot to tell you. She came by the other day!"

"Was she meeting your mom or something?" I ask, confused.

"No, she brought me the menus we used to collect. You remember, the ones where we put the ratings on? She said that they were important to you and that you'd want me to have them."

"She said that?" My stomach does a flip.

"Yeah," Anna says in her *no-duh* voice. "Why do you sound so surprised?"

"Because we sort of got into a fight about it."

"About the menus?" Anna asks.

"Yeah. Well, not really a fight. You know my mom; she doesn't really give you enough of a chance to talk for you to tell her you're actually upset."

"What happened?"

"She called and asked me about packing things up. She made it sound like she wanted to donate my whole room and start fresh in London. Like she was going to pick and choose what she deemed important to move from my room. I was already freaked out about moving, and then she was going on about not only not letting me come home to help, but also scrapping my stuff. Then, she had the nerve to say she was going to throw out our menus, and I snapped at her. I thought she didn't care. But …"

"You must have gotten through because she was pretty serious when she gave them to me."

"So, she actually listened," I say, feeling completely taken aback.

"Apparently. Although I don't know why you made such a big deal of it. Half of these places aren't even open anymore."

I smile, trying to untangle the knot in my stomach. I probably need to call my mom.

"That's true. Plus, we can start a new pile when you visit. There are lots of places I want to check out."

"I can't wait! What are you doing this weekend?"

"I'm actually at Harry's country house with Noah and Mohammad. It's our midterm break, so we're spending a few days here, then going back into the city. Harry has to go with his parents to Shanghai on Wednesday, and then my mom and dad get here."

"I can't believe it's that quick."

"I know. I'm just happy to be out of the city for a few days. Anyway, what else is new? How have things been going with Jordan?"

"We're good! I'm going to his swim meet next weekend. I think he's going to ask me to be his girlfriend."

"Anna! That's so cool."

"I know," she gushes. "I didn't think I would be this happy about it. Usually, boyfriends are more of a strategic play for me …"

"But Jordan's different?"

"We actually talk," Anna says seriously.

"That's what you said about the first night you met, right? You drank champagne. Talked. *Kissed.*"

Anna giggles. "Okay, so there might have been more kissing than talking," she admits. "But he's actually someone I like hanging out with. And that's saying a lot because, usually, I just want a boyfriend to go on dates with."

"I'm happy for you. I can't wait to meet him!"

"Same. When I'm there, we'll have to figure out when we can get together next. Maybe my parents will let me travel over spring break. We could meet in the Swiss Alps!"

"Sounds like a plan." I smile into the phone. "I love you,

Anna."

"Love you too. I'll message you my flight booking."

"Sounds good. Talk to you later."

"Bye."

I click off the call and lean back against the wall. I can't help the smile that pulls at my lips. I'm happy that Anna's happy. And that she's going to come visit. She's always been one of the most positive people I know.

I slide off the wall and walk back into the living room.

"How was she?" Noah asks when he sees me.

"She's good. Looking forward to visiting. Going to book a flight for Thanksgiving," I say, sitting down next to him on the couch.

"Now, that's an American tradition I can get on board with," Mohammad says.

"Same for me," Harry agrees. "But don't tell anyone I said that."

"Why not?" I ask.

"Harry doesn't want to be associated with anything American," Noah interjects.

"Apart from Miss America," Mohammad replies. "I don't know why people have such a problem with America anyway. It's great. You've got Disney, Florida, California, *California girls,* Route 66."

"You're really picking and choosing there." I laugh.

"I think I'd like it there," Mohammad says.

"You can't go on an exchange," Harry cuts in. "You belong in London."

"You'd be bored without me, I know." Mohammad smiles.

"Who else would I party with but you two?" he says, glancing between Noah and Mohammad before looking to me. "And, of course, you."

"Lucky for you, I'm no longer going home," I say.

"London's become your home now. You're going to have to accept it," Mohammad says.

"I have," I try to tell him, but he just shakes his head, apparently not agreeing.

"Have not," he remarks.

"Have too," I say, sticking out my tongue at him, causing Noah and Harry to laugh.

But Harry quickly collects himself.

"All right, I say we all go have a lie-down, relax, and then meet for drinks." Harry stands up.

"Drinks at seven-thirty. I can do that." Mohammad beams.

"I've decided it's a formal night," Harry says, extending his hand out to me.

"Have you?" I ask, taking his hand as he pulls me up from the couch.

"I figured we should do something to celebrate. You're always telling me it's important to make new memories. Better memories," Harry says, his blue eyes glued to mine.

My stomach flips. Because his words and my hand in his are both reminders of our past together.

Of our relationship.

"Apparently, memories in which we will be well-dressed." Noah's voice pulls me out of my thoughts, and I drop Harry's hand.

"Not excited to dress up?" I tease, already knowing the answer is no.

"Ecstatic," he replies, flaring his nostrils.

"But you'll do it for me," Harry says with a grin.

"I will," Noah agrees.

"Are we going out for dinner or having it here?" Mohammad asks.

"We'll dine here. But we can always go into the village later if you're up for a night out."

"Is the village big?" I ask. "I mean, we didn't really pass anything on the drive in."

"Nah, it's tiny," Noah answers.

"There's a pub though." Harry yawns as he checks his watch. "Right, I'm off to bed."

"So, back down here at seven-thirty?" I confirm.

"Seven-thirty it is," Harry replies.

Seems to be working.
6:00PM

WHEN I GET to my room, I find my suitcase empty. Everything is folded and hung. All my bathroom products are lined up neatly in the bathroom. There's nothing for me to do, except relax.

And call my dad.

And get ready.

And think about Noah.

I fall onto the mound of pillows on the bed, taking in the room from a new view. There's so much red and black and items on every table that grab my attention. A unique sculpture. A stack of books. You'd think with the patterned carpet, red-and-white bedding, and large red fans, the room would feel stuffed.

Overdecorated.

But it doesn't.

I glance at a white fireplace that seems to get lost on the wall. The ornately carved black bed spindles. It's bold and outrageous at the same time as being delicate and tasteful. It's such a mix.

And I'm immediately reminded that this is usually Harry's room.

That, normally, he would be the one in this bed. With this view.

But instead, it's mine.

He said he's letting me stay in his room because he can't face his upcoming trip. And partially, I believe that.

But another part of me wonders if there's something more. This room—his room—it reminds me so much of his family's room at the club. Where we had our date. Where my parents are going to join.

So much of my life has Harry in it.

He shows up at my hotel. He's always at Noah's. We have class together. We're at his house. He's on the phone with my dad. He's wrapping me in a hug. He's telling me that we don't know our future. He says we're best friends—

A knock comes from the door, snapping me out of my thoughts.

"Come in," I call out, not sure who to expect.

Maybe it's a maid. Or Mohammad coming to bug me.

But it's Noah.

I quickly move to sit up, but the sheets are silky, and my fingers slip on the bedding.

"Hey," I stutter as he steps into the room, closing the door behind him.

In a few quick strides, he's joining me on the bed, pulling me into a hug.

"I was missing you," he breathes out against my neck, causing goose bumps to rise down my arms.

"Yeah?" I smile, getting lost in his warm embrace.

"Yeah," Noah says, pulling me into a soft, slow kiss.

I pull him closer to me, wanting more. Opening my

mouth to his. But Noah pulls back.

I look at him, confused. Noah just smiles.

"Are you getting settled all right?"

"Settled?" I say, my brain feeling like a scrambled egg. Because is that what he really wants to do right now? *Talk?*

"There wasn't much to settle. They unpacked for me," I comment.

"Usually do at places like this," Noah says.

"Places like what?"

"Well, here. Or maybe on a private yacht."

"They didn't unpack me at the Bvlgari."

Noah props himself onto his elbow. "Did you ask?"

"Fair point," I say, giving in. "I don't know. I find it a little weird. I don't really like the idea of people going through my stuff."

"You're private." Noah nods in understanding. "Was there anything you didn't want them to see?"

"Like what?" I ask, running my fingers through his chestnut hair. "I brought regular stuff. Dresses, hangout clothes. Lots of sweaters." I'm about to add that I brought the necklace Harry got me for my birthday, but I decide against it.

"And anything for under them?" Noah asks, causing me to still.

I bring my eyes to his. "You mean … lingerie?"

A smile pulls on Noah's lips, and I know the answer is yes.

"Sorry to disappoint, but I didn't pack anything special," I say, being honest.

"Everything you wear is special, Mal," Noah says, pulling me back to his lips.

He gives me a deep, open-mouthed kiss. I pull my head back slightly.

"If you keep kissing me like that, we're not going to make

it downstairs for drinks," I mumble.

"Then, we'd better control ourselves," Noah says, suddenly sitting up and turning toward the bedside table.

I look over at it, leaning over him, and realize there's a bag on it that wasn't there before.

"What's that?" I ask as Noah reaches for it.

"Mum asked me to give this to you," he says, handing me a small pink gift bag.

"What is it?" I ask, untying the bow that's keeping it closed.

"I don't know. She told me not to give it to you until we arrived."

"Did you peek?"

Noah's face flashes with shock. "Of course not. It's not for me."

"I would have peeked," I say, my mind racing as I open up the bag.

Immediately, the smell of pumpkin and cinnamon fills the air around us.

"Oh, yum!" I moan out upon seeing Mia's cookies. They're made into cookie sandwiches with maple syrup glaze.

"Oh, not fair," Noah says, reaching for the sandwich.

"No, no, no, mister. This is all mine," I say, setting the cookies down. I look into the bag and see it's not empty. I pull out a book. "Aw, that's sweet of your mom."

I flip over from the back cover to the front cover and instantly drop it.

"Oh, wow," Noah says, picking it up. "Another historical romance. I had no idea my mum has read so many of these books."

"I can't believe she sent one with you!" I reply when a note sticking out of the book catches my eye. I pull it out as Noah flips through the book. It's a note from Helen.

"What is it?" he asks.

"A note from your mom," I say, reading it. *"Something to keep you company and busy during your trip. Be good.—Helen."*

My mouth instantly falls open.

"Interesting." It's all Noah says.

"Does your mom really think that a romance book and some cookies will distract me from the fact that I'm in a parentless house, with you, for the entire weekend?"

"I thought you made her promises?" Noah asks, reading over the note himself.

"I did, which is why I don't get the last-ditch effort to rein me in," I say, pointing to the book and cookie bribe.

"So, you're not going to eat or read?" Noah asks, his dark eyebrows rising up.

"That's beside the point," I say, reaching for a cookie. I open up the plastic wrap surrounding it and take a bite. "Oh, wow."

I lick my lips, remembering how good these cookies are.

Noah watches me, a smile pulling on his lips. "The bribe seems to be working."

I roll my eyes at him, but I can't totally deny that Helen's plan isn't working a little. Because this cookie is definitely a distraction to the fact that Noah is lying on my bed.

"Do we have to get ready soon?" I ask, trying to find a clock.

"Nah," Noah replies without even looking at his phone or watch. His eyes never leave mine.

"You mentally prepared to dress up tonight?" I ask, taking another bite.

"Harry's excited, so I'm happy."

"So, you'll go along with it?" I ask.

"I always go along with what he wants," Noah says.

"You do," I reply, examining what's left of the delicious

cookie. I've practically inhaled it.

"You going to share?" Noah asks, looking from the cookie to me.

"These are way too good to share." I laugh, jumping up off the bed.

"You aren't going to give me any?" Noah asks, his mouth sliding open. "Not even a crumb?"

"Nope." I grin.

"What if I take it from you?" Noah questions.

"You wouldn't," I reply, narrowing my eyes at him.

"Wouldn't I?" His words are cool and stern, and they make me actually think he would consider stealing it from me.

I look around the room, weighing my options. I could make a run for it, get caught, and lose the rest of the cookie altogether.

I could offer to split the remaining half with him, but then I'd have to watch as he sits and soaks in his victory.

And that would just be annoying.

Or I could give him the whole thing, making him feel so guilty that he ends up giving it back to me.

Noah takes a step toward me. Our eyes lock, both narrowing, and then it dawns on me. If I'm going to win, I'm going to have to cheat.

As Noah watches, I shove the entire thing into my mouth. His eyes go wide in shock as I chew, but quickly, he's standing directly in front of me.

"It's a shame. It would have been fun to share," he says, taking my hand into his.

He looks at me through his thick, dark lashes before bringing my finger to his lips. He sticks it in his mouth, sucking the little bit of leftover icing off of it. I watch with fixation as his pupils dilate. He retracts my finger, sending a warm tingle through my body.

"I promise I'll share the next one," I say, breathless, my full attention on his lips now.

He licks them once and then pulls me toward him.

Noah doesn't kiss me right away. He lets his lips dance close to mine, and it sends my thoughts swirling. When his lips find mine, his kiss is soft and gentle. I start to open my mouth, ready for more, when my phone rings. Noah glances in its direction, but I grab on to his cheeks, wanting him to stay focused on me.

He gives me another gentle kiss but then pulls away again.

I groan, annoyed at the interruption.

"It's your dad," Noah says, picking up my phone.

"Just ignore it."

Noah shakes his head and hands me the phone. "Answer it."

I let out a sigh before deciding Noah's right. I answer the call and bring the phone up to my ear. "Hi, Dad."

"How's my girl doing?" my dad asks, excitement evident in his voice.

"I'm alive," I say, trying to be chipper.

"Well, that's good news," he replies, not missing a beat.

"It is," I say, moving to sit down on the edge of the bed.

"So, you got in all right today?" he asks.

Noah comes to sit next to me and strokes my hand.

I press my lips together, trying not to get distracted.

"Mmhmm. We drove out after Noah's football game."

"And how was it?" he asks, apparently not satisfied with my half-hearted answers.

"The big topic of conversation today is how well he did. It was an amazing match," I say, causing Noah to smile next to me as he continues to rub my hand.

"That's great to hear," my dad says cheerfully.

"Yeah," I reply, watching Noah slip his fingers from my

hand to my forearm, causing my eyes to flutter shut.

"Well, your mother has me hunkered down at home, looking online at fabrics and couch styles today."

I open my eyes and can't help but laugh into the phone. "Sounds fun."

"Not exactly. But she's happy. And we agreed we'd be done by four and go out for a celebratory drink."

"Aw, that's nice."

"It is. We miss you, Mal."

"I miss you too."

"So, everything is good?"

I get up from the bed, knowing that I need to focus on our conversation and not on the way Noah makes me feel.

"Everything is good. Today, we've just been hanging out at the house. This place is gorgeous. And it's been the nicest day. We had lunch outside, and I learned to play croquet," I tell him.

"You're really branching out," my dad says, admiration in his voice. "A weekend in the country is a far cry from lunch at the Boathouse in Central Park. I'm proud of you."

"Thanks, Dad," I say, my heart melting a little.

Normally, I'd find a statement like that weird. After all, as long as I'm proud of myself, does it really matter if he is? But it's my dad.

And it does mean something to me.

"Speaking of the house and Harry, I've been talking to a friend in London. He's agreed that The Arrington Club is the one we'll want to join, so you'll have to pass that message along."

"You like Harry, don't you?" I try not to groan.

"He seems like a well-rounded boy."

"Well-rounded?" I laugh.

"Why do you sound upset by that?"

"I'm not upset, but, Dad, meeting at the club for drinks? Have you forgotten he's sixteen?" I point out.

"Would you rather I not take interest in your friends?"

I roll my eyes. "No …"

"Mal, I hope to meet all of your friends. Harry. Noah."

"Mohammad and Naomi too," I insist.

"Your mother and I are looking forward to us being together again. To getting settled. To meeting your friends. And to starting our new life. We all have different things we're looking forward to. For me, one of those things happens to be the club."

"Well, it is really nice. You know Harry's family donated a room," I say, quickly turning back to look at Noah. He's still on the bed, but I can tell he's listening intently.

"Well, that is unique." And my dad sounds impressed.

"Yeah. All right, Dad, well, I should probably get ready for dinner now," I say, trying to get him off the phone.

"Sounds good, Mal. Give us a call tomorrow."

"I will."

"Love you."

"Love you too," I say, hanging up.

A shadow falls across Noah's face when I get off the call, causing my stomach to flip. I walk over to the bed and pull my legs up, so I'm sitting crisscross.

I watch Noah suck in his cheeks, his forehead creasing.

I stay silent, not sure what he's thinking.

"Harry kissed you last night, didn't he?" Noah finally asks.

I think back to last night, to seeing Harry in front of the Bvlgari. I remember clearly how we walked toward each other. How he pulled me into a hug and then gave me a peck on the lips.

"It wasn't like that," I start to say, but Noah's face darkens. I cut off my words, knowing that if I try to deny the kiss, I'll sound like I'm lying to him. I let out a heavy breath, bringing my gaze to Noah's. "Yes, he kissed me."

Noah nods but doesn't say anything.

"Does that bother you?" I ask hesitantly.

"It's not the best feeling in the world." Noah shrugs.

I grab on to his hands, pulling him toward me. "I didn't ask him to. And I didn't … I didn't kiss him back. It was a peck."

"Harry told me it wasn't anything. A brief moment, but that he wanted to be honest with me about it anyway."

I raise my eyebrows in surprise. "That's big of him."

"Apparently, he thought it was enough of a kiss to tell me."

"Do you think I would do that?" I ask him seriously.

"No."

"Because I wouldn't," I reply. "Honestly, I'm annoyed he even told you."

"Annoyed?"

"Yeah. That means he put thought into it. It wasn't just a *thankful to see me* peck then."

Noah quickly shakes his head. "I don't think that's right either."

"What do you mean?" I ask.

Noah's brown eyes shift to the corner, and I can tell he's thinking about his words.

"If anything, he probably did just give you a quick kiss in the moment. Knowing Harry, he wouldn't have thought about it before. Usually, things just happen. He didn't tell me to make me jealous."

"Because he doesn't know about us yet." I nod, understanding.

"I think he felt embarrassed more than anything. He …"

Noah stops, pressing his lips together. "We shouldn't be talking about this. I've just now realized why he told me, and I feel like a tosser for saying it."

"Saying what?"

"It made him feel vulnerable. He ran to you and felt relief in your arms. He fell back into an old habit."

I think about what Noah said. About falling back into old habits.

"You mean, needing me as more than a friend?" I dare to ask.

"I think just needing you."

"Regardless, I want *you*," I say, taking his hand in mine.

"Your dad asked about Harry?"

I nod. "I'm sorry about that too."

"I told you this morning, there's nothing to be sorry about."

"Well, I am. If he should have spoken to anyone, it should have been you."

"And why's that?" Noah says, wrapping his hands around mine.

"Because ... you're the one he should worry about," I reply with what I hope is a sexy smirk.

Noah smiles, bringing my palm up to his lips to kiss it.

"I'm sure he just wanted confirmation that you'd be treated well. Cared for while you're away," Noah says.

"It's ridiculous. And traditional. It's not like I'm something to be handed around. I can take care of myself," I huff.

"If I had a child, I'd want to know their friends. Especially if they were going away with them on a trip."

"I think my dad cared less about me coming to London alone than he cared about me going out to the country for a few nights."

"We both know it's not because of the trip," Noah says

knowingly.

"No, I guess it's not. It's about being alone with someone I have feelings for."

"Parents generally worry about those things," Noah agrees.

"I know, but this is new between us. And even though the feelings have been there, I didn't think we would take that step this weekend. Besides, I've heard you talk about sex. It's special. *Sacred*. It's not something to be rushed. It's this huge deal to you. So, I figured that you wouldn't want to, uh, have that happen at Harry's house."

"Hmm."

"Hmm what?" I ask.

"Sometimes, you really do make me sound dramatic."

"Well, you are dramatic."

"I can't believe my mum talked to you about sex," Noah says.

"It's either you or me. One of us was going to get the safe sex lecture."

"It's just a shame you got the lecture but aren't allowed to indulge in the reward of it."

My mouth falls open at his words.

"Noah Williams, are you trying to say that you wanted to get into my pants this weekend?" I cross my arms over my chest, raising an eyebrow at him.

"Course not." Noah shakes his head. "But I figured you'd try to get in mine."

"You make me sound terrible." I laugh.

"I always told you that you have a lot of energy. It's just a matter of where you put that energy. I'm hoping now, it won't go toward being angry with me."

"It's kind of funny. You're sort of right."

"Mmhmm. Obviously, I've thought about it. And after

Harry told me about this weekend, well, the thought that we'd have some time together did cross my mind."

"It crossed mine too," I admit. "But this is a friends' trip, right?"

"Right," Noah agrees. "Although I still think we're allowed our moments."

"Yeah?"

"We're technically on holiday. Aren't we supposed to enjoy ourselves?"

"I don't see why not," I say, causing Noah to smile.

"You like the idea then?" Noah asks, his hands finding my waist.

The feel of his fingers sliding against my skin turns my mind to jelly.

"Mal?"

I flick my gaze up to his. "The idea of what?" I finally ask.

"Of this," Noah says, pulling me to him.

To his lips.

He places a tender kiss on my mouth, and I immediately want to drown in the feeling. But his lips on mine send a jolt through my memory. My mind remembers what Mohammad said earlier.

And I pull away.

"I can't believe you told Mohammad that I wouldn't make a move," I say, looking up into Noah's eyes.

"Well, you wouldn't, and you had loads of opportunities."

I let out a surprised laugh. "Loads, huh?"

"Loads," Noah confirms, nodding his head as a smirk dances on his lips.

"If I recall, you had loads of opportunities that you passed up too."

Noah drops his head down to my neck, peppering warm kisses across my skin.

"You're right. You were practically throwing yourself at me. I'm not sure how I resisted for so long," he says in between kisses.

"Noah!" I laugh and push against his chest, trying to move him back away from me.

But he's so heavy that he doesn't go anywhere. His lips firmly stay on my skin.

"It's true. I love the way you taste. It's surprising really, that I was able to make it so long. Now that I know what you taste like, there's no going back."

My face flushes as Noah's tongue dips out of his mouth, meeting my skin. I let out an unsteady breath.

"You think?" I barely get out.

"Absolutely."

Noah's lips trail across my neck and over my jaw, his teeth grazing against my skin. I bite my lip, desperate for a distraction. But then something Noah said about Harry flashes through my mind.

"Noah, can I ask you something?"

"Yeah."

"Our friendship is important to you, right?" I ask, looking up at him.

Noah pulls back. "Of course."

I glance away, thinking about how things used to be between me and Harry. We were together, and everything was great. But then it wasn't. And our friendship barely made it through that. And then there's me and Noah. Everything with him is more. Everything feels bigger. Which means, if anything happens, our friendship probably won't survive it.

"What's on your mind?" Noah asks, recapturing my attention.

"Just nerves, I think."

"You can tell me," he insists.

"What if we ruin our friendship, Noah? I mean …" I shake my head, feeling overwhelmed at the thought.

"It's worth it." He grabs on to my waist, pulling me back against him in a hug.

I hug him back, but I can't shake the feeling. "Is it though?"

"Yes."

"I don't want to lose you," I say, pulling him closer.

Noah lets go of me and lays down, propping himself up onto his elbows. I do the same. He looks down over me, worry washing over his face. "Are you regretting this?"

"I don't regret anything. I just, well, our breakup last week did a number on me."

"Our breakup?" Noah's dark brows dip in with his question.

"Our friendship break," I explain. "You were mad at me. I was mad at you. Anyway, now that things are good again, it makes me wonder if we are pushing our luck. Are we allowed to ask so much of one another?"

"I'd give you everything."

"And what happens if it blows up in our faces?" I ask, trying to make sense of it all.

"You're worried about the illusion of loss. We're getting more from one another, not losing our friendship. It's only going to get stronger because of this." And it's a typical Noah answer.

"So, kissing will solve all of our past problems?" I ask, raising an eyebrow at him.

He lets out a chuckle. "Most of our problems revolved around wanting more from one another."

"What happens if I start spazzing out about something? Usually, I just tell you because we're friends and we can talk. But now, what happens if I feel like I can't tell you something because our friendship has changed? You're going to have different expectations about me now."

"You can always speak to me. About anything, Mal. You know that, right?"

I let out a sigh, knowing that he's right. This is all just in my head, and if I follow the path to the end, I'll end up talking myself out of something really good. Something that I want. All because I'm scared about the future.

"Yeah, I do."

"You know you talk to me with more than your words."

"What do you mean?" I ask, not following.

"Even when we're kissing, I can tell how you're doing. I can feel you. If something's wrong, even if you don't tell me, I'm going to know."

"I'm not sure that's reassuring," I say, rolling my eyes at him.

Noah pulls back an inch before bringing his hand up to cup my cheek. His warm palms keep me from looking away from him. "Can I ask you something?"

"Shoot," I reply.

"Would you rather us go back to being friends? Do you really think that was easier? Because if you do—"

I quickly cut Noah off, "That's not at all what I want." I adamantly shake my head, trying to show him I'm serious.

He holds my gaze, his expression becoming firm and set. "You're scared of losing me. I understand that. But I can promise you, Mal, you won't. I'm yours. I ... love you. And I know that scares you. I know you think love is unstable and combustible. And I know that I haven't always been consistent with my feelings in the past ..." Noah's forehead creases as he breaks his eyes away from mine.

I reach out to him, my hands falling onto his forearms. "I don't think you're going to change your mind."

"I'm not," he says.

"I'm just trying to wrap my head around … *us,* I guess." I shrug, hoping that he understands. "And what these changes mean."

"You don't have to figure everything out yet." Noah's fingers lace through mine, and he squeezes my hand.

I want to nod, agreeing with him. But I can't. "Mentally, I sort of do."

"What are you worried about?" Noah finally asks.

"Honestly, I'm scared that I'm going to disappoint you. I'm scared of how much I care about you. Everything scares me. And on top of that, the one person who I could talk to about this, well, it's you. So, I'm in a pickle."

Noah's worried expression falls away from his face and is quickly replaced by a wide, full grin.

"A pickle, huh?" he says, sounding amused.

I want to be annoyed that he finds this funny. That he isn't taking me seriously. But he's so happy that it's hard for me not to be happy too.

I crack a smile, but I cross my arms over my chest, so he knows I'm serious. "Yes, a pickle. And I don't know what to do about it."

"Pickles are delicious. I'd suggest eating it," Noah says, kissing me once on the forehead before moving his lips back to my neck.

A flush spreads across my cheeks as his tongue finds my skin again.

"I don't even like pickles," I argue.

"Well, I do," Noah says, his mouth grazing my skin. "And I have a solution to your problem as well."

Noah's hand grasps at my neck, tilting my head back and to the side. I let my eyes slide shut, my *problem* suddenly seeming irrelevant.

"Mmhmm?" I ask, trying to think straight.

"You should think of me as your boyfriend," Noah says, his tongue flicking across my neck.

My eyes fly open, his statement snapping me out of the moment.

"*My boyfriend?*" I repeat.

Noah breaks his lips from my skin.

"Either that or as your best friend who enjoys kissing you," he says with a smirk, looking up at me. "Whichever is easier to wrap your head around."

I narrow my eyes at him, trying to figure out if he's serious.

Because boyfriend!

"I don't know how I feel about either of those options," I say, but quickly, his mouth is back on my neck, moving over my jaw and up to my lips.

"In both cases, there is nothing to be worried about. Whether I'm your boyfriend or best friend, you can talk to me. That's sort of the point," Noah insists.

"I thought the point of having a boyfriend was getting flowers and chocolates and kisses?" I tease.

"I thought the point was that we were more than friends," Noah replies, dropping a kiss onto my lips.

"And what does being more than friends entail?"

"I'd rather show you than tell you," Noah says, his hands sliding around my hips until he's grasping my butt. I suck in a breath of air as he pulls my hips to meet his. "How does that sound?"

"Good," I say, breathless. "That sounds really, really good."

You look smashing.
7:30PM

AFTER AN INTENSE make-out session with Noah and a quick change and primp, I'm trying not to fall as I not-so-gracefully attempt to run down the stairs in my heels. After forcing Noah out of my room, *and my bed*, I had a cold, hard reality check when I saw my reflection.

My hair was a disaster.

My eyeliner and mascara were smudged.

And I only had ten minutes to make myself look presentable!

I brushed out my hair and decided to go with a smoky eye, cleaning up the mascara under my eyes but leaving the smudges above. I added some more shadow to the corners, a swipe of mascara and a lathering of lipstick, hoping that would be enough to salvage the situation.

I slipped into the first dress I could find in the closet—a thick-strapped black V-neck that tapers in at the waist before flaring out at the skirt and a pair of silver heels. I accidentally stabbed myself, putting in matching silver earrings, but I know Mohammad will appreciate that I took the time to accessorize.

I'm still trying to clasp a bracelet onto my wrist as I rush into the drawing room.

"Fucking hell, you look smashing."

Harry's voice grabs my attention, pulling my eyes up from my wrist. He's seated on a formal sofa, Mohammad in the chair opposite him.

Harry stands and comes to greet me at the doorway.

"Thanks." I smile at him.

"Need help?" he asks, nodding toward the bracelet.

"If you don't mind," I say, holding it out to him. "It's got a weird clasp."

As Harry clips it into place, I take a chance to look at him. He's wearing a navy suit with a navy-and-cream patterned shirt. The blue in his clothing always manages to pull out the blue in his eyes.

"You look amazing," I say as Harry finally secures the bracelet to my wrist.

"What about me?" Mohammad whines from his chair.

I give him my full attention. He's wearing a black-and-brown Gucci shirt that's tucked into black pants.

"I love your shirt," I admit, walking toward him.

Harry follows behind me.

"Thanks." Mohammad beams. "I was thinking about wearing it for my date with Naomi."

"Your date?" I ask, sitting down. "Also, shit, I forgot to text her."

"That's all right," Mohammad says, waving me off. "I took care of it."

"Took care of *what*?" I ask.

"Our boy's secured himself a date," Harry says, high-fiving Mohammad.

"Seriously?" I ask.

"Seriously. I phoned Naomi. Told her that when I get back, I want to go on a date. Said hearing that she phoned you and not me made me jealous," Mohammad explains.

"Holy shit!"

"I know!" Mohammad agrees.

"You really put yourself out there." I try not to coo.

"I was direct. And girls find direct sexy," Mohammad states confidently.

"Girls do find it sexy," I agree. "I'm proud of you."

"Proud of him for what?" Noah asks, rushing into the room.

I turn in the direction of his voice and immediately notice the flush on his face. It's probably because he's late.

And he *hates* to be late.

He showered. His chestnut hair looks darker than usual, and it's gelled to the side. He has on a white button-down, tucked into gray slacks. My heart feels like it's going to leap out of my chest at the sight of him.

He looks freaking gorgeous.

"Getting a date with Naomi," Harry answers.

I hold Noah's eyes, my mind fixated on how good he looks. About how all I can think about is undoing his shirt, button by button, and attacking him.

"You look beautiful, Mal," Noah says, sitting opposite me.

I grin at him, a little prideful that the reason he's late is because of our make-out session.

"Thanks," I reply as Gerald brings in a tray with four martini glasses on it.

"I thought we could drink something different tonight," Harry says as Gerald hands us each a glass.

"Martinis?" Mohammad asks, giving the drink a sniff.

"Exactly," Harry replies.

"Now, you're really like James Bond," I tease Mohammad, reminding him of how he fantasized about being a spy.

"Cheers to being here, mates," Harry says, raising his martini glass. "I needed this."

We all take a sip of our drink. Noah's face is unreadable. Mohammad puckers his lips together, looking like he just ate something sour.

It's not my favorite drink, but it isn't bad, so I take another sip.

"You never said how your parents took you wanting to go away. I'm surprised your dad let you leave," Noah says.

"I told my parents that Mallory and I needed a weekend away," Harry says, setting down his glass. "I snuck in the part about you two later."

"Wait …" Mohammad says, setting down his glass too. "They still think you're a couple?"

Noah's face fills with surprise.

My glass starts to shake in my hand.

"I didn't say it directly, but I figured they'd find it odd if we broke up right after the party and then went away for the weekend together."

"That would be weird," Noah mumbles.

"This is so messed up," Mohammad says, flaring his eyes.

"It's not messed up. It's just a game I had to play with my parents to get us here for this weekend," Harry responds.

"But Mallory isn't a game," Noah says with a frown.

"Noah, it's fine. I don't care what he had to tell his parents. I'm just happy we are all here together," I say, trying to avoid a friendship disaster. Because I can see that Noah is getting worked up about this, and the last thing we need is for him to blow up at Harry right now. "If it takes some fibbing to get here, then I'm all for it."

Noah exhales, his chest falling. "Wherever you three are, I am too," he finally says.

I shoot him a sympathetic smile.

"So, did you tell your parents we arrived?" I ask Harry, desperate to change the subject.

"We don't keep in touch like that."

"You're still mad about the trip to Shanghai, aren't you?" Mohammad asks, getting right to the point.

"I don't feel good about it," Harry admits.

"How do you feel?" Noah asks.

"That's a big question for such a small martini," Harry says.

He crosses and uncrosses his legs, looking uncomfortable, before finishing off his martini and then waving Gerald over and asking for a refill.

"We're a sad lot," Harry says, licking his lips. "We're on holiday. In the company of a gorgeous woman. And look at us … fucking pathetic."

"That's life," I comment, not sure what else to say.

"I think we should get it all out now, before dinner," Harry says, sitting up.

"All what out?" Mohammad questions as I start to panic, afraid Harry already knows about me and Noah.

"Why we're here. How I'm feeling. How *you're* all feeling." Harry sighs. "I thought coming here was a good idea because Mallory and I had talked about it, and she told me she wanted to make my bad memories here good."

Mohammad furrows his brows, looking hurt. "But we've had some great times here," he counters.

"We have," Harry agrees.

"Do you want to change those?" Noah asks.

Harry shakes his head. "Never. But they aren't *all* good. I remember once, I broke one of my dad's crystal glasses. It was an accident. I was a kid, and he'd asked me to make him a drink. When he heard the sound of glass shattering, he stormed into the room. He was so upset, and I cried all night."

I grab on to Harry's hand, giving it a quick squeeze.

"We'll make new memories then," Mohammad says optimistically. "Like when we were in Mallory's bath after your parents' party!"

"Hopefully, we don't create any more memories like that." I laugh.

"Why not? I had fun," Mohammad says.

"I'm sure you did. You were drinking champagne and eating falafel in my bathtub! That's pretty much your *idea* of heaven!"

"True." Mohammad laughs.

"Shit, we never showed Noah the photo of you in the bath," Harry says, his blue eyes brightening.

"I don't think that's necessary," I say, shaking my head.

"Definitely necessary, Princess of the Bathtub." Harry laughs, pulling out his phone.

"I'd like to see," Noah says a little too seriously, quickly setting down his martini.

"Come on. Let's not." I try to grab Harry's phone out of his hand, my face flushing. But before I can get it, he tosses it to Noah.

"Noah!" I whine. "Give it back."

Noah's eyes go wide as he looks at the picture. "You're plastered. And wearing a tiara."

"I hate you both." I sink down into the sofa, feeling mortified.

Because the last thing I want is Noah seeing an embarrassing photo of me.

"Don't hate me," Harry says, throwing his arm around my shoulders. "It's a great picture. I had a smashing time that night."

"You don't look too upset in the photo," Mohammad says, looking at it with Noah. "You're smiling."

"Okay, fine, maybe I was drunk. Honestly, I don't remember."

"That's because you took shots at the club. Naomi told me you two snuck drinks without me," Mohammad says pointedly.

"We didn't *sneak* shots. She made me take a shot. There's

a difference."

"Two shots, neither of which was with me." Mohammad scowls.

I roll my eyes at him.

"Wait, Mohammad, is that falafel on your face?" Noah asks, looking more closely at the photo.

"Wait, what?" Mohammad immediately reaches for the phone.

"Doesn't feel so good, does it?" I tease.

Noah hands Mohammad the phone.

"I still can't believe you all took a bath without me," Noah says, looking directly at me.

"We tried to get you to stay," Harry says.

"It's not like I wanted to," I explain. "But Harry made it clear it was either that or he was going to wake up the entire hotel, trying to get in the pool."

Because it wasn't all just fun and games that night.

Even tipsy, I knew I had to be strategic.

Harry was a boy on a mission, and I knew I was going to have to compromise.

"Really?" Noah asks.

"Yep."

"And he would have done it too." Mohammad smirks.

"Either way, it was a great ending to a shit night. It was fucking numbing, being paraded around by my dad."

"Your dad surprised me," I admit, taking a sip of my martini.

"It probably comes as a shock to most people that he's hotheaded. You'd never know," Harry says dramatically, flaring his nostrils. "Not someone as respectable as Mr. Brooks, exporting tycoon."

"Harry," Noah says.

"Right, enough talk about Dad." Harry glances away but

then quickly looks back at me. "How about you, Mallory? Have you checked in with your dad?"

I roll my eyes. "Yep," I mumble.

"What's that look for?" Mohammad asks.

"He's just being weird. I think he's excited about the move or something. I don't know …"

"Don't know what?" Noah asks.

I turn to Harry. "He's just so … annoying. And I think he likes you."

"How rude of him," Mohammad teases.

"Well, I'd rather hope so!" Harry says, looking at me with a confused expression.

"He just keeps going on about the club. And my mom won't stop going on about decorating and joining a health club and my exercise routine and buying me a new wardrobe. Someone needs to tell them to stop! It's like they've completely decided their life here before they've even gotten here. I don't know …" I grumble.

"Good, get the anger out," Mohammad encourages.

"I'm not angry," I try to disagree, but I know he's right.

"You are," Noah says. "Why are you angry?"

"Does the fact that they're joining the club bother you?" Harry asks seriously.

"Well, what about your parents? What if they meet?" I ask him.

"My parents put on a great act. And it's unlikely they'll meet."

"It's a possibility though. I don't know. It just feels like … I don't know how I feel. I'm probably overthinking this whole thing," I tell them.

"They're probably just excited," Noah offers. "Once they get settled, everything will calm down."

"You're right," I concede.

"You should be looking forward to it," Mohammad says.

"I guess it feels like two different worlds. My parents and New York are one. And then you guys and school, here, is another. And I'm trying to figure out how they come together in my mind."

"Do you think your parents will start to run in the same social circles?" Noah asks, looking between Harry and me.

I pull my lips to the side, wishing that I didn't already know the answer. "It sounds like it."

"Don't forget, my parents are hardly home," Harry points out.

"That's true," Mohammad agrees.

"I bet your parents would like to meet Mohammad's parents too. And Naomi's," Noah says encouragingly.

"And yours," I say, thinking back to breakfast this morning. About how serious Noah was when he said he wanted our parents to meet. I can't help but smile, thinking about us all together.

"I want dibs on seeing the place first though," Mohammad cuts in. "And meeting the 'rents."

"Planning on charming them?" I tease. I glance at Noah, immediately noticing he looks lost in his own world.

"It's a given!" Harry chimes in.

"Probably," I agree. "At least my mom. Once she finds out your love for Harrods, there's going to be no escaping her."

"I don't think I'd want to," Mohammad admits.

Harry chuckles, settling back into the couch.

"Harry," Noah says, sucking his cheeks in.

"Yeah?"

"You know that no amount of new memories will get rid of your past, right? This weekend away, this trip, it's you running away."

Noah's words send a shock wave through me. I snap my head up, not believing he actually just said that to Harry.

"Don't say that," Harry replies.

"You are though. It's all right. It's nothing to be ashamed of," Noah states.

"I'm not ashamed," Harry replies.

"As much as I wish we could change things with one weekend, we can't," Noah says.

I look at him, trying to figure out why he's telling Harry this.

Why isn't he being supportive?

Why can't he just pretend everything is fine?

Is that really too much to ask?

"I know we can't," Harry admits.

"Yes, you can," I insist.

Because Noah was wrong to say that.

"Mal." Noah shakes his head at me.

"Noah's right," Harry tells me. "I do have to face facts."

"No, you don't."

I look at Mohammad, hoping he will chime in. But he stays silent.

"That's what you two have in common," Noah states, looking between me and Harry. "You both are always wanting to run away from your problems."

Forget how hot Noah looks tonight. Because, right now, I want to strangle him.

"Not everyone has their life figured out. You shouldn't judge Harry or me for doing things in our own time," I say, looking directly at Noah.

Because I don't run away from my problems.

Well, maybe I do, just a little.

But that's because life can be hard. And confusing. And eventually, I always come face-to-face with my issues. But

Noah, he wants you to stare at your fears and deal with them the moment they arise. Not everyone is like that.

Not everyone has that strength.

"I know that," Noah says to me. Then, he turns, looking directly at Harry. "But friends tell each other the truth."

"I respect you for that," Harry replies, tilting his chin up at Noah.

I look between them, not at all understanding what is going on.

Is this a bonding moment? Is Harry upset?

Before I have a chance to find out, the butler steps into the room, clearing his throat.

"Excuse me, but if you're ready, we can move into the dining room. Dinner is served."

"Perfect timing. I'm starved!" Harry stands up from the couch like the intense conversation never happened.

I down my martini then set it on the coffee table before following Harry into the dining room.

The table is so beautiful.

There are tall tapers held in modern candelabras, interspersed between informal floral arrangements in a riot of rich autumn colors. Our place settings feature simple white stoneware dishes that are surrounded by an array of gold flatware and cut crystal goblets.

"Can we sit anywhere?" I ask, not sure what to make of tonight.

"Wherever you'd like," Harry replies, walking around the table to an open chair.

Mohammad goes with him, leaving Noah and me to sit next to one another on the opposite side.

As we sit, Harry clears his throat and picks up the printed menu from the table. "I helped plan the menu for tonight."

"Did you?" Noah asks with interest.

"Well, I approved it," he says casually.

I grab the menu, scanning over it.

Champagne, crostini with duck confit, and Camembert cheese and bread to start. Beef Wellington with double cream mashed potatoes and roasted vegetables, followed by a chocolate torte, topped with strawberries and fresh cream.

"Damn," I mumble.

"I love coming to your house," Mohammad says, rubbing his hands together like he can't wait to get started.

I'm worth the wait.
10:30PM

AFTER ENDING DINNER with a glass of port wine and the chocolate torte, it's sort of hard to be mad at anyone. I was going to talk to Noah about what he said during cocktail hour, but I decided against it.

Because, well, we all had a great time.

Ate amazing food.

Drank a lot of wine.

"You all look lovely tonight," Harry says, taking a sip of port.

We're seated in the living room now, the fireplace lighting the room.

"Not like we had much of a choice in the matter," Noah teases, folding onto the sofa.

"Please, you love looking smart," Harry says, waving him off.

"It's unfair really," Mohammad says, going to stand in front of the fire.

"What is?" I ask him.

93

"Looking this good." He turns around to admire himself in the gold-framed mirror on the wall.

"Oh, come off it." Noah laughs from the sofa.

"It's true. It should be a crime to look this good," Mohammad replies, running his hand back through his hair.

"You do look devilishly handsome," Harry agrees.

"Too bad Naomi isn't here to appreciate it. Although even if she were here, I'm not sure she'd appreciate it," I tease. "She was pretty annoyed with you earlier."

"Please. The fact that she was mad at me is a great sign," Mohammad disagrees.

"How is that a good sign?"

"It's a great sign," Noah confirms.

I swirl around and look at Noah in shock. "What?" I laugh. "How?"

"She obviously wanted to see him this weekend," Noah replies.

"Exactly," Mohammad says, agreeing. "She's only mad because she thought we'd go on a date and she'd get to snog me again. Can you blame her for being salty about it?"

Mohammad's practically beaming now.

"You'll be lucky if she waits around for you until we get back on Tuesday," I say, playing devil's advocate.

"She'll hold out for a piece of this," Mohammad says, running his hands down over his chest seductively.

"Oh. My." My eyes go wide as I watch him.

"He isn't wrong," Harry confirms.

I roll my eyes and walk over to the couch, taking a seat next to Noah. He glances at me, a warm smile pulling at his lips.

"You might be onto something though. Naomi is probably missing me. I mean, what woman wouldn't be?" Mohammad asks, turning away from his reflection. "Maybe I should send her something to remind her I'm worth the wait."

"That doesn't sound good," I comment, taking a sip of port.

"Oh, it will be good." Mohammad grins, his eyes lighting up.

"What are you thinking?" Harry asks, perking up.

Mohammad purses his lips and looks around the room. "I'm thinking a photo."

"Please don't send her something inappropriate," I comment, glancing over to Noah.

"There's nothing inappropriate about this body," Mohammad fires back. But a second later, he's adjusting his shirt. "Anyway, I'm thinking something suave."

"Let me," Harry says, taking Mohammad's phone from him.

Mohammad outstretches one hand, bringing it to his chin as he tries to eye the camera sexily. Then, he switches up the pose, turning to his side so Harry can get a different angle.

Noah busts out laughing, but neither Harry nor Mohammad cracks a smile. Harry hands him the phone when he's finished, letting Mohammad scroll through the pictures.

"Well, if that doesn't appease her, I don't know what will." Mohammad smiles. "Sent."

"You'll have her going wild, mate. Look at you," Harry says, giving Mohammad a firm pat on the shoulder.

"I thought you were saving this outfit for your date?" I ask.

"Sometimes, you just look too good to not take a photo and share it with the world," Mohammad says. "It would be selfish to keep this sexiness to myself."

Harry chuckles but high-fives Mohammad anyway.

"Someone should keep their sexiness to themselves," I say, sipping on more of the port.

It's sweet but strong, and combined with the warm sofa, Noah next to me, and the fire going, it makes me feel like I've fallen into heaven.

Mohammad waves off my comment but comes to sit across from me and Noah. He puts his elbows on his knees, his expression turning serious.

"So, I've been thinking … we need to make a formal *boys' club* and then induct ourselves into it."

"But we're already in it. Why do we have to induct ourselves?" I ask him.

"It sounds like a good idea," Noah chimes in. "How should we do it?"

I glance at him, surprised he's on board. But when I see his empty port glass and relaxed face, his participation starts to make more sense.

"With tattoos," I chant.

All three of them look at me in unison.

Noah furrows his brows. "Something less permanent maybe," he says, patting my knee. "But I appreciate the enthusiasm."

"What about a contract?" I suggest.

"Less formal," Harry counters.

I roll my eyes, annoyed they don't like any of my suggestions.

"I've got it," Mohammad says excitedly. "Blood!"

"Mohammad! That's a terrible idea," I disagree, shaking my head over and over.

"I'm with Mallory on this one. She's terrible with blood," Noah adds.

"Spit then," Mohammad grumbles.

Noah raises his eyebrows in interest, like he'd actually entertain the idea.

"I like it." Harry grins.

"Is it ironic that I'm a girl in the boys' club?" I ask, a pout forming on my lips. "Because my dad said something about a girl not being able to be in a boys' club, but I want to be in the boys' club."

"Aww." Harry pats my head in sympathy. "We can call it anything."

"How about *The Club*? Or maybe something based on location and our pact, like ... *The Country House Pact*?" Mohammad offers.

"*Blood Brothers*," Noah says, glancing at me. "Well, minus the *blood*." He says the last part as a whisper, like he thinks, somehow, I'm scared of hearing the word *blood*.

Although a shiver does run through me at the name.

"*Spit Brothers*!" Mohammad laughs. "I mean, Spit Brothers and Sister."

My eyes go wide at Mohammad's suggestion.

"How about we just ... leave it at friends?" I offer.

"Mallory's right. We can always decide later," Harry agrees.

"True," Mohammad says, looking at his phone, which reminds me that I need to text Naomi—even though Mohammad said I didn't need to.

I OPEN UP a new message.

> **Me:** *Heard you've got a date next week and possibly a weird photo of Mohammad posing by the fire. He was trying to impress you!*

I send the message off, hoping any message is better than none. Mohammad turns on music and stands up. He walks over to the fire, grabs the bottle of port, refills his glass, and starts to sing.

Harry joins him, singing along.

Noah scoots closer to me. "You look so beautiful tonight," he says, leaning his head against my shoulder.

I smile and have to fight off the urge to run my fingers through his hair. "Thank you."

Noah lets out a giggle and nuzzles my shoulder. My eyes fly wide open in shock.

Because did Noah just giggle?

"Mal," he says, shaking my arm. "Are you upset about earlier?"

"You mean, about the *you run away from your problems* comment?" I ask, raising an eyebrow at him.

Noah's eyes go wide, and he sinks further down into the sofa. "Apparently, the answer is yes."

"I'm not mad. I just don't understand why you can't be supportive."

"You want to protect Harry," Noah says, shaking his head like that's a bad thing.

"What's so wrong with that?" I ask, looking at Harry. He's got his arm around Mohammad's shoulders as they sing.

"Sometimes, the best service you can do for your friend is tell them the truth."

"And sometimes, people just need time," I counter.

"You keep saying that." Noah exhales loudly.

"I'm not talking about me."

Noah looks at me, and his eyes have a sadness in them I didn't expect. "No?"

"Of course not."

"We aren't always going to agree," he says softly.

"I know that."

"But I still respect you. I know what you're trying to do for Harry."

"He's the one who asked us to be here. It wasn't the other way around, you know?"

Because, for some reason, everyone's acting like it was my idea to come here. I know that I mentioned coming here to Harry when we were together, but that was different.

It was in a different context, and since then, things have changed.

But Harry and I have talked about that.

"I know." Noah grabs my hand. He squeezes it quickly before placing a kiss on my cheek. "It's been a long day."

"You tired?"

Noah nods, his head falling back onto my shoulder. I cover him up with a blanket, letting him rest against me as I listen to Mohammad and Harry sing. Eventually, they must see that Noah's fallen asleep because they bring their palms together and put them up to their cheeks, like they're lying down on a pillow.

I just smile.

"Let's play checkers," Harry suggests, bringing the game over to the coffee table between the sofas.

"It's so on." Mohammad grins, his eyes lighting up.

As they continue, they start to play dirtier and dirtier.

They both try to cheat and then get mad at the other for cheating.

And it's actually hilarious.

But then I start to get tired.

"Come on. Let's get you to bed," I say, gently waking Noah up.

He rouses, pulling his head off my shoulder.

"I'm going to take Noah to his room and then go to bed," I tell Mohammad and Harry. "Are you two staying up?"

"I'm challenging Mohammad to another battle," Harry says, not at all looking tired.

"All right." I laugh, giving them each quick hugs.

"Time for bed," I say, taking Noah's hand and pulling

him up from the couch.

"Bed?" Noah asks, his cheeks pink from being asleep.

"Bed," I repeat. I hold on to his arm, leading him through the house and up the stairs to his bedroom.

"Thanks," Noah says in his room, a little more awake.

I watch him strip off his clothes, leaving on only his underwear before he falls back onto the bed. I'm slightly in awe of how beautiful he looks.

"Oh, this is nice," Noah says, stretching out.

I swallow, trying to focus on his face and not his bare stomach.

"I'm glad. I know you're tired. Sleep good, okay?" I lean down and give him a kiss on the cheek.

I turn, ready to leave him to sleep when he grabs on to my hand.

"I thought we might be on our first date this weekend. Not … here."

"Yeah?" I ask, looking down at him.

"Yeah. Do you want to run in the morning?" he asks, sounding tired again.

"You should sleep in," I tell him.

Noah nods. "You know, I'm only one room over from you again."

"Just like when I lived at your house," I say with a smile.

"Does that make you happy?"

"Of course it does." I sit down on the edge of the bed and bring my forehead to press against his.

Noah takes my cheek in his palm and gives me a warm, long kiss. I break our lips apart.

"Do you want me to sleep with you?" I ask him.

Noah brings his eyes up to mine, his dark lashes catching my attention.

"Sleep together?" Noah asks, his eyes scanning over my

body.

I bite my lip, doing the same. I can't help but take in his tight stomach. The muscles in his chest. The way his straight collarbones cut across, disappearing into his thick shoulders.

"I mean, sleep together, like in the same bed," I clarify, suddenly going red.

Noah gives me another kiss.

"I do," he says, but I can hear the hesitation in his voice.

"But?" I ask.

"But I know Harry will have us up early, and I haven't spoken with him yet," Noah replies.

I search his eyes, wondering if he's just using that as an excuse.

I nod anyway, moving to get off the bed.

Because, deep down, I know Noah's right. Harry walking in to find us in bed together wouldn't be good. Instead of allowing me to get up, Noah wraps his hands around my waist and pulls me next to him, and then he rests his head in the nook of my arm, his cheek lying against my chest.

When he wraps his arms around me, he lets out a deep, contented sigh.

"Our first night in bed together, and we cuddle," Noah mumbles, sounding amused.

"You're sleepy. You need rest," I reply, running my fingers through his soft hair. I've thought about touching it so many times; it almost feels surreal that I now can.

"I'm not *that* tired," Noah says, his grip on my waist tightening.

"No?" I ask, holding back a gasp.

"No."

Noah draws me down to his lips. His hands shift at my waist, and he rolls me onto my side. My palms come up to his shoulders before sliding across his chest.

We kiss for a long time, Noah's warm breath and soft kisses sending tingles through my entire body.

Eventually, my eyes start to get heavy, and I know that I should go to bed. I give Noah one last kiss and then get up, adjusting my dress.

"Mal," Noah says.

"Yeah?"

"I'm going to tell Harry. After tonight, you're not sleeping alone again while we're here, okay?"

My heart feels like it's going to burst in my chest at his words. Partially out of fear of him telling Harry. But also because that's all I want. To be in bed with Noah and for him to never let me go.

"You promise?" I ask.

"Promise," Noah says back. "Good night, Mal."

"Good night, Noah."

SUNDAY, OCTOBER 20TH
Loses his shit.
7:15AM

"IT'S TIME TO party!" Mohammad's voice fills the room.

I roll over in bed, trying to shield myself from the noise. I feel the bed give as Mohammad bounces up and down next to me, causing my body to dip and rise.

"Wake up. Wake up. Wake up!"

I swat my hand out in his direction, hoping he'll stop.

"Shh," I whine as I burrow myself in the bed, pulling the comforter up to cover my face. I instantly relax in the little cocoon, feeling like I could fall back asleep.

Maybe if I don't engage with Mohammad, he'll get the point.

I love him.

But I love sleep more.

"Miss America, there's no time like the present," Mohammad sings.

I try to block out the noise, but it doesn't really work, especially when he starts poking me through the covers. I want to let out a groan, but I know he'll just see it as a sign that he's wearing me down.

That victory is in sight.

So, instead, I stay quiet.

Mohammad grumbles, and then there's movement on the

bed as he gets up, causing me to let out a sigh of relief.

He got the hint!

I hear the door open and shut, feeling happy that I get to go back to sleep.

I'm readjusting my pillow, smashing my cheek into it when a sudden chill of cold air hits my skin. I squeeze my eyes shut, annoyed at the change in temperature. But then I realize that someone is sliding into bed with me. A moment later, the covers are back on top of me, and a set of hands wraps around my waist, pulling me against a firm chest.

I try to blink my eyes open, but they don't want to work.

"It's our first day of freedom in the countryside. You can't spend the day in bed."

But this time, it isn't Mohammad speaking.

It's Harry.

His lips must be right at my ear because his voice is warm and low, and I can feel his hot breath bounce onto my skin.

"Harry?" I whisper his name and push my lips out into a pout.

"Mohammad sent for reinforcements," he says back, nuzzling my neck.

I relax against him.

"And you agreed? You're usually on my side." I wipe at my eyes, trying to get the sleep out of them. But it doesn't work.

"That's when I'm hungover or avoiding going to class," Harry informs.

"Vacations are meant for rest." I pout, rolling over and shoving my head against his chest. Maybe if I snuggle with him, he'll let me stay in bed.

Harry sucks in a breath, and I can feel his chest still. But just as quickly, he wraps his arms around me and pulls me even closer.

"Trying to keep me in bed?" he asks, stroking my back.

"Don't make me get up," I mumble.

"You're doing a terrible job of waking her up!" Moham-mad's annoyed voice comes from somewhere above the covers.

Harry laughs. I try to ignore them both.

"She's not as easily woken as me," Harry says.

"Are you both trying to spoil the day?" Mohammad huffs out. And I can clearly hear the annoyance in his voice.

I lift my head, forcing my eyes to open. Mostly so I can roll them at Mohammad's little tantrum.

Harry laughs, apparently watching me.

"Should we come out from here before he actually loses his shit?" Harry whispers.

I take in his clean face and bright blue eyes and feel more awake.

I flare my nostrils but nod and then push the covers off of us.

"*You. Are. So. Annoying,*" I say to Mohammad.

He's standing over the bed and looking at us with an intense stare.

"There's no grumbling on holiday," he states.

Harry sits up next to me. In the light, I see that he looks as tired as I feel.

"If this were a true vacation, I'd be allowed to sleep in," I counter, moving my attention back to Mohammad.

I bring my hands up to my hair, self-conscious over the abrupt wake-up.

"And Harry, as the host and homeowner, is overruling your request," Mohammad counters.

I raise my eyebrows at Mohammad.

"What, did you fall on a crown this morning?" I scoff.

Because he has way too much attitude and *energy*. And I'm feeling … tired. And a little hungover.

"We probably do have a crown lying around here some-where," Harry contemplates as Mohammad throws open the curtains.

I shield my eyes, wanting to cry.

"Come down for breakfast. Then, we're going shooting," Mohammad yells before running out of the room.

"What is up with him this morning?" I ask, shaking my head.

Because Mohammad is on a different level today.

"He's just excited," Harry tells me.

"Have you woken up Noah yet?" I ask.

"We did." Harry yawns with a smile, then leans back, resting his head against the headboard. "He's out for a run."

"He is? He should have woken me up."

"I think he knows better than that," Harry teases.

I grab the pillow out from behind my head and smack him.

"My point," he says, sticking out his tongue at me.

I push out a pout, still wanting to go back to sleep. But based off Mohammad's energy, I know there's no chance of that.

"All right, I guess I'll change and then come down."

Harry leans over to me, giving me a kiss on the cheek. "You can come down in your pajamas. I am."

"I appreciate that," I mumble, closing my eyes for just a minute.

"Sleepy?"

"Extremely." I nod. "And I hate happy people in the morning. They're annoying."

"You'd better prepare yourself for Mohammad then." Harry laughs.

"It's like he's on a sugar high or something." I shake my head in disbelief.

"We had an eventful morning," Harry tells me, getting up.

"Oh?" I ask curiously.

"I'm sure you'll hear all about it at breakfast," Harry says, making his way to the door. "See you down there."

A second later, he's gone.

I pull the sheets over my head and let out a groan.

Eventually, I drag myself out of bed, brush my teeth, ignore my hair, and throw on some lip balm. By the time I make it down the stairs and into the large dining room, it feels like I've completed a marathon.

Mohammad and Harry are already at the table. Mohammad is in his usual morning look—silk shorts and no T-shirt. Harry has on sweats and a tight long-sleeved shirt.

I fall into an open chair and motion toward Mohammad's plate. "What do you have there?"

"Tea and toast," he cheerfully replies.

"What more could you want?" I grumble.

"Someone's charming this morning," Harry says, looking at me from across the table.

Mohammad tells Harry, "She just needs a coffee."

Harry looks past me toward the end of the table. I follow his gaze, my vision quickly filling with a woman. She comes to stand at my side and pours me a cup of coffee.

"Do you want a cappuccino? Juice?" Harry asks, looking from me to who I'm assuming is one of the servers. "The chef can make you anything."

"Uh ... a cappuccino would be great. And an orange juice?" I ask her.

She nods before turning on her heels and leaving.

"I love having a staff," Mohammad says, happily sipping his tea.

His enthusiasm is contagious, and I crack a little smile.

When the server comes back, she brings my drinks and Harry's breakfast. Unlike Mohammad's somewhat-healthy toast, Harry's plate is piled high, full of … grease.

"Harry," I scold, looking at his plate with shock.

He follows my gaze down to his food and grins. "Delicious, yeah?" he says, bringing a spoonful of beans to his mouth.

I have to swallow down a gag.

His plate is all brown.

Sausage, toast, reddish-brown beans.

"We really need to work on your diet," I comment.

"What are you talking about? This is a well-rounded breakfast. I thought you'd be proud," Harry counters.

"You need fruit. Or at least some juice to get that all down," I reply, a shiver running through me.

"You know Harry; he doesn't believe in a balanced diet." Noah's voice comes from behind me, and I spin around in my seat to find him leaning against the doorframe, wearing a black workout tee and running shorts.

"One day, it will catch up with him," I say, trying to keep focused on the conversation.

But Noah looks *good*.

Really good.

And it's very distracting.

"Maybe." Noah laughs and smiles, obviously in a happy mood from his run.

"You going to stand in the doorway all day?" Mohammad asks, barely looking up from his toast.

"I need to shower first," Noah says.

"Eat first. We don't have much time," Harry tells him, glancing at a clock on the wall.

"I might stink," Noah counters. But he comes into the room anyway.

"I thought you were going to wake me up," I say to Noah as he takes a seat.

"I didn't have time. I had to shower before my run," Noah says, glaring at Mohammad.

"What?" I ask, looking between them.

"It was fucking hilarious." Harry laughs, his whole body shaking.

"What was?" I ask Noah.

He shakes his head at me, pushing his chin up in annoyance. "I won't say."

"I will!" Mohammad interjects. "We put whipped cream on Noah's hand and then blew on his face until …"

"Until he went to itch his nose and got it all over his face," Harry says with a chuckle.

"My bathroom is a disaster!" Noah says, his eyes flaring.

"Your bathroom?" I ask, trying to follow along.

"After I woke up, Harry decided to chase me into the bathroom with the can of whipped cream. He got it everywhere." Noah shakes his head.

"I think you're forgetting the part where you stole the can from me and covered me in whipped cream," Harry points out.

"You deserved it," Noah replies, but he's smiling, and I know he had fun regardless.

I look between the three of them, wondering how they even have energy for this conversation this early. Normally, I'm happy to be up early and run, but today, I was tired.

It was probably the sunshine from yesterday.

And the alcohol.

But I could have slept even longer.

"Good thing you didn't wake me up like that," I comment, taking a drink of my cappuccino.

"You would have been *so* mad," Mohammad says, a look

of fear flashing in his eyes.

"It would have been bad," Harry agrees.

"Definitely," Noah says, eyeing my orange juice.

I slide it over to him, knowing that he probably needs it more than me right now. He shoots me a quick wink.

"So, how was your run?" I ask.

"Refreshing." Noah smiles, taking a big gulp of juice. "The air here is great. And all the space makes it easy to get lost in the rhythm. I like it."

"I'm sure it's a lot better than running in the city," Mohammad says.

"Yeah, it can break up your pace. But running in the park is nice," Noah says, glancing at me. "But I still have to practice today."

"I'd argue with you on that, but I know I'd lose," Harry remarks, waving the server over. "What do you two want to eat?"

Noah looks at Harry's plate.

"I'll have the same as him," Noah says, shocking me.

"Really?" I blurt out.

Noah nods, apparently sure.

"And you?" the server asks me.

I look across the table, finding jam and toast already there.

"Uh … can I have a smoothie?" I ask, knowing it will be good for me.

"Of course. What kind would you like?"

"Uh …"

"What about strawberry banana?" Noah suggests. His voice grabs my attention, and all I can seem to focus on is how he said the word banana.

Bah-naan-ah.

Noah's accent is so soft, and my eyes immediately slip down to his lips.

"Mal?"

"What?" I ask, flicking my eyes up to meet his.

Noah's forehead creases, like he thinks I've lost it. "The smoothie?"

"Shit, sorry. Yeah, that sounds great. Thank you." I give the server an apologetic smile.

"I'll have one too," Noah adds.

"You all right there?" Mohammad asks, his brows furrowing in.

"Yeah," I lie, embarrassed I just got distracted by Noah. *Here.* In front of everyone. "I was just thinking about … football."

"Football?" Noah asks with interest.

"About you practicing while you're here."

"It won't take too long. I wouldn't worry about it," Noah says.

"You're very dedicated," I comment.

"I love it."

"And you're bloody good at it," Harry agrees.

"Do you think you'll play at university?" I find myself asking.

"He could easily join a league," Mohammad answers.

"I could …" Noah says, weighing his head back and forth like, somehow, this is a new idea to him.

"If you're going to play pro, I wouldn't go to university at all," Harry says to Noah.

Noah's eyebrows shoot up in surprise.

"Huh," Noah says, sounding stunned. "I've never actually thought about that before."

"Playing professional?" I ask.

"Yeah."

"Do you think you'd enjoy it?" I ask seriously.

"Enjoy it?!" Mohammad erupts. "Professional footballers

here are like gods. They have the hottest wives, get to travel the world, have people chant their names, and the pay is ridiculous! Who *wouldn't* enjoy it?"

I wave off Mohammad, turning back toward Noah.

"Truthfully, it has never crossed my mind. But, yeah, it would be a different option to consider."

"Figures," Mohammad says, biting into his toast. "Noah could get into any university he wants with his marks, but he probably won't go. I, on the other hand, will be forced into it by my parents and will probably disappoint them when I don't get accepted where they *think* I should."

"Nah, mate. You'll get in wherever you want. But no point in worrying about it now. It's ages away," Noah disagrees.

"You're right," Mohammad says. But I can tell he's down about the fact.

I know he wants his parents' approval.

We all do.

Noah looks from Mohammad to me, his lips pulling to the side. I can tell he's worried about him.

"You have so many talents. Whatever you decide you want to do, we'll help you get there," I say encouragingly to Mohammad.

"Mallory's right. We're in it together, yeah?" Noah asks.

"Of course," Harry agrees. "And really, I'm going to be the one who needs help. Knowing my family, I'll end up at Oxford. And I won't be going there alone. I'll have to insist that one of you comes with me."

"Oxford?" I ask, raising an eyebrow.

Impressive.

"If I'm lucky, they'll let me stay in the city before going to university there."

"We could all stay in the city," Noah offers as the server

comes back into the room, bringing our smoothies and Noah's food.

"I don't know. The more I think about it, the more I like this *California plan*," Mohammad says, finishing off his toast.

"Weren't you the one going on about the *boys' club* last night?" Harry asks Mohammad. "And yet you'd abandon us so soon?"

"You could come visit," Mohammad says to Harry.

Harry frowns, obviously not liking his answer.

"As long as I'm in a city, I'm happy," I cut in, trying to defuse the situation.

"In a city *together*," Harry says under his breath.

I glance over to Noah. He's happily sipping on his smoothie and completely missing what's going on.

I tap my elbow against his.

He looks at me in confusion, his brows weaving together. I flare my eyes at him before motioning toward Mohammad. Then Harry. Harry keeps glancing over at Mohammad while eating his breakfast.

"So, you said we're going shooting this morning?" Noah asks.

Harry's blue eyes brighten, and he sets down his fork.

"I can't wait," I add with a cheerful smile.

"It will be a cracking time." Harry grins. "You'll want to change into what we bought the other night for it."

"We're going to look smart," Mohammad says, finishing off his cup of tea.

"Did you already have a shooting outfit, or did you go and buy a new one?" I ask Mohammad.

"I've got clothes from our other visits," he tells me.

"Aww. I can't wait to see you all dressed up. I'm sure you'll look great." I give him a grin.

"Speaking of which, we'd better get changed. The car's

picking us up at half past eight," Harry says, pushing his plate away from him.

He and Mohammad are quickly up and out of the room. I stay in my seat and wait for Noah to finish his breakfast before we head to our rooms.

"So, you packed a shooting outfit too?" I ask him when we get to the stairs.

"Harry insisted that we do it properly. Seems a bit much, but I wasn't about to tell him no."

"I'm not exactly sure about the whole shooting part, but I am excited for the clothes," I say with a laugh.

"I'm sure you'll look great," Noah says as we make it to the top of the stairs.

"Thanks." I flush. Noah starts to walk in the direction of his room, but I don't want him to go. "Do you want to come and see my outfit?"

Noah turns toward me, his eyes finding mine. "Sure."

I take his hand before I lose my nerve and lead him into my room. When we get inside, I close the door behind us and walk over to the wardrobe, where my shirt, vest, and pants are hanging.

"We're going to melt out there," Noah says, sitting down on the edge of my bed.

"Really?" I ask, pulling out the clothes.

"Yeah. There's a bit of a heat wave this weekend."

"Can't complain about that," I say, laying my outfit on the bed. "Well, what do you think?"

Noah glances at the outfit next to him before his eyes find mine again. "Aren't you going to put it on?"

"I'll change in a minute." I drop down onto the bed next to him.

"I thought you wanted my opinion?" Noah asks, his brows drawing in.

I take his hand in mine again, ignoring his question.

"Your accent kills me, you know," I say, his fingers feeling warm on my skin.

When I saw Noah at breakfast, all I wanted to do was get him out of his workout clothes. I couldn't let myself think about it when I was sitting across from Mohammad and Harry, but now …

"Kills you?" Noah asks.

"I love it," I say, scooting closer toward him. "I mean, I like your voice. And certain words you say, they're really cute."

Noah licks his lips, his brown eyes growing darker as he looks at me. And I can see the flicker of interest flash across his face.

"What's your favorite word to hear me say?" he asks.

"I don't know. I only notice it sometimes. But I really noticed it when you said banana at breakfast."

"Were you thinking about me during breakfast?"

And the way he says breakfast causes goose bumps to crawl down my arms.

He says everything so softly.

Bah-naan-ah.

Breck-fust.

"That's another one," I comment, my gaze slipping to his lips.

"What?" Noah asks, dropping his eyes to my mouth.

"Breakfast," I answer. "Everything you say sounds so soft."

Noah laces our fingers together. "Do you think I'm a softy then?"

"You're definitely a softy below that rigid exterior."

"The only thing you don't want soft." Noah winks, causing me to flush.

I bite my lip.

"What about you? Do you have a favorite word that I say?" I ask him.

Noah's eyes roll up to the corners as he thinks. "Hmm. I do like when you say *honestly*."

"Honestly?" I laugh. "Why?"

"You're always so serious when you say it. And the way you say it makes it sound so final. *Like, Honestly, Noah, can you believe ...*" he says, imitating my voice.

And it's a freakishly good imitation, except for the fact that he made me sound ridiculous.

"You make me sound like an airhead." I laugh, swatting at him.

"Nah. It's cute," he disagrees.

I smile at him, wanting to get lost in his eyes. In his lips. But I know I need to change clothes.

"Well, what do you think?" I ask, motioning to the outfit.

"I think you'll look perfect," he says, but I can hear hesitation in his voice.

"But?" I ask, looking at him.

"But you didn't bring me in here to show me your outfit, did you?" Noah asks, pulling me toward him.

"Of course I did," I say as he moves me onto his lap.

"You did?" he asks, his brows drawing together.

I shake my head at him. "No," I say. Because, really, I wanted a minute alone with him.

I wanted to kiss him.

I lean in and press my lips against Noah's. He kisses me back gently, sending a wave of emotion through me. I wrap my arms around his neck, pulling him closer. Noah grips my waist, causing an unexpected moan to erupt from my mouth.

"I knew you just secretly wanted to kiss me," he says against my lips.

"Did not," I disagree, but my lips are still on his.

All I can think about are his firm hands at my waist and how I feel like my chest might explode.

"Did too."

Noah catches me rolling my eyes and leans back, so there is space between us.

"You know, you can't exactly win this argument," he says with a smirk.

"Why not?" I ask, rubbing my hands across his chest.

Noah's cheeks flush, and I can tell he's getting distracted. His eyes drop down to watch my palms slide across his shirt. But then he flicks his gaze back up to mine.

"Because admission through action is still admission. You can deny it with your words, but your body is telling me a different story," Noah says, pulling me higher on his lap so my chest is almost flat against his.

"And what story is that?" I ask, barely getting the words out.

"That you want me." Noah playfully runs his palm down over my chest, making my skin feel like it's on fire.

"I thought you said I already have you?" I say seriously.

Noah grows serious too, his hand stilling. "Of course you do."

"Good," I say, pulling him back to my lips.

Why are you so good?
8:30AM

WHEN I COME downstairs, the boys are all dressed and ready to go.

Harry looks like a model. He's standing in the entryway

in a three-piece suit that he has tucked into short boots. Noah looks equally as gorgeous. He has on a flannel shirt underneath a hunter-green vest with matching pants that he has tucked into boots too. All three of them are wearing boots, just like me.

But Mohammad definitely looks the suavest.

He's wearing a plaid jacket, navy pants, and a coordinating tweed cap.

"You all look dashing," I say as I join them.

"We do our best. But I think the prize goes to Mohammad," Harry says. "He's properly turned out."

Mohammad practically blushes.

"You do look amazing," I tell him.

"Sorry you had to wait on me." I look down at myself. "I had trouble getting on the wellies."

"They're a pain," Mohammad agrees.

"Don't worry; we're right on time," Harry says, leading us out the front door.

Noah walks next to me and whispers, "You look gorgeous."

I smile brightly at him.

"You like it then?" I ask, remembering the hassle of putting it all on. I'm wearing my own jeans with socks and wellies with a white long-sleeved shirt under a navy vest.

"I like *you*," Noah says, his hand finding mine. His fingers graze my palm as we walk across the gravel drive toward a waiting Land Rover.

"Yeah?" I barely get the words out.

Noah always causes my head to spin.

He looks amazing, and he smells really good, like he just got out of the shower. But I can always find him underneath.

"Isn't it obvious that I fancy you?" he asks.

"Nope," I tease. "I think you should make it extremely

clear."

"Always wanting action." Noah laughs. "Harry would say, *how American of you.*"

"What can I say? He's right. I'm demanding," I say with a shrug.

But Noah doesn't look too upset about it.

"Very," he says, shooting me a wink as we follow Harry and Mohammad into the car.

It only takes about twenty minutes to get to where we're going, and I spend most of the drive looking out the window. It's cooler than it was yesterday but still gorgeous.

And the change in scenery is amazing.

You never realize how chaotic the city is until you get out of it.

As we unload ourselves out of the car, a man comes to greet us.

He's older and shorter than the boys, but he looks active for his age. His brown jacket and pants get lost in the landscape, and he gives off an air of relaxed confidence.

"Welcome back," he says, shaking Harry's hand.

"It's nice to be back. We've got a new one with us today," he says, motioning toward me.

"Hi," I say, shaking the man's hand. "I'm Mallory."

"Nice to meet you, Mallory. I'm Fred. I'm the keeper here, and I'll show you how clay pigeon shooting works."

I nod, knowing that I need to pay attention.

"There are different types of clay pigeon shooting, but Harry has requested the sporting layout. It's a more difficult setup for beginners, but it's the most realistic style."

"What's the sporting layout?" I ask.

"The targets will be expelled from traps that are set up in various locations to make it feel like you're hunting, as opposed to standing in a line, in one spot, and shooting."

"Okay," I say, trying to follow along.

"But before we get to that, I'm going to give you a quick gun safety course and teach you the terms we use."

He motions for us to follow him, so we walk out into an open field, forming a half-circle around where wooden stands are set up.

He takes us through a course on gun safety and shows me how to use the control that releases the target. Apparently, the shooter has to call for a target before it's released from what's called a trap.

They've got over sixty targets—or clay pigeons—coming from eight stands. We're required to wear earmuffs, and we have to watch out for the recoil of the shotgun.

"Why don't you do a few practice rounds here before we go out?" Fred says, handing me a shotgun that's open and unloaded. Anytime a shotgun is carried, it has to be like that for safety. He shows me how to get in the correct position and how to load the gun.

Once I get set up, he backs away.

"Now, you'll yell out *pull* when you are ready for the target to be released from the trap," he explains, "but first, I want you to do a practice shot, so you know what to expect."

I fire, adrenaline rushing through me.

For the next shot, he has me yell out *pull.*

I aim for the target, but I miss. By about a mile.

"That's great, Mallory!" Harry calls out once my gun is down at my side and open again.

"I missed." I laugh.

"We're still proud," Mohammad says with a grin.

"I didn't account for the fact that you've never shot before," Harry says, walking over to me and pulling me into a hug. "And know that anytime you're uncomfortable with the noise or you don't want to shoot, you don't have to. You can just follow through the course with your partner and not shoot, or we can always leave."

"Thanks, Harry." I grin. "But I think this is going to be fun."

"All right, let's break off then. Noah and Mallory can pair up, and I'll be with Mohammad," Harry says to Fred.

Fred agrees, then turns to me and says, "I'll go through the course with you."

We move farther into the open field until Fred stops us. Noah goes first, calling out *pull* but missing the shot.

I go next, missing too.

But then Noah hits one.

And then another.

And another one after that.

"Why are you so good?" I pout.

"Harry always has us doing things like this," he replies. "Turns out, I'm a pretty good shot."

"Really?"

"Of course. We don't just sit around when we come out to his country house. His family has very clear expectations for us."

"Harry likes this, doesn't he?"

"He loves it. Especially now that it's his idea and he's here with just us. I think he likes that he can show you another part of his world."

"I never realized how many talents you had," I comment. "Football. Statistics. Shooting."

Noah laughs. "We've all had lessons. And you're doing great."

"I am not. I've missed every time!" I laugh along with him. "But I am having fun. And I like being with you."

We work halfway through the course, Fred showing me what to do every time and always staying at my side.

"If you'll wait here, I'll see how Mohammad and Harry are getting on," Fred says, stopping us.

"Of course," Noah says as Fred hurries off.

I think about Harry now, about how well he's probably doing. About how much he enjoys this. And it makes me sad that his father can't see how amazing he is.

It makes me sad that Harry doesn't think he's good enough.

For his family.

For anyone.

"Noah, do you ever worry about not being good enough?" I ask as we wait.

"Good enough at what?"

"I just mean, in general."

"It's easy to get lost in what other people want for you," he says, thinking. "You're talking about Harry? About not being good enough for his parents?"

"I'm just … talking."

I don't want to answer Noah's question. Because I don't pity Harry. That isn't love. Not real love. To pity someone, to want to take care of them, is to not respect them. It means I don't respect his independence.

And I do.

But it makes me wonder what I would be like if I were in his shoes.

If, day after day, I was made to feel like I wasn't good enough. Like I was a disappointment to my family. Would I believe it? Would I be messed up because of it? Or would I be even harder on myself because of it, always trying to reach a goal that was somehow always out of my reach?

"Do you worry about that?" Noah asks me, breaking into my thoughts.

I flare my eyes, thinking through that one. "Sometimes.

But I think I have pretty high standards for myself. Maybe I set them because I'm scared to be criticized. Or I hope that, because my standards are high, I won't have the option to fail."

"Failing is a part of life."

"Says the boy who excels at everything," I say with a laugh.

Noah smirks, his cheeks warming.

"I don't excel at everything," Noah replies.

"Give me one example, apart from History."

Because I can't think of one thing that Noah is *actually* bad at. He's thoughtful, he works hard on most things, and he's great at Statistics, at football.

"My communication skills could use work," he says. "Especially when it comes to you."

And his answer takes me by total surprise.

"To me?" I ask.

"In my mind, everything is clear now. But I know I'm not always the best at conveying how I feel."

"Do you worry about that?" I ask, really looking at Noah. Because, suddenly, he seems younger, especially when his cheeks go a shade of pink with my question.

He blinks, his dark lashes grabbing my attention.

He brings his gaze to meet mine. "Not usually. I've told you how I feel now, so I hope it's obvious," Noah replies, looking more relaxed.

"You're not the easiest to read," I admit. "But I try to pay attention."

I can't help it when my eyes slide down over his body. He really does look gorgeous today.

"You don't pay attention," he says, moving toward me. "You get distracted."

He dips his chin, looking down his nose at me.

"Well, you're distracting," I force out. I try to keep my voice firm, but it barely has any volume when it leaves my lips.

"You're distracting too, you know," he replies, taking another step closer and bringing his hand to mine, letting his fingers graze my palm.

Butterflies erupt in my stomach at his touch.

"And I've always told you, whatever happens now is up to you."

"Up to me?" I question.

Noah glances over my shoulder, biting his lip.

"I know I teased you before. At first, it wasn't exactly nice, but I had to feel you out."

"Feel me out?" I raise my eyebrows at his word choice, but Noah doesn't crack a smile.

"Yeah, you know, figure you out. I had to push your buttons to find them."

"Circle the prey. Get to know the enemy, so you can be strategic with the kill." I flare my eyes, rambling on.

That finally gets Noah to smile.

"You were new. Different. *Beautiful.* And very demanding. I was at a loss. Still am most of the time."

"Really?" I ask, surprised. "You always seem so sure—of everything."

"I am." Noah nods.

"I'm not like that."

"You're surer of yourself than you think. Especially when you're determined."

"Talking the day away?" Harry says, joining us.

Noah takes a step back from me and smiles at Harry.

"I was getting sick of beating her." Noah shrugs. But the corners of his eyes crinkle up, and a wide smile sets onto his face.

"You did not just say that!" I laugh.

"It's true. Fred told me." Harry nods adamantly, seemingly amused.

"Fred's a traitor," I try to say with a straight face. But I can't help but crack a smile.

"We're switching partners for the last half. Noah, it's you and Mohammad."

Noah nods and runs out to meet Mohammad.

"Enjoying yourself?" Harry asks, looking me over.

"It's a lot of fun," I admit. "I just wish I were better."

"With practice, you will be."

"I'm not sure I can consistently practice this in London," I tease.

"Maybe not. But if you keep coming out to the house with us, you'll get more and more experience," he tells me.

"That's true," I admit as Fred rejoins us.

Harry is up first, and he's kind of amazing to watch. I'm not sure I've ever seen him so focused.

On anything.

Usually, he's laid-back and so relaxed. But it's obvious Harry takes this seriously.

When my turn comes up, I aim, call *pull*, and fire.

And I finally hit one!

I want to jump in the air and yell for joy, but I know that's not allowed. Fred takes the shotgun from me, opening it for safety. Harry sets his down on the ground, and a second later, he's picking me up.

"That was great!" he says, spinning me around.

"Did you see that?" I try not to scream out.

"What a shot," Harry replies. And he's beaming.

Eventually, my feet find the ground again, and my celebratory adrenaline rush settles down. Fred gives me back the shotgun, and Harry and I keep going.

"Usually, after shooting, we go to the pub, but I've had Muriel arrange lunch for us at the house," Harry tells me as we move through the grass.

"Really?"

"Yeah. I thought you might like to go into the village later, so we can stop at the pub then," he explains.

"Any excuse you can get to go to a pub," I tease.

"I do love a good pub." Harry grins sheepishly. "And having you there, it will bring back some memories."

"Of us in the pub?" I ask.

"On that ever-fateful night at the pub, in which I stumbled upon an angel," Harry says dramatically. "Drinking cider no less."

"It takes some guts to kiss an angel upon first meeting," I say, remembering how Harry kissed me within minutes of talking to me.

"Liquid courage," Harry replies with a wink.

"Were you drunk?" I ask.

"I was sober enough to notice you," he replies seriously.

"And my shitty cider."

"That was just an in," Harry says, patting me on the shoulder.

My mouth falls open. "Wait, seriously?"

"Sometimes, you can be so dense. Of course it was," Harry replies.

I blink, impressed.

Because I never would have figured that out.

"Damn. Props to you."

"Props to me." Harry gives me a smirk.

WHEN WE FINISH the course, we meet back up with Noah and Mohammad. They are both smiling widely and look like they've had a great time.

Fred takes our shotguns and gives us all handshakes and hugs.

"You boys ready?" Harry asks, throwing his arm over my shoulders.

I grab on to his wrist, my cheeks warming as he leads us back to the waiting car.

"Let's go home."

Just like that.
11:00AM

"THAT WAS AMAZING, Harry!" I haven't stopped grinning since we got back to the house. "I didn't know you'd be so good!"

"I'm a great shot. It's my only saving grace for when I go out with my dad," he replies, pulling off his wellies in the mudroom.

Noah leans against the wall and does the same.

"You didn't do too bad either," I say to Noah, giving him a smile.

"You think?" Noah shoots me a wink.

"Well, I did! It was ridiculous." Mohammad pouts, pulling off his jacket and hanging it on the coatrack.

"You didn't do bad," I reply, trying to keep his spirits up.

"You weren't even partnered with me," he fires back.

"Lucky I wasn't. You don't take losing very well," I counter.

"You can't *lose*. It's not a competition," Noah corrects.

"Either way, I could have done better," Mohammad mutters, sitting down on a bench against the wall.

"Are you usually better?" I ask, curiously.

Mohammad's eyes roll up to the corners as he contemplates my question. "Define *better*."

Harry laughs, throwing his arm around Mohammad's shoulders. "Mate, you did great."

"You think?" Mohammad asks, looking up at Harry with big puppy-dog eyes.

Obviously, his ego is wounded.

"I know so. You and I were neck and neck. And I've had proper training."

Harry leads Mohammad out of the mudroom, patting his shoulder as they go.

"He's bent out of shape over that," I comment once they've left. Then, I sit down and pull off my wellies.

Noah leans his shoulder against the wall and focuses his attention on me. "He'll get over it. And hopefully soon, or we'll never hear the end of it."

"I'm sure with Harry in his ear, his ego will be back in no time," I say wryly, causing Noah to laugh. "Either way, I had a great time."

"So did I." Noah smiles, his eyes dropping to scan across my body as I stand up. "You did brilliantly out there."

"Really?" I laugh. "I tried not to think about it. Just focused on having fun."

"You let loose," Noah confirms, pushing off the wall. "I loved seeing you happy."

Noah takes my waist in his hands, pulling me against his firm chest. I respond by putting my arms around his neck.

"Well, get used to it. I'm happy, Noah. Really happy."

Noah's smile turns into a full-fledged grin. I tilt my chin up as he brings his lips down onto mine. It's a soft kiss, but it's perfect.

I pull back, lacing my fingers through his.

"Come on. We'd better go find them. See what's next on

the agenda!" I say brightly.

Noah squeezes my hand and nods.

"I think they went into the living room," he says, leading the way.

"It's been a full day, and it's only eleven o'clock!" Mohammad says, looking at the time.

"Plus, Noah went for a run this morning," I comment as we join them.

"It was a quick run, no biggie," Noah says, downplaying it.

"You really are efficient with your time," Harry says, sitting down on the couch.

"You always have time. It's just a matter of how you spend it," Noah replies knowingly.

"Well, I plan to spend my time here with a glass of liquor in my hand and you three by my side."

A wide smile settles on my face.

"Not exactly healthy," Noah chastises under his breath.

"Isn't Mallory always saying we need balance in life?" Harry counters. "I think a holiday and rest will do me some good in the grand scheme of things. Especially with the upcoming stress."

"Think you'll come back from Shanghai with gray hairs?" I ask, sitting down directly across from Harry.

"I've been thinking—" Harry starts, but Mohammad cuts in.

"Uh-oh," Mohammad says eerily. "That can't be good."

Mohammad grins in anticipation, waiting for our laughter of approval, which, in turn, causes me to laugh. Harry just rolls his eyes.

"You were saying?" Noah asks Harry.

"I plan on coming back from Shanghai with a reward," Harry says.

"A reward?" I ask.

"I've decided if my parents are making demands on me, I should make demands on them."

"Like how you asked to come here?" Mohammad asks him.

"Exactly. If my dad wants to be a prick, fine. Let him be a prick. But I'm going to get something out of it."

"What do you want?" Noah asks with interest.

Harry purses his lips as he thinks. "I haven't decided yet."

"A yacht!" Mohammad shouts.

Harry weighs his head back and forth, like he's actually contemplating the idea. I look at Noah, my eyes going wide.

"That seems a bit excessive," Noah says, trying to keep them grounded.

"Does it?" Harry asks seriously.

"What about a car?" I suggest.

"A car?" Noah gapes at me.

A grin bursts onto Harry's face. "Yes, and not just any car. A fucking Aston Martin V12 Vantage!"

"Oh, yes," Mohammad squeals, clapping his hands together like he's five. "Gorgeous and fast with curves in all the right places."

"Do you even know how to drive?" I ask, rolling my eyes.

"Besides the point," Harry says, waving off my question.

"I think that might be too big of an ask," Noah states.

"Can you really put a price on abuse?" Mohammad interjects.

My hand flies up to cover my mouth.

"Mohammad! You can't go around saying stuff like that," I chastise. "It's insensitive."

"What? It's true! And bargaining with Mr. Brooks wasn't my idea; it was Harry's," he says with a pout.

"Don't hassle him. He's right. You can't put a price on it.

Even though I'm trapped in this family, I can still bargain to make my life a bit cushier," Harry agrees.

"That seems like a bad idea," I say.

"Says the girl who would rather be disinherited than give in to her family's demands," Harry replies.

My mouth falls open.

Again.

"It's not a bad thing. Just very American," Harry says, standing and walking over to me. He pinches my chin fondly. "Honestly, I admire your strength. It's just not an option for me."

"Enough," Noah cuts in. "We're supposed to be relaxing."

But he looks anything other than relaxed.

"You're right," Harry agrees. "I'm going to let Muriel know we're ready for lunch."

"Wait, before you go, let's take a photo for Helen," I say, getting up from the couch.

I gather us all together and snap a selfie.

"I'm going to send this photo to your mom," I say to Noah.

He looks over my shoulder, watching as I type out the message.

Me: *We're about to have lunch and wanted to say hi! You'll be so proud. We went clay pigeon shooting today, and I learned how to shoot!*

I hit *send* just as Noah grabs the phone out of my hand. I glance over my shoulder, annoyed.

"Mallory!" Noah says, shaking his head at me.

"What?" I ask.

"You did not just send that to my mum." His forehead creases, and he looks like he's about to lose it.

"Uh ... I'm pretty sure I did. Why? What's wrong with

it?"

I take the phone back from him and look over the text and photo. But I can't find a problem.

Mohammad grabs the phone from my hand, and immediately, his eyes go wide.

"She's going to freak," Mohammad says.

A second later, Noah's phone rings. He glares at me before answering the call.

"Hello?" he says into the phone.

Both Mohammad and I listen in.

"Yes, Mum, I know," Noah sighs before running his hand back through his chestnut hair. "Yes, she was safe."

Noah starts to pace, causing me to frown.

Why is Helen freaking out?

"Yes. Yes, I understand. Hang on …" Noah walks over to me and holds out the phone. "She wants to talk to you."

"You're in trouble," Mohammad sings out.

I flare my eyes at Noah. Because I don't want to take the phone!

No, I mouth silently.

Noah places the phone in my hand anyway.

I clear my throat and brace for an attack.

"Uh, hello?" I say to Helen.

"Mallory James," she starts.

I swallow a gulp of air, knowing that if she's using my full name, I'm in deep trouble.

And I probably should keep my mouth shut.

"Mmhmm?" I ask through sealed lips.

"What were you thinking?" she screeches into the phone.

My eyes go wide at her outburst, and instantly, my stomach drops.

"I—"

Helen cuts me off, "Exactly, you weren't! You could have

been injured—or killed!"

"But the boys …"

"Don't make this about them," she says, stopping me. "I told you to be safe. And what do you decide to do? Engage in a dangerous sport—that's what!"

"But Harry planned it," I try to explain. "And Noah didn't say you'd be upset. They said they've been shooting before! And he knew we'd be going."

Both Mohammad's and Noah's mouths fall open as they listen. I walk away from them, needing space.

I move to the corner of the room and look out the window.

"They've all had proper training and gone out with Harry's father. You, on the other hand, haven't been trained," she cries out.

My stomach twists.

"I'm sorry, Helen. I was with Noah most of the time. And, Fred, the keeper, gave me a lesson on safety, and he was always there." I stumble over my words, realizing that she's *really* upset.

And the last thing I wanted to do was disappoint Helen.

She lets out a sigh. When she speaks again, her voice softens. "I'm sorry that I yelled. Oh, Mallory … I just worry about you. You can be so impulsive. And that, combined with a gun, well …"

My mouth falls open.

"You have to have a little faith in me," I tell her, immediately feeling hurt.

Does she really not trust me?

"Of course I do, dear. But your mother and father aren't here yet. And seeing as I've been responsible for you for the past few weeks, I felt it important that someone tell you to never do that again."

"I'm sorry I worried you," I say back.

Because that's what her freak-out is really about.

"I care about you, and I expect you back in London on Tuesday in one piece. Understood?" she asks, only she sounds choked up now.

And it makes me smile.

"I understand."

"Good. Now, promise me you'll never pick up a gun again."

"I don't have any intention …" I start, but she cuts me off.

"Mallory," she says impatiently.

"I promise. I will never pick up a gun again without having more training and your approval first," I reply, deciding it's better to just tell her what she wants.

"Thank you," she says, relief flooding her voice.

There's a pause, and I'm not sure what to say.

I decide to change the subject.

"So, how was Mia's date?" I ask, hoping she'll just go along with it.

"She came home on a cloud," Helen says warmly.

I hear the clink of glasses in the background and assume she's unloading the dishwasher. I can picture her holding her phone between her shoulder and her chin as does her chores.

"Aww. I'm glad," I reply. "Are you two still reading Sherlock Holmes together?"

"We are. I'll finish up the book today while Gene works on repairing the upstairs sink."

I immediately look up at Noah, remembering what he told me about his parents. That every Sunday, Gene helps around the house.

"What's wrong with the sink?" I quickly ask.

"The tap isn't working correctly. Mia said it started leaking. And every time I walk past the bathroom, I hear it," she says, disappointment thick in her voice.

"That's not good."

"No, it's not. But Gene is on the job," she says brightly.

"I almost forgot. Thank you for the book."

"I hoped it would keep you entertained *and* out of trouble," she says.

"And it will," I assure her.

"All right, dear. Give the boys my love and make sure to have Noah phone tomorrow. We love you."

"I love you too."

Helen hangs up, and the second she does, I'm searching the room for Noah. He's seated on the couch, watching me in amusement. I'm across the room in a second and throwing his phone at him.

"What the hell?! Why did you do that?" I growl.

"Me?! That was all you!" Noah replies.

"He's right," Mohammad says, deciding to chime in. Which is *definitely* a mistake.

I swirl in his direction.

"I don't remember asking you!" I shout, fuming.

Mohammad holds his hands out in front of his chest in defense as Harry rejoins us.

"Whoa!" he cuts in. "What's going on?"

Neither Noah nor Mohammad says anything.

"I just got bitched out by Helen for going shooting," I tell him.

Harry moves toward me, placing his hand on my arm. "She was upset?" he asks, looking concerned.

And it immediately calms me down.

"She was furious. She yelled at me." I feel a pout form.

"Aw, no," Harry says, pulling me into a hug. "Don't worry; she'll get over it."

"You did give a good diversion," Noah finally says.

I pull away from Harry and look at him.

"You think?" I ask, feeling a little better.

Noah nods approvingly. "Completely. Mum can always be sidetracked. You played her well," Noah says with admiration.

"I didn't play her," I disagree.

"You totally did," Mohammad cuts in.

"Well, it was either that or listen as her head exploded," I reply, shaking my head. "The whole implied *don't shoot a gun because you're a girl* felt a little sexist though."

Noah rolls his eyes. "Mum's traditional—you know that."

"I think it had more to do with your lack of experience," Mohammad disagrees.

I raise an eyebrow, looking in his direction.

Because how could he know that?

"Wait, were you listening?" I ask, my eyes going wide. Because I was all the way on the other side of the room!

Mohammad grins, his pearly whites coming out. "I've got good ears."

"Intrusive ears! That was a private conversation."

"Not *that* private. I could hear Helen yelling at you through the phone."

I shoot Mohammad a glare, then turn my attention back to Noah. "Your mom is like a hawk."

"She overreacted," he replies.

"She *knows*," Mohammad says seriously.

"I went from living in a house in New York that was constantly empty with no rules to living in a house with your mother," I say, thinking out loud.

"You like that she hovers," Noah replies.

Harry takes my hand and leads me to the couch. "Why don't you sit and relax? Cheese toasties and tomato soup are on the way," Harry says, but he doesn't join me on the couch.

I'm about to ask him where he's going, but I watch as he makes a beeline for the bar cart.

Mohammad watches, too, and is up in an instant and at his side.

Which leaves just me and Noah seated.

I turn my attention back to him and his statement.

"I don't like that she hovers. I'm not used to having a mom who cares so much. A mom who overreacts, sure. But not one that treats me like a child."

"You really don't get along with your mum," Harry says, turning to look over his shoulder at me.

"It's not that we don't get along. We're just different people," I reply. "Different people from different planets."

Harry and Mohammad return back to the seating area, each carrying two drinks. Harry hands me a glass.

"There's nothing that a little whiskey won't dull," Harry says, holding his glass up in a toast.

Mohammad and Noah both extend their arms up. I roll my eyes but then finally do the same.

"To dulling the pain with good friends and even better alcohol. Cheers."

I laugh, taking a drink.

Harry is grinning as he drops onto the couch beside me. "It's mad, the amount of shit that's happened since you've been here," he whispers to me.

And I can't disagree with him.

"To me or you?" I ask, wondering which one of us he's referring to.

"To me," he says.

"You have sort of fallen apart in front of me," I tease. "I mean, only a few times."

Harry laughs. "Maybe once or twice."

"Once or twice?" I push.

"All right, maybe more than that," he says, a smile curling on his lips. He searches my face. "Hasn't anyone told you it's not nice to kick a man whilst he's down?"

"I didn't know you were down," I reply, taking in his calm demeanor and relaxed features.

Harry smiles.

"Here, I'm not." He glances at Noah and Mohammad, looking appeased.

"You having fun?" I ask, taking another drink.

"Loads actually." Harry quickly rises from the couch to stand and looks at me. "Want to play billiards?"

"Sure," I reply, looking from Harry to Noah and Mohammad, who are in the middle of a conversation. "You guys want to play?" I ask them.

"Maybe in a bit," Noah says, glancing up to me.

I lead Harry into the attached room and watch as he racks the balls.

"I'm glad you like the house," he says.

"Harry, this isn't a house. It's an *estate*," I correct, leaning against the table. "It's one thing to be modest. But it's a whole other thing to be oblivious."

"Do you think I'm oblivious to my life of luxury?" he asks, moving around the billiards table toward me. When he gets to my side, he hands me a cue stick.

"I think you know just as much as me that this place is on a different level."

Harry looks around, taking in the filled walls and thick leather couches. The room is filled fully and exudes a warmth that Harry's place in London never has.

"It is beautiful," he agrees, his eyes slipping back to me.

"It is. But only because of the people inside of it." I hear myself say the words, and I don't know where they came from. My gaze meets Harry's, both of us knowing the importance of this time together.

Because, in a few days, he'll be gone.

And then gone again over summer.

And then maybe gone again for college.

And the idea of Harry leaving ... it doesn't sit well with me.

It doesn't sit well at all.

Harry pushes a strand of hair out of my face, his blue eyes holding mine. "Getting all mushy on me now?" he asks, his hand staying on my face.

"A little," I admit. "I don't want you to leave."

"I'm not leaving yet." Harry puts some space between us. I nod, watching as he lines up his cue stick before striking the balls.

"And we have that party," I say, watching Harry sink a shot.

"Exactly. We need to get you thinking like a socialite."

"And how do I do that?" I ask, lining up my shot.

"You'll want to comment on the age of the house. The gardens. Ask if they produce anything on the land. When do they holiday in the area, what's their favorite pastime to engage in," Harry explains.

"Spoken like someone who's talked the talk before." I laugh.

"I'm just trying to prepare you for the *riveting* conversations to come," Harry says, flaring his eyes.

"You're pretty good with people. I don't see you having any trouble with conversation."

"Not usually." Harry grins and pushes his blond hair out of his eyes before taking another shot. "Maybe you can come back for the holidays."

"The holidays?" I ask.

"Yes. You could spend winter break here," Harry says, motioning to the house. "This is usually where we spend Christmas. Every so often, we might celebrate on some exotic island, but I'm assuming this year, they're going to want to sell the whole *family effect*."

"How about I join you for that exotic island trip?" I reply. "I could definitely picture myself tanning while it snows on my friends in New York."

Harry laughs. "We could make that happen."

"It sounds nice, but I'm not sure how my parents would feel about me being gone for the holidays."

"Your parents would be invited, of course."

My eyebrows shoot up in surprise. "That sounds like a bad idea. Doesn't it?"

"How come?" Harry asks.

"With the divorce, do you think you'll even come back this year?"

Harry sucks in a breath. "You have a point. Maybe we won't be here. It's funny; I've always hated it. I get bored out here without the boys …"

Harry's face flashes with pain.

"But there's comfort in the familiar?" I say.

Harry audibly exhales. "Who knows? Maybe I'll request my own holiday. We can keep up the whole act and tell my parents we're jetting off together. Go to that exotic island to ring in the new year," he suggests.

"We can't lie to everyone. Or to ourselves," I try to say delicately.

"I know."

"Besides, don't you want to ring in the new year with a kiss in the city or something? Not stuck on an island somewhere with me?"

"If we were on an island and the clock struck midnight

and we were all alone, you really wouldn't kiss me because of everything?" Harry asks.

I search Harry's eyes. "I don't know."

"I know you would. Which is why taking you to an island for New Year's sounds like a bad idea if I intend on keeping my friendship with Noah," Harry says lightheartedly.

I smile back at him, glad that he isn't making this weird.

"So, no island for me?" I tease.

"I'd take you regardless." Harry winks. "No one would blame me."

I shake my head at him. I'm not sure if he's teasing, but it doesn't really matter.

Because we're having fun again.

We're joking.

And it feels really good.

Noah knocks on the door before he enters.

When he sees me, he immediately smiles.

"Lunch is ready," he tells us.

Muriel has set the table in the dining room for lunch, and it's almost a waste. In under five minutes, we all finish our food, hungry from the morning out.

"DO YOU GUYS want to go get some fresh air?" Noah asks once we're finished and back in the living room. "I'm going to go for a walk."

"Sure," I reply, my eyes on Noah.

He nods at me before looking to Harry and Mohammad.

"I'll pass on the walk," Harry replies, plopping down on the couch.

"Mohammad, what about you?" Noah asks.

But one look at Mohammad, and I already have the answer. He's sprawled out on the couch, looking way too comfortable to move.

"What?" Mohammad asks, apparently not paying attention.

"Do you want to go for a walk?" I ask him.

"We just went for a walk." He waves us off. "I'll stay in."

"Okay." Noah nods. "See you in a bit."

Noah stays at my side as we walk out through the French doors.

"I'm sorry my mum upset you," he says once we're alone.

"She didn't upset me—"

"She did," Noah says, cutting me off, "and I'm sorry. I know your independence is important to you."

"It is," I agree.

Noah grabs on to my hand.

"It didn't feel good, having her question that, did it?" he asks.

"Not really." I give his hand a squeeze. "But I know she just cares about me and my well-being. I can't fault her for that."

Noah smiles at me as we cut across the grass. I notice the football net set up and think back to what Mohammad said about Noah playing later in life.

"So, you really are serious about football," I comment, motioning toward the net.

"I feel good doing it, yeah."

"Do you see yourself continuing it after school?" I ask.

"I've never really considered it," Noah admits.

"Really?"

"I could see it. I'm just not sure where I'll end up with that stuff," he says.

"Sometimes, I wonder if I hold on to my dreams so hard because I'm scared of feeling in limbo," I admit.

"It's okay to know what you want though," Noah tells me as we walk.

"It is. But I also think there's a lot of strength in admitting that you don't know. Being able to face the confusion with a high head is ... scary."

"You like having a plan. It's who you are." Noah wraps his arm around my waist as we walk.

"Do you care if you have one or not?"

"I don't necessarily have a plan, but that doesn't mean I haven't thought about it. I've played out a lot of scenarios in my head. The way I think things will go. The routes I might take to get to my goals and how those might stray. It's important to think through things," Noah tells me.

"And you thought *I* was the planner." I laugh as we approach a pond. It's beautiful, set right in the middle of freshly cut grass.

"Oh, you are." Noah tickles my waist.

I laugh at the sensation, but quickly, Noah's fingers still, and he pulls me closer to him.

"You know, Mohammad told me when I first got here that you didn't like change and that you'd probably take a long time to warm up to me." I bring us to a stop, pulling Noah down so we can both sit in the grass.

"Well, you weren't in the equation," Noah replies with an agreeing nod.

"And now?" I ask, tugging at a blade of grass.

"You've kind of single-handedly thrown my equation right out the window. Though I think it's a good thing, Mal. Another one's arisen in its place."

"And you're happier with this new equation?"

"It took me a while to warm up to it. But now, I'm very happy." His eyes slip down to my lips, but quickly, his gaze is over my shoulder.

Just when I think he's about to kiss me, I hear Harry shouting from behind me.

"Let's go!" he yells out, and I watch Noah's eyes go wide and a smile break out on his face.

I turn to see Harry running across the grass in nothing but his underwear. He has a floatie around his waist and two pints full of beer spilling out as he runs.

"What the hell?" I laugh.

Mohammad is in his underwear, too, carrying a flask and running behind Harry like a madman.

"Come on," Noah says, pulling me after them.

I watch as they both run straight toward the pond. Harry reaches the dock first, and I wholeheartedly expect him to run straight across it and jump in, two pints, floatie, and all. But he sets down the pints, strips off the floatie, and *then* makes a run for it.

He jumps into the pond, making a huge splash.

"Strip off!" Mohammad says, tossing the flask to Noah before running and jumping into the water.

"Oh fuck!" Harry yells as Mohammad's splash soaks him.

Mohammad pops up in the water. "It's freezing!"

"Come on!" Harry yells to us as Noah drags me to the pond.

When we get there, Noah starts stripping. His shirt comes off first, and I have to turn away from him *and his chest.* I squat down and dip my finger into the water.

"You guys are crazy! This water is freezing," I reply, shaking my head.

"You're getting in," Noah tells me.

"No way," I disagree, standing my ground.

"Oh, yes way," Noah replies, taking off his pants so he's left standing in only his underwear.

"Hurry up! Mohammad and I will rate your cannonballs!" Harry yells.

"I'm not getting in that water," I call out, crossing my

arms over my chest. "Just because you two have decided to do something idiotic doesn't mean I have to!"

"Noah, throw her over your shoulder," Harry calls out.

I drop my mouth open and glare at him.

"Looks like you've got two options. Strip and run in yourself or get thrown in, fully clothed," Noah replies seriously.

I whip my head in his direction. "Neither of those things is happening," I reply firmly.

Noah takes a step toward me, and instinctively, I move back a step.

"It's your choice, Mal," Noah says, dropping his voice. "I'd rather carry you in myself, but I think you'd rather go in on your own. What do you say?"

"I say, there's always a third option," I reply. And then I start sprinting in the opposite direction.

"We've got a runner!" Harry shouts with a laugh.

I push myself as hard as I can, but quickly, hands are around my waist, and I'm actually being picked up and thrown over Noah's shoulder.

"Put. Me. Down. This. Instant!" I smack against his butt with each word.

"Fully clothed it is!" Noah shouts, walking out onto the dock.

"Fine, fine, fine!" I reply, letting my hands drop. "You win, okay?"

Noah sets me back down, barely looking winded from chasing me. I glare at him before spinning around to Mohammad and Harry to do the same to them.

"Hurry up," Mohammad says impatiently.

I roll my eyes but pull my shirt off over my head and drop it onto the dock. Harry swims over to the dock, grabbing one of the pints and his floatie, situating himself in it.

"Don't get in until she's in. She's already proven she's a runner!" Harry laughs.

"She can't outrun me," Noah replies over his shoulder.

I let out a groan but unzip my pants.

"Hand me the flask," Mohammad says, swimming toward us.

Noah hands it to him as I strip off my pants. I try not to think about Noah's eyes as I mentally prepare for this.

"All right, let's go," Noah says, ushering me down the dock.

"In my own time," I reply, annoyed.

"Chop-chop," he insists with a grin.

I decide to change tactics. I turn to him, pushing out my bottom lip.

"Noah, it's so cold. Don't make me," I say, batting my eyelashes at him.

Concern flashes across his face. He steps toward me, his hands outstretched. I let his fingers barely touch my arms before I turn, pushing him off the dock and into the water.

"Oh shit!" Mohammad yells, his eyes practically on fire.

Noah's head pops up, and he sputters out water.

"What the fuck?" he says, wiping his face.

"She got you. She got you bad," Harry says, raising his glass to me.

I do a little curtsy, proud of myself.

"You're done for now," Noah says. And he's already swimming for the dock.

I take off running, but soon enough, wet arms wrap around me.

"Think about what you're about to do!" I scream as Noah drags me back to the dock. "I'll never forgive you for this!"

A second later, he's tossing me into the water. I gasp, feeling like I was just shoved into an ice bath.

I kick to the surface and immediately scream, furious.

"This water is freezing!" I say, but a second later, Noah's jumping in next to me. I shield my eyes from his splash, but the second his head pops back up, I swim over to him and dunk him back into the water.

"She's trying to drown him." Mohammad laughs, taking a swig from the flask.

"I'm not trying to drown him. I'm *going* to drown him!"

"I'm putting my money on Mallory," Harry says from his floatie.

I glance up at him, noticing he's already drunk half his pint.

Noah and I scramble in the water until, finally, I'm out of breath.

"You're so strong." Noah cough-laughs, spitting up water.

I kick away from him, prepared for a secret attack at any time.

"That's what happens when you mess with the bull!" I tell him, quoting one of my dad's many weird sayings.

Harry busts out laughing.

"Yeah, yeah, yeah," Noah says, swimming over to the dock.

When he gets there, he pulls himself out of the water and downs half of a pint, then swims over to me with the flask.

"Want some?" he asks. "It will warm you up."

I want to argue with him, but at this point, I don't even care.

I'll take anything.

I grab the flask and down a shot, feeling a little better. But not much.

"Aren't you frozen?" I ask Mohammad, hoping he's on my side.

"It's cold," he admits.

"But fun!" Harry calls out.

"I thought you two would be napping or something. How'd you go from saying no to a walk to jumping into a freezing cold pond?"

"Harry suggested it," Mohammad tells me.

I look at Harry in question.

"I figured, *why not?*" Harry says, like that's somehow an answer. He finishes off his pint the same time that Noah does.

"Well, we've run dry," Noah says, slamming the pint glass down on the dock.

"One more cannonball, and then we need refills," Harry says to Noah.

Noah's eyes light up.

A moment later, he's up and running down the dock, away from us. Then he turns, sprints toward us, and jumps into the water, tucking his knees to his chest.

He makes a huge splash before popping up.

"Brilliant!" Harry yells, paddling himself toward the edge of the pond in his floatie.

"Ten out of ten," Mohammad agrees.

Noah looks at me, pushing wet hair out of his face.

"It was *all right*," I reply, still not over him throwing me in.

"Into the house we go!" Harry says. He's already on the grass, dragging his floatie behind him.

Mohammad, Noah, and I all swim to the dock, grab our clothes, and run after him.

As we run into the house, soaking wet and practically naked, I try to keep from slipping on the slick floor.

"I can't believe you did that," I grumble, still annoyed with Noah.

Noah follows me into my bedroom, watching as I pull clothes out of my drawers.

"I felt like a man's man." Noah smirks, looking way too pleased with himself.

I roll my eyes. "Your mom would be so proud," I deadpan.

"Probably."

"What do you think—should I call and tell her that her lovely son threw me into a pond today?" I threaten.

I quickly move into the bathroom, closing the door behind me. I strip off my wet bra and underwear before toweling dry.

"Not to mention the fact that the water was freezing. She'll probably worry we're going to get sick," I call out from the bathroom.

I quickly pull on jeans and a sweater, then open the door.

"I think she'll have more of a problem with the fact that you were in your knickers," Noah says, looking me over.

And even fully dressed, I feel naked in front of him.

"So, we shouldn't tell her?" I ask distractedly. Because now that I'm not freezing and focused on getting dry, I notice that Noah is still only in his underwear.

And he looks amazing.

I step toward him, wanting to touch his creamy skin. I put my palms flat on his chest, my hands sliding up and around his neck.

"I wouldn't," Noah says, placing his hands on my hips. "But knowing you, she'll find out today."

My mouth instantly drops open.

"I can't believe you!" I yell, but quickly, I'm silenced by Noah's mouth on mine. I try to talk through closed lips. "Kissing won't fix this."

"It's not my fault you're upset by the truth," he says, pulling me tight against him.

"I'm upset by you," I mumble against his mouth.

"I can tell," he replies as he pushes me back onto the bed. "But I have a question."

"What?" I ask, looking up at him.

"If you're cross with me, then why are you still kissing me?" he asks with a smirk.

"I've changed my mind. I don't want to kiss you," I say.

"You don't?" Noah asks, lying on top of me. "Not even just a sweet little kiss?"

I bite my lip, annoyed he's going to make me say it.

And I already know that I am.

"Ask me," Noah insists.

I want to roll my eyes in response, but his fingers find their way to where my jeans meet my sweater, causing me to feel breathless. All I can focus on are his hands on my skin.

"I told you from the beginning, I'd have you begging before I gave in," Noah says softly.

"I can't believe you!" I say, shoving him. "I'm not begging."

"Sure I can't change that?" Noah asks, his finger sliding across my stomach. "Think about Friday. I'm pretty sure someone brought up being my girlfriend before we even properly kissed, or am I wrong?"

"And what about our first kiss?" I counter.

"Well, I had you yelling at me for that one," he says with a grin.

I shake my head at him.

"Don't worry, Mal. There are a lot more things I can have you begging me for."

Noah's voice is so low and warm that all I want to do is nuzzle up to his chest and stay there. He lets his body weight settle on mine. All I can think about is kissing him. But at the same time, I don't want him to think that he's won.

"Do you really think so highly of yourself?" I ask.

"No. I just know you. Besides, teasing you is half the fun. You get so worked up," he says, dropping a kiss on my neck. "The more drawn out, the better. Or so I hear."

"And what makes you think I won't have you begging for me?" I raise an eyebrow in question.

Noah's brown eyes sparkle. "I wouldn't beg, for one."

"And two?"

"For two, silly girl, sex isn't a bargaining chip. Or something to be used or thrown around lightly."

"What's it for then?"

Noah pulls his head back, so he's looking down at me. "Love. Pleasure. Expression."

I frown. "So, let me get this straight. You're allowed to tease me because it's fun, but I'm not allowed to tease you because this is too serious of a matter?"

Noah sucks in his cheeks. "You're such a brat."

"I might be a brat, but at least I'm right," I reply.

Noah rolls his eyes. "Fine, you might be right. Although I don't think I would have to beg at all, Mal."

"You don't think so?"

"Nope." He brings his lips down against mine in a light kiss. "You already want me. All I would have to do is strip us both down and …"

"And what?" I ask, my body pounding.

"And bring us together, fully."

"Just like that, huh?" I ask.

"Just like that."

A man crush.
2:30PM

AFTER NOAH NOT-SO-KINDLY teased me, *and my body*, working us both up into a frenzy, he gave me a few hot kisses and then told me he needed to change.

Which left me speechless.

And in a puddle.

A turned-on, annoyed puddle that is now desperate to get Noah naked and to finish the job.

I've never wanted someone so badly. And I don't really know what to do with myself.

Half the time, I want to smack him—for doing things like throwing me into the pond—and the other half of the time, I want to figure out a way to seduce him, so he'll finally give in to me.

I walk downstairs, not sure what my next move should be.

Or if I even need a move.

Maybe I need to just wait, let things play out. Noah can talk all he wants about teasing me and holding out, but when it comes down to it, I'm sure he wants me as much as I want him.

Doesn't he?

I go downstairs and into the living room, finding Mohammad on the couch. He's on the phone, and he doesn't look happy.

I make sure I'm quiet as I sit down across from him, but a second later, he's ending the call.

"I don't understand why my mum can't just leave me alone," he groans.

"What's the matter?" I ask, noticing Harry's been sitting

silently, listening to him too.

"She's insisting that I work on my coursework. Now." Mohammad rolls his eyes before dramatically tossing his phone onto the couch next to him.

"Perk up, mate," Harry says, getting up and patting Mohammad on the back. "Just lie."

"I can't lie," Mohammad says with another huff.

"And you shouldn't lie," I add in agreement.

Mohammad looks toward me, his eyebrows shooting up. "No. I actually *can't* lie. She wants me to message back proof—and soon."

"Well, shit," I mumble, thinking of what to do. "I guess we should all just go get our homework then."

"You don't need to do that," Mohammad says, shaking his head.

I pull my lips to the side. "If you have to study, then we might as well study with you. I'll have to do it later anyway."

"Really?" Mohammad asks.

"Yeah. Besides, if I wait until I'm home to do it, I probably won't even get it done. With moving into the new apartment and all that, it's probably better if I get it out of the way here."

"Such a good student," Harry says in admiration.

"What's going on?" Noah asks, walking into the room.

"We're going to work on coursework now to appease Mohammad's mum," Harry explains.

"Cool." It's all Noah says before turning around and walking back upstairs.

Both Mohammad and I follow him. When I get to my room, I quickly collect my things and check the time. It's two-thirty here, which means, at home, it's nine-thirty. And my parents are definitely up.

I decide to give my dad a call.

"Hey, Dad," I say when he answers.

"Hey, sweetie. How are you?" My father's voice booms through the phone, and I immediately feel like he's here with me.

"I'm good. Just got back in from swimming, actually."

"Swimming? Don't tell me they have an indoor pool," my dad says excitedly.

"Not exactly." I laugh. "We ended up swimming in a pond."

"A pond? It's the middle of October, Mal." I can hear the concern in his voice.

"We've had a heat wave this weekend. It's been gorgeous out," I say, but I may not mention the fact that the water was freezing.

Because I don't need another scolding today.

"That's good for being in the country then."

"It's been so nice," I agree.

"What else have you been doing today?"

I fall onto my bed, letting my legs dangle off the side as I look up at the ceiling.

"We started with a big breakfast this morning. Moham-mad woke everyone up early. He's thrilled to be here. And so am I, but I didn't need to be woken up before eight on a Saturday to be informed of it."

My dad laughs. "You're not a morning girl," he says.

"I'm definitely not. But either way, I was up and ready for breakfast by the time Noah got back from his run. I told you he runs, right? We could all go together sometime."

"You've mentioned that," my dad replies.

I wait for him to say something else, but he doesn't.

"Anyway, he got back, we had breakfast, and then *drum-roll* ... we went clay pigeon shooting!"

I smile at the ceiling, knowing that my dad's going to be

impressed.

He lets out a wholehearted laugh. "That sounds nice, Mal. Did the boys have fun?"

I furrow my brows, confused at his reaction. Because why isn't he more excited? And why did he laugh?

"Yeah, of course they did," I say, but then it suddenly hits me.

He thinks I'm joking.

"That's great to hear."

"But, Dad, it wasn't just the boys. I shot too," I explain.

My dad clears his throat. "You shot a *gun?*"

"Yes! That's what I'm trying to tell you. I didn't just tag along. I got to shoot the clay pigeons too. With a shotgun! Thank goodness they were just clay. I would *never* have done that if they were real. Honestly, I don't even know why they're called pigeons. They don't look like them."

"I'm impressed, honey ... and a little terrified," my dad says, cutting in. "You know, you probably should have checked with your mom and me before doing that."

"If you're going to yell at me, you're a little late to the party. Helen already chewed me out about it," I mumble.

"And did you learn a lesson?"

"Yes. Apparently, girls aren't allowed to do things boys would do without first asking permission."

"Mal," my dad says sternly.

"I'll ask next time," I say, giving in.

"Thank you. All we care about is your safety."

"You really do sound like Helen," I reply.

"Your mother and I can't wait to see you on Thursday."

"It's going to be here before you know it. Are you excited to start off in the office Monday?" I ask him.

"I am, sweetie. It's all worked out for a reason, hasn't it?"

And I can't disagree with him.

"I think it has."

"And … how are things with Noah?"

My dad's question surprises me. Because, up until now, he really hasn't taken an interest in Noah. Even though I'd like him to.

"Really good, Dad." I smile against the phone. "I can't wait for you to meet him. I think you'll have a lot to talk about. He's so smart. Great at Statistics too."

"I'm sure we will," my dad says quickly. "And how's our boy Harry doing?"

I try not to roll my eyes. "He's great. Nothing could bother Harry right now. He's happy to be here. And you'd be proud; we're about to do our homework. On holiday. Can you imagine?"

My dad laughs into the phone. "I'm proud of you, Mal, for staying on top of your schoolwork. And I want you to know, I'm not worried about you being away. I know with Harry there, you're in capable hands."

"Uh, thanks …" I'm not sure what else to say.

Because *capable hands?*

He can't be talking about Harry. And what is with my dad's infatuation with him?

"All right, sweetie, get to work! You'll call us tomorrow?"

"I'll call tomorrow," I say on autopilot.

"Love you," my dad says.

"Love you too." I hang up and feel struck.

Does my dad have a man crush on Harry?

Send the text.
2:45PM

"SO, WHAT DO we plan on accomplishing?" I ask, laying all of my books onto the oversize dining table.

"I've got Stats, Chemistry, and Art," Noah says, sliding into an open seat.

I nod, turning to Harry.

"I'm not participating in this," he says, waving his hand in the air.

"Don't you have history homework?" Mohammad asks, looking up from his notebook.

Harry looks at Mohammad, frowning. "How do you know that?"

"Because I have History before you," Mohammad reminds him.

"Oh, with Sarah!" I say.

"And Olivia," Mohammad adds.

"Right ..." Harry says, clearly not remembering our earlier conversation.

"How is Miss Gunters doing?" Noah asks Harry.

"Slowly breaking my heart. Fucking assigned us coursework over break too," Harry grumbles.

"The nerve," Noah says.

"Exactly. It's bollocks," Harry says seriously.

"That's the homework you should tackle then," I suggest. "Face your fear head-on."

"Someone's gone motivational," Mohammad teases.

"Well, if we have to do homework on a Saturday, we need to try and find a silver lining."

"Make her stop," Mohammad says, covering his ears as he

starts to fake cry.

"Now, you're just being dramatic." I flip open my textbook and try to ignore him.

Noah pats Mohammad on the shoulder.

"The more you get done now, the less you'll have to do when we're back," he encourages. "Plus, it will get your mum off your back."

"True," Mohammad says, perking up a little.

"Think about it. If you not only get your extra credit done, but also all your coursework, you'll have the rest of the break to spend with us and Naomi," Noah suggests.

"Keep talking," Mohammad says.

"And … you'll also have studied and prepared for the upcoming week. So, I'm sure you'll impress your professors."

"We do have to study for Latin," I agree.

"By the time we get back next week, I will have forgotten what I studied now anyway," Mohammad says, continuing to pout.

And avoid working.

"I'm going to start on Stats," Noah says, burying his head in his textbook.

"Are you starting the first half of our review?" I question. Noah nods. "Want to work on it together then?"

"Sure," he agrees.

I scoot my chair closer to his, looking at his open textbook. I pull out my review and immediately remember how much I hate Statistics.

"Did you bring your history textbook?" Harry asks Mohammad.

"It's right here," Mohammad says, sliding it to Harry.

"Won't you need it for your extra credit?" I question.

"I'll start on Latin instead," Mohammad says. He flips through it mindlessly, looking sad and lost.

"Just let him be," Noah whispers.

"I'm not getting involved in that," I reply quietly as Noah and I get started.

When I glance up at Mohammad, he's writing now, and he seems to be engrossed in his Latin textbook. Maybe he's copying down vocabulary for our quiz.

I look at Harry. He has his head down in Mohammad's history textbook.

And I'm slightly impressed that he's actually studying.

"Do you know how to do this equation?" Noah asks, pulling me back into our review.

But eventually, I get bored.

"I THINK I'M going to start brainstorming ideas for Art," I tell Noah, moving my chair away from his.

I get out my notebook and tap my pen against it.

I've been thinking about making Noah something since Mohammad and I planned to break into his locker and fill it with granola bars.

Noah's always doing things for me.

And I want to do something sweet for him.

I bring the pen up to my lips, biting on the end of it as I think.

Maybe I'll do a coupon jar. One time, Anna made her then-boyfriend a coupon jar for Valentine's Day. She wrote little romantic things they could do together on slips of paper and then put them in a jar. He could pull one out and collect whatever was written on it.

I think of things I'd want and write them down.

A free massage.

Breakfast in bed.

I get half my notebook page filled with ideas when Noah gets a text. I immediately wonder if it's from Helen.

"So, Mr. Hard Worker," I say, closing my notebook, "is your mom nagging you like Mohammad's?"

"About school?" Noah asks, looking up from his phone.

"Yeah."

"Nah."

"Does she ever?"

Noah exhales slowly as he thinks. "Not really. I mean, when I don't do great in a subject, she will. But for the most part, she lets me be."

"It's not fair," Mohammad says.

"How come?" I ask.

"Probably because I tell her not to worry about it. I'll find a career that suits me," Noah answers.

"You won't have any trouble doing that," Harry chimes in.

"Yeah. Or I could become a footballer and support Mum in her old age," Noah says. His eyes quickly find Mohammad, and he gives him a small nod.

"Have you tried that one on her?" I laugh.

"She'd be thrilled. They're well off," Mohammad interjects.

"Do you actually think that would be right for you?" I ask.

"Who knows? I try not to think about the future too much," Noah admits.

"You're great at it though," Harry says, looking to Noah.

I nod enthusiastically. Because Noah is good.

Really good.

"I'm decent," Noah agrees.

"You're more than that," Mohammad says.

"I appreciate the support," Noah says, flushing. He glances down at his textbook, avoiding our eyes.

"I know that I don't actually know anything about it, but

you could always teach me sometime. At least that way my compliments could have their intended full effect." I smile at Noah, hoping to pull him back out of his shell.

He immediately looks up at me.

"I could train you," Noah says. "You're pretty determined. I bet you'd be a killer on the field."

"With my luck, I'd end up in a fight and get kicked out of the game. Or I'd get injured. I'm not very coordinated."

"Maybe stick with running," Mohammad cuts in. "I couldn't deal with the drama that would unfold on the field if you played football."

My mouth drops open.

"What?! It's true. You cause havoc wherever you go," Mohammad says pointedly.

I roll my eyes at him.

"Anyway ... speaking of sports, do you have tennis practice over break?" I turn from Mohammad to Harry. "Or squash?"

"Hell no," Mohammad replies, his head back down in his Latin book.

And I have to admit, I'm impressed.

"They don't have anything mandatory," Harry answers.

"But it's implied," Noah says. "If you want to be good, you've got to stay on top of your fitness."

"My fitness is fine," Harry says.

"No, your game is fine," Noah disagrees.

"Exactly."

"I think you're missing his point," I chime in.

"His point is being ignored," Harry says, shooting Noah a wink.

Noah shakes his head disapprovingly.

"Finished!" Mohammad says triumphantly, slamming his textbook shut.

"With studying Latin?" I ask excitedly.

Mohammad looks up at me, a confused expression on his face. "What? No. With this!"

He holds up a piece of paper, a single sentence written out on it in Latin. I snatch the paper out of his hand, trying to make sense of it. But I don't recognize any of the words.

"What does it say?" I ask, confused.

"It says, *Your sweet, juicy lips feel perfect on mine.*"

"Ugh, Mohammad!" I drop the paper.

"Naomi will eat it up," he says with a wide grin. "I'm going to text her a photo of it and tell her to translate it."

"You really are smooth," Harry compliments.

Mohammad smiles at him before pulling out his phone.

"So, you *haven't* been studying like the rest of us then?" Noah says, clearly annoyed.

"I've got other priorities," Mohammad replies, snapping a photo.

"The whole reason we're even sitting here, studying and doing our homework, is to support you," Noah fires back.

And I can tell he's moving from annoyed to mad.

Mohammad doesn't pay him any attention. But Harry notices.

"Send the text, mate, then you actually need to do your History, so we can get on with our plans today. Maybe go into the village?"

Mohammad clicks his phone off and looks at Harry.

"Shit, you're right," Mohammad says as Harry slides him back his textbook.

And to all of our surprise, he actually starts working.

Noah pushes my review toward me, motioning for me to work on it.

I nod in happy thanks because Noah is in no mood to be told *no* right now.

"Are you still writing ideas down for your art project?" Noah asks, noticing me writing in my notebook again.

"Uh, yeah," I fib, even though I'm still working on the coupon list.

"Any favorites?" He leans toward me, and I quickly slam the notebook closed.

"Tons of options," I reply nervously.

"Really?" Noah says. And I know he's suspicious.

"Yes … I'm thinking a clay Medusa."

Noah purses his lips, but he doesn't say anything. He goes back to working on his review.

My mind quickly slips back to Mohammad texting Naomi when I remember that it wasn't just me and Naomi who were supposed to hang out together this weekend.

It was me, Naomi, and Olivia.

And I probably need to text her.

I open up a new message on my phone.

Me: Hey, I'm sure Naomi's told you, but I'm out of town this weekend. Want to meet up next week instead?

Olivia: You're at Harry's house.

I press my lips together, wondering if she's going to be upset by it too.

Me: Yeah, just for a few days.

Olivia: I don't blame you. I'd get out of the city, too, if I could.

Me: Things not going good at home?

Olivia: Always something. Next week is good.

Me: I'm sorry.

Olivia: Don't be sorry. What do you think about a

girls' night out?

Me: *I think it sounds like a great idea.*

Olivia: *Will you still be at the Bvlgari?*

Me: *Yeah, my parents get here Thursday, and we're staying through the weekend.*

Olivia: *Perfect. We can stay there.*

Me: *Have you been staying at Naomi's?*

Olivia: *Off and on.*

Me: *That's good.*

Olivia: *Yeah. Call when you're back in town.*

Me: *I will.*

I click off my phone, setting it in my lap.

Olivia took the news that I was gone and at Harry's pretty well. Maybe she really is okay with it. Or maybe she just has a lot going on in her life.

Either way, I'm glad that she wants to still meet up when I'm back.

"How are we doing?" Noah asks, pulling me out of my thoughts.

Harry holds up a drawing.

"So, you haven't been productive," Noah says with an eye roll before turning to Mohammad.

"I'm ... finished," Mohammad says, scribbling quickly in his notebook.

"That was fast," I comment.

"Turns out, the extra credit wasn't that hard," he says, proudly holding up his filled notebook page.

"That's great," Noah says, finally cracking a smile.

Mohammad snaps a photo. "Just have to send this pic to Mum, and then we're good."

"What did you work on?" Harry asks Noah.

"I got the first half of our review done," Noah says, his voice filled with pride. "It wasn't as hard as I'd thought it would be."

Harry fist-bumps Noah from across the table before looking at me. "What did you work on?"

"Um ..." I say, feeling all eyes on me.

Noah glances down at my notebook. A second later, he's reaching for it. I scramble, grabbing it and clutching it against my chest so he can't take it. Because the last thing I want is for him to start reading these things out to Mohammad and Harry.

"It's a personal project," I say, standing my ground, not wanting them to start prying.

"Personal project?" Mohammad repeats, looking confused.

"Are you telling me, in all that time, you didn't do any homework, except for what I helped you with?" Noah asks. He blinks quickly, like that will somehow help him process the news that I was being a bad student during our study session.

"I thought about Art," I say. "But then I messaged Olivia and ..."

"So, you weren't *really* working," Mohammad cuts in.

"You messaged Olivia?" Harry asks.

"Yeah. We had talked about getting together this weekend, so I figured I should let her know that I was out of town."

"I still think that's a bad idea," Noah says as he collects his homework into a pile.

"Us being friends is a good thing," I disagree. "At least, it beats fighting with her."

"Well, now, you have nothing to fight over, so ..." Mohammad says, holding his hands out like he's solved all our problems.

All three of us turn and glare at him.

"Jeez, *sorry* for telling it like it is. Now that you two broke up, of course she'll be friends with you."

"See, Mohammad has it right," Harry says, agreeing with him.

I look between the three of them, feeling hurt.

"So, none of you think I should be friends with her?" I ask.

Why can't they just be supportive?

It's not like Olivia is my favorite person, but I would rather be her friend than her enemy.

"I'd warn against it," Noah answers.

"I agree. Olivia only causes drama," Harry states.

I roll my eyes and look at Mohammad. "You too then?" I ask.

"Hell no. I'm all about the drama. Be friends with her. Fight. Make up. Just as long as you let me watch," he says with a sheepish grin.

I immediately scrunch my nose up, a sour expression coming onto my face. "Mohammad, ew!"

Harry busts out laughing.

"What? That catfight was hot!" Mohammad tells us.

"It was childish," Noah disagrees.

"It's not like I started it," I cut in.

"No, but I had to finish it. Or did you forget that I was the one who had to drag you away from her?" Noah raises an arched eyebrow at me.

"And I was the one who was assaulted!"

"Exactly! If anyone should just let it rest, it's you," Noah says, clearly thinking he's right.

But what Noah doesn't get is that I can't hate her.

Maybe it's because I feel sorry for her.

For losing Harry.

For what her family is going through.

For my coming between her and Naomi.

"Everyone deserves a second chance. And I honestly believe that us being friends will put the drama in the past."

Harry starts to open his mouth, but I hold up my finger, stopping him.

"You don't have to agree with my decision, but you have to respect it, okay?"

Harry frowns, but he doesn't say anything.

"We do respect you," Mohammad says, looking equally as sorry.

"We do," Harry agrees.

I turn to Noah.

"Noah?" I ask.

Noah flares his nostrils like he wants to fight me on this, but then his face softens.

"I do respect you *and* your decisions," he says, placing his hand on my shoulder and giving it an affirming squeeze.

"So, what's the game plan?" Mohammad asks, quickly changing the subject and lightening the mood.

"I say, we get cleaned up and go into the village," Harry answers. "A reward, as promised."

"You really are motivated to have us out and about on this trip," I say, fighting off a yawn.

"It's alcohol-induced," Noah explains.

"He's right. It's probably going to be short-lived, so might as well enjoy it while it lasts," Harry agrees.

"Are you saying that tomorrow you're going to be useless?" I tease.

"Who knows what tomorrow holds?!" Harry says, getting up from the table. "I'm going to have a fag and change."

He leaves his notebook and pen on the table, gives us a nod, and then heads outside.

"Finally, we're free," Mohammad says, outstretching his hands into the air as he does a catlike stretch. "Be back down in ten."

Before we can reply, Mohammad is out of the dining room and running upstairs.

I think we all know that ten minutes isn't much time for him to primp.

"I should change too," I say.

"You know, now, you're going to have to take more time out of the break to do your coursework than if you had just done it now," Noah says, grabbing my attention.

I look over at him, finding a face full of disapproval.

"You're really worked up over this," I reply, collecting my things.

Noah does the same, walking beside me as we head upstairs to change.

"I'm not worked up. I just think it was a bad use of your time."

"I told you, I was working on something."

"Yeah, *something*. And if you had been doing your homework like the rest of us, you wouldn't have to worry about it when we get back."

"I'm not worried about it." I can't help but laugh out the words.

I don't understand why Noah is so bent out of shape about this.

Noah looks at me in question, not at all amused.

I sigh.

"Seriously, Noah, it will be fine."

He shakes his head. "You're going to be busy, Mal. With your family. With coursework …"

I take in his expression, finally realizing what this is about.

"You think I won't have time for you?" I ask, blinking up at him.

Noah winces at my words. His forehead creases as he looks down at me. "I'm not worried. I just know you're going to have a lot going on."

"Are you saying that if I want to come over and work on my review with you, you'll say no?" I smile at him, trying to get rid of the grim expression on his face.

"Are you saying that you'll only come over because I can help you with Stats?"

"I told you before, I miss living with you. If I could, given the choice, I'd move back in."

"Yeah?" Noah asks, sounding slightly vulnerable.

I take his hand. "Of course. I was living the life at your house. I got a great family to live with ... I got free back rubs ... delicious lunches made for me ... help with my homework ... a cute boy in the next room over." I grin at him. "So, I can promise you, even if things get busy with the move, I'm going to be over there every free chance I get."

"For the delicious lunches," Noah says, grinning at me.

I shake my head at him. "No. I'll be there because of *you*."

"Mal," Noah says, holding my gaze.

"What?"

He bites his lip before dropping his mouth down toward mine.

I'm about to meet his lips when I realize that we're standing in the hallway.

I pull away.

"What is it?" Noah asks, searching my face.

I press my lips together and glance over his shoulder to the staircase.

"Noah, have you told Harry yet?" I ask, suddenly feeling

antsy.

"No. We've just been having fun."

I look away, my stomach doing a flip.

"You're overthinking it," Noah tells me.

"I'm not." I shake my head at him.

"You are." He lets out a heavy breath, takes my hand, and leads me to his bedroom. He closes the door behind us before pushing me up against it.

His fingers find their way into my hair, his brown eyes drilling holes through mine.

"Talk to me, Mal."

"I want this. I want *you*. But my mind won't stop. We have to tell him. I want to. But at the same time, I don't. And I don't understand why I'm feeling so overwhelmed by it all."

"I'm going to tell him, and I promise you, it will be fine." Noah strokes my hair. "I promise, okay?"

"Okay," I agree.

But I don't feel any better about it.

"Does your mind ever stop?" Noah asks, looking me over.

"Never," I say flatly.

"You sure about that?" Noah's mouth is on mine. He pushes my back up against the door, grabbing on to my wrists. His mouth opens to mine.

And then all I can feel is warmth.

And suddenly, with one kiss, one action, Noah proves me wrong.

And it's maddening.

I've never met someone who could make me feel like this.

I've always had faith in my reactions. I take pride in knowing myself. In knowing who I am. But sometimes, with Noah, it feels like I know nothing. Sometimes, it feels like he knows me better than I know myself.

And … that's a little scary.

But I guess some people are able to see you clearly. They can see the future you want for yourself, helping you build it. They can see the possibilities of your life and how beautiful it's going to be. They can see the lies you tell yourself and encourage you to be honest. They find all the ways that you limit yourself, and they urge you to push past them.

They shatter everything you thought you knew, and they do it so easily, with a smile on their face.

And Noah does that.

I tell him my mind never stops.

And then he shows me that it actually can. One kiss from him is all it takes to switch it off.

It's the first belief I had about myself that Noah just shattered.

And I have a feeling that it won't be the last.

Missed our friendship.
4:00PM

"HOW DID A trip to the village end up with us at the pub?" I ask.

"Well, it's a small village," Harry replies.

"We could have gone shopping," Mohammad grumbles.

"Trust me, I've brought you to the liveliest part of it," Harry replies, leading us into a small, badly lit pub.

"Only part of the village Harry's been to at least," Noah jokes.

I look around, expecting to be wowed. There are a few people in the pub, but I'd say it's severely lacking in excitement.

"What about the bookshop? We could always stop there

after. And I saw a cute little café," I comment, immediately wanting to leave.

"You shouldn't read on this trip. The whole point of a midterm break is *not* to read," Harry says. His face goes sour at the idea of reading for pleasure.

"Like you read for class," Mohammad says, teasing Harry.

"I would be reading fiction," I clarify.

Harry looks back at me like I'm speaking a foreign language.

"For fun," I explain.

"Read for fun? That's hilarious!" Harry laughs, waving me off as he goes to the bar.

"Maybe they'll have one of those books your mum lent Mallory," Mohammad says.

"I'm sure they'll have historical romances," Noah replies seriously.

"Actually, Noah's mom …" I start to say, but Noah interrupts me.

"So, what does everyone want?" he asks, flaring his nostrils at me.

I look at him, confused.

"Noah's mum what?" Mohammad asks.

"She recommended another book for Mallory. You two could probably find it at the bookshop after, if you want," Noah says.

"The bookstore is closed today. I saw the sign," Harry cuts in. "You could check it out on Tuesday though."

"Why Tuesday?" I ask.

"It's closed Sunday and Monday," Harry answers.

I roll my eyes. "Everything here is closed half the time. It's ridiculous. I have no idea how people manage to make a living or stay afloat with the hours they operate!"

"Someone's a little salty about it," Mohammad says.

"I'm not salty. I just don't understand why everything isn't open when it should be. The weekend is the exact time you wouldn't want to close. It's when people are actually free to come to your shop," I explain.

"Not how we operate here. Everything in the States is go, go, go," Harry says.

"It's the same in London," I counter.

"True, but you are in the countryside, Miss America. Things are bound to be different," Mohammad tells me.

"Mohammad's right," Harry says, turning toward me. "Now, what do you want to drink?"

We order food and drinks at the bar before ending up at a small table in the corner. A few more people slowly trickle in, making it fun to people-watch.

"I still can't believe Mia and Sophia are a couple," Mohammad says, taking a dramatic sip of his Coke.

"Your fault for not listening." Noah scowls. "I tried to tell you."

"You're just mad that I came between you two," Mohammad says, pointing between me and Noah.

"I was mad that you were making up facts!" Noah disagrees.

"Making up facts." Mohammad laughs. "Come on! All the signs were there. Sophia was friendly with you. She was always at your house. I could smell the sexual attraction oozing off her."

"Oh my God, stop," I tell him. Even though Sophia and I sort of made up and I'm happy she's with Mia, the last thing I want to hear is her *supposed* past sexual attraction to Noah.

"Fine, maybe not oozing. But there was attraction there," Mohammad states.

"For my sister," Noah says, running his hands back through his hair.

173

"Wrong sibling, right house. I wasn't that far off," Mohammad says, taking another sip of his soda.

"Mia told me that Sophia was upset about the idea of her going away to art school. Has she talked to you about it?" I ask Noah.

"They're not going to last," he says, "so it really doesn't matter."

"Trouble in paradise?" Harry asks eagerly, suddenly interested in the possible prospect of gossip.

"Mia isn't going to let herself get tied down," Noah replies.

"What if it's love?" I ask.

"I know they love one another," Noah says seriously. "But sometimes, love isn't enough. Life just isn't that simple."

"Life is never simple," Harry agrees.

"Did she tell you about her date at least?" I ask. "She mentioned they were going to the Saatchi Gallery after your match."

Noah shakes his head.

"Maybe I should message her." I pull out my phone and open a message before I realize I don't have her contact information.

"Hey," I say to Noah, "give me your sister's number."

"What for?" he asks, surprise flashing across his face.

"For future reference. She probably wants someone to gush to about Sophia. And if Sophia is her best friend and she went on a date with her, well, she definitely can't gush to her about it then."

"Did anyone just follow that?" Harry asks, looking bewildered.

"I did!" Mohammad says triumphantly as our food arrives—bowls of soup for me and Mohammad, chicken breast and potatoes for Noah, and fish and chips for Harry.

"Why are you so concerned with my sister's love life?" Noah asks, narrowing his eyes at me.

"Mia and I bonded," I reply, dunking a piece of bread into my soup. "Plus, if it gets me free cookies in the future ..."

"Now, we're getting to the truth," Noah says.

"What free cookies?" Harry asks with puppy-dog eyes.

"Just something Mia made," I say.

"That's not fair." Harry shoves a chip in his mouth.

"Life's not fair," I say.

"You're starting to sound like Harry." Noah laughs, looking between us.

"I'll show you unfair!" Harry counters. "Let's play darts."

"We just got our food," Noah argues.

"Mohammad, you want to play?" Harry asks.

"Aren't you going to eat?" I question, looking at his plate. "Speaking of which, we really need to work on your diet. You should be eating the rainbow."

"He's got green on his plate," Mohammad says, sticking up for him.

"I don't trust anything that's not a shade of brown," Harry says, teasing me.

"The peas don't count," Noah comments, looking up from his food. "Harry won't eat them. They're merely there for decoration."

"All right, fine, let's play darts," Mohammad says. "But we have to take breaks to eat."

"Done," Harry says.

The dartboard isn't far from our table. Noah and I watch as they collect the darts before getting into position a few feet back.

I look at Noah. He's eating his food, slowly chewing, barely paying attention.

"Noah."

He looks up at me. "Yeah?"

"I really missed you last week." My stomach twists as I think about how bad things got between us.

"I was upset," he states.

"I know. But I missed our friendship. Missed talking to you. Hanging out with you. It was terrible. I felt like I'd lost more than my best friend when I came back to school."

Noah grabs my hand under the table. "But things are better now."

"I know." I smile. "I just want you to know how much I missed you and our friendship."

"It was a bad week."

"Terrible," I agree. I glance over, finding Mohammad and Harry enthralled in their game. "Plus, I don't want you to think that it's only physical. Mohammad alluded to that before, that I was just trying to get with his—well, our—English rose."

"Wait, I'm the English rose?" Noah asks, setting down his utensils.

"Apparently, you're a rose, and I'm a chicken. At least, according to Mohammad."

"Figuratively, you mean," Noah says.

"No, literally," I say with a smirk.

"A rose and a chicken. What a weird combination." Noah chuckles.

"Very weird. Mohammad and I talked about it in Latin. He was thrilled he got to kiss Naomi at the party, and when Naomi told him to walk her out to get a cab, it was so we would have a chance to be alone."

"Have you spoken to her about us?" Noah asks with interest.

I immediately flush. "Sort of," I admit.

"You cracked to her too, huh?" Noah says, a silly grin

coming onto his face.

"All right, maybe a little."

"I'm assuming Mohammad knows as well?"

"Well … he might know a few things."

"Uh-huh." Noah laughs.

"Yes!"

Harry's shout pulls me away from the conversation.

I'm assuming that means he has won.

"I won't challenge you to another game to save you from embarrassment," Harry says cockily to Mohammad as he comes back to the table. "Which means, Noah, you're up."

Harry sits down and starts in on his chips.

Mohammad rolls his eyes, but Noah gets up and grabs the darts.

"You have fun?" I ask Harry.

"I think I would have had more fun beating you." Harry smirks, his blue eyes lighting up.

"Really?" I ask, raising an eyebrow at him.

"I think so. I'd say we're a well-matched pair, wouldn't you?" Harry says wittily.

"Maybe at playing darts," I reply.

"Or maybe in life," Harry counters.

"It was never going to work between us. You and I both know that."

I dunk a piece of bread into my soup, surprised at how easy this conversation is. A week ago, we could never have talked like this.

"Why not?" Harry asks with a pout.

"Because you need someone who jumps when you snap your fingers," I reply honestly. Because I think Harry needs to hear the truth. He's on too much of a high from winning at darts, and there's no telling when he'll come down from it.

"You make me sound demanding," Harry says.

"Slightly. But you're also fun, energetic, indecisive, and unconvinced."

"Just listing it all out." Harry laughs. "I like that. I think part of the fun with you was winning you over."

"It was a challenge."

"You never really put up a fight. About anything," Harry disagrees.

"What about when you wanted me to leave school and I wouldn't?" I ask, clearly remembering the fallout we had from that.

"And you shouldn't have. I was being a prick."

"I was your girlfriend, Harry. I should have. I shouldn't have thought twice about it."

"Maybe," Harry admits, biting into his fish. "But as my mate, you knew it was self-destructive. And you weren't going to support that."

I let out a sigh. "I wasn't good to you either."

"I was going through a lot, as were you," Harry says. "Living at Noah's. Leaving London after three weeks. We wanted things to be fun and simple when they never really could be."

"Circumstances definitely got in the way." I laugh.

"Noah did too," Harry says, his eyes finding mine.

I chew on my lip, not sure what to say, finally settling on, "Harry, you told me before that someone who is broken can't love. Did you really mean that?"

Harry nods, and it causes my stomach to twist.

"Did you really think that you were going to hurt me?" I ask him.

"I knew I would. And I did," he says. "I didn't want to, but it's like watching a car crash. You see it coming toward you, and you don't want it to happen. But at the same time, you know there isn't anything you can do to stop it. You just have to watch everything fall apart."

"Have you moved past it?"

"Us?" Harry asks, taking a drink of his soda.

I nod.

"No, not exactly. I've moved past the drama of everything though. I want to have fun. I don't want to hurt anyone. It's like I told you at the cocktail party."

"Told me what?"

"Use this time to your advantage," he says. "Have fun with things. You're living in London now. You're part of the boys' club. Settle into your new life and then figure out what you want. Explore your options."

"With you?" I ask. Because Harry's looking at me like he could swallow me whole. And I wasn't prepared for him to be so ... open about his feelings.

"If you want," he says with a grin.

"I can't do the no rules thing, Harry. It's not for me."

"There's nothing to do. Stop putting so much pressure on yourself. You are enjoying yourself here, aren't you?"

"Of course I am."

"Good. We need to start having fun together again. I can't wait to come back from Shanghai. My parents will be appeased, and I can see you around more. Especially if your parents join the club."

"It's so strange that my parents are joining. I never thought they'd join someplace so ..."

"Posh?"

"Exclusive," I reply.

"It's an escape. Plus, I've got tons of good memories there. Like our date."

"That was there," I reply.

"It is one of my better memories." Harry smiles. "Feeding you chocolate-covered strawberries and then ..."

Harry's eyes are sparkling now.

"That was …" I clear my throat, not sure what to say.

"Hot?" Harry finishes.

"It was special," I say after trying to find something else to call it.

"Special is one word for it," Harry says, biting his lip.

I look away from him, searching the pub until I find Noah and Mohammad. They seem to have paused their darts and are at the bar.

"Want anything else?" Harry asks me. "I'm going to grab another soda."

"I'm good. Thanks."

I stare blankly at the table after Harry gets up. I don't know how I'm feeling or why he said any of that. Harry wasn't the best boyfriend, but I know he cared about me. He told me he loved me. And I know that he meant it. Meanwhile, I was a terrible girlfriend. My focus wasn't always on him because I was infatuated with Noah.

Maybe it's because he's flirting with me now. Or maybe it's because he seems more grown up. But Harry doesn't hide anything. He's open about how he feels. About what he wants.

And for the first time, I wonder if Harry really is growing up.

"You all right?"

I jump at Noah's voice.

"Fine," I reply, noticing Harry and Mohammad are still at the bar.

"Mal?" Noah asks.

"Just thinking," I say, but really, my head is spinning.

Noah looks at me from across the table, then slides his hand on top of mine. "Get out of your head."

"And go where?" I ask, pulling my hand away from his.

Noah winces. "Be here."

"But Harry …" I start, immediately cutting myself off.

"Harry what?"

"You don't get it," I say, shaking my head.

"Then help me get it."

I shake my head at him again. And then again. Because I can't help him understand. Even I don't understand.

Did Harry really think he was going to hurt me? Is that why he always pushed me away? And what does it say about me, that I'm still here, lying to Harry about Noah?

What does it say?

Lovestruck.
6:00PM

"CAN YOU BELIEVE those girls?" Mohammad says when we get back to the house. He lets out a low whistle, falling onto the couch.

I plop down next to him. "What are you talking about?" I ask.

"Weren't you paying attention at the pub?" Noah asks, sitting down in the chair opposite us.

"Apparently not." Harry laughs, running his hand back through his hair. He pours himself a drink, taking a large gulp.

"You really need to start paying attention," Noah says, shaking his head.

"For your information, I wasn't not paying attention. I can't focus on everything all at once," I reply, crossing my arms over my chest.

Because what is his problem?!

He doesn't need to always call me out.

At the pub.

Now.

It's like he wants to constantly, over and over, push me past my limits.

He wants me to get out of my head.

He wants me to pay attention to him.

But I'm one person!

"Whoa. You two need to chill," Mohammad says, snapping me out of my internal dialogue.

I look up at him and try to push out a breath. But I'm still annoyed. With Noah. With Mohammad telling me to chill.

"I am chill," I mutter under my breath.

"You were in your head at the pub," Noah says, obviously disagreeing.

I glare at him, suddenly getting the urge to strangle him. Or at least injure him.

Okay, maybe not injure him.

But at least wipe that knowing look off his face.

"Who fucking cares? You're missing Mohammad's story," Harry interjects, downing his drink. He licks his lips, then refills the glass.

I furrow my brows, watching him pour what's at least another double. When he's finished, he walks to the couch and extends his hand out to me. The crystal glass is pinched between his fingers, and he nods for me to take it.

"Drink—now," he instructs.

I frown at him, but I take the glass anyway. I take a small sip. Harry looks at me disapprovingly. I roll my eyes and take a bigger drink, emptying half the glass.

Harry's lips curl up at the corner.

He takes the glass back from me, walks over to Noah, hands the glass to him, and says, "Finish the rest."

Noah looks from Harry to me, then back to Harry, like

he's trying to figure out what to do. Finally, he takes the glass without question and downs the amber liquid.

"Good." Harry adjusts his jacket, places the glass onto the coffee table, and then takes a seat.

"So, I'm going to pretend that we just didn't witness … whatever that was," Mohammad says, motioning between me and Noah, looking freaked out. "And I'm going to continue with my story."

The drink that Harry gave me settles into my stomach, and it makes me relax. I rest my head back against the couch and give my full attention to Mohammad.

"About the girls?" I ask.

"They were all over us!" Mohammad replies, his eyes lighting up.

"I'm not sure about that …" Noah dares to disagree, but Harry shoots him a look that shuts him up.

"Wait, at the pub?" I ask, completely confused.

"Like I said, you were distracted," Noah states.

And I try not to growl at him.

"Yes, at the pub. They were all over me and Harry," Mohammad says with a smile. He leans back and throws his arms out, resting them on the back of the couch.

"Are you sure you didn't imagine it?" I tease.

Because Mohammad looks way too happy.

"Harry has their numbers," Mohammad replies triumphantly. "Is that proof enough?"

I look from Mohammad to Harry, my stomach instantly twisting.

"You do?" I try to keep my voice steady, but something in me feels like it wants to snap. And it catches me off guard. I sit still for a moment, trying to figure out what I'm thinking.

What I'm feeling.

But then I just grow annoyed again.

Because was Noah right?

Was I really that distracted at lunch?

I look at Noah. His expression is unreadable. I quickly glance back to Harry, my mind moving to the girls.

To the idea of Harry flirting with someone else.

I swallow hard.

I've thought about Harry and Olivia getting back together. I know she loves him. And I know that Harry loved her at one point. But anytime I've thought about it, it's been theoretical.

Hypothetical.

A possibility that isn't likely to happen.

But suddenly, the realization settles in. That, eventually, Harry is going to be with someone else. And not just hypothetically.

Physically.

And the thought doesn't settle well. I've felt terrible about Noah and me all weekend. I've felt guilty. Because Harry has made it clear he wants our friendship to be open. He doesn't want me to close myself off to a future with him. To the possibility of him.

But after everything that Harry's said and hinted at, he had the audacity to get a girl's number basically right in front of me?

"Mallory, did you hear me?" Harry asks, snapping me back to reality.

"What?" I refocus my eyes, wondering where I just went.

"I didn't ask for them," Harry says, his eyes locked on me. "They gave them to me."

"But you accepted?" I state, instantly feeling territorial.

Hurt.

And I don't know who I'm more upset with.

Harry, for doing that.

Or myself for caring.

And I don't know which is worse.

"On Mohammad's behalf." Harry smiles genuinely, easing a little of the tension in my body. "I made it clear I wouldn't use them."

"You'd be mad not to," Mohammad says disapprovingly.

"I'm not looking for a woman," Harry replies, his gaze catching mine before continuing his conversation with Mohammad. "But you're still a free agent."

"But you're not," I say more to myself than to anyone else.

"Are you going to call them?" Noah asks with interest.

"Call them?" I repeat, trying to process everything. But then I realize they've moved on to Mohammad, and something shifts in my mind. "Wait, what about Naomi?"

"Would you relax? I can appreciate some fit birds and not do anything about it. I was simply being a good wingman." Mohammad beams.

"Except I wasn't trying to get their numbers," Harry replies.

"Well, you have them now," Mohammad shoots back.

"There's nothing wrong with either of you getting their numbers. You're both single," Noah states.

And I don't know why, but his comment sort of pisses me off.

"Mohammad isn't *single*," I disagree.

"He is single," Harry says, agreeing with Noah.

I cross my arms over my chest, annoyed that he isn't taking my side.

"And like he said, he wasn't trying to get their numbers. He was trying to get them for me even though I didn't want them," Mohammad says.

"Exactly." Noah's nodding and smiling along with Harry

like, somehow, they're all on the same page.

I turn to Mohammad and raise my eyebrows at him in question, wanting an answer.

"I'm *definitely* single." Mohammad says the words more to himself than to anyone else. And he actually sounds freaked out by the prospect of not being single.

"So, if Naomi asked you to be her boyfriend, you'd say no?" I ask, testing him.

"I'd probably say yes," he answers.

I hold my hands out in front of me while shaking my head. Because boys make no sense. Doesn't he see that flirting with girls while he likes someone else is wrong?

Isn't it?

"Mallory thinks you can't chat up other girls while you're dating Naomi," Noah states, reading my mind.

"It was harmless chat." Harry shrugs, his blue eyes sparkling. "For both of us."

"Is anything you do really harmless?" Noah remarks, a smirk playing on his lips.

"You have a point." Harry chuckles. "But am I really to blame?"

"If anyone's to blame, it's Mohammad," I interject.

"It's not my fault women flock to me," Mohammad replies, sounding pleased with himself.

"Flock to you?" I let out a sharp laugh at the ridiculousness of his statement.

He shoots me an evil glare before going on. "They do actually flock to me. I can pull anyone, and with Harry at my side, the girls can't stay away."

"So, you flirted with them," I say, knowing that neither of them is as innocent as they're leading on.

Mohammad would chat up a wall, and Harry, well, he really can win anyone over with his charm. And I know they both enjoy the attention.

"Not intentionally," Mohammad replies. "They just started chatting with us and, well ..."

"It's not Mohammad's fault," Harry insists. "He was born naturally smooth."

Mohammad looks at me with big puppy-dog eyes, nodding in agreement. Noah just laughs.

I roll my eyes at both of them, deciding to drop it.

Whatever Mohammad wants to do is up to him. If he asks for my advice, then I'll tell him. If he wants to date Naomi and flirt with other girls at the same time, then that's his choice.

A bad choice, if you ask me. Which he hasn't.

"And it's not your fault either, is it?" Noah chimes in, looking at Harry.

"Nope," Harry says, getting up to refill his drink. "I won't put in the work of flirting if I don't see a reward."

Harry fills up his glass and then takes a gulp. Swallowing, he tilts the glass to the side and looks at the liquid.

"Are you saying you'll only flirt with a girl if you think you'll get her in bed because of it?" I ask, raising my eyebrows in question.

"Absolutely," Harry says, walking back over to the couch.

"That's terrible!" I let out a surprised laugh and quickly cover my mouth with my hand, thinking back to how we kissed within minutes after meeting.

"It's strategic," Harry disagrees as he takes a seat. "And effective."

"Flirting is foreplay," Noah agrees.

I glance at him, catching his brown eyes. He's looking at me knowingly. Like he wants me to disagree.

Like he wants to prove me wrong.

"You don't have to tell me that," Mohammad says, sliding

his phone out of his pocket. "I've already got the ball rolling."

I want to ask what he's talking about, but I can't look away from Noah.

His dark eyes hold mine.

"What ball?" Harry asks.

"The *flirting is foreplay* ball," Mohammad answers.

Noah gives me a shadow of a smile before moving his attention to Mohammad. I do the same.

"You putting moves on Naomi?" Harry asks eagerly.

"Oh, yeah. You should see the shit I'm writing." Mohammad grins.

"The question is, how is she replying? Getting any pics?" Harry asks, waggling his eyebrows.

I swat at him.

"What? It's just a question! Men are visual," Harry says in his defense.

"It's because we're more animalistic. If we can see it, we can picture it." Mohammad grins deviously as Harry lets out a low growl.

Oh my.

"Women are just more creative. We don't need photos to imagine things. We can create the images in our head," I point out. "And honestly, we're more likely to picture a life with you outside the bedroom."

This comment causes Harry to frown and Mohammad to say, "The first thing I think about when I see a fit bird is that I want to shag her. Are you saying that girls immediately think about what our life could be like together?"

"Exactly! Of course, we take notice if we're attracted to them. But for the most part, we think about what dating them would be like."

I glance at them, getting confused and blank stares in return.

"What do you mean, *dating*?" Mohammad asks.

"For example, we think about what it would be like to go out. How they would fit into our lives. What our friends would think. How they'd act in front of our friends ..." I go on.

"That's *way* too much work to put in," Mohammad says, his expression souring.

"Yeah, of course it's a lot of work. Why do you think girls get so invested so quickly and then get upset when it doesn't work out? For the most part, we've planned our entire future with you. So, when things end, you not only took, well, yourself from us, but you've also taken a dream future," I say matter-of-factly.

"That's mad!" Harry says, cutting in.

"Tell me about it," I agree.

"Are you like that?" Mohammad asks, looking struck.

"Maybe not to the extent of some girls. I like to consider myself a bit more of a realist, but, yeah, in some capacity, I think about what it would be like if I was with that person."

"So, when you met me, your initial thought was, *What would it be like if we dated?*" Harry asks.

"Not right away. When we met, things were different. I didn't think I was going to get a future with anyone here. I thought I'd have a few weeks of fun, and that would be that," I say truthfully.

"Hit him where it hurts," Mohammad says.

Noah lets out a chuckle.

But Harry just waves them off.

"At least she's honest, boys. If anything, it's a compliment that she knew I'd be a good time. Can't argue with that," Harry boasts.

"Little did I know that we'd go on to date," I say, trying to bring the conversation somewhere more upbeat.

Because I can already tell what Harry is doing. He's going to write himself off as *fun*, pretend to be proud of it when, really, that's the last thing he wants.

"And that I'd make a shit boyfriend. Always fulfilling my potential," Harry says jokingly.

"You do have a talent of getting in your own way," Noah adds.

I glance between Harry and Noah.

Will Harry take what Noah said badly?

Harry just laughs.

"Oh shit," Mohammad gasps, capturing the attention of everyone in the room.

"What's wrong?" I ask, worried something's happened.

But when my gaze lands on Mohammad, his eyes are bright with excitement.

"Things with Naomi are heating up," he says proudly.

"No fucking way," Harry says.

"Are you doubting my skills?" Mohammad asks, eyeing Harry.

Harry holds his hands up in concession.

"Look for yourself." Mohammad tosses his phone to Harry, a smug smile on his lips.

"What did she send you?" I ask.

"This isn't dirty," Harry says, throwing Noah the phone next.

"What isn't?"

Noah looks at the phone and immediately looks confused.

"It's a photo of Naomi. A selfie," Noah answers, handing me the phone.

I take a look at the picture and see Naomi looking beautiful. She has on a bubblegum-pink dress that's both sweet and sexy at the same time.

"She looks fit," Mohammad cuts in, grabbing the phone

back from me as it buzzes again. "And the fact that she's sending me photos now is a great sign."

"Didn't you send her a photo yesterday?" I ask, clearly remembering Harry and Mohammad's *photo shoot*.

"You have to use your assets to your advantage," Mohammad says, like that's somehow an answer to my question.

"What's my best asset?" Harry asks.

"Definitely your chat," Mohammad replies.

"Hmm, maybe." Harry's eyes narrow as he considers Mohammad's compliment. "Mallory, what do you think?"

"What my best asset is?" I question.

"What *my* best asset is," Harry corrects.

"Well, it's definitely not your humbleness," I joke.

Noah lets out a laugh at my comment.

But I let my eyes linger on Harry.

I look at him. Really look at him.

Harry's gorgeous.

He's funny.

He doesn't lack for conversation.

Maybe it's a combination of everything that makes Harry so charming.

He's easygoing.

He makes you feel relaxed.

And then there are those blue eyes that somehow have the ability to show his emotions more than the rest of his face. Even when he smiles, his happiness shows in his eyes.

And then I finally answer his question. "Harry, I think your best asset is that you have the prettiest blue eyes. They make you feel like you're standing in the rain."

"Standing in the rain?" Harry asks.

"Well, that can't be good." Mohammad laughs.

"No, it is," I say. "They're refreshing. They're light, but they have lots of depth."

"What about mine?" Mohammad asks me.

"Your eyes are beautiful too. They're like … a chocolate hug."

"Oh, I like that." Mohammad grins.

"And you have eyes that look like … a storm," Noah says, catching my gaze.

"A pretty storm," Harry corrects.

"They're different. Almost gray," Mohammad says.

"What about Noah's?" Harry asks.

"Easy," I answer. "His are like sunshine. There's so much gold in the brown, and they get darker and lighter throughout the day."

Noah smiles at me, and I have to force myself not to grin back at him.

"So, we're rain, a hug, a storm, and the sun. Interesting …" Mohammad says. "I wonder if I can figure out what Naomi's eye color is like."

He pulls out his phone and says, "Do you think that girls get off more on hearing our voices than receiving photos?"

"One thousand percent. Especially when it's new and we're trying to get to know you," I say.

"Hmm … I think I'm going to ring Naomi then. Tell her what her eyes look like to me or some shit like that," Mohammad says, a devious smile settling on his face.

"You know when I say talk, I actually mean, talk," I tell him.

Mohammad frowns. "I am going to talk to her."

"I think what Mallory means," Noah says, "is that women want to hear about your feelings, not what you're thinking when you look at their photo."

"So, I shouldn't describe to her all the different ways I want to shag her?" Mohammad asks the question seriously, but a moment later, he's sticking out his tongue at us.

Harry and Noah erupt in laughter.

I just roll my eyes at him, trying not to smile.

"I'll be back!" Mohammad says, sprinting out of the room.

"I told you, you shouldn't meddle," Noah says to me when Mohammad's gone.

"I didn't. I just gave him advice."

Noah shakes his head. "I've never seen him so …" He pauses, apparently at a loss for the word.

"Lovestruck," Harry says.

"Exactly," Noah agrees. "It's not like Mohammad."

"Isn't love good for us?" I ask.

"For us, maybe. But for Mohammad … I'm not sure," Harry says, looking lost in thought.

I weigh my head back and forth, not sure I agree with them. I think it's just new for them. They're in that awkward dating stage where they both like one another but don't really want to admit it to one another, yet they can't help but admit it to everyone but the other person.

"Anyway, I was thinking about tonight," Noah says. "How do you feel about watching a movie? Something relaxing."

"Yeah?" Harry asks.

"Yeah. Let's just chill," Noah says.

"Sounds good," Harry agrees.

"Sound okay to you, Mal?" Noah asks, turning his attention to me.

"Sounds perfect. If we're staying in, I think I might go change into something comfortable."

"We can even make some food," Noah suggests.

"What kind of food?" Harry asks.

"Aren't you full from the pub?" I ask them both.

"I can always eat," Noah answers.

"What about pizza?" Harry says excitedly.

"It doesn't sound like the healthiest option," I interject.

"But it sounds delicious," Harry counters. "Besides, we're on holiday."

"Are you okay with that?" I ask Noah.

"I think we deserve to treat ourselves," Noah says, a sparkle in his eyes.

I exhale, realizing pizza and a movie is definitely going to turn into a splurge night. Which honestly doesn't sound too bad.

"All right. I think it will be fun," I agree.

"It's decided then. I'll go talk to the chef and tell Muriel the plan," Harry says, getting up.

"Wait, Harry. Was dinner already being prepared?" I ask.

"No. I told them, if anything, we might want a late snack since we ate out."

"Okay, cool," I reply, feeling better.

"Don't worry; nothing will be thrown out." Harry laughs.

"I just didn't want to be inconsiderate."

"I appreciate that." Harry nods. "Why don't you two change and then come down to the kitchen? I'll go and find Mohammad and tell him the plan!"

Kissing haze.
7:30PM

I'M CHANGING INTO my pajamas when a knock comes from the door. Before I have a chance to reply, Noah's in my room, shutting the door behind him.

"Come to check out my pajamas?" I ask, looking down at the cute purple set I have on.

Thankfully, I thought to pack them. I figured we'd have a chill hangout night, and since we aren't at my hotel anymore, I knew I couldn't just hide under the plush bathrobe if I looked ridiculous. And knowing that Noah would see me …

Noah creases his forehead as he sits down on the edge of the bed.

"Is everything okay?" I ask, realizing he looks stressed.

"Do you think I can flirt?" he asks.

It takes me a minute for his question to register.

"What?" I ask, sitting down on the bed next to him. "Where is this coming from?"

"Do you think I can flirt?" he repeats. "What you and Mohammad were talking about earlier, how girls like vocalization, I realized I've sort of been shit at that. At telling you exactly how I feel."

I grab on to Noah's hand.

"You can absolutely flirt. If anyone can't flirt, it's me," I reply.

"No," Noah says, agreeing. "But you've got good chat. And you're sexy, like all the time."

I blink.

Did Noah just call me sexy?

"You're not the typical flirt. But you definitely do flirt. Although instead of flirt, you might say dominate," I reply, thinking about Noah. "You're always so intense."

"Really?" Noah asks, a smile creeping onto his face.

"You leave me in a wordless puddle most of the time," I admit.

"I get you that wet, huh?" Noah grins.

"I said a puddle," I correct.

"Mmhmm." Noah looks me over. "Not a flirt … please. You smell amazing. You act like you look ridiculous or you don't know how beautiful you are, but I see right through it."

I laugh, moving my hand to cover my mouth. "You think I'm downplaying it?"

"I think you pretend like you're not sexy, but you are," Noah says, placing his hand on my knee. He inches closer toward me, causing my body to still. Noah takes both of my hands in his. "Mal, what happened at lunch?"

All the air in my lungs deflates with his question.

"You had to bring it up." I glance away from him.

"Bring up what?" Noah asks.

"Sometimes, I'm going to be in my head. I know you don't want me to overthink things, but it's part of who I am," I reply.

"Will you tell me what you were thinking about?"

I shake my head. "It's not going to do us any good, No-ah."

"It was about Harry."

I swallow, wishing he wouldn't push this.

Why can't he just leave it be?

"Noah, we don't need to talk about *everything*."

"We need to talk about this."

"I just … I just wish that I had been a better girlfriend to him, okay? It made me wonder if I wasn't so focused on you, on avoiding how I was feeling, if things might have been different for Harry. If I wouldn't have hurt him so much."

"It's okay to tell me that," Noah says.

"Not really, Noah." I shake my head. "I don't regret anything. And I don't want you to think that I do. But I can't help wondering how my actions affected him, you know?"

"I told you that you could always talk to me. Tell me anything."

"There are some things I wouldn't want to know," I disagree.

"Like?"

"Like I wouldn't want to hear that you feel bad for how you treated your ex or something. I guess I figured you'd be the same," I answer honestly.

Noah smiles.

"What?" I ask.

"That makes you a good person, Mal."

"Then, why did you get so upset with me about it?"

"Because you were shutting me out."

"I ..." I start to say *I wasn't*, but I know I was. "I'm sorry, Noah. I didn't mean to."

"It's all right. I understand why you didn't want to tell me. But it's not a big deal to me, Mal. I know you want this." Noah's mouth quickly finds mine. His thumb starts to stroke my skin as his lips part, his warm breath enveloping me.

I grasp his shoulders, feeling my worries float away as he kisses me.

EVENTUALLY, NOAH GOES to get changed for the movie.

And I walk out of my room in a kissing haze.

Everything looks shiny and blurry and ... better.

Noah's lips have that effect.

He makes me feel like I'm flying and falling, all at once and for who knows how long?

And the thing is, I should care.

I should care that I almost run into the door when I leave the room and that I stumble, walking down the stairs, luckily grabbing on to the handrail. I should care that he has this effect on me.

But for some reason, I can't bring myself to mind.

If I fall, I fall. But at least I'll do it, having experienced this.

Having felt this happy.

I amble toward the kitchen, feeling slightly drunk. Or

high. I don't know what it feels like to be high, but I imagine it's something like this.

It's all fun and games and happy and exciting until you accidentally run into the edge of a marble table in the hallway.

"Shit," I mumble.

"Are you all right?" Mohammad says, suddenly at my side. He grabs my elbow, looking me up and down.

"Fine." I smile at him and have to hold back a laugh.

Because I literally just walked into a table.

I press my lips together, trying to think of something that's not funny.

Mohammad squints his eyes at me. "What's going on?" His voice is full of suspicion.

"Nothing." I laugh, shaking my head.

Mohammad drops his arm. I try to walk away from him, but everything still feels slightly off its axis. Like the hallway is wobbling. I laugh, realizing how ridiculous I sound.

"Okay, something is *definitely* going on," Mohammad says, glaring at me. His eyes are narrow slits, and his expression makes me laugh even more.

"Nothing is wrong."

"You ran right into a table! Where's your head at?" Mohammad continues, ignoring my statement.

"My head is here." I point to my head and stick my tongue out at him at the same time.

Instead of finding it funny, he just looks at me with even more suspicious eyes.

I roll mine at him as we find our way into the kitchen. It's empty, and I take a seat in a free chair, falling down in a huff.

"What do you want me to say?" I ask, looking up at Mohammad.

He leans his back against the counter and crosses his arms over his chest. He looks like Noah when he isn't going to let something slide. When he's extremely determined and serious. I glance across Mohammad, instead seeing Noah in my mind. And I'm instantly taken back to kissing him upstairs. To his hand slipping down to my waist.

I smile again.

"That's it!" Mohammad yells, pushing off the counter. "Spill!"

"Fine! I was just distracted," I admit, looking up at him. I'm not going to give him any more information than he asks for. Mostly because I know it's going to annoy him.

And that's pretty entertaining.

Mohammad starts to pace. "Distracted is an understatement," he says more to himself than me.

And he really is giving me crazy Noah vibes right now. A laugh escapes me. I immediately bring my hand to my lips, covering my mouth. Mohammad snaps his head in my direction. My eyes go wide.

But then recognition flashes across his face.

"Wait ... where's Noah?"

I blink, trying to look indifferent, and then shrug in response.

"You don't know?" Mohammad questions, looking at me.

"How should I?"

I know that I should just tell Mohammad that I was distracted from our kiss, but he looks too happy at this game of inquisition for me to spoil his fun.

"Because you're one room over from him," Mohammad goes on. "So, one would assume that you would know if he was in his room. But if you're denying it, then that means you have something to hide. Am I right?!"

I crack a smile. "Maybe."

Mohammad grins back. He pulls a free chair up next to me, looking like he's won the lottery.

"I knew it. You were with him, weren't you?"

"I was changing," I reply, avoiding his question. But the smile doesn't leave my lips.

"So you say," Mohammad says enthusiastically.

"I can't help it if in that same time period, I might have gotten a few kisses," I reply.

"We're in a lot of trouble if just a few kisses does this to you," Mohammad replies, tapping me gently on the forehead. "You're useless."

"I am not!" I laugh out in surprise.

"You are. You're stumbling around, running into things. I told you, love makes people go crazy. I'm telling you, you might want to rethink this whole *love* thing."

"And how exactly does one *rethink* love?"

Because Mohammad sounds ridiculous.

"You have to stomp it out with some cold, harsh reality, likely in the form of facts."

"What kind of facts?"

"For example, you're only seventeen. Even if this is your first love, it's not likely to be your last. In all truthfulness, you'll probably have some big fight because you and Noah are seriously intense, and it won't end well. So, you shouldn't injure yourself or lose your head in the meantime. Or you can remind yourself that Harry is still an option. Who knows? One day, you two could end up hitched with kids, and you'd feel a little silly, looking back on being at his house, which is now your house, and lusting over his best friend."

"Mohammad!" My hand flies up to cover my mouth. "You can't say any of that!"

Mohammad rolls his eyes. "I'm just trying to give you some perspective, so one day, you don't walk off a cliff or something because little love birds are spinning around in your head, distracting you." Mohammad spins his finger in the air, apparently showing me the love birds.

I frown at him. "I'm not going to walk off a cliff. Besides, there aren't any cliffs to walk off of in London," I reply, flaring my eyes.

"You're right; your demise would be more pathetic than that. I can see the story now. *American tourist hospitalized after walking in front of a double-decker bus. When witnesses were interviewed, they said the girl strode right out into the middle of the street with no regard for oncoming traffic.*"

I stand up from my seat, officially *un-lovestruck.*

"All right, all right. I get your point," I say, waving him off.

I move over to the cabinets, opening random ones to see what I can find. I need something to snack on right now, so I don't have to sit and dwell on Mohammad's *insightful* words.

I grumble, finding only plates and glasses.

"What are you looking for?"

The voice isn't Mohammad's, and I quickly swirl around, finding Harry behind me. His cheeks are pink, and I quickly notice the freckles sprinkled across his nose. He has on a white T-shirt and pajama bottoms, and he smells like cologne.

"She doesn't know what she's looking for right now," Mohammad says from the other side of the island.

Harry tilts his head at me in question. I glare over my shoulder at Mohammad, who replies by sticking out his tongue.

I want to tell Harry that anything I can throw at Mohammad will do. Something that would injure him a little, but not draw blood. Like a butter knife.

Instead, I say, "Food. A drink. Preferably both."

"I think I can handle that," Harry says, shifting past me. A second later, his head is stuck in the freezer, and he's pulling out frozen pizza boxes. "Mohammad, can you find some baking trays?"

"Sure thing," Mohammad replies.

Harry opens the boxes, removes the plastic, slides the frozen pizzas onto the counter, and then turns back to me.

"Next is you." He pinches my chin before going to the pantry. When he returns, he's got a bottle of wine in his hand.

"It's been so long since I've had a good frozen pizza," Mohammad says, laying out the pizzas on the trays before popping them into the oven. "Do you have any chocolate around here?"

"Needing something sweet?" I ask Mohammad as Harry starts to open the wine.

"Badly," Mohammad replies.

"Go look in the pantry," Harry instructs. He uncorks the wine and then sets a timer for the pizzas on his phone.

"We could always make a banana split," Harry says, bumping his shoulder against mine.

"Like we had at the diner." I can't help but smile.

"I remember how much you loved the banana," Harry says, his voice dropping.

I swallow, nodding. "I do love my fruit."

"I'm pretty sure you enjoyed watching me eat the whipped cream even more though," Harry says, his gaze falling to my lips.

I pinch my lips shut and keep my focus on his blue eyes. I don't let my eyes wander across his face to his firm jaw and pink lips.

"Harry …"

"Tell me I'm wrong," Harry replies, searching my eyes.

I don't say anything back. I'm not sure what to say. Mostly because when Harry says things like this, when he's … sexy, well, it takes me by surprise. I never know if he's teasing or joking or if he always just falls somewhere in between.

"Jackpot," Mohammad says, rejoining us.

I gladly turn my attention to him. He's got a box of popcorn in his hand.

"What can I do?" Noah asks, walking into the kitchen. He's changed into navy pajama bottoms and a T-shirt.

And he looks amazing.

"Popcorn duty," Harry says, motioning toward Mohammad.

ONCE WE HAVE the pizzas cooked, the wine in a decanter, and Noah's popcorn made, we move into the living room.

"This might be the best night," Mohammad says, shoving a handful of popcorn in his mouth.

"You like snacking?" I ask, curling up on the couch while Harry turns on the television.

"I love it. There's nothing like a night in with the boys. And of course, you, Miss America." Mohammad gives me a sheepish smile.

I smile at him but quickly steal a handful of popcorn from the bowl, sticking out my tongue.

"Are you two going to behave yourself, or am I going to have to separate you?" Noah asks.

"I think separate," I reply.

Noah laughs as he sits down on the couch and pours us each a glass of wine.

"What kind of movie are we in the mood for?" Harry asks, standing with his hand on his hip as he looks through the options.

"Something funny," Mohammad calls out.

"What about a romance?" I jokingly offer.

"Noah?" Harry asks.

"Whatever you want," he replies, taking a sip of his wine.

"Funny it is," Harry says, deciding on a movie.

He turns down the lights before joining us on the couch.

"Can I have some pizza?" I ask Harry.

He hands a piece to me and then one to Noah. I take a sip of wine and a bite of pizza, and it's the best combination. As the movie starts, I watch Noah. This reminds me of the night we finished off the bottle of wine at his house.

And I remember how much I wanted to be with him.

I lay my head against his shoulder, feeling content. Noah glances over to me, a smile on his face.

HARRY MIGHT HAVE actually chosen the stupidest movie. Both he and Mohammad can barely eat; they're laughing so much. Noah laughs every once in a while, but I think it's honestly because his focus is more on the popcorn than it is on the show.

Eventually, he finishes the bowl.

"We're out of popcorn," Noah announces.

"And wine," Mohammad says.

"Harry, want to come help me? We can open another bottle of wine too," Noah says.

Harry nods and is quickly up from the couch, grabbing the empty decanter.

"Bring back candy," Mohammad calls out as they head to the kitchen.

Almost fifteen minutes later, they come back. Noah has two bowls of popcorn and sets one of them in my lap. He hands the other to Mohammad.

"Where's the candy?" Mohammad asks, looking between them like he was somehow forgotten.

"Figured this was the best of both worlds—sweet and salty," Noah says, motioning to the popcorn. It's drizzled with chocolate, and my mouth starts to water.

I take a bite and immediately feel like I'm in heaven.

"Yum," I mumble, inhaling another mouthful.

Harry leans over Mohammad and Noah to hand me a glass of wine, and that's when I notice that something seems off.

His complexion has gone white.

"Everything all right?" I ask, wondering what's up.

"All good," he replies, giving me a forced smile.

He passes out the rest of the wineglasses before leaning back on the couch. I throw a piece of popcorn at him, hoping to get a smile.

He does, but I notice it doesn't reach his eyes.

"Is everything all right with Harry?" I whisper to Noah.

"He's all right," Noah answers, not giving me any more information. "Do you like the popcorn?"

"It's delicious. The chocolate was a great idea."

"I'm glad you like it," Noah says.

I take a few more bites, offering some to Noah, which he happily accepts. And I try to stay focused on the movie, but every time I glance over at Harry, he looks the same.

Blank expression.

Wineglass in hand.

Eyes on the television.

He hasn't even touched the chocolate popcorn.

Something is definitely wrong.

No more nights alone.
11:15PM

"THAT WAS REALLY fun." I smile to Noah as we head upstairs.

Harry eventually fell asleep during the movie and then excused himself early when he woke up, but Mohammad managed to stay awake for all of it. By the time the credits came, all the pizza, popcorn, and wine were gone, and we were all yawning and ready for bed.

"It was fun. I wasn't a fan of the movie though," Noah admits.

"What would you have picked?"

"Something with more action."

"You're not really into funny movies, are you?" I ask.

"Nah." Noah shakes his head. "But Mohammad and Harry love them."

"I'm not the biggest fan either."

When we get upstairs, I walk toward my bedroom door.

"I'm going to brush my teeth. All that sugar," I say, flaring my eyes at Noah.

He nods. "When you're done, why don't you collect your things and bring them to my room?"

"Wait, really?" I ask in surprise.

"I talked to Harry." It's the only thing Noah says, but it causes my heart to lurch in my chest.

Because he talked to Harry?

"Wait, Noah." I walk toward him and grab on to his forearm. "What?"

Noah creases his forehead. "Why do you look surprised?"

"You told him about *us*?" I ask, immediately feeling sick.

"Yes, I told him. I told you I would."

I glance away and bite my lip. "How did he react?"

Noah looks around the dark hallway before pulling me into his bedroom and closing the door behind us.

"He knew it was coming."

"I don't think he did, Noah." I shake my head at him.

"What do you mean?"

"He's been ... suggesting things," I say, trying to figure out how to word this. "I just think that Harry would rather things between all of us be loose. You know, noncommittal."

"*Noncommittal?*" Noah tilts his head in question.

"Harry keeps going on about us having fun together. He talks about us not knowing about our future ..."

"He isn't wrong. No one knows the future," Noah says.

"No?"

"Well, it's not a guarantee," Noah says, taking my hand. "However, I know that I want you. Always."

I pull Noah to my lips, needing him.

He kisses me, and for a moment, I can forget that he told Harry. That Harry is probably upset.

That this is the first of many people we will start telling about us.

But Noah pulls back. "You're stressed?" His brown eyes fill with concern.

"You can tell?" I ask.

He nods. "Why don't you let me draw you a bath?"

"I'm not big on baths."

"I am." Noah's words take me by surprise.

"You want to take a bath together?" I ask.

"Why not? It could be fun. Besides, I think it's fair," Noah says, his hands slipping around my waist.

"Fair?" I ask.

"Because you took one with Mohammad and Harry." He looks me up and down. "Although I think this one will be more fun."

Noah drops my hand and pulls his shirt off over his head, causing my mouth to fall open. My eyes scan down over his chest to his abs, butterflies erupting in my stomach.

"Come on," Noah says, leading me into the bathroom.

He closes the door behind us before starting the bath. I sit down on the edge of the tub as he works, dimming the light and grabbing us towels.

It's hard to think straight when he's shirtless, and I know I'm about to see more of him naked.

Noah finishes his tasks and stills in front of me.

His hands move, and his fingers start working on the tie on his pajama bottoms. Slowly, he pulls them off, his eyes staying on me the entire time.

My heart starts to pound in my chest, and I stand up.

Noah hooks his fingers into the sides of his boxers like he's going to pull them off. I lick my lips, ready to see all of Noah.

To *experience* all of him.

But he moves his fingers away.

"I'll wear my boxers in," he says, nodding at me like I'm next.

"Okay," I mumble.

Noah walks up to me and wraps his hands around me. His fingers hook into the fabric of my shirt before he pulls it off, over my head.

I bite my lip and fumble out of my pants until I'm only in my underwear and bra.

"You can stay covered if you want," Noah says, looking me over. "But you don't have to. You never have to cover up in front of me, you know."

I press my lips together, debating what to do.

"Why are your boxers on then?" I ask.

"Because I want to hold you," he says, slowly getting into the tub. "And I think if I didn't have these on, things might go differently."

I follow Noah into the tub and sit, so I'm facing him.

"Noah, you're too big for this tub." I laugh, trying to get comfortable.

"Am not," he says, shaking his head in disagreement.

But I know he knows it. His knees are bent, and I'm

pretty sure I'm sitting on one of his legs.

"Are too."

"Are you having a good weekend?" he asks once we get settled.

I push my hands through the water and think about the weekend so far. It's been good with the boys. And things with Noah and me have been good.

"Honestly, yeah."

"You sound surprised."

"I wondered if things might be hard or weird with us since everything is new. I didn't know how it would be, being more than friends here. Especially with our friends," I admit.

"Because our friendship was hard sometimes?"

"More like impossible." I slink down into the tub, growing comfortable.

"I struggled," Noah admits. "But it's because I knew how I felt. I never wanted to be just friends."

"Now, we're not." I smile at him.

Noah smiles back before sliding his hands over my knees.

"Let me see your toes." Noah smirks.

"What? No." I laugh.

"Come on," Noah says, grabbing my ankle in the water. He pulls my foot up, placing it on his chest. "Look at those monsters," he teases.

"Do you like them?" I ask, wiggling my toes against him.

"Definitely." Noah starts to tickle my toes, causing me to kick up water.

"Noah! That tickles." I laugh.

"It's supposed to." He grins.

"Stop it, or I swear …" I laugh, trying to escape his grip.

"What are you going to do about it, all the way over there?" Noah challenges, raising his eyebrows at me.

"You're being a brat," I reply.

I shift in the tub, and he lets go of my foot. I turn around and slide in between his legs until my back is against his chest.

Noah's hands find their way to my bare stomach, and he draws circles on it, his hand barely grazing my underwear. I let my head fall back against his chest.

"It's just like being in a swimsuit, right?" I ask, wondering how Noah actually feels. I slide my hands down his legs, wanting to get him out of his boxers. I want to forget everything.

My parents moving.

The fact that he told Harry.

I want to drown in Noah.

"Do you want the honest answer, or do you want me to tell you what I think you want to hear?"

I smile. "Tell me what I want to hear."

"It's just like a swimsuit," Noah says into my ear.

"And the truth?" I ask.

"The truth is, it's taking everything in me not to peel these wet clothes off you and drag you into the bedroom."

I bite my lip again, my whole body flushing.

"Are you sure that's not what you want to do?" I ask.

Because I want Noah to make a move.

I want him to take control.

Noah exhales shakily, and I can tell he's considering what I said.

"Let's just enjoy this," he says, wrapping his arms around me. "You've had a busy day; you need to rest."

I relax into him, knowing he's probably right.

"Says the boy who woke up at dawn to run before Harry and Mohammad's full day of events."

"I have to stay in shape over break."

"With Harry's schedule for us, I'm not sure you'll even need a workout to stay in shape. I don't know if today could even be categorized as vacation; it was so busy!"

"Harry has kept us busy," Noah agrees.

"I figured he'd be in his underwear the whole time, playing video games and trying to feed us cold pizza all weekend. I didn't expect all of this. He's put in a lot of effort to make this weekend special."

"I think what you said about making new memories really stuck with him."

And I immediately feel bad.

"I'm sorry about that. It's something I said when …"

"When you two were dating." Noah nods. "You don't have to apologize."

"I don't want to talk about Harry right now," I say, trying to get comfortable against Noah.

"Why don't we go get ready for bed?" Noah suggests, rubbing his hands down my arms.

"Yeah," I reply.

We both stand up, but Noah's the first out of the bath. He wraps a towel around me before grabbing his own.

I watch him strip off his wet underwear once his towel is secure at his waist.

"One sec," Noah says, leaving me to go into the bedroom.

I take the chance to strip off my bra and underwear, wrapping the towel around my chest.

Noah knocks on the bathroom door.

"Come in," I call out.

When he comes into the bathroom, he's in a pair of shorts and a tee, and he has another outfit in his hand. His eyes slip down over my towel before landing on my underwear on the floor.

"I brought you these to change into," he says, handing me the clothes.

"Thanks."

"I'll be right outside," he says before leaving the bathroom so I can change.

I drop the towel and quickly pull on his clothes, feeling like I'm drowning in them. They're too big, but they're comfortable.

Plus, *they're Noah's.*

I walk into the bedroom, finding him standing not far from the door. He grins when he sees me.

"You look great in my clothes."

"You think?" I smile back.

"Mmhmm," he says, his eyes dilating.

"So, tonight …" I say, wondering what's going to happen.

"Tonight, you'll sleep with me," Noah states.

He doesn't ask if I want to or offer for me to stay.

No.

He tells me.

"Oh, you think?" I partially tease, wondering how serious he is about this.

"I know." He nods.

"And what if I want to sleep in my own room?" I question, my eyes sparkling.

Noah shakes his head. "Not going to happen."

"Oh yeah?"

I look between him and the door and make a run for it. But Noah quickly catches me. A second later, he picks me up and then walks over to the bed, tossing me on it before falling down on top of me.

"No fair!" I say as he pins me down.

"I made a promise to you last night. No more nights alone, remember?"

"I remember."

"So, you'll stay with me?" Noah asks.

"Do I have a choice?" I smirk.

"Sometimes, you really do have too much sass for your own good." Noah tickles me, his fingers moving from under my arms to around my neck.

I laugh and easily push Noah off me.

"I'll stay," I reply, rolling onto my side.

Noah looks at the ceiling, his hand finding mine. I watch his chest rise and fall as he breathes.

"It's the first time we've ever been able to sleep together," Noah says. "I mean, in the same bed."

"I know. We're lucky to get this time together."

He rolls onto his side to face me and brings his hand down onto my hair, pushing it back off my face.

"It will be different when we get back—with my parents being here, and I'm sure your mom will have more rules for us," I tell him.

"Especially after you caved about us."

"Hey, I took one for the team." I push him gently. "It was either you or me she was going to talk to."

"That's fair," he agrees, glancing down. "Here, do you want under the covers?"

I nod, so he pulls the blanket up around us. But a second later, he's uncovered and stripping off his shirt.

And then his shorts.

I swallow as he tosses them both on the ground.

Because now, he's only in his underwear.

I look over him, my mind going blank.

Am I ready for this?

"Mal?"

"Yeah?"

"Come here," he says, pulling me to him.

To his lips.

He wraps his arms around me. His skin is soft and warm from the bath, and it seeps right through my clothes. When he tightens his grip on my waist and deepens the kiss, it sends my body into overdrive. I push and pull against him, wanting more.

Very quickly, my top is gone. But I barely notice. Because all I can think about is that Noah is warm and hot and intense, and I want everything from him.

He pulls back, looking me over. "You're so beautiful," he says, which makes me pause.

Because I realize this is the first time that he's seen me topless.

I flush, pulling him back down to me.

To my lips.

And then Noah is on top of me.

His chest against mine feels like perfection.

And we kiss for a long time.

His hands trail over my chest.

Across my belly.

I touch his bare stomach, dragging my hand down to his boxers. Noah shudders, his breath coming out in unsteady exhales.

"You should probably keep your shorts on," he says, his voice deep and gravelly.

"You didn't keep yours on," I point out, playing with the edge of his underwear.

"That's because I can control myself," he says.

"That's debatable."

"More control than you," Noah says, but then he gives me a steamy, open-mouthed kiss.

"I have no self-control," I agree, loving the feel of his weight on top of me.

"I know." He smiles. "Which is why one of us needs to keep a clear head."

"Because you want to wait? How long do you want to

wait?" I ask, trying to figure him out. "And weren't you the one saying to stop focusing so much on sex? Stop focusing on it. Maybe … let it happen?"

"Using all of that against me?" Noah laughs as he sits up, so he's straddling me.

"I have no choice."

"There are certain things I want to do before we do that," he says.

"Like what?"

"Well, I'd like to be alone."

"We are alone," I tell him, propping myself up onto my elbows.

"I mean, just you and me."

"You mean, not at Harry's?"

"No."

I chew on my lip. "What else do you want to do?"

Noah's face brightens.

"You only want to know, so you can check the boxes and get me out of my underwear," Noah teases.

"I can't deny that," I say with a laugh. "And I respect that. It's just more tempting than I thought."

I motion to his naked chest above me and let out a dramatic sigh.

"Being in bed with me?"

"Yeah."

"I know how you feel," he says with a nod.

"Then, it's a clothes on kind of night," I tell him, sitting up and looking for his shirt.

"Whoa, whoa, whoa," Noah says, grabbing my hands.

"What?"

"Let's not get crazy. I think I can manage with the shirt off," he says, running his hand down over my chest.

"So, you're all right with this then?" I ask.

"Definitely fine with it."

"And how about kissing? Are you okay with that?" I tease.

"I think I can manage," he says, his mouth crashing against mine.

MONDAY, OCTOBER 21ST
Love is tricky.
8:00AM

HARRY.

It's the first thought that pops into my head when I wake up. When I wake up in bed. *With Noah.*

I look up at the ceiling, trying to figure out how I feel. My mind is empty. There aren't any thoughts swirling around. I'm not confused. Or conflicted.

I know exactly what I want.

Who I want.

I roll my head to the side, looking over at Noah next to me. He's still asleep, his breathing coming out in a steady flow, causing his chest to rise in a rhythmic motion.

In and out.

Over and over.

He's lying on his back, the covers only rising halfway up his stomach. They stop short of his chest, his rounded shoulders and creamy skin on full display.

My gaze moves from the line of hair leading up to his belly button to his firm stomach.

His broad chest.

Eventually, I find my way to his face—his long, dark eyelashes capturing my attention.

Noah's hair is a mess, and it's the only thing that keeps

me from thinking that this is a dream.

Because Noah is perfect.

And I got to wake up with him.

Me.

It's almost too much to wrap my head around. Last night, having him lying on top of me ... every day just gets better and better.

But then I think about Harry.

About how Noah told him about us yesterday.

I think about how Harry must be feeling. And I immediately feel guilty again.

I could never regret being with Noah. It would be impossible. After all, you can't regret something that feels like part of you. Something that feels right. And being with Noah? Nothing has ever felt so right. But what I do regret is lying here, looking at this perfect boy, knowing that half of my heart is out there, somewhere else in the house, probably hurting.

And I need to address it.

I slide my hand onto Noah's chest, my palm immediately warming.

"Noah ..." I whisper out his name.

I don't want to wake him up, but I also don't want him to wake up without me here. Not after last night.

"Hmm?" Noah lets out a quiet grunt, his dark brows pulling together. He takes in a long, slow breath, his hand finding its way to rest on mine.

"I need to go talk to Harry."

Noah's forehead creases, and he slowly opens his eyes.

"Now?" he asks, his voice thick from sleep.

He blinks a few times before looking up to me. I hold his gaze.

"Yeah. I just ... I want to make sure he's okay."

Noah drops my hand before sitting up in bed. He licks his lips and pinches the arch of his nose, forcing his eyes shut and then open again.

"Are you okay?" he asks.

"I am."

Noah pulls his lips to the side. "Are you regretting us, Mal?"

My head jerks in his direction. "What? No."

Noah's forehead creases again, and I instinctively reach out to him. I take his hand in mine, shaking my head.

"Noah, waking up with you this morning, it was perfect. And last night …" I look into his brown eyes, hoping that he understands.

"I know." Noah smiles. "I loved kissing you last night, and I really love waking up with you."

I smile back, but quickly, my mind flashes to Harry.

"But I need to go talk to Harry. I won't be long."

I kiss Noah slowly on the lips. His breath is warm, and it causes me to lay my hand on his chest.

Noah's lips part mine, his tongue grazing my bottom lip. I have to hold back a moan as I fold in toward him, my fingers pressing into his bare skin. Noah responds by deepening the kiss. His fingers find their way into my hair, and for a moment, I'm able to forget the conversation I know I need to have.

When Noah's kissing me, there isn't room for anything else. *There isn't room for anyone else.*

In my mind.

In my heart.

Or my body.

He occupies everything. Demands everything.

I bite Noah's lip, my body aching for more.

But he pulls away.

His brown eyes are clouded with desire from our kiss.

"You stopped," I say more to myself than him.

"You wouldn't have," Noah replies.

I press my lips together. Because he's probably right. I wanted to lose myself in him. But Noah's never let me run away from anything. He always wants me to face my problems. To talk to him.

To talk to Harry.

I give him a pathetic excuse of a smile, trying to rally. But suddenly, the effect of our kiss is gone and is replaced by discomfort in my stomach. Noah grabs my hand and brings it to his lips, placing a quick kiss on my knuckles.

"Take your time," he says.

I nod, then get out of bed, trying to be quiet. Even though Noah's awake, I'm hoping he will fall back asleep. I decide to stop in my room and change into my own pajamas.

I know that I should look at myself in the mirror.

Brush my hair. My teeth.

But ever since I woke up, I've had this knot in my stomach.

I know that Noah thinks everything is okay because they talked, and maybe their relationship is fine. But what about me and Harry?

Are we fine?

When I get to Harry's room, I don't bother knocking. I peek my head inside and find his bed empty. The sheets are thrown to the side, a mess of pillows sprinkled across the bed.

I step inside, wondering if he's in the bathroom.

Or maybe he's up, somewhere else in the house. But then I see the patio door is open. I walk outside and find Harry sitting in his bathrobe, smoking a cigarette and drinking a cup of coffee.

He looks up at me. His eyes are red, like he didn't get

much sleep.

"Mallory?" Harry asks.

"Whatcha doing?" It's all I can manage to say.

He holds up his coffee cup and cigarette. "Want one?"

"I don't mind waiting until breakfast," I say, not wanting to be a bother.

Harry tilts his head, waiting for me to change my answer.

"I'll always take a coffee," I reply.

"Sit. I'll make you a cup."

Harry rises from his chair, setting his lit cigarette down in the ashtray. After he goes inside, I expect him to call Muriel to let her know, but instead, I hear a coffee machine grinding.

"You have a coffeemaker in your room?" I call out to him.

"It's convenient," he says.

When he comes back, he has a blanket draped over his arm, coffee cup in hand. He sets down the cup on the table between us.

"Here, it's cold out," he says, handing me the blanket.

I give him a sympathetic smile and accept it.

Because he's right; it is chilly.

Harry tightens the robe around his waist, picks back up his cigarette, and inhales a drag.

"My ex-girlfriend is now dating my best mate. I never thought I'd be able to say that," he says.

I drop my eyes, wishing I could make this better.

Make this easier.

But I know I can't.

"Not saying it doesn't make it any less real."

"I know," Harry agrees, bringing his coffee cup to his lips. "Maybe me going to Shanghai is good timing then."

"You leaving is never a good thing," I disagree.

"You sure about that?" He turns and really looks at me.

"I'm positive. I love you, Harry. I don't want you to go." I reach out and grab on to his hand.

"So, you'll miss me?" he asks, giving me a hint of a smile.

"Definitely."

Harry breaks our hands apart before taking another sip of his coffee. I do the same.

"I understand why you're doing this, you know. Exploring things with Noah. It's all good. Just ... don't forget what I said. Our futures aren't set in stone."

I nod. "Trust me, you aren't getting out of my life that easily. We will always be there for one another."

"That's true," Harry says, ashing his cigarette. "Makes it slightly awkward that you're my date tomorrow night then, doesn't it?"

"Honestly, I don't think so."

Harry's blue eyes find mine. "I thought you'd tell me you wouldn't go," he admits.

"Of course I'll go. I told you I would. But ..."

"But then that's it," Harry finishes. "I understand."

I look out at the garden, not sure what else to say. I don't know where to start. Or if I even owe Harry an explanation. I probably do. And at the same time, I probably don't.

"Noah's not like us," Harry says, his brows weaving together.

"No, he's not."

"He's sure of himself. Laser-focused. I don't blame you, you know. I chose Noah, too, when he told me he loved you. My immediate response was to not hurt him. Then, I went and broke up with you." Harry shakes his head.

"You two always choose one another. It used to scare me a little. I thought I would end up slipping through the cracks, but ..."

"But not this time," Harry says seriously. "Noah would never let something small come between us. He never has. No matter how much shit I pull, he doesn't say a word. But you … you're not something small to him."

I stay silent.

"I was surprised though when he told me."

"I figured we should talk about it," I say.

"Not much to talk about. I was the one who told you that you two should date and figure things out."

"Do you regret that?" I ask.

Harry smiles at me. "Actually, no. I'm too prideful. This probably isn't the right thing to say, but I've never been good with words. I think if we got back together one day in the future, I wouldn't want this hanging over us."

"You mean, Noah?"

"Yeah. And if you two are some predestined pair, like he thinks, then, well, I guess I need to be happy for you both. So, either way, you two dating helps us figure all that out."

"I can't believe you just said *predestined pair*." A laugh escapes my lips.

"It burned, coming out," Harry replies, taking a drag of his cigarette. But at the same time, he shoots me a wink.

"I bet it did." I smile and take a sip of my coffee.

Because I think everything between us is going to be okay.

"It's strange, isn't it? I told you that I loved you. I love Noah. Noah loves you. I know you love us both … love is tricky," Harry says.

"Love is … love. I think I'm just the one making it tricky. Constantly messing everything up," I say, my stomach falling.

"Blame the hormones." Harry smiles. "I always do."

"Yeah?" I ask, wondering if he's just telling me that to make me feel better.

"Of course." He nods firmly.

"Maybe we should make it into a slogan then. *The hormones made me do it.* What do you think?"

"*T-H-M-M-D-I,*" Harry says, sounding each letter out. "Hmm. I think that might be a tough one to get people to latch on to."

I laugh, watching Harry's blue eyes lighten up. His cheeks have grown pink, and he looks better than before. Movement in the garden captures our attention.

It's Noah.

He must be out for his morning run.

"He's so motivated." It takes me a minute to realize I said it out loud.

"He's always been like that," Harry states. "Always so serious."

I look over at him, noticing the irony.

"And then there's us. Coffee and cigarettes," I say, causing us both to laugh.

"We all wake up for something," Harry replies, taking another sip of coffee. "Noah's reasons just happen to be healthier."

"What do you wake up for?" I search Harry's face.

"Deep question." Harry clears his throat.

"One you'll answer?" I ask.

"I wake up for my mates. And I do love a good time." He gives me a grin.

"I know you do," I say, smiling back at him.

"It's always been like that, since we were young. Noah shows me unconditional love. His family too. I remember waking up one morning to a note from my mum. It was when she had just started working more with the company. Dad was out of town already. She told me she'd be gone for a few days. She only called me once after a week, telling me she wouldn't be back for a few more days." Harry shakes his head. "I tried to play it off as a feat. You know, no parents. House to myself. The staff was there, but they had their purposes, and I could dismiss them when I wanted."

"She just left you?"

"Yeah. I would hang around Noah's house after school, staying for dinner until Helen would send me home. I dragged my feet, but I would always go. I didn't want to cause trouble or anything. Halfway through the first week, Noah showed up at my door though. The house was empty, my parents still gone. He took one look around, packed my duffel, and took me back to his house. Never said another word about it. I stayed with him until Mum got back."

"He's a good friend. And he loves you."

"A great friend." Harry nods in agreement.

"What happened when your mom got back?" I ask.

"I felt abandoned. I was going to tell her how upset I was, but when she got back, she was happy. *Really* happy. Happier than I'd seen her in years. She hugged me, apologized for the delay, and I couldn't bring myself to do it. So, I hugged her back and got used to being alone. Turns out, being alone leaves you with a lot of free time. Especially time to think. So, I convinced myself that their absence was a gift and that I should take advantage of the freedom. I had money. My mates. My family name. What use were parents really? I didn't need them; I had a whole staff. So, I started filling my time. I partied. Got a girlfriend. Let my marks go in school."

"You started slipping."

"Yeah. And then I became a constant disappointment to my dad. After all, he thought I had everything a kid could dream of. Why couldn't I just keep myself out of trouble? Keep my grades up? But the more I got in trouble, the more I heard from them …"

"You wanted attention."

"I've always loved attention." Harry smiles. "Anyway, I came to terms with it. My dad's disappointment and abuse.

Letting my grades go because I always knew I'd have money. I let myself party because I knew, one day, I wouldn't have a say in my future. I was fine, living like that."

"What changed?" I ask him.

"You got here." Harry's response is immediate.

"Me? How?"

"I was a shitty boyfriend to you. I didn't realize that my actions could really hurt someone else until I hurt you. With Olivia, I had done what I wanted, you know? We hooked up, went through the motions, fought, made up. But she never seemed hurt by it really. If anything, she'd liked the drama. Me always going back to her. But with you, I could see how much I hurt you. I could see that you wanted better for me. I didn't know how to deal with that," Harry admits.

My heart aches at his words.

"I do want better for you, Harry. But I truly believe that comes, first and foremost, from being better to ourselves."

"I want to work on it."

"I'm proud of you, Harry. And I really appreciate you sharing that with me. It means a lot."

"Don't they say, sharing is caring? I always thought they were talking about a shower or a bed, but ..."

"Always cheeky." I laugh and take Harry's hand into mine. "Look, whatever happens in Shanghai, with the divorce, with your parents, I'm here for you, okay?"

"I appreciate that," he says, squeezing my hand before glancing away.

And I can tell this makes him uncomfortable.

"And I'll need you to be there for me too," I tell him, moving the attention to me. "With my parents arriving soon and moving into the new place, it's a lot of change."

"You need me?" Harry asks with surprise.

"Of course I do."

"What about Noah? I mean …"

"Just because things between Noah and me might change doesn't mean I don't want or need your friendship anymore. I'm always going to depend on you, Harry. Sometimes for a good time. And other times to just hang out. Talk about the serious, boring stuff."

A mixture of emotions flashes across Harry's face before his eyebrows shoot up in what looks like surprise.

"I'm not sure I've ever been needed before," he says, suddenly looking relieved.

"Are you okay with it?" I ask, trying to gauge what he's feeling.

He looks at me, his face lighting up. "You can count on me," he says.

I smile at him. "And you can count on me too."

I stand up and pull Harry into a hug, trying to figure out why this is so hard. Harry holds me for a while, but eventually, he breaks us apart.

"Why don't I get cleaned up for breakfast? We can meet in the dining room?" Harry asks.

"Sounds good."

Getting naked.
8:30AM

WHEN I GET upstairs, I go straight to Noah's room to see if he's back from his run. I can hear the shower running in the bathroom, so I knock on the door.

"Noah?" I call out.

"Come in."

I turn the handle and walk into the steamy bathroom.

"Good run?" I ask, leaning against the counter.

Noah pulls back the curtain. "Great. How'd you know?" he asks. His body is still hidden, but his head and shoulders are on full display.

"I saw you," I answer.

"Watching me?" Noah laughs, dropping the curtain.

He moves back under the shower, probably washing his hair. And the fact that he's a few feet away from me, wet and naked … well, it's very distracting, and it causes my stomach to erupt with butterflies.

"How's the shower?" I ask.

"Feels great. How was the talk?"

I shake my head, trying to focus on his question. But the room is filling up with steam. And it would be so easy to strip naked and join him in the shower.

"It was hard. But good," I finally answer.

"Are you glad you talked to him?"

"I needed to," I reply. "I have other things on my mind right now though."

"Like what?" Noah asks.

Getting naked. Joining you in the shower.

But Noah said he wants to take it slow.

"You," I finally say.

Noah pulls back the curtain. Again.

But this time, I see more of him. I watch the water roll down his chest until it disappears behind the curtain.

"You could join me if you want."

I flick my gaze up, finding Noah's eyes on me.

"But I thought you said …" I start, but Noah cuts me off.

"It's just a shower. Like the bath," he states, his brown eyes sparkling.

Except it wouldn't be.

Because he'd be fully naked this time. And so would I.

And I know the minute we see one another like that, I'm not going to want him to stop.

Am I ready for this?

Here?

Now?

Definitely.

But is he?

"I think that's a bad idea if you want to take things slow." I grip on to the edge of the counter, the words tasting sour as they come out.

"Hand me a towel then?"

"Nope," I reply. Because if Noah wants to wait, that's fine. But I'm not going to make it easy on him.

"Seriously?" He laughs.

"If you want one, come out and get it," I challenge. Because I know Noah.

And he never backs down from a challenge.

I grab the closest towel I can find and hold on to it for dear life.

The water stops, and Noah pulls back the shower curtain. He doesn't try to hide behind anything—or cover himself. My heart wants to rip out of my chest at the sight of him. My eyes start at his rounded shoulders, move down to his flat stomach, his hips, and then ... even lower.

Noah steps out of the shower and strides toward me, water dripping off of him.

I am definitely ready for this.

"Think I wouldn't do it?" he asks once he's right in front of me. He only leaves a few inches between us.

I swallow hard.

"I knew you would," I mumble, fighting the urge to gawk at him.

"Are you going to give me the towel, or are you holding it

hostage?" Noah holds out his hand, waiting. And I can tell he's amused.

"I think I should keep it," I reply, deciding to go for it. Because Noah is in no rush to hide himself from me.

If anything, he's enjoying this.

So, I might as well too.

I glance down, goosebumps rising across my skin.

Noah looks beautiful.

I can easily see the definition of his muscles below his creamy skin.

"Is this making you reconsider saying no to joining me in the shower?" he asks, his fingers finding my wrists.

At his touch, I feel breathless.

I nod in reply.

Noah leans in and kisses me. It's a kiss that I can feel in my entire body.

His lips are so warm and soft. And I never want them off of mine.

But then they are. Noah smiles as he grabs the towel from my hand and wraps it around his waist. I'm about to ask him to kiss me again when he lifts me up and sets me on the counter, and then he pushes his hips between my legs and looks at me.

"Tell me about your talk," he says.

"We saw you running," I decide to start with.

"Yeah?"

"Yeah. I told Harry the truth. That things between me and you have changed, but that I still care about him and that I don't want our friendship to be affected. I think we're in a good place. And it felt like he did too."

"And how did that make you feel?" Noah asks.

"I'm glad he knows. But honestly, it's hard. I care about him. I never want to make him feel less loved."

"I know. And he knows that too. It's easy to see you care for him. He knows that you do."

I nod because I know that Noah is right.

But it doesn't make things easier.

A tear slips down my cheek.

I immediately suck in a breath of air, wiping it away.

Noah cups my cheeks, sympathy flashing across his face. "Mal …"

"I'm sorry. I think this might have been harder for me than I realized." I wipe another tear away, not sure where they are coming from.

"Harry is okay. Wanting this … it's not a bad thing. It could never be bad."

"I just feel so guilty," I finally admit.

"I know."

Noah's words take me by surprise.

"You do?"

"I can tell."

"Then, why don't you tell me to not feel guilty? You never said anything."

Noah rubs his palms against my arms. "I would never tell you to feel a certain way. Your emotions, they're your own. You have a right to them. A responsibility even."

"You think you don't affect my emotions?" I question.

Noah smiles. "I'm sure I do. But ideally, what anyone else says or does shouldn't affect them. So, I can't tell you how you should feel. I might have an opinion on it, but it's irrelevant."

"Noah …" I plead.

"I hope that you don't feel guilty though," he says, his eyes coming up to meet mine. "I'm happy we are figuring things out."

"Is there anything to figure out?" I boldly ask.

"Honestly?"

"Honestly," I reply.

"No."

"Then, are we hiding?" I ask.

"We're being respectful to our friend. That isn't wrong; that's a good thing. And now, Harry knows, so everything is out in the open."

"I know. And … it kills me."

Noah's face flashes with frustration. "He's not a little boy, Mal. He can take care of himself despite how he might act sometimes."

"I know. I just don't ever want to hurt him. And I could see this morning, he was hurt."

"He's got both of us in his life, and he's grateful for that. He told me so last night," Noah says, wrapping his arms around my waist and pulling me into a wet hug.

"I'm glad," I say, hugging him back. "Do you regret any of this? After telling Harry?"

"Never, Mal. I'd do anything to see Harry happy, but I won't give you up. I can't." Noah holds on to me tighter.

"Has he asked you to?" I ask, confused.

"No. But I see how he looks at you. I know things have changed between you two since you broke up. You're better friends now that he's not being a shit boyfriend. And I'm sure that's confusing for you both."

"I know how I feel," I say, pulling back to look at Noah.

"I know you do." And suddenly, his sullen expression disappears and is replaced by a wide, amused smile.

"What's that look for?" When he doesn't reply, I say, "Come on. Tell me!" I push against his chest, my fingers pressing into his wet skin.

"You're just very obvious with how you feel. It's so easy to tell."

"I forget I'm an open book to you," I say, rolling my eyes.

"It's a good thing. I like knowing how you're doing," he tells me. "And you're pretty obvious when you're checking me out, for example."

"I am not obvious." I shake my head at him.

"So obvious." Noah laughs.

"Would you rather I not check you out?" I raise an eyebrow at him.

"Silly question."

"Maybe I should get off this counter. Leave the bathroom. Prove my point," I reply.

"Another silly idea," Noah says, eyeing my lips.

"Am I just full of them this morning?" I ask, searching his face.

As Noah nods, I watch his eyes dilate.

"Maybe it's best you stop talking," he says, his mouth finding mine.

Before I know what's happening, his hands are wound tightly around my waist, and my fingers are pushing back through his chestnut hair. Noah pulls me toward him, so my legs are wrapped around his waist.

He holds on to me with one hand, bringing the other onto my thigh as he deepens our kiss. Then, he slowly slides his hand up until it's between my legs on the outside of my pajamas.

I let out a moan, causing Noah's whole body to tighten. He moves his hand against the fabric as our tongues intertwine.

Noah's touch makes me feel like I'm on fire.

But suddenly, he stops kissing me.

"Do we need to go downstairs?" he asks against my lips.

"What? No?" I pant out.

"No?" Noah asks, giving me another kiss.

I shake my head, trying to clear it.

What is he asking?

"Of course not," I say, wanting him to refocus. But then his question finally registers. "Oh …"

Noah pulls his head back, his chest rising and falling quickly.

"Harry did say he wants us to meet him downstairs for breakfast."

"Is he in his room?"

"Yeah."

"I'm going to go talk to him," Noah says, sliding me down off the counter.

"Really?" I ask, trying to stay upright. I feel wobbly on my feet.

"Yeah. And you should go wake up Mohammad."

"I'm sure he's already up."

"You could catch him up quickly, before breakfast," Noah says, pulling me back to his lips for a slow kiss. "I should probably get dressed."

"Do you have to?" I push out a pout as a last-ditch attempt to keep Noah here with me. In nothing but a towel.

But I know he's right. We need to get downstairs.

"Don't worry; you'll get to see me in less than a towel soon." Noah winks at me.

"Promise?" I ask too quickly.

"Promise."

Babying him.
9:00AM

AFTER TAKING WAY too long with Noah, I rush to change before barging into Mohammad's room. And I'm not surprised to find his bed empty.

He's probably already downstairs.

I turn around to leave when Mohammad calls out, "Who is it?"

I make my way to the bathroom door. "Mallory."

Mohammad throws open the door, and I'm immediately engulfed by his cologne.

"Is breakfast ready?" he asks, checking his reflection in the mirror.

"About," I answer. "But that's not why I'm here. Well, it is. But also for another reason …" I go on.

"Get to the point."

I walk into the bathroom and sit down on the edge of the tub.

"Noah talked to Harry last night."

I brace for impact, but Mohammad barely bats an eye.

"About?" he asks, running his hands through his hair.

"About *us*. About me and Noah."

Mohammad stills before spinning around to face me.

"Oh shit." His eyes go wide, and I can tell he's about to freak out.

"It went okay, I promise," I say, trying to calm him down.

"Seriously?" Mohammad asks, not believing me.

"For the most part. Noah told me last night that he talked to Harry. Said he took it well," I explain.

"And did he?"

"Well, that's what Noah said. But I knew he had to be hurt, so I went and talked to Harry about it this morning."

"What did he say?" Mohammad moves and motions for me to follow him into the bedroom. He leads us to two chairs in the corner, so we can sit.

"It was hard. Harder than I thought, honestly. I felt like I was hurting him. And I don't like disappointing him."

"You can't worry about that," Mohammad says.

"That's what Noah said. But I do care. I care about Harry a lot."

"I know you do," Mohammad says.

And it starts to frustrate me that he and Noah sound exactly the same.

"I don't think you do," I reply.

"You worry about him like a child though. You want to take care of him. Protect him," Mohammad tells me.

And part of me knows that he is right.

"I know that I want Noah. There's no question of that …"

"Do you want me to say it?" Mohammad cuts in.

"Say what?" I ask, looking at him.

"What your problem is."

I pull back in surprise. "Let's hear it."

"You have trouble distinguishing types of love," he explains. "Platonic. Romantic. You love them both, and you don't know what to do about it. So, you're flailing."

"Way to hit me where it hurts." I cross my arms over my chest.

"It's going to hurt worse," Mohammad says, continuing. "You need to set boundaries with Harry and make it clear to everyone that you and Noah are a couple. No more of this wishy-washy bullshit."

"Damn," I say, slightly impressed.

"Tell me I'm wrong," Mohammad says. "Tell me Noah doesn't want you to be his girlfriend."

"He does, yeah."

"But?"

"But I told him we needed to get through this weekend before we announced anything. I told him this weekend, the focus should be on Harry, not our change in relationship status."

"Except your talk with Harry proved that's not really true. You're better off, being up front."

"Well, it's out now," I mumble. "And anyway, I was trying to be supportive of Harry."

"No, you were babying him again," Mohammad disagrees.

I roll my eyes, annoyed that Mohammad is probably right.

And I really don't want him to be.

"Look, even if you were Harry's girlfriend, babying him doesn't do him any good. We only change because we want to. If you stopped having so much sympathy for him …"

"I know. I know." I hold up my hand, stopping him. "You're right."

Mohammad's eyebrows shoot up. "You usually don't admit when I'm right."

"Well, I'm not on a winning streak right now, so better to admit defeat and learn something in the process."

"That's big of you," Mohammad says, looking at me weirdly. "Are you feeling all right?" He puts the back of his hand against my forehead, checking for a temperature.

I swat his hand away. "I'm not sick."

"You're acting strange."

"I'm just …"

Mohammad gets up and pulls me into a hug. I squeeze him, wishing that this were all just easier. I know at this point, it's me, making it hard for myself, but it doesn't change how I feel.

"I know," Mohammad says, rubbing me on the back. "I'm here for you, okay?"

"Okay," I mumble against him.

And I don't let go.

You cheated.
9:15AM

"I THOUGHT YOU were getting dressed for breakfast?" It's the first thing that comes out of my mouth when I see Harry seated at the dining table, still in his robe, sitting next to Noah.

"I considered it, but eventually, I decided against it," Harry replies. "After all, how many Monday mornings can you get up, smoke a fag, wear your robe to breakfast, and know that you don't have any classes for the entire week?"

"You make a good point." I laugh, sitting down at the table.

After talking to Mohammad, I feel better.

I don't feel perfect yet, but I know that I will get there.

And after almost crying twice this morning, I need to pull myself together.

"He's taking the holiday seriously," Noah says, motioning to the table in front of me. "We ordered you both cappuccinos."

"Nice," Mohammad says, happily taking a sip of his.

"Thanks." I smile at them, my heart wanting to burst.

Because everything really is going to be okay.

"Of course I'm taking this holiday seriously. It would be a travesty to not take full advantage of it," Harry states.

"I agree," Mohammad says.

I look over at him, noticing foam on his top lip.

I cover my mouth with my hand, holding back a laugh.

Mohammad looks back at me and frowns. "What?"

Harry sits there, chuckling, bouncing up and down in his seat.

"You've got a little foam," Noah says, pointing to his own face.

Mohammad wipes it off before tossing out an eye roll. "You three are childish."

We order breakfast, and I'm surprised how quickly it's brought out. I got avocado toast and some juice. Harry, Mohammad, and Noah all got full English breakfasts. Plus, Noah ordered chocolate milk.

"We should play some football today," Harry says, dropping three cubes of sugar into his tea.

"Yeah?" Noah asks. He scoops beans onto his toast before bringing it to his mouth.

"Yeah, let's get outside," Harry continues.

Mohammad looks up at Harry in surprise. "You want to play football? I don't think I've ever seen you play football."

"Of course I've played," Harry replies. "We can do some one-on-one."

"Uh-huh," Mohammad says suspiciously. "And who will go first?"

"You and Noah. I'll be the ref," Harry explains.

"Of course you will." Mohammad laughs. "Leave it to you to pick the easiest job."

"Either way, it sounds fun." Noah grins.

TWENTY MINUTES LATER, Harry has us all outside. He and I are in lawn chairs, and Mohammad and Noah are on the field. He is the self-appointed referee and even has a whistle.

"Ready?" Harry yells out.

Mohammad and Noah are both wearing joggers and sweatshirts. I changed into workout clothes and a jacket.

I'll probably do some yoga later, and it seemed like a better idea than sitting around in jeans.

"Ready!" Noah and Mohammad call back.

Harry blows the whistle, signaling the start to their game. Noah and Mohammad fight over the ball.

"Here we are, sir," Gerald says at Harry's shoulder. He's got a tray with two champagne flutes on it and a blanket draped over his arm.

"Thank you, Gerald." Harry accepts the champagne glasses, handing me one. It's orange and fizzy—obviously a mimosa.

"It's a rather cool morning. I thought you might need this," Gerald says, offering me the blanket.

"Thanks." I smile at him before draping the blanket over my lap.

I watch Harry take a sip of his mimosa. For some reason, he didn't change into workout clothes, and he looks slightly ridiculous, sitting in his underwear and robe.

Especially now that he's got a whistle hanging out of his mouth and a glass of champagne in his hand.

Harry starts whistling at the boys. "I saw that," he yells out.

Mohammad turns and glares at him. But a second later, he's running across the grass with the ball.

"I think this power could go to your head," I say to Harry.

He grins at me. "Easily."

I take a sip of the mimosa, but honestly, it feels a little too early to be drinking.

Instead, I lean my head back against the lawn chair and watch Noah and Mohammad fight over the ball.

Mohammad pushes Noah down into the grass.

Harry whistles.

Noah trips Mohammad.

Harry whistles.

After twenty minutes of Harry whistling, I finally snap.

"Give. Me. That!" I say, pulling the whistle out from his lips and tossing it into the grass.

Harry looks at me, appalled. "What was that for?"

"Do you know how annoying that is to sit next to?" I say, flaring my eyes at him. "I told you, you are power-hungry."

"I was just doing my job," Harry disagrees, finishing off his mimosa.

Mohammad runs up to us. "I'm out," he says, pulling me up out of my lawn chair and grabbing the mimosa from my hand. Then, he leans back, looking way too content.

"Hey! You can't just steal my spot."

"Can and did," Mohammad says, covering himself up with my blanket.

Mine!

I start to lunge at him, but hands wrap around my waist, stopping me. I turn around and look at Noah.

"Why don't we play?" he suggests.

"I'm not going to win," I reply.

"It's not about winning. Let's just have fun," Noah offers.

I glare at Mohammad, annoyed he stole my seat.

"You've got this," Mohammad calls out, raising my champagne glass in the air as he sends me off.

"I'm going to kill him," I mutter.

Noah laughs, but he grabs ahold of my hand. I look down at our clasped palms as he leads me out to where the ball is on the grass.

"Why don't you start first?" Noah nods at the ball. "Try and get it in the goal."

I roll my eyes, knowing that isn't possible. Not with how good Noah is.

But then I remember that Noah will probably go easy on me.

And maybe I can use that to my advantage.

"All right," I reply, dribbling the ball toward the goal as Noah comes up in front of me.

I manage to make my way close enough to the goal that I know if I get a clean shot, I can kick it in.

But Noah is all over me.

And he's about to steal the ball.

I immediately stop and bring my hand up to cover my mouth, and then I make a horrified expression. "Noah, look!" I point, knowing all I need is one good distraction to get the ball past Noah.

He stops, his expression going white as he follows the line of my finger to the edge of the grass where I'm pointing. And it gives me just enough time to kick the ball past Noah, putting it straight into the goal.

Noah's head snaps back to me and then from me to the net and the ball. Then back to me again.

"You cheated," he says blankly, in shock.

"No, I diverted your attention," I reply smugly.

Noah frowns at me. "I was seriously worried."

"Not my fault you got distracted."

Noah raises his eyebrows at me. But then his expression shifts. "If you want to play dirty, we can play dirty." He smiles, running to grab the ball.

"I never said that," I reply, shaking my head at him.

Because this is *not* going to be good.

He kicks the ball back to me.

"Why don't you try again?" Noah urges me on, nodding his head at the ball.

I pause and try to figure out what to do.

Maybe I can take the ball and run in the opposite direction. Or maybe I can fake an injury. Then, when Noah's helping me, I'll instantly spring up and kick it in for a goal.

I decide to start simple and dribble it toward the goal. But immediately, Noah steals it from me. I grab on to his sweatshirt to try and stop him, but he slips out of my grasp.

And then he scores.

At the same time, the whistle goes off.

"Foul!" Harry yells out. He's still in the lawn chair, wrapped up in a blanket, but he has the whistle back in his mouth.

I notice that the lawn chair next to him is empty. Mohammad must have gone inside.

"Agreed!" Noah calls back.

I glare at Harry before turning and glaring at Noah.

"You said you'd go easy!" I pout, pushing out my bottom lip at him.

"I said that before you cheated," Noah replies. "I have no sympathy for you."

"Well, you should."

"Why don't we just take turns, passing the ball?" Noah suggests.

"Because I can't beat you? No, thank you," I reply, shaking my head. "Let's go again."

Noah laughs. "Next goal wins, and then we pass the ball, okay?"

"Scared of being decimated in front of Harry?" I tease.

"Decimated?" Noah laughs out. "Yes, I'm terrified."

I run to grab the ball from the goal, hell-bent on winning, then drop it down in front of Noah and immediately go for it. We fight over the ball, our feet getting close together. So, while he's focused on trying to get the ball without tripping over me, I give him a hard shove and push him over.

"Holy shit!" Harry calls out as I kick the ball across the grass.

Noah's already back up, but it's too late.

I kick the ball into the goal, scoring.

"You really are a cheat!" Noah says, wrapping his arms around my waist and picking me up.

"At least I won," I say with a laugh.

"I don't know if I'd consider that winning," Noah replies, setting me back down.

"Well, I do," I reply once I'm on my feet. "And now, I'm ready to play pass."

"I'm sure you are," Noah remarks, shaking his head at me like he's disappointed.

But I know he's not.

He's impressed. Even though I cheated, I won.

And Noah *hates* losing.

"Mallory, your phone's going off," Harry calls out as Noah kicks me the ball.

I kick it back to him before running across the grass. I grab my phone off the edge of the lawn chair, seeing a stream of text messages.

Mohammad: SOS

Mohammad: Come inside and help me.

Mohammad: Now!

Mohammad: Also, I'm in my room.

"Who is it?" Harry asks.

I roll my eyes and remember the deal Mohammad and I made last week. Technically, I still have to respond to his SOS texts—at least until Tuesday. And apparently, he knows his time to abuse them is almost up.

"It's from Mohammad. *Apparently*, he needs me."

"Go find him," Noah says, suddenly at my side.

"You sure?" I ask.

"Yeah." Noah nods. "Harry and I can play a little one-on-one."

Harry looks at Noah in surprise.

"What do you say? Are you up for a game, Harry?" Noah asks.

"I can't very well turn you down." Harry grins.

He gets up from the lawn chair and ties his robe into a double knot.

"Have fun," I call out.

I text Mohammad as I walk back inside.

Me: *What do you need help with?*

Mohammad: *I need input. Stat.*

I'm about to text back, *With what?* But I'm already inside, and I'm better off just going to his room and finding out. I take the stairs two at a time and go in his room.

"What's the emergency?"

"I need to know what you think of this photo," Mohammad says, rushing up to me.

And he's only in his underwear.

He holds out his phone.

I take it and look at the screen.

But I immediately wish that I hadn't.

"Mohammad!" I squeal, covering my mouth with my hand.

"What?" he asks nervously. "Good? Bad?"

He's looking at me frantically, like he's trying to gauge my reaction.

"You're naked!" I say, feeling horrified.

Mohammad looks at me like I've gone crazy.

"I'm not naked. Not totally. See, my bits are covered with my hand," he says, pointing to the screen.

"I am not going to look again," I tell him, trying to divert my eyes from his almost-naked body in the photo. He's

245

holding the camera in one hand, holding his junk in the other.

And to make it worse, it's a mirror selfie.

"You need to be objective," Mohammad says sternly. "Now, tell me, do you think I look hot?" He hands me back the phone.

"Hot?"

"Yes, hot. Personally, I think it's a great photo. But usually, all of them are. After all, I'm very photogenic. But one can never be sure, which is why I need the second opinion. And what do you think about the angle?"

Mohammad is literally spazzing out.

It's not very often that I see him look so frantic.

I pull my lips down in a frown, already freaked out by what he's asking me to do. But Mohammad's my best friend.

And if he needs me to look at his photo, then I have to look at his photo.

I glance at the phone and try to be objective.

"Well, I can see your abs," I comment, trying to be helpful. But then I realize they're Mohammad's abs. And that he's not wearing any underwear.

I hand the phone back to him, still too freaked out.

"I agree," he nods enthusiastically.

"What is that for anyway?" I ask, a shiver running through me.

"I'm sending it to Naomi," he replies like my question is ridiculous.

"Wait … has she sent you anything?"

He waggles his eyebrows. "I don't kiss and tell."

I raise an eyebrow at him. "Yes, you do."

"Fine, she sent me this hot photo. She looks banging. Was heading out for brunch with her gran." Mohammad pulls up the photo to show me and lets out a slow whistle.

"And you decided to respond to her daily update text with

a naked photo?" I ask, trying to follow along.

"Obviously. And I'm hoping she'll reply in similar form."

"Don't tell me you think she'll actually send you one?" I ask, slightly horrified.

"It could happen. And once she does, then she'll finally get a glimpse of the crowning glory."

Mohammad is beaming.

"You would not send her a dick pic, would you?"

"I would."

"And what happens if that gets around somehow?" I ask, trying to be practical.

"Easy. You always follow one rule. *If it's below the waist, you don't show your face.*"

"The better advice would be to just not send the picture," I disagree.

"Says the girl who's getting action on her holiday. The rest of us have to deal with wanking off in the shower to a photo their girl sends of her and her gran. Do you know how hard it is to simultaneously undress someone in a picture while also trying to mentally block out the old person who happens to be in the photo with them? Do you?"

I blink. "I can't say I do. Wait, did you just call Naomi *your* girl?"

Mohammad flushes.

"Moving on ..." he says. "Anyway, I want to give her a taste of what she can look forward to when I'm back."

"Can I make a suggestion?" I ask, bracing for Mohammad to bite my head off.

But he doesn't.

"What are you thinking?"

"Maybe you should save the photo for once you're back and after you've done stuff. It might be a bit presumptuous to assume she'd want to see that—at least just yet. Besides, isn't it better to have the big, naked reveal in person?"

Mohammad weighs his head back and forth.

"I'll consider it," he replies. "Speaking of naked reveals, when are you and Noah biting the bullet? At least two of the four of us should be getting some action this week."

"So far, we're four–nil," I reply.

"Hmm." It's all he says.

"Hey, Mohammad," I say to him.

"Yeah?"

"Promise me you'll treat Naomi right. And promise that you'll let her treat you right too."

"What do you mean?"

"I mean, we both know that she's a sweetheart. And inside, you are too."

"Oh, gross." Mohammad gets a sour expression on his face.

"I'm serious. Of course, I want you to get action, but more importantly, I want you to get action with someone you like. And someone who likes you back."

"Doesn't that seem a little *quaint*?" Mohammad questions.

"It seems like good advice that you should take," I tell him.

"Advice being given to the advice-giver … I don't know how I feel about that."

"I'd take it. Besides, sex seems to be on all of our minds these days."

"We're young, fit, and horny. Of course sex is on our minds."

"It's kind of funny because it was never on my mind in New York. Sex wasn't even on my radar," I say, sitting on the edge of the bed.

"Really? You didn't date."

"Sure, I went on a few dates. But I was focused on school. And Anna and I, we went out, partied and stuff, but relationships weren't such a big thing."

"It's us British boys, babe. We're on another level," Mohammad teases.

At least, I think he's teasing.

"Probably." I laugh.

"Want to know something kind of pathetic?" Mohammad asks, lying down next to me on the bed.

"Yes." I grin and lie back, rolling in his direction.

"Before you and Naomi, I never really considered being friends with girls," he admits.

"Really?"

"Yeah. I mean, Olivia was around with Harry. And I was always looking to get some action. I've always been good at chatting girls up and whatnot, but I never considered seriously dating a girl. Let alone being best friends with one like I am with you."

"We aren't this whole other species, you know," I say, raising an eyebrow at him.

"You're close," he replies.

"Well, I think it's a good thing. It brings balance into your life. And honestly, that's not completely true for you. You have three sisters you're great with."

"Yeah, but sisters are different. I see them as evil little princesses up in some tower. I will always protect them."

"High school girls aren't all that different."

"They're way more complicated. And trust me, if I treated a hot rando like a princess, she'd mug me off. Women are difficult. They want to be equally sought after and ignored."

"I think we just say that. And maybe at the beginning, we do like a little intrigue. It's exciting. But once you know someone, if you like them, it's always good to show them.

Treat them well. Be kind to their heart. You know?"

Mohammad looks at me like I've gone full alien on him. And honestly, did I just say that?

"Okay, I even freaked myself out with that one," I say, not sure where that came from.

Mohammad's eyes light up. "Do you know what you sound like?" he asks knowingly.

"Don't say it."

"You sound like a woman in love!" he yells out.

And the shame I feel is immediate.

"Yeah, yeah, yeah. Let's just move on from that," I try to tell him.

"You're sappy," Mohammad says, shaking his head.

I roll my eyes. "Can you please put on some pants, so we can go downstairs? When I left, Harry and Noah were about to start a one-on-one match."

"Shit, I have to find out how that ended," Mohammad says, running into the closet. "Two secs."

Time alone.
11:30AM

WE HEAD BACK downstairs to find Noah and Harry coming in from outside. They're both covered in grass. But they're both smiling from ear to ear.

"Have fun?" Mohammad asks.

"Loads," Harry answers.

"This one is just as bad of a cheat as you," Noah says to me while pointing at Harry.

"Looks like you two were rolling around in the grass." I laugh.

"Yeah, and now, I'm in desperate need of a shower," Harry says. His blond hair is a disaster, and his robe is hanging open.

"Probably a good idea," I reply.

"See you in a bit." Harry nods at us before walking off in the direction of his bedroom.

Noah, apparently, isn't interested in a shower because he says, "Let's play some billiards. What do you say? You up for it, Mal?" he asks.

And his eyes are all over me.

I'm not sure if it's the testosterone running through him or the fact that it's been a whole ten minutes since he's seen me, but he doesn't try to hide the desire in his eyes.

"Oh. My. God," Mohammad says, pushing his nose up in the air.

"What?" Noah asks, turning to him.

"This is disgusting." Mohammad shakes his head like he can't do this. "I'm going to go find … fuck, something else to do for a bit."

He turns on his heels, leaving the room.

"Mohammad," I call out, not wanting him to feel excluded.

"It's fine," he says. But he doesn't turn back.

"Well, way to make it weird," I comment to Noah once he's gone.

"I didn't mean to," Noah replies, pulling me toward him. "But I couldn't help it. You look amazing."

"Amazing?" I question, looking down at myself. "I'm in workout clothes."

"I know." Noah smiles.

"But what about Mohammad?" I ask, suddenly aware that Noah didn't try to hide his feelings in front of him.

"He's got to get used to it. We're going to be a couple,

Mal. Even when we're all together."

He runs his hand back through my hair, calming me down a little.

"That's fine, but when he comes back, let's just do our best not to make it awkward."

"I'm not walking on eggshells anymore," Noah says firmly. "They can either be happy for us or not be. It doesn't concern me."

"Noah …"

His face softens. "But I'll try to be respectful when we are in group settings."

"Thank you." I smile.

"But until then …" Noah says, biting his lip.

"Until then what?"

"Until then, we should take advantage of this time alone," he replies.

My eyebrows immediately shoot up. "Really?"

"Why not?" Noah smiles at me.

And he doesn't have to tell me twice. I take his hand, lead him into the billiards room, and close the door behind us. A second later, his mouth is on mine. He picks me up and carries me over to the sofa. I fall back onto it as Noah crawls on top of me.

"You weren't kidding about not wasting time," I say as his lips find mine.

He doesn't reply.

Probably because his hands are all over me, moving across the outside of my clothes. But even with all this on, it feels like there's nothing between my skin and his palms.

I feel on fire.

Every time Noah touches me, I'm overwhelmed.

He trails his lips down across my jaw to my neck.

I gasp as his tongue finds my skin. My hips roll up toward

him, and Noah responds, flexing his hips against mine.

It feels like a wave pushes through me, and I find myself wanting more and more.

I bring his mouth back to mine, my hands sliding across his back.

I pull him closer to me, loving the feeling of his hips against mine. He cups my cheek in his hand before biting on my lip.

I let out a moan.

Noah's hands start to move everywhere. His fingers play at the edge of my sweatshirt. At the top of my pants. But they never move further than that. I slip my hands up under his shirt, letting myself feel his bare skin.

"We probably shouldn't be grinding like this, here," Noah mumbles, suddenly rolling off me.

I want to agree with him.

I know I need to think straight.

But honestly, in this moment, I don't really care.

Everything is pounding.

"You're right." I blink up at the ceiling and try to slow down my heart rate. Because he makes a fair point.

"Feeling better with a little air?" Noah asks me.

"No. I think you should ask me a question to distract me or something," I say. "All I can think about is kissing you again."

Noah grins.

"Okay. Uh … are you happy about seeing your family next … shit, this week?" Noah asks, propping himself up onto his elbow.

"My mom's thrilled," I answer.

"And you're not?"

"I want to be."

"Feeling stressed about it?"

"I just … I don't feel like they get any of this. How big this move is. Obviously, I'm happy, but they make such lightness of it. They say it's great, and they're so happy and optimistic … I don't know … it's annoying."

Noah glides a strand of my hair away from my face.

"It's terrible when people are happy," he whispers.

"You know what I mean."

"Can I ask you something?"

"Yeah." I nod.

"What do you want?" Noah asks.

"What do you mean?"

"I mean, what would make you happy? Do you wish they weren't excited or what?"

"It feels like a game, Noah. It doesn't even feel real."

"Because everything is too perfect, you feel like they're being unauthentic?"

"Exactly. All of these moving parts. Shopping for new furniture. Getting new clothes. This whole move. I feel like I have to be excited because they expect me to be. I have barely gotten to take a breath to figure out how I feel. But I can't. I can't even be excited—truly excited—because it's just expected. And then I get mad at myself for not being happy when I know they are," I huff.

"Do you wish you had gone home?"

I pull Noah closer, kissing his neck. "No. At least, not permanently. But maybe to pack my own things. To have a chance to say good-bye to Anna. Visit my favorite restaurant one more time."

"You're sad," he says, rubbing a circle across my back.

I pull my lips to the side, not sure what to say.

Because he's right.

"Which is crazy. My parents are happy. I'm happy too. I'm here with you. With Mohammad and Harry. That means everything to me."

"The good news is, you aren't shunned from the city. You can always visit. And you know, if you decide you miss it enough, you can go back after graduation. For college or work."

"I couldn't leave you here. Besides, New York isn't my home anymore. London is. It's not something that makes sense. I think I'm just really bad with change."

"What can I do?"

"Hold me." It's all I say. And it's all I have to say.

Noah wraps his arm around me, pulling me against his warm chest. "Mal?"

"Yeah?"

"I can't lie to you. Change, it's inevitable. But ... you have me. I know I always tell you I want you to stand on your own feet, and I do. But that doesn't mean you can't lean on me for things."

"I can depend on you?" I ask, looking up to Noah's warm eyes.

He nods.

I smile. "That kind of helps."

"Kind of? Only kind of?" Noah laughs, tickling at my waist.

"Okay. Okay. It helps a lot!" I laugh.

Noah grins at me. "So, London feels like your home, or I do?"

"I can't reveal everything so soon."

"You won't tell me?" Noah's mouth falls open.

"Nope. I have to keep you on your toes."

"Wow. Never playing fair." Noah shakes his head, but he pulls me back against his chest. His fingers work their way down through my hair.

"Noah?"

"Hmm?"

"You're my home," I say against his chest.

Noah squeezes me tighter against him. "Thank you for telling me that."

"You don't have to thank me. It's the truth."

"Regardless, Mal, it means a lot."

Noah pulls me to his lips, pressing another kiss against mine when my phone buzzes in my pocket.

I pull it out and check it, noticing a text from Harry.

"Harry messaged all of us. Said to meet downstairs at one o'clock for lunch. Apparently, he's taking a nap."

"Well, that gives us some free time then," Noah says.

"Anything you want to do?" I ask.

Noah looks down at himself. "I probably need a shower."

"I should shower too. Get changed out of my workout clothes."

"Cool." Noah takes my hand and leads me out of the billiards room when a brilliant idea pops into my mind.

"So, we should shower together then?" I ask, hoping that the answer is *yes*.

Just this morning, Noah was telling me to shower with him. I didn't because I thought he wanted to wait on things.

But after our make-out session on the couch, I know that Noah wants me.

It's easy to tell.

And I want him too.

So, what's the problem?

"I think that would lead to other things," he replies, his expression growing serious.

Exactly.

"Isn't that what should happen?" I ask.

"Why don't you shower and then come over to my room? We can hang out."

"*Hang out?*" I gape at him. "I don't want to *just* hang out."

Noah chuckles. "What do you want to do then?"

I narrow my eyes at him.

Because is he actually kidding?

I let out a pathetic sigh. "I guess I'll just shower and come to your room then," I say, feeling broken.

When we get upstairs, Noah gives me a chaste kiss on the forehead before leaving me in my doorway.

I head into my room, annoyed. Because why is Noah so yes and no with me?

One second, he wants me to shower with him. The next, he doesn't.

I guess I knew from the beginning, that's just what Noah's like.

He goes up and down like a yo-yo.

It's what makes him so passionate one moment. But then another … not so much.

Once he decides something, it's decided.

But until then, everyone's left hanging.

Well, not everyone.

Just me.

I shower and wash my hair. And I take my sweet time when I get out, putting on body lotion and brushing my teeth.

After all, I'm in no rush.

We've got tons of time before lunch, and it's not like I'm rushing over to a naked Noah, who's waiting in bed for me.

If anything, he's probably at the desk, working on more homework.

And the second I get in there, he'll tell me to turn around and go get my statistics review, so I can finish it while we have some free time.

I let out a groan and decide to blow-dry my hair—*since why not?*—and put on a fresh coat of mascara. I leave my face bare and throw on one of the dresses I packed. Usually, I wouldn't go for a dress just to hang out, but I've gotten used to wearing skirts at school, and they're very comfortable. I layer a sweater over it to give me some warmth and quickly check my phone before heading to Noah's room.

I don't bother knocking.

"Hey," I say, finding him splayed out on his bed, dressed in jeans and a T-shirt, his focus on his phone.

"Hey," he says happily, tossing his phone to the side.

He gets up and walks over to me. He takes my hand and leads me to the edge of the bed.

"You look beautiful," he says, kissing me.

"You look nice too," I try to reply, but his mouth is on mine.

He gives me a stream of warm, slow kisses. But he doesn't do anything else.

He doesn't throw me back on the bed.

He doesn't try to take off my dress.

He doesn't even attempt to touch the bare skin of my thigh.

No.

Noah keeps his hands on my arms and his mouth firmly on mine.

I break our lips apart, putting some space between us.

Noah smiles lazily, like he couldn't be happier.

I crawl onto his bed, so I'm sitting crisscross in the center.

"Should you call your parents?" Noah asks, reminding me of my promise to check in with them daily.

"No." I shake my head, wishing things were different.

"What's on your mind?" He scoots over next to me on the bed.

"Noah, what do you think about doing … *more*?"

"More?"

"Like, sexually."

Noah blinks, surprise flashing across his face.

He doesn't say anything for a minute. He looks lost in thought.

"Mal, when you're with the right person, it doesn't matter how little or how much you do. There really isn't a difference. Last night, just having you in my bed felt amazing."

"Even though we didn't do anything?" I ask, flushing. Because I haven't even touched Noah yet. I haven't explored his body the way I want to.

"I feel you in my whole body when we kiss," Noah says, shaking his head in disagreement.

"I thought you said once we started, you wouldn't be able to stop."

Because that's what I want.

I want Noah to undress me. To kiss me. To hold me. And to let me finally experience him.

I've never taken that step with anyone before.

But I want to with him.

Noah furrows his brows and lets out an unsteady breath. "I'm doing my best to stop."

I look up at him, holding his gaze. "I don't want to stop."

"I can tell," he says, a shadow of a smile flashing across his face.

"But you do?"

Noah licks his lips, and his dark lashes hold my attention as he blinks.

I can tell he's thinking about his answer.

"I told you before, when I'm with you, I will demand nothing short of everything because our bodies will require it. But when I said everything, I meant, everything. And you aren't there yet."

"I am, Noah." I shake my head, growing frustrated.

Because he's said this before.

And I don't understand why he keeps saying it.

Why does he think I'm not ready for him?

How could he think that I'm not there yet?

He's all I want.

He's all I can think about.

A pained expression flashes across my face, and I look down, wanting to hide it from Noah.

He puts his finger under my chin, causing me to have to look at him. "You're close, Mal. I can see that."

"I don't know what else to do. I don't know how else to show you I want you, except by, well, showing you."

I look up at him, realizing that's what I have to do.

I have to literally show him.

I pull Noah to my lips, kissing him gently. I give him a moment to adjust to having my mouth on his. I know he likes to take me in. I know he likes it when I kiss him slow. I pull my face back, letting a sliver of air come between our lips. I give him just enough distance to miss me. To want my lips back on his.

Noah's fingers slide around my waist, his breath warming my cheek as he exhales. His eyes flutter open, and I watch him glance across my face. His gaze slips down over my lips, to my pink cheeks, up to my eyes. I hold his gaze, wanting him to understand.

I am there.

Noah nudges my nose with his. I smile, my palms finding his arms.

Because if he wants me to show him, to make a move, I will.

I'll show him that I am there.

That there isn't anyone else.

I slide my hands up his arms until I reach the edge of his rounded shoulders. I pause, letting my fingers dig into muscle before wrapping my arms around his neck. I run my fingers through the back of his silky hair, turning his head slightly so his lips are exactly where I want them.

Then, I kiss him again.

And this time, I don't break our lips apart. I kiss his bottom lip. His upper lip. I let my tongue explore the space in between them, opening his mouth to me. My fingers tighten in his hair as I taste him.

He tastes like salt and water and air and warmth.

He tastes like everything I could ever need.

And it's all right here, available for the taking.

Noah's offering himself to me. His body. *His heart.*

I press my chest against him, my tongue slipping into his mouth.

Noah lets out a deep groan, his body shuddering against mine. The sound of it sends tingles all the way from my chest to my toes and then back up again. Goose bumps rise on my arms. Noah's hands move from my waist down to my backside, and he pulls me closer and higher up, until I'm seated in his lap.

His fingers dig into my skin, and I moan into his mouth.

I feel desperate for him.

And I know this is exactly where I'm meant to be. Wrapped around him. His hips tipped toward mine. Feeling his fingers digging into my skin.

Feeling … *him.*

Feeling all of him.

Noah bites my bottom lip gently, pulling me out of my thoughts. He breaks our lips apart, and I open my eyes to see his flushed cheeks.

Noah opens his eyes, too, his gaze flashing across my face.

"You are very persuasive." Noah chuckles, his lips pulling up into a one-sided grin.

I look at the dimple it forms on his cheek before looking up to his eyes.

"I want to show you I am ready, Noah."

Noah exhales, his chest falling and then rising again.

"At least ready … for *that*," he says, looking down—at my body. At our touching stomachs. At my legs wrapped around him.

I glance back up, trying to figure him out. But then it flashes into my mind.

The reason why Noah would want to stop.

The reason why he wants to wait.

It's so simple.

"Noah … are you trying to protect yourself?" I suddenly ask.

His forehead creases as he glances away. I can feel his fingers loosen their grip on me.

"That ship sailed a while ago, I think," he finally responds.

"But?"

Noah searches across the room until his eyes come back to mine. His expression is serious now, his eyes set in determination.

"When we finally sleep together, it will bind us. Sex is more than sex. It's more than this urge, this need. Sex is meant to express … love."

My eyes widen.

"Oh," is the only word that I can find, and it's all that comes out of my mouth.

"So, until you're at that point, I'd like to wait," Noah says firmly.

I squint my eyes, not understanding. "But, Noah, I do—"

He cuts me off and shakes his head, "Mal, we've got time. Loads of time."

I sigh, my shoulders falling. Because I want to tell Noah how I feel.

I mean, I know how I feel. I love him. I knew I loved him, even when I thought I was going to leave London. The last week we spent together, our good-bye, it broke my heart.

I flick my gaze down and refocus on Noah. On how it feels to have my body on his.

"Sometimes, I just feel like all we have is now. This moment, you know? And I've never felt that way before, so desperate for someone," I admit.

A shadow of a smile flashes across Noah's face, and I know he's pleased. But quickly, he pulls the smile off his lips.

"That's just your body talking."

I want to roll my eyes. Because he's wrong.

"And you're always on my mind," I add.

Noah kisses me on the forehead, then taps my chest. "You need to think about your heart. And you need to consider mine."

I press my lips together, not sure what to say.

I'm not sure there is anything to say.

Noah brings his hand up to my cheek, tucking a piece of hair behind my ear. "Your heart belongs to more than one person. We both know that."

I bring my hand up to cup his, my forehead creasing. "It's not the same with Harry," I tell him.

"I understand that. But I know what is in my heart. I just want you to take the time to figure out what is in yours."

I drop his hand and slide off his lap. "Did Harry tell you what he told me?" I ask, my mind instantly going back to a conversation we had. Because Noah sounds exactly like him right now. And it makes me wonder who this is coming from.

Noah. Or Harry.

"What did he tell you?" Noah asks curiously.

"It was … at the party. He said that I should explore my feelings for you. But … well, he also said that we don't know what the future holds. Or what we will want."

Who we will want.

"He's right. It's like I tell you, we've got time to figure all that out."

"So, you two have discussed this?" I question angrily, my stomach flipping.

"No. But he isn't wrong," Noah says hesitantly.

I want to turn away, frustrated.

But instead, I shake my head and look at Noah. Really look at him.

Is he not sure about us?

About me?

"You wouldn't have asked everything from me if you weren't sure, would you have?" The question falls out of my mouth, surprising even me. "I mean, is that what you're saying? Do you think we—you—need time to make sure this is right? You're scared that I'll hurt you … you're scared that we'll change in the future, and then you won't want me anymore. Is that how you feel? Are you scared we're going to ruin things?"

Panic quickly rises in my chest.

Because is this what Noah is so concerned about?

Noah pushes my hair away from my face before pulling me against his firm chest. His hand falls onto my head, holding me against him. I squish my eyes shut, forcing myself to relax. To listen to his heartbeat.

To fall into the rhythm.

To fall into him.

"We aren't going to ruin anything. This is too good, too beautiful, to be bad. I promise, Mal. But I'd be lying if I said I wasn't nervous. But it's a good nervous. I'm hopeful. About you. About the future. Let's just enjoy this."

I nod against him, knowing he's right.

Somehow, Noah is always right.

I pull back and look up at him. His forehead is creased, and concern is written across his face.

"I'd never ask for your heart without giving the matter serious thought. You know that, yeah?" he says.

I let out a sigh, nodding. "It kind of comes with the Noah description. *Does nothing without thinking it over at least a million times. Takes lots and lots of convincing to give in to simple pleasures,*" I tease.

"I appreciate the sarcasm," Noah says, but a smile comes onto his face.

"One of my many talents." I lean in and kiss him.

He bites my lip, causing me to laugh.

"Feel better after talking?" he asks, pulling away.

I pull my lips back into a flat smile. "Yeah, I do."

And it's the truth.

At least now, I know why Noah wants to take things slow.

Although I'm not sure if that makes things better or worse.

"Good," Noah replies.

"And I think I'm beginning to understand you more," I comment.

"Oh yeah?" he asks, his eyebrows rising up in interest.

"Yep."

"Well, come on. Let's hear it."

"Well, it all comes back to that first week of school really, when you told me in the bathroom that you'd have me begging for you before you gave in."

Noah tilts his head in intrigue, his eyes growing darker and brighter, all at the same time.

"Anyway," I continue, "that's what this is. You're just going to make me work for it. And honestly, I'm fine with that. I like a challenge. And like you said, more time will just give me more opportunities to show you how I feel. And to make it very, very hard for you to say no to me. And to what my heart wants."

I grin at Noah and watch as his entire face lights up.

"That's your plan, huh?" he asks, letting out a deep, vibrating laugh.

"That's my plan," I confirm confidently.

A wild card.
1:00PM

AFTER OUR TALK, I'm sort of relieved when we go downstairs to meet Mohammad and Harry for lunch. I'm ready to be back with them as a group. To get my mind off of everything Noah said.

About me not being ready.

About Harry.

I push it all out of my mind when we walk into the dining room. The table's already set, and Harry's already seated at it.

This time, he's dressed.

But he looks sad.

Really sad.

"What's wrong?" I immediately ask, glancing at Noah with concern.

"Spoke to my parents," Harry says.

It's all he says, but it's enough.

"What happened?" It's Noah who asks the question this time.

Harry shakes his head. "Nothing particular happened. I just sometimes wish things could be different. I wish I didn't have to bargain with my parents. I wish I could tell them I'd like our family to stay together. That I don't always want to disappoint them. But it's wishful thinking on my part. I don't actually have any happy memories of my family."

Noah walks around the table and pulls Harry into a hug.

Harry holds on to him from his chair, and I notice that his eyes look bloodshot.

I take a seat across the table from him, wishing there were something I could do or say.

But there isn't.

Because Harry is just a child. If he were an adult, I think he'd come to realize he has to love himself even though his parents don't. He has to respect himself even though his parents don't. He has to make a life that he is proud of—for himself, no one else.

But he's just a teenager who doesn't know better yet.

"In their eyes, I'm selfish for putting up a fight about this trip."

"Mate, you deserve better. And you can't lead a pretend life; eventually, it will catch up to you. Maybe not at first, but eventually, it will," Noah says, taking a seat next to Harry.

"But what if I get into it and enjoy it? Will I turn out like him?" Harry asks.

"Of course not. You're a better man than he could ever dream of being. But, Harry, it's going to start with an internship. And then a job. And then who you date. They're going to try to choose a life for you. But instead of rebelling, you need to stand up to them, if you want part of the business."

"You're strong, Harry. I know you can handle it," I add.

Harry gives me a sympathetic smile. "I'm sorry to have started lunch off like this."

"Don't apologize," Noah cuts in.

"I suppose I'll see how Shanghai goes."

"It sounds bad, but you're going to have to negotiate with your dad," I say. "He's a businessman. Tell him if he wants you to do the internship, then you get a gap year. It will give you time to decide if you want to join the company or go to university. And show your dad you're not messing around."

Harry's eyebrows shoot up.

"That's not a bad idea," Noah agrees.

"My family is all about legacy. We all know they won't cut me off even if they threaten to."

"Exactly," I agree.

"Thanks, guys," Harry says to both of us.

"Don't worry about it," Noah replies.

"Honestly, I don't want to do this," Harry says, motioning to the table. "Let's go put on a movie and have lunch in the living room."

"You sure?" Noah asks.

"One hundred percent. I can't be bothered right now," Harry says, getting up.

"I'll go let Muriel know," Noah says, standing.

I get up, too, when Mohammad pops his head into the dining room.

"Sorry, sorry. I know I'm late," he starts to say. But once he catches sight of Harry's red eyes, he closes his mouth.

"Don't worry about it. We're doing lunch and a movie," Harry says, draping his arm over Mohammad's shoulders.

I follow them into the living room and get settled in on the couch as Harry picks out the movie.

"All right, I let Muriel know," Noah says, joining us on

the couch.

"Perfect. I found a great option," Harry says. He gets up quickly, dims the lights, and then tosses all of us blankets.

"Thanks." I smile, snuggling next to Mohammad.

He leans in and whispers in my ear, "Please promise me you won't be one of those touchy couples. It freaks me out."

"I'll do my best," I whisper back.

"Uh-huh. I know you, Miss America. You get ruffled, just thinking about him now. But I don't want it to be weird," Mohammad says, a shiver running through him.

"I'm sorry earlier was weird," I whisper back.

Mohammad shrugs. "It was. But if it were Naomi and me, you wouldn't blink an eye."

"Probably not, but still."

Mohammad smiles at me before turning his attention to the movie.

TWENTY MINUTES INTO it, Gerald brings in our food. We have warm bowls of pasta with crusty bread and butter.

We all slurp it down happily.

"This is so much nicer than eating at the table," Harry says.

"It was a good idea," I agree.

Before the movie is even halfway over, Harry falls asleep. Mohammad isn't far behind him.

"Should I put on another movie?" Noah asks when the movie ends.

"Might as well," I whisper, looking between Mohammad and Harry with a smile.

"I think they're worn out from the weekend of events," Noah comments, selecting a movie.

"I think we all are."

"I feel pretty good," Noah replies, hitting play.

Mohammad stirs as the movie starts, and his head flies up abruptly. "What did I miss?"

"Just the movie." I laugh, patting him on the arm.

"I think I need a nap," Mohammad says, getting up. "See you in a bit."

"Sleep good," I reply.

Harry wakes up not long after and decides to do the same, leaving me and Noah in the living room.

"Do you want to finish the movie?" I ask Noah, unsure of what he wants to do.

"Nah." Noah pauses the movie. "I've seen it before anyway. Why don't we go up to my room and relax?"

"Yeah?" I ask, biting my lip.

"Yeah."

"I'M SO HAPPY that we're on break. Friday was *rough*," I say to Noah when we get to his room, thinking back to our last day of classes.

"You were exhausted," Noah agrees, his eyebrows rising up.

"I know. It was terrible! I had to force myself to stay awake though." I shake my head.

I was tired and hungover and very, very confused about my feelings.

And that was all before the day even started!

"You didn't do a very good job of it. You kept falling asleep in Stats," Noah reminds me.

My lips pull down into a frown, and I have to fight off the urge to glare at him. "Hey, I tried my best. But Statistics is boring. And I was so tired."

Noah laughs, his brown eyes growing lighter. "I'm not sure Mr. Johnson would have called you out on it anyway. If anything, he'd have just woken you up and reminded you that you were in his class."

I can't help but smile as the image of Mr. Johnson pops into my head. Crossed ankles. Fancy socks.

"I wasn't worried about that," I say, waving him off. "It's that I fell asleep for, like, a minute, and started daydreaming about …" I quickly end the sentence, pinching my lips shut.

Because shit, shit, shit.

What is wrong with me?!

I was daydreaming about him.

I had to do my best to stay awake, so I wouldn't have any more unwanted sex dreams.

"Kept daydreaming about what?" Noah asks, urging me to continue.

I feel like a deer caught in headlights, and I try to force my eyes to close slightly, so I don't look so freaked out. I lick my lips before looking away from Noah, a flush spreading across my cheeks.

"About me?" he asks, his voice rising.

I look up at him to see a wide smile settling on his face.

"Oh, now, I have to hear this."

I take a step away from him, trying to calm down my cheeks. "Noah, no. It's embarrassing."

He turns me to face him, and I'm greeted with a sincere expression.

I let out a long exhale. Noah's not going to drop this, and I know I'm going to have to cave and tell him about my dream. I cross my arms over my chest, thinking back to class on Friday. How Noah basically asked me when I was planning on letting him into my bed.

I flick my gaze up to his. "Well, after your cocky little response to my note, obviously, I thought about us being in bed together," I answer matter-of-factly.

Maybe my straightforward response will put an end to his

questions.

Noah's lips curl at the corner, his mouth pulling up into a lopsided grin. "That was the point," he says.

I snap my head in his direction, surprise flooding through me. "Really?"

"Seriously, Mal?" Noah says with disbelief. "Yeah, of course it was."

He shakes his head once before letting out a soft, quick exhale, like he's holding back a laugh.

What he says finally settles in.

"So, you did have a goal!" I laugh out, pointing my finger at him.

Because I was right!

And I feel slightly victorious in the fact that he's finally admitting it. Even if it is a few days too late.

Noah grabs on to my hand, lowering my pointed finger, drawing me to him. "You walk a fine line between being annoyed, mad, and turned on. They're your personality traits. I'm just doing what I can to work with your limitations."

A smug smile slides onto Noah's lips, and I raise an eyebrow at him.

"You're seriously not going to get any more information from me, flattering me like that."

Noah grabs on to my other free hand, lacing his fingers through mine.

"So, we were in bed …" he says, urging me on.

I roll my eyes but go with it. "Yeah. You were kissing me, and then I was taking off your tie. Then your shirt," I say, thinking back to the daydream.

"Want to show me?"

"Show you?" I ask as Noah's hands find my waist.

He pushes me back down onto the bed.

Oh.

Oh!

"So, my shirt was gone," he says, pulling his shirt off over his head.

I suck in a breath, my gaze moving across his pale skin. His rounded shoulders. His firm chest. His flat stomach. My eyes focus on the dark line of hair trailing down below his naval …

"Mal?"

I bring my gaze up to his. "Yeah?"

"So, you took off my shirt. Then, what?" He sits down next to me on the bed, his leg bumping against mine.

"You took off my shirt, and your hands were everywhere," I explain.

"I can imagine that," Noah says, breathless, his eyes slipping down over my dress.

My cheeks flush.

"Then, what did I do?"

I sit up straighter, trying to keep my thoughts organized.

And focused.

"Well … since I was in school, obviously, in my dream or whatever, I had on my uniform. So, next, you took off my stockings."

"Poof, they're gone." Noah smiles, looking down at my bare legs.

I laugh, biting back a smile. "Convenient."

"And then?" he asks, his eyes trailing back up to my face.

I press my lips together, wondering where this is going. Wondering if I should answer.

"And then your hands slid up my thighs."

Noah sucks in his cheeks, his tongue coming down to graze his bottom lip. His eyes shift back to my legs as his palm moves onto my thigh.

"Like this?" He looks at me through dark lashes as his

hand slides up my leg.

My eyes flutter shut.

"Keep going," Noah instructs.

"Your hands slid up my thighs until one hand found its way under my skirt," I say, remembering. Trying not to confuse my dream with what's happening now.

Noah's hand trails further up my leg until his palm moves under my dress. His fingers graze my inner thigh, sending a jolt through me.

"Then, what did I do?" he asks, trying to keep his voice steady.

"You kissed me."

Noah shifts, bringing his lips down onto mine. They're soft and warm. His free hand cups my cheek while the other stays at my thigh. Noah kisses me once before putting space between our lips.

"And then ... you ..." I try to go on, but all I can think about is Noah's hand on my leg. How his fingers keep shifting and grazing the soft skin of my inner thigh.

"I what?" he asks, his fingers stilling.

I pull my face away from his, so I can see him. So I can see his eyes. So I can try to figure out what I'm getting myself into here.

"You moved my underwear aside."

Noah's eyes widen, but a moment later, a grin slides onto his face.

"You really were having a wet dream, right then and there, weren't you?" Noah says happily.

I cover my face with my hands, mortified.

"Don't be embarrassed. It's a real turn-on."

I don't say anything back.

I don't even know what I'm supposed to say. *Because it's true!*

I was having a sex dream.

Right then and there.

In statistics class.

Sitting *next* to him.

I let out an annoyed pout, trying to hide behind my hands.

"Mallory," Noah says softly.

I peek at him through my fingers, and when he catches my eye, he pulls my hands down away from my face.

"What?" I ask, wishing that he weren't making fun of me.

"After … after I moved your underwear to the side, what did I do?"

"You … well, I woke up."

Noah's brows draw in.

"So, the dream ended?" he asks, sounding confused.

"Yes."

Noah nods, understanding. But then his expression shifts. "And does this have to?" His eyes darken as he asks the question.

I can see his pupils growing wider, hear his breathing becoming shallower.

Noah's fingers flex on my thigh, and I suck in a gulp of air at the reminder of exactly where his hand is at.

At what he's asking.

I clear my throat and shake my head. "No," I barely whisper.

Noah leans toward me. "So, I can … do this?" he asks, his fingers finding the fabric of my underwear. He doesn't move them, but he doesn't have to.

I suck in another breath, my head falling back. My chest is pounding as Noah moves his fingers against the fabric, his lips finding mine. He's hesitant at first, but quickly, his lips separate from mine, his tongue dipping into my mouth. He pulls me further onto the bed, trying to kiss me and touch me, all at the same time.

Eventually, I'm lying flat on my back, his body next to mine. His fingers are back on the fabric, his lips teasing mine with kisses. He drops one kiss after another onto my mouth, but he never stays there long enough for me to deepen it. I push myself up toward him, the sensation of wanting more taking over.

Noah breaks our kiss. "Mal?"

"Yeah," I reply, my whole body buzzing for more.

"How are you feeling?" he asks, his eyes sweeping down over me.

"I feel like you need to get my underwear out of the way." My voice sounds thick, filled with something I don't quite recognize. *Desire?*

Noah grins. "I can do that."

"Thanks," I mumble, pulling him back down to my lips. And this time, I don't let him leave.

His mouth opens up to mine. And his fingers eventually work their way around my underwear, and when they do, everything changes. He kisses me and touches me in a rhythm that I can't seem to predict. His whole body grows warmer. His mouth wetter with each kiss.

Usually, I know what to expect. The movement of hands. My body's reaction to them. The building of sensations. I know all of the points along the way.

But with Noah, I feel like I don't know anything.

He's a wild card.

I can't predict his next move, the next feeling or sensation that floods through me.

He changes things so quickly that my body can barely keep up. As his hand moves between my legs, his mouth trails down over my cheek. My jaw. He sucks on my neck, sending sparks through me.

When he lets out a soft moan against my skin, the sound vibrates through me. I pull him back to my lips before my hands move instinctively to his jeans.

They need to be gone.

I want him closer.

I want *all* of him.

I try to pull his jeans off but fail. I probably should have reached for the button or zipper, but I can't think straight. I can't focus on one thing. I just know that I want them gone. I end up pulling Noah on top of me, my fingers digging into his shoulders. I push my hips up against his, his hand still between my legs.

Noah moans into my mouth but pulls back.

"Whoa," he says, letting out a shaky breath.

And when I look into his eyes, I notice there isn't any gold in them; they're so dark.

"What?" I ask, practically panting.

"It's getting a little … intense."

"That's good. We shouldn't stop," I tell him, trying to pull him back to me.

Noah lets me bring him down to my lips, but I can feel him smiling as I kiss him. I let out a small grumbling, wishing he would refocus. Wishing his fingers hadn't stilled.

"We should though," he says in between kisses.

"We shouldn't," I disagree.

He pulls back. "We'll get to everything eventually. But for now, let me just enjoy this, okay?"

I want to pout.

To say no.

But he's looking down at me so sweetly that I can't disagree with him.

So, I nod.

Noah doesn't say anything else. His lips find mine again. His tongue dips into my mouth. His fingers start moving. He stays on top of me, and I can't help but move my body directly under his. My fingers dance across his back, running from his tapered waist up to his broad shoulders.

And when Noah grinds against me, my head starts spinning. I can feel him against me. *All* of him. And the thought of his body so close to mine makes me ache for the clothes between us to be gone. For there to be nothing separating us. I wrap my legs around his waist, trying to get closer. His lips feel amazing. And his hands on my skin … I've never felt so charged.

Noah's rhythm shifts, his body speeding up on its own. I feel his hips flex. His hand moves faster. His chest rises quicker. His kisses become deeper.

I try not to lose myself to it.

To him.

But I feel myself building and building. I have too much want. Too much need. Too much energy. And it has nowhere to go. I can't do anything but give it to Noah.

I feel myself start to shake under him. I squeeze my legs against his sides. My nails grasp at his shoulders as I feel myself falling apart.

"Noah," I start, breaking our lips apart. But before I can say anything more, my breath is gone. Everything in me gets pulled back in to a pinnacle. Into a single moment before shattering. Before crashing outward.

I blink, feeling so overwhelmed with emotion. I'm too full. Too alive. Everything feels possible and new and there. I try to focus on Noah's face, but I can only make out his outline above me. It's like I'm in a dream. Like I'm floating.

But slowly, he comes into focus.

His eyes are practically black, and he's looking over my

face with flushed cheeks and pink lips.

He licks those lips, watching me, as his hand slips out from my underwear. But he doesn't move off of me.

"So, you ..." Noah starts but then clears his throat.

"Yeah." I nod.

He nods back, bringing his finger to graze my bottom lip. "And is it always that ... strong?"

My heart is still pounding in my chest as I answer, "Not usually, no."

Noah brings his lips down onto mine, giving me a hard kiss before sliding off of me.

He rolls onto his back and looks up at the ceiling. I glance over at him. He's beaming.

"Why are you smiling?" I laugh, noticing his grin.

"Can't I smile?" he says, his grin not going anywhere.

"If anyone should be smiling like that, it should be me," I say. But I can't even smile. I can't move. I feel overwhelmed by him. By this.

Noah glances at me again. "You look more like you've just had an out-of-body experience than anything else." He chuckles.

"I kind of did," I admit, looking back up at the ceiling.

"I knew it would be powerful, but that was ... cool."

"You did not just say my orgasm was cool," I mumble, covering my eyes with my hands.

"Well, it was." Noah laughs.

"I figured, if anything, you'd say it was a gift or something." I laugh along with him, rolling onto my side.

"A cool gift," he teases, rolling over to look at me. But then his face grows serious. "I've thought about us being together before. I just never realized how intense it would be, even without the sex."

"Honestly, after that, I'm not sure if I could handle sex

with you," I reply. "That was … well, it was different than any time before."

"But you enjoyed it?"

I pull Noah to my lips. "I really enjoyed it."

"Good," he mumbles against my mouth, and then he wraps his arms around me, pulling me flat against his chest. "Because I plan on making you do that again."

Serious business.
6:00PM

"WHY DO YOU want to go back to the pub?" I ask Harry the question even though we're already on our way back into town.

He sent out a text message, telling everyone in the house to meet out front in ten, dressed and ready to go.

When we all got out front, there was a car waiting, and I didn't get a chance to ask Harry where we were going before we were ushered inside it.

"It's trivia night," Harry replies.

He's riding shotgun. I'm in the back, wedged in the middle seat between Mohammad and Noah.

"Trivia night …" I draw my brows in.

I didn't know Harry was interested in trivia.

"How'd you know?" Noah asks, leaning forward to talk to Harry.

Harry turns over his right shoulder and nods toward Mohammad.

"I saw a sign posted about it when we were there yesterday," Mohammad answers.

I look over at him. He's got on a pressed polo with blue

jeans and a puffer jacket. He smells like shampoo and cologne. And his hair is done perfectly.

He looks good.

Suspiciously good.

"Are you sure you're not just trying to catch another glimpse of those girls?" I raise a questioning eyebrow at him.

"Trivia night is serious. Has nothing to do with the girls," Harry interrupts.

"Besides, Harry has their numbers. If we wanted to see them, we'd just hit them up," Mohammad replies.

"Then, why are you all done up?" I ask. Because he definitely didn't have enough time to shower and primp after Harry messaged.

"You've always got to look good. You never know who you'll meet," Mohammad says seriously.

"You sound like my mother," I reply.

"Your mum sounds like she gives sound advice," Mohammad fires back.

I have to hold back from rolling my eyes at him. I glance over to Noah instead.

We were still in bed when we got the text message, and I had to quickly run to my room, throw on some jeans, fix my hair, and make sure I didn't look like I had just been rolling around in bed for the last hour.

Which I had been.

I grin at Noah, feeling so much better about ... well, everything.

He's finally trusting me, I think. And I'm starting to trust him more.

I think what happened between us this afternoon shows that. And I couldn't be happier.

I have to fight the urge to take his hand in mine. Even though it's not a big thing, it's still fresh for Harry. And apparently, for Mohammad too.

Noah smiles back at me.

I hold his gaze for a moment before asking Harry, "Are you any good at trivia?"

"I'm just there for a good time. It's Mohammad you should be worried about," he replies.

"Really?" I ask Mohammad.

"I like to win." He shrugs. "And usually, I can pull us through. Depends on the competition."

"We've played before," Noah says, flaring his eyes. "It was an intense evening."

"So, I'm going to have to take this seriously?" I ask.

In response, I get a, "Nah," a, "Probably," and an, "Absolutely."

"Okay then …"

I LOOK OUT the window, watching as we make our way into town. When we get to the pub, we all unload from the car and follow Harry inside.

"Two times in one weekend. Aren't we lucky?" an old man says from behind the counter.

"Gregor, good to see you, mate!" Harry clasps hands with a tall, broadly built man across the bar.

Gregor's cheeks push up into round, rosy hills as his mouth forms a full smile.

"Good to see you, Harry. Angie told me you came round yesterday." He holds up his finger for Harry to wait, and a moment later, he's around the bar and pulling him into an encompassing embrace. "Here to cause a little trouble?"

He looks from Harry to Mohammad and Noah, recognition sparkling in his eyes.

"I don't go out, *looking* for trouble." Harry laughs out.

"Trouble just always happens to *find* you!" Gregor finishes before letting out a hearty laugh. "You kids in for trivia night?"

"Wouldn't miss it," Harry replies. He opens his mouth to speak again but then quickly shuts it and turns to me, Noah, and Harry. "Do you want to grab a seat? I'll order us drinks, yeah?"

"Sounds good." Noah's the first to reply.

Mohammad and I both nod in agreement before Noah leads us through the pub toward an open table in the corner.

We all strip off our jackets, hanging them over our chairs.

"Big crowd," I comment, taking in the tables filled with small groups.

Even though there aren't that many people, it's still more than the first time we were here. It was practically empty.

"Trivia is serious business," Mohammad replies, echoing Harry's earlier comment.

Noah lets out a chuckle before shaking his head.

"I love this place," Harry says, walking up to the table.

"Who was that?" I ask as he gets settled in his chair.

"Gregor. He's the owner and a personal friend. Has helped me through some hard times," Harry replies.

"Yeah?" I ask.

As Harry thinks, his blue eyes look unfocused. "Yeah, I've been coming here since my parents bought the place. Even when we were younger, Mum would let us walk into town if we promised to ring her once we got here. Gregor always let us use his phone," Harry explains.

"So, he *really* knows you," I reply as Gregor brings over a tray full of pints.

"Here we are," he says, passing them out.

I accept a cold glass and give it a quick sniff.

It's cider.

"Enjoy," he says, giving us a discreet wink.

"Now, I see why you love it here." I laugh, taking a sip.

"He's seen me at my best and worst. If we got bored at the house, we'd come here and play darts for hours, and Gregor would sneak us some pints."

"This was the first place I ever got pissed," Mohammad says, taking a drink.

Noah laughs. "We were so scared Harry's mum would find out. Had to call her and tell her we'd be late and that we were eating dinner here, which we did."

"But only to sober Mohammad up," Harry adds.

"That's true." Mohammad laughs.

"At least they do a great roast," Noah says with a grin.

"Speaking of which, should I order four roasts before trivia?" Harry asks.

"I'll do it," Noah says, standing up.

"Cheers," Harry says, taking a gulp of his pint. "You know, one of my first kisses was here."

I watch Noah walk to the bar, but ... *what did Harry just say?*

"You got kissed here?" I ask.

"Yep. Mohammad tried to convince me that I couldn't get a real *woman*." Harry grins.

"He did though," Mohammad says, clinking his pint against Harry's.

"What do you mean, *a real woman?*"

"An *older* woman." Mohammad waggles his eyebrows and sticks out his tongue.

"Older?" I repeat, shocked.

"One of the bar staff," Harry explains.

"I lost fifteen quid that day," Mohammad says, his face souring slightly.

"It was worth it though, wasn't it?" Harry grins, and it causes Mohammad to bring out his megawatt smile.

"Definitely!" He laughs.

"How old was she?" I croak out.

"I don't know," Harry says. "Maybe thirty."

"Thirty!" I try not to shout. "That's illegal."

"It was a kiss." Mohammad rolls his eyes at me. "And anyway, I'm sure she didn't get any pleasure from it. She probably just knew that she'd make Harry's night."

"My year," Harry corrects. "And for your information, she got pleasure."

"I think that might be a stretch," Noah says, sitting back down.

"You knew about this?" I ask.

"He was there," Harry says.

"How did that even happen? What approach did you take?" I ask, feeling very, very confused.

"Yeah, what approach *did* you take?" Mohammad parrots back.

Harry rests his elbows on the table, scooting his head closer toward ours. We all do the same, leaning in like he's going to tell us top-secret information.

"Well, if you must know, I walked up to the bar, slapped my hand down, and told her I wanted a pint and a kiss," Harry says.

"That did not work!" I laugh, imagining a young Harry doing just that.

Harry shrugs, a sly smile on his face. "I can't reveal my secrets."

"The only way that would have worked is if you'd slipped her a crisp twenty," Mohammad replies.

Noah busts out laughing when our food arrives.

"That was quick," I say more to myself than anyone else.

The plate is piled high. There are carrots, potatoes, obviously roast, stuffing, a piece of weirdly shaped puff pastry, and it's all smothered in gravy.

"Oh my," Mohammad says, his eyes lighting up.

"This looks like the meal of your dreams," I say to Harry. Because everything is brownish-orange.

"Roasts are the best." Harry nods, digging in.

Noah leans in toward me. "That's called a Yorkshire pudding," he says, pointing to the piece of pastry.

I nod and decide the best thing to do is just dig in.

I take a bite of potato and am actually surprised.

It's delicious.

"Wow," I mumble, licking my lips.

"Good, right?" Harry says before taking another bite.

"Really good," I agree.

"So … have you heard from Olivia?" Mohammad asks me. And his question catches me off guard.

"Just the other day. Have you?" I ask Harry.

"We don't message," Harry responds with disinterest.

"Did you ever reach out to her about …" I immediately cut myself off. I know that I alluded to Harry what was going on, but I'm not sure if the boys know. And it's not really my place to tell them.

"About her family? Yeah, I did," Harry says.

"That's good."

"Is that what her breakdown was about?" Mohammad asks, a lightbulb going off.

"Breakdown?" Noah asks.

"Yeah! Did you hear about it?" Mohammad asks excitedly.

"No. What are you talking about?" I ask at the same time Noah shakes his head.

"Harry, you neither?" Mohammad asks.

Harry holds his hands out in surprise.

Mohammad looks at us like we are aliens, astonishment

flashing across his face. "It was wild! Apparently, Olivia had a standoff with her dad in front of the school. Even yelled at him in front of a group of girls and started crying. Can you believe that?"

My stomach drops.

"Wait, seriously?" I ask, covering my mouth with my hand.

"Yeah. Someone messaged me about it Friday night. Apparently, it was this whole thing."

"Why didn't you tell us?" Harry asks, his face going white.

"You've been so anti-Olivia. I wasn't going to chance mentioning her," Mohammad says, his tone growing serious.

"It's true," Noah agrees.

Harry looks to Noah, his lips turning down into a frown.

"Before I leave, I'll check in with her," Harry says.

"I can't believe that Naomi never mentioned it. And neither did Olivia when we messaged yesterday."

"Maybe she thought you had already heard," Mohammad suggests.

"Maybe," I reply.

I pick at my food, feeling bad for her. She really has been going through a lot.

I glance at Harry.

He looks worried by the news.

Really worried.

And I'm not sure what to make of it.

But two more ciders and a game of trivia take my mind off of Olivia.

"Fuck, I hate losing," Harry says, running his hands back through his hair. "I need a fag. Anyone want to join?"

"I'll come," Noah responds.

"Why don't we all come?" Mohammad says. "Then, we can get the car back."

"Good plan." Harry nods.

We all say our good-byes to Gregor before leaving. I pull my coat tightly around me as Harry lights his cigarette. The heat wave must be over.

It's officially autumn.

The street glows under the streetlights, and I look in the window of the pub, feeling happy. I glance around the town, realizing my parents would probably love this place. It's quaint and charming.

We'll have to have a family weekend somewhere like this. Maybe over Christmas.

But then I think about my dad. And how I haven't called him yet.

"Shit, I haven't called my dad today," I say to the boys.

"You should probably call," Noah says.

"When we get back to the house, I will."

"Call while I finish," Harry says, holding up his full cigarette.

I get out my phone, deciding I might as well get it over with.

It rings, but no one answers.

"He must be busy," I say, ending the call.

A second later, I get a text.

Dad: Hey, sweetie. Sorry, we have the movers at the house. How's the trip?

Me: It's good. We just played trivia in town, and now, we're headed back to Harry's.

Dad: Sounds fun!

Me: We didn't win, but it was fun anyway.

Dad: Thanks for checking in. Give us a call tomorrow?

Me: Sounds good. Have fun packing!

Dad: *We will. Your mom and I can't wait to see you this week.*

Me: *Me too. Love you.*

"Everything okay?" Noah asks me.

"I'm seeing my parents this week," I reply. "The movers are there now."

"Only a few more days now," Noah replies.

"At least we still have another full day here," I comment, wrapping my arms around his waist.

Noah tucks me against his side. "We do."

I glance over to Harry, watching as he ashes his cigarette.

Only a few more days …

A plan for my life.
10:00PM

WHEN WE GET back to the house, Mohammad makes us all a cocktail as we get settled into the drawing room. Harry starts a fire. Noah and Mohammad look through Mohammad's phone, trying to find a playlist.

I take a sip, not sure what to make of Mohammad's drink.

But Mohammad seems to like it. He takes a large gulp, looking satisfied.

I lean my head back against the couch, thinking about my life here. About Noah's question of if I missed New York. I told Noah that I felt like I was pretending to be happy even though I am happy.

Very happy.

And I need to figure out why.

I think it has to do with not saying good-bye to Anna. I

feel like my parents disrespected me by just uprooting my life without telling me. Yes, it all worked out for the best, but what if this wouldn't have been best for me? They should have at least asked me before springing something so big on me.

Maybe I just need time.

Or maybe, like I'm always telling Harry, I need to take some ownership of my life.

I sit on the couch, having a realization.

"I think I need a new plan," I say.

"A plan for what?" Mohammad says absentmindedly, but Noah looks at me with genuine interest.

"A plan for my life," I answer, still thinking. "You know, Headmaster Compton said I could always go talk to the school counselor."

"You're going to see a shrink?" Harry asks, looking appalled.

"Not a shrink," I reply. "And I wouldn't be using the counselor in the sense of talking about my problems. I would have him help me make a new plan. Be strategic about my life."

"What about your old plan?" Noah asks.

"Well, my old plan was business school in New York before working there."

"Has that changed?" Harry asks with interest.

I shrug, genuinely not knowing.

Has it?

"Maybe. I mean, for one, I don't live there now."

"So, you would sell real estate here?" Mohammad asks, putting down his phone.

"I could."

"What about going back to America for university?" It's Noah who asks the question this time.

"I … I have no clue. I wouldn't rule it out, but if I want

to live here long-term, then I'm not sure why I would."

"Making a new plan sounds like a brilliant idea," Noah says, giving me the best smile.

"Yeah, I think that might help me adjust to things," I agree.

"If you get a life plan, does that mean I need one?" Mohammad asks, pouring himself another drink.

"I thought you already had your plan figured out?" Noah says to him. "Matchmaking, right?"

"Who knows?" Mohammad replies.

"You know, you're only seventeen. You don't need a life plan," Harry says.

"I think I do," I disagree. "It's just who I am."

"Well … if you want to talk to someone, I told you before, my family has a shrink on retainer."

I can't help but laugh. "Thanks for the offer."

"All right, now that we're properly pissed, I'm going to ask the question," Mohammad says, slamming down his empty glass.

And it immediately worries me.

"Uh-oh," Noah says, flaring his eyes at me.

"This can't be good," I mumble.

"Ask!" Harry shouts.

"What are the thoughts on you and Olivia?" Mohammad asks Harry.

"Oh, Mohammad!" I shake my head at him.

"What?" he replies defensively.

"That's insensitive," Noah agrees.

"Harry, have I offended you?" Mohammad asks him.

"Nah." Harry waves his hand in the air. "But to answer your question, I don't have thoughts on her."

"You know their history," Noah says.

"I know," Mohammad replies. "But I already know the

topic is going to come up."

"What? Why?" I ask.

"Because if there's one thing we can count on, it's that women will be women," Mohammad says, like, somehow, that's an answer.

"What do you mean?" Noah questions.

"And if I'm *seeing* Naomi—" Mohammad starts.

"Dating," Noah coughs under his breath, sending Harry into a fit of giggles.

Mohammad goes red. "If I'm seeing Naomi, then I know it's going to come up."

"What is?" Harry asks.

"Double-dating," Mohammad explains.

"Been there and done that with Olivia. I'm good," Harry replies.

"Harry …"

"I got dumped a week ago. Let me heal my ego before you hand me back over to her," Harry says.

"I think I was the one who got dumped," I point out.

"Besides, why would I agree to that?" Harry goes on.

"You don't have to," Noah cuts in.

"I'm just preparing you. What happens if Naomi will only go out with me if you go out with Olivia?" Mohammad asks, pushing the subject further.

"Then, she's not the right girl for you," I state. "Besides, it won't come to that. She likes you."

"You say that now. But trust me, the second my phone password becomes her birthday and I know all the names of her dogs and her favorite Starbucks order, I'm done for."

"Does she have dogs?" I ask.

"That's not the point," Noah cuts in, apparently coming to Mohammad's defense.

"Then, what is?" Harry asks.

I look over at him, realizing that he's just as confused as I am.

"The point is that women say one thing, let you believe it's true for a while, and then once you're in a compromised position, they change the game," Noah says.

I look at him in surprise. "I thought love wasn't a game."

"Love isn't. But dating ... that's a whole different story," Noah says, blowing out a heavy breath.

"He's right. Two different things," Harry chimes in, now somehow agreeing with him.

"So?" Mohammad asks. "Double date?"

"That's a hard no," Harry replies.

"Even if I got you some of your favorite whiskey? Followed by a pizza? And then lots and lots of mind-numbing FIFA?" Mohammad says, trying to sweeten the deal.

"Seriously?" I ask.

Because Harry isn't going to ...

"I'll consider it," Harry replies with a smile.

"Good to know." Mohammad grins. "You're such a good mate."

"I know." Harry smiles.

"Way to stand your ground," I say to Harry.

"He wasn't going to give up. Better to have a win-win."

"I think you could have struck a better bargain," I disagree.

"How would you know? You don't even bargain!" Mohammad fires back.

"Of course I do."

"Not really," Harry agrees. "You demand and expect to get what you want, and then you get salty if told no."

My mouth falls open. "Oh, thanks for that," I say. "Noah?"

He shrugs at me, looking amused. "They're not wrong."

"And on that note," I say, getting up. "Bed for me."

"Nooooo," Mohammad groans.

"Yes! I'm tired," I reply.

"Let her sleep," Harry cuts in.

"Fine. But set an alarm for sunrise. I want to meet down-stairs for it," Mohammad says.

I shake my head at him. "That's not happening."

"I'm serious," Mohammad says. And he sounds like it. "It's either that or a bucket of ice water."

"You wouldn't," I say.

"He would," Noah chimes in.

"See you at five!" Mohammad sings out.

Noah gets up too. "We should all head to bed."

"Probably right," Harry agrees.

Noah takes Harry's hand and helps pull him up off the couch. I walk over to Mohammad and give him a hug.

"Good night," he says to me.

"Good night."

Harry's next. I wrap my arms around his waist and rest my head against his chest.

"Sleep good," he says warmly.

"You too."

I walk upstairs with Noah and then start to head to my room.

"What are you doing?" he asks, grabbing on to my hand.

"Getting my pajamas," I tell him.

"You can wear mine tonight, if you want." Noah's eyes focus in on mine. He rubs his fingers against my palm before leading me into his room.

I can still taste Mohammad's cocktail on my lips, and I feel flushed as Noah closes the door behind us.

"Let's brush our teeth first," Noah says, ushering me into the bathroom. "I can't get the taste of the cocktail out of my mouth."

"Me neither." I laugh.

Noah hands me the toothpaste. I grab my toothbrush, which has somehow ended up in his bathroom, and brush my teeth, watching in the mirror as Noah does the same.

He keeps his eyes on me the whole time, and once we're finished, I can't help but wrap my arms around his neck.

"Today was nice."

"It was," Noah agrees. "Know what's also nice?"

"What?" I ask.

"The sunrise isn't until closer to seven-thirty."

I immediately smile and bring Noah to my lips.

"You smell good tonight," I say in between kisses.

"You do too."

Noah pulls his shirt off over his head. I run my fingers along his collarbone as we kiss. Noah shivers at the sensation.

I move my lips off his, kissing down his neck and across his chest.

"Wow," Noah mumbles.

I look up and watch his eyes slide shut.

I start to kiss lower, working my way down onto his firm stomach when his hands find mine at his waist.

"We should get into our pajamas," he says, pulling me back up.

"Noah," I say, stopping him.

"Yeah?"

"I won't wear them."

It takes Noah a minute to understand what I mean. And it's easy to see his face change from trying to hold it together to when he finally lets himself go.

Suddenly, he's kissing me.

His hands are everywhere.

They're pushing through my hair and wrapping around

my sides.

"Fuck," he whispers, his tongue finding mine.

His kisses slowly undo everything in me. Each one is better than the last. Who would have thought he would have such a delicious mouth? Or be kissing me this freaking hotly?

I think, in the beginning, I got it all wrong.

I thought Harry was the sexy and flirty one. I figured his good looks and charm would make him ... well, passionate. But Noah ...

With every day I get to know him, he somehow becomes sweeter but more intense. One second, he is bringing me coffee, and the next, he is pushing me up against the wall. I can't figure him out at all. Which is probably why he has my head and my body spinning.

Suddenly, his hands are undoing the buttons on my jeans, and he's pulling down my pants.

Then, my shirt is gone.

I'm in nothing but my underwear.

It's then that his lips leave mine. They sprinkle kisses across my chest. Down over my stomach. His fingers slide against the outside of my bra, and I can tell he wants that piece of fabric gone too.

Finally.

This is what I've been waiting for.

Noah takes me out to the bedroom and pushes me down onto the bed. His hands are everywhere, caressing my skin as he climbs on top of me. I don't even have a chance to appreciate the feel of it before his chest is pressing against mine. He pins my hands above my head with one of his hands, and the other finds its way to my stomach.

I press my lips together, suppressing a moan.

My head is spinning at how his body feels on top of mine.

I push Noah off me and roll onto my side, unhooking my

bra before giving him a chance to say no. Noah's eyes go wide as I toss it onto the floor.

My hands move to his jeans, and I quickly undo them. Surprisingly, Noah helps as I pull them off him. Before he can say anything, my lips find his, and I press my body against his. And he wraps his hands around my waist.

But my fingers keep coming back to the edge of his underwear.

I blink up at Noah, hoping what I'm about to do is okay.

But I don't ask. I just push his underwear down. I give him a second to pull away, but he doesn't.

And then I'm touching him for the first time without anything separating us.

His mouth falls open, his golden eyes landing on me.

I move my hand, letting myself get lost in him. In the way he's looking at me.

Noah starts breathing heavily, his eyes falling shut. I lick my lips, my heart pounding in my chest. He opens his eyes back up, looking me over. He sucks in his cheeks once before rolling on top of me and kisses me hard, his tongue parting my mouth as his fingers find their way into my underwear.

I moan into his mouth, my hands sliding up onto his shoulders. My palms slide down his back and past his waist. I grab on to his butt as he presses his hips against mine.

At some point, my underwear comes off.

And I can feel Noah against me.

All of him.

My mouth falls open at the idea.

That this could be it.

"Do you have—" I start to say, but Noah pulls back and trails his mouth down over my neck.

He kisses across me, his tongue making circles against my stomach. Then, he kisses across my hips, his lips finding their way between my thighs.

I let my fingers push through his hair. I try to grasp at his shoulders. But no matter where my fingers go, they feel rigid.

My whole body does.

Noah's lips are soft and then firm, and no matter how much I shift, he keeps me pinned down.

"Noah, I'm ..." I say, my body vibrating.

He nods, lacing his fingers through mine.

"Are you sure you want—" I start, but he won't stop.

His soft lips. His warm breath. His tongue. It's all too much. I bend toward him, feeling my body giving in to the sensation.

I bite my lip, trying to stay quiet.

But it's all too much.

I moan, squeezing Noah's hands until my body stills.

Noah kisses up my stomach, trailing his lips across my chest and up to my neck before looking down at me with a flush. His breathing is ragged, his chest rising and falling quickly against mine.

"How are you feeling?" His dark eyes find mine; his lips are parted. And he looks incredibly sexy.

"I feel ..." I try to find the words. "I feel flushed. And breathless. I feel perfect, Noah."

He smiles above me before dropping his lips down onto mine. I bite his lip gently.

"And how are you feeling?" I ask.

He pulls back, his eyes sparkling. "I was just thinking actually."

"Thinking?" I laugh. "Aren't you supposed to *not* be thinking at times like this?"

Noah props himself up onto his elbow, his fingers trailing down my sternum to my belly button.

"Actually, I was wondering something," he corrects.

I look up at him in interest. "And what were you wondering?"

"I was wondering," he starts, his fingers slipping further and further down until they cause me to suck in a shaky breath, "if I could make you do that again."

I blink up at him, my heart rate already speeding up. Noah dips his head down, his lips coming to my ear.

"What do you think? Should we find out?" he asks, excitement in his voice.

But he doesn't let me answer before he's rolling back on top of me, his lips on mine.

TUESDAY, OCTOBER 22ND
You are naked.
6:45AM

THE ALARM RINGS, stirring me awake.

I pull the blanket over my head, trying to block out the noise. But it doesn't do any good. That annoying tone never seems to end.

I reach my hand out to the bedside table, tapping around until I turn the alarm off.

Actually, I don't remember setting an alarm.

I roll over, ready to go back to sleep when I realize that I'm not in my bed. I slowly open my eyes, finding Noah asleep next to me.

I look down over myself, the weight of last night settling into me.

Because Noah and I are in bed together.

Naked.

Like, *naked*. There are no ifs, ands, or buts about it. Well, except for my butt. And Noah's butt. So, technically, there are two butts, and they aren't at all covered!

I press my eyes shut, my mind slipping back to last night. To Noah's mouth all over me. He was demanding and so freaking hot. Every part of me was pounding, wanting more and more.

And I almost got it.

Noah and I almost had sex.

My eyes fly open.

Because, holy shit, we almost had sex. Like, sex, sex.

I mean ... Helen would be furious. And I don't even know how I would feel now, lying here awake before him if we had done it. I've been trying to get him to cave for days.

I mean, a girl can only take so much. And Noah was right. Sex is something private and between two people.

What Helen doesn't know won't hurt her.

I roll my eyes at myself, knowing that isn't true. Helen *would* care. I would care.

And we didn't actually have sex. Although I don't think we were too far off. But Noah never gave in.

And I didn't push him.

Well, maybe I did a little. But he was pushing my body, wanting more and more from me. And I gave it to him. Over and over.

He really did have me begging for him.

Just like he'd told me when I first met him.

And he still does.

I turn my head and look at him—well, at his back.

I can see the outline of his shoulder blades. The back of his arms. His thick, dark hair. My eyes follow the line of his spine, watching it dip in the same place where there are two dimples set above his round butt. I peel my eyes away from him, biting my lip. Before I have a chance to think about what I should do, I reach out and shake him.

"Noah," I whisper, trying to get him to wake up.

"Hmm?" Noah stirs, rolling over to face me. His eyes are still closed, but he wraps me up in his arms, pulling my naked body against him.

I try not to freak out at the fact that he's bare. *Everything ...* is touching me.

And is there anything hotter than a sleepy boy who can't even open his eyes but somehow still manages to wrap you up in his arms?

The answer is no.

There isn't.

"You're so warm," he mumbles.

I roll onto my back, weighing my decisions. Maybe I should just start kissing him. *Everywhere.* Then, we can get the sex thing out of the way. It's like some invisible line we're dancing around. And I want it gone.

But I also need to respect Noah.

And probably myself. I remember how he talked about sex being an exchange. A sharing of emotions. And feelings.

He wants us to take our time. But honestly, at the pace we're moving … it can't be far off.

"We need to get dressed," I say out loud.

"We don't," Noah disagrees.

"We do. The alarm went off," I say, trying to sit up. But Noah holds me tighter, keeping me put.

"Stay in bed."

"If we don't get up and go meet them, Harry and Mohammad will come looking for us. And I'm not sure either of them will be prepared for what they might find. Me and you. *In bed. Naked.*"

Noah's eyes peel open, and he pulls back the covers, looking down over me. "Shit, you *are* naked."

"What? Did you forget?" I laugh.

"I was just tired before, but now that you said that …" Noah pulls me toward him, wrapping his hands around my waist.

"Noah, last night was …" I start, a smile forming on my lips.

"I know. You're amazing." Noah smiles before kissing me.

"Me? I think you took the flag on that one," I reply.

"I'm really happy." Noah smiles again.

I lean back and brush his hair off his face.

"So am I. Last night, it was hard to stop," I admit.

"I told you it would be."

"But we did. And as painful as it is for me to say, I think you were right."

"About what?" Noah asks.

"About taking our time. Everything has felt amazing. But I'm glad we didn't last night. Sometimes, I just feel frantic for you, you know? Like I just want more and more and more."

Noah chuckles, his eyes lighting up. "I know the feeling. That's why it's important we are conscious of the steps we take."

"Do you think we're taking it slow enough? I mean, we're naked and in bed together, and there are few boxes left unchecked. Well, only one box really. For both of us."

"I can't believe you just compared exploring our bodies and feelings to checking boxes." Noah outright laughs this time.

"It's either that or the bases analogy," I point out.

"We're trying our best. I want to get to know your body, what you like, before …" Noah sucks in his cheeks, his fingers moving at my waist. The sensation makes my eyes flutter.

"Before we …"

"Yeah."

"I think you're getting a pretty good idea of what I like." I grin at him.

"Do you feel good?" Noah asks, the corner of his lips pulling up.

"I feel perfect."

"That's good. I want you to feel comfortable. Happy about things."

"Trust me, I am. What about you?"

"I've got you in my bed. I'm not sure I could be happier." Noah gives me a silly smile, raising his eyebrows at me.

"Good to know," I say. And I have to fight the urge to pull him to my lips. "Time for sunrise?"

"Check the clock," Noah replies.

My forehead creases, but I do as he said, checking the time.

I flare my eyes. "Noah, the sun doesn't rise for another half hour!"

"I know. I set it early," he says, giving me a mischievous smile.

Oh!

I grin, pulling him toward me.

Noah kisses me, but his lips are gentle on mine. I try to open my mouth against his.

"Mal …" Noah says.

"Yeah?" I ask, running my hands up his chest and across his shoulders.

"I set it, so you'd have time to get coffee."

I break our lips apart.

"Oh. I thought you set it early, so you could appreciate having me naked in your bed."

"If you keep it up, we won't leave this room," Noah says, looking over me.

"Promise?"

Noah sucks in a breath, pulling me to his mouth. I sit up, sliding myself on top of him as we kiss.

Which, in retrospect, probably wasn't the best idea.

Because all I can feel is Noah's naked body against mine.

I let out a sigh, slide off him, and roll onto my side.

"What's wrong?" Noah asks, his eyes dilated again.

"I think I'm more animal than you or something. All I

can think about is …"

"Sex?"

I push out a pout. "It's annoying."

"You need to focus on something else. It's just a trick your mind plays. It sees something it wants and won't let off until you have it. Which, in this case, is sex."

"What are you saying?"

Because, sometimes, Noah makes no sense.

"I'm saying … let's say we had sex right now. After, your mind would move on to wanting something else, maybe related to me or maybe not."

"Don't blame my mind. This is your fault!"

"My fault?" Noah laughs out.

"Yes. Your fault."

"And how exactly is this my fault?" Noah brings his hand up to my cheek and runs his fingers through my hair, pushing it back off my face.

"You've had my body in a frenzy for weeks. And then, suddenly, we go from nothing to everything in a matter of days. And once I get close to finally getting all of you, you hold back," I state matter-of-factly.

Because that's the truth.

And sometimes, the truth hurts.

"That doesn't sound too fair," Noah says, actually agreeing with me.

"It doesn't, does it?" I say, a smile slipping onto my face.

"Do you have a solution then?" he asks.

"Yes, I do actually. Well, at least, I did …" I reply. Because, somehow, my plans always seem to backfire.

"Are you going to let me in on it?"

"Well, I planned on seducing you, obviously. But since we just had the whole we'll wait until we're both ready and respect one another's decisions and bodies talk, I feel a little guilty about that plan."

Noah pulls a strand of my hair away from my face, examining it between his fingers. I thought he'd laugh at what I said, but he doesn't.

"I want this, you know."

"I know." I nod. "I was only teasing."

"You know I want you—badly—right?" Noah asks, his gaze locked on my eyes.

"I want you too."

"Do you remember when we were dancing? When you told me that the only thing keeping you from falling apart was not giving in to the physical?" he asks, rolling onto his back.

I swallow, remembering.

It was Thursday night at the club, when Mohammad and Naomi left me and Noah on the dance floor.

"Of course I remember." I push up onto my elbows and look down at him. "Wait, Noah, is that how you feel?"

"I want to show you how I feel. But you need to be ready. *Sure*. Not only for yourself, but for me too."

"Your heart speech yesterday. Can I ask you something about it?"

"Ask."

"If I reach that point, where I know exactly what's in my heart and what it wants, when I'm a hundred percent sure, how do you want me to tell you?"

Noah turns and smiles at me. "You can't ask that question," he says with a laugh.

My mouth falls open. "What? Why not?"

"One word: romance. If you reach that point, Mal, tell me however you want. Tell me in your own way. Any way you want. Be creative."

I roll my eyes.

"Well, I tried that method already, and you wouldn't

accept it."

"What method? Assaulting me with your body?" Noah chuckles. "That wasn't a profession of love. It was a sneaky—and very tempting—attempt to get into my pants."

I laugh, completely surprised by Noah. "You really are going to make me work for it, aren't you?"

Noah looks at me disapprovingly.

"Fine, you're going to make me think deeply in my heart about my wants and desires," I correct. "And then, once I do, sex will happen, right?"

"Shit, speaking of that, remember how you said you wanted a different term for the sex bridge? How you didn't like bridge?" Noah asks.

"Yeah?"

"Well, I've come up with a term for it."

"Really?"

"Yeah. I think you should think of it as a gift instead. As an effect."

"What do you mean, as an effect?" I ask.

"Well, generally, when you love someone, you think of them. And you give them material gifts. You give them the gift of time. Your presence. Your body. So, sex is an effect of love. It's a gift given …"

"Like a result." I nod, following along.

"Basically." Noah nods.

I grin. "I like that."

"I'm glad." Noah gives me a warm kiss before getting out of bed.

He walks over to the dresser and pulls out underwear, a T-shirt, and joggers from the chest of drawers. But all I am paying attention to is his naked backside.

I bite my lip.

"Hey, Noah," I call out.

"Yeah?"

He turns to look at me.

I bounce out of bed, the soft rug hitting my bare feet as I stand up, fully naked in front of him.

"I have a gift for you," I say, trying to keep a straight face.

Noah busts out laughing, causing me to laugh too. He pulls on his boxers before walking over to me.

"Cheesy?" I ask.

"Cheesy," Noah agrees, setting his hands at my hips. "But I liked it."

"I had to try." I smile up at him.

"It was a good attempt," Noah says with a nod. "Come on. Let's get you in some clothes."

I turn around and start to walk back to the bed to grab some clothes when Noah smacks me on the butt.

I gasp, swirling around to look at him. "You did not just do that!" I say, my mouth falling open.

"I did." Noah grins, shoots me a wink, and then walks into the bathroom. "Oh, wow," he says.

"What?" I ask, pulling on his shorts and T-shirt. I need to change into my own clothes, but I'm not going to chance running into anyone in the hallway, not fully dressed.

"You gave me a love bite," Noah calls out.

"A love bite? What are you talking about?"

He comes out of the bathroom and points at his neck. I walk up to him, noticing a small bruise just to the left of his Adam's apple.

"A hickey," I say, the term he used mentally clicking. "My bad."

"You need to be more careful," Noah scolds. He pushes my hair away from my face, glancing at my own neck.

"I am careful! It's not my fault you bruise like fruit," I reply.

"Oh, it's mine then?" Noah asks, a sparkle in his eye.

"Absolutely. You're to blame—always."

"Hmm. That doesn't seem quite fair ..." Noah says, shaking his head.

"Doesn't it?" I ask, pulling him to my lips.

"Your tactics won't work. You messed up with this one," Noah says.

He kisses me but then quickly pulls away.

A second later, he's back in the bathroom, looking at his neck in the mirror.

"Is it really that big of a deal to you?" I ask, joining him in the bathroom.

Because way to get bent out of shape over nothing ...

"It is what it is," Noah replies.

"I can cover it up with makeup?" I offer.

Noah lets out a deep, echoing laugh. "I think I'll manage without it."

"Up to you. Just be prepared for Mohammad to question you," I say, pointing out the obvious. Because Mohammad won't be able to resist.

"He wouldn't bring it up," Noah disagrees.

"Mohammad?" My eyebrows shoot up in surprise. "Of course he would. I love him, but he has no shame."

"It will be fine."

"Are you worried about Harry seeing it?" I can't help it when the question comes out of my mouth.

Noah looks at me with scolding eyes. "I'm worried about my mum. As you should be."

"Oh ..." The thought of Helen seeing a hickey on Noah's neck immediately brings me back to reality. "We're definitely going to have to cover that up if it's still there tomorrow morning. And I promise to be more careful."

Noah gives me a genuine smile before brushing his teeth.

When he's finished, he cleans his brush with water before setting it back down on the counter.

"I'll go get you coffee while you get changed," he says.

My heart immediately goes warm.

"I love you," I say, smiling up at him.

Noah's face flashes with surprise.

"I mean, I love *that*," I say, floundering. Even though I do love Noah, when I tell him for the first time, I want it to be special.

Really special.

"You mean, you love coffee." Noah chuckles, causing me to flush. His hand comes up to my cheek. "It's all right, Mal."

"I do love coffee," I agree.

"Amongst other things." Noah smirks at me. "See you downstairs."

He looks lost.
7:20AM

WHEN I GET downstairs, changed into workout clothes for the morning, I pick up a blanket from the living room and wrap it around my shoulders before heading outside. I find Mohammad already seated on one of the benches.

I walk up next to him and wrap the blanket over his back, so we're both tucked under it before I sit down.

"Morning." I smile.

"Morning! I'm glad you made it," he says happily.

"I wouldn't have missed it."

Mohammad raises an eyebrow at me, apparently not buying it.

"All right, fine. If sunrise were at five a.m., I probably

would have. But luckily for us, as it gets closer to winter, the sun rises later and later."

"Lucky for *you*." Mohammad laughs. "Where's Noah?"

"Getting coffee. Have you seen Harry?" I glance around the garden.

The morning light is just coming up, but the sun hasn't fully risen.

"Not yet."

"I'm sure Noah will find him," I reply.

"I can't believe today is our last day here. This weekend flew by."

"It really did," I say, the realization settling in. "Harry and I have that party tonight."

Mohammad turns to me. "Are you prepared for it?"

"What do you mean? It's just a party."

"Yeah. One that you and Harry are going to *alone* while pretending to be a couple." He flares his eyes at me.

"It's not a big thing. Besides, Harry knows about me and Noah now. There aren't any secrets."

But Mohammad doesn't look convinced.

"Whatever you say," he replies.

I pull the blanket closer around me, not sure what to make of Mohammad's question. Or the fact that today is our last day here. Which means, tomorrow, we'll all go back to London and Harry will leave for Shanghai.

The patio door opening pulls me out of my thoughts.

"Morning."

I hear Harry's voice before I see him. A second later, he and Noah are taking a seat across from us. Harry seems bright and energetic, and it instantly makes me happy.

"Morning." I smile widely at Harry.

"Sleep good?" Harry asks.

"Great," I say, not missing a beat. I have to fight off the

urge to look at Noah, knowing if I do, my cheeks will go immediately red.

"I slept like a rock," Mohammad agrees.

"Same," Noah adds, looking directly at me. "I started to make coffee, but Gerald insisted on bringing us out a pot."

"Can't complain about that." I smile.

"Gerald doesn't make coffee often," Harry says, "but when he does it's truly incredible. You're in for a treat. Now, where is this sunrise?"

Mohammad pulls out his phone, checking the time.

"It should rise in that direction," he says, pointing toward our left, "any second now."

We all look out, waiting. Because the land around Harry's house is low and mostly flat, we will actually be able to see the sunrise in the distance.

Gerald brings out a tray with a silver coffee service, sets it down on a side table, and then starts pouring.

"Thanks," I tell him when he hands me a cup. I take a sip and immediately want to melt.

Because Harry was right.

This coffee is amazing.

As I take another sip, the sun starts to peek over the horizon.

"Wow," I mumble, leaning in closer to Mohammad. "This was a great idea."

"Yeah?" Mohammad asks, looking over at me happily.

"Yeah. I would much rather be here than getting another hour of sleep in bed," I reply.

I glance to Noah. He looks beautiful in the morning light, sitting next to Harry. I move my gaze to Harry. He's looking toward the sunrise, but he looks lost.

"What's on your mind?" I ask.

Harry looks at me as I speak, and I nod my head at him,

so he knows the question is for him.

"Shanghai," he answers honestly.

"Try not to worry about it," Mohammad says, his lips pulling down in a frown.

"I think it's a good opportunity," Noah interjects, clapping Harry on the shoulder.

"What do you mean?" Harry asks.

"See what you make of it. Speak with the people at the office and get a real sense of what it would be like, interning there. Better to know now than ignore the situation while you're there and then end up there, unprepared."

Harry looks at Noah in understanding. "You're right. I'll just feel it out."

"Exactly. A few of your smiles and some smooth talk will go a long way," Noah agrees.

"So, I've got a game plan …" Harry says, looking more upbeat.

Noah nods. "I think you need one."

"It sounds like a good idea," I encourage.

And Harry smiles. He actually smiles.

"Thanks," he says.

We watch the rest of the sunrise in silence, enjoying each other's company. Because after today, things are going to be different.

For all of us.

Harry will be in Shanghai, looking at where he could one day be interning.

Noah's asking for my whole heart; he wants our parents to meet and for us to tell everyone about our relationship.

My parents will be arriving from New York.

Even Mohammad has a possible love interest waiting for him back in London.

I don't think any of us ever thought we'd be in the situations we're in. They're full of opportunity.

Possibility.

But possibilities also come with unknowns.

And unknowns can lead to heartbreaks.

Disappointment.

Possibilities mean that, one day, you'll have to make a choice about who you are and what you want for yourself, for your future.

But for now, all we have to focus on is our last day here, together. And that starts by watching the sunrise.

Completely mystified.
9:30AM

AFTER WE WATCH the sunrise and eat breakfast, we all sit at the table, deciding what to do.

"I'll request lunch outside," Harry says, informing us of the plan.

"Isn't it too cold?" I counter.

"They'll put up heating lamps," he tells us.

"Any other plans besides that?" Noah asks, finishing off his orange juice.

"Thought we'd have a chill day before tonight," Harry says, sounding noncommittal.

"Hell no, this is our last day. We've got to utilize it!" Mohammad chants out, causing both Harry and Noah to laugh.

I smile at Mohammad, loving his enthusiasm.

"Does drinking and eating count?" Harry asks bashfully.

"Of course it does," I tease.

"I don't know. I've got some energy this morning. Maybe

I'll exercise," Mohammad says, taking us all by surprise.

"I thought you liked to do your workouts alone?" I ask him.

"Usually, I prefer to do exercises in my room—you know, the standard push-ups, sit-ups, squats. It's foolproof." Mohammad beams. "But I'd be down for something different this morning."

"I could lead a group session," Noah says excitedly.

"I haven't agreed to any of this," Harry cuts in.

"Well, what exactly do you want to do?" I ask, wondering what Harry's ideal day is.

"Like I said, eat and drink," Harry repeats.

Mohammad waves him off.

"But … if you guys want to exercise, then we will. But I'm going to make a game out of it," Harry says.

"That doesn't sound good," I say under my breath.

"What are the rules?" Noah asks.

"I'm thinking … wrestling." Harry grins widely.

"Oh, yes!" Mohammad smiles and rubs his hands together like he's got some evil plot brewing.

"What do you say?" Harry says to Noah. "You up for getting a little dirty in the grass?"

"Definitely," Noah agrees.

"What about you?" Harry asks me next.

"Mmhmm … yeah, I'm thinking no." Because wrestling with these three sounds like a disaster waiting to happen. "But I'll do some yoga outside."

Harry weighs his head back and forth. "All right, fine. I'll get changed then." He rises quickly from the table and is out of the room in a flash.

Mohammad glances down at his pants. "I should probably change too," he says, getting up.

"Sounds good," Noah says.

We're the only two in workout clothes, so neither of us needs to change.

IT'S NOT LONG before Harry comes tearing back into the dining room, wearing shorts and a sweatshirt that are a good two sizes too small for him.

"What do you have on?" I laugh, noticing that his pants barely come down to his ankles.

"I figured the best way to win my match is by distraction," Harry admits.

"Yeah?" Noah prompts, not looking convinced.

"That, and I didn't pack enough workout clothes." Harry rolls his eyes.

"I think you look great," I cut in. "I actually like the look. It's giving me *Grease* vibes. When everything was short and tight."

Harry grins. "It does show off my figure," he says, his blue eyes sparkling.

Once Mohammad is changed, we all make our way outside. Harry and Noah decide to go first, and I have to fight the urge to sit and watch them. Instead, I move a little farther away and get started on yoga.

I lie on my back, pulling my legs in toward my chest before taking it into a twist. I do cat and cow poses to make sure my spine is loose before pushing up into downward dog. I take myself through one flow, peeking over at Noah and Harry every chance I get.

Noah currently has Harry in a headlock.

I look back down at the grass and try to clear my mind.

"Stick that butt up!" Mohammad shouts, walking up to me.

"Mohammad"—I laugh, waving him away—"I'm trying to focus."

"I am focused and completely serious," he says, squatting next to me like he's my workout coach. "Now, pull your chest toward your knees. Extend those legs. And it's time to flip the dog!" He laughs, not able to control himself.

"Oh my God, how do you even know these positions?!" I burst out laughing and have to come down onto my knees.

"It's yoga," he replies. "It's all *tight clothes and butts in the air*. I've done my research."

"He jacks off to yoga videos," Harry calls out jokingly.

Well, I think he's joking.

I look over, noticing that he and Noah have taken a break.

"Seriously?" I tease, turning my attention back to Mohammad.

"No," he says, waving Harry off. But both Harry and Noah come over to join us. "Well, maybe once. It started off innocently enough ..."

"I love this story." Noah smiles, sitting down next to me.

"Let's hear it," I prompt.

"I was just trying to figure out what all the fuss was about. Figured if all the girls were raving about it, I needed to see what the deal was. Especially after I saw a few girls walking down the hallway after yoga class in those tight outfits." Mohammad grins shamelessly.

"Of course you did." I laugh.

"Anyway, I figured I'd watch a few videos. Get good at the poses and then crash the class. So, I went on Google, found a woman teaching a class, and was completely mystified. She was hot. Like, *hot*."

"And thus the ..." I say.

"Self-pleasure." Harry giggles.

Mohammad rolls his eyes. "Of course I got hot and bothered. I mean, the positions. The butt in the air. The tight clothes. The breathing," Mohammad says, sounding more and more breathless himself.

"All right, rein it in," I tell him, my eyes going wide.

"Anyway, after all that, I realized I could skip the class and just watch the videos at home instead." Mohammad smiles.

"He even came over to show us," Harry says, looking to Noah.

"I remember," Noah says, losing the color in his face.

"It wasn't that big of a deal," Mohammad says, shaking his head.

"It was a nightmare!" Noah replies.

Mohammad rolls his eyes before glancing at me. "I went to Noah's to show them. Decided to pull it up on the telly for the big full-screen effect when Noah's mum came out of nowhere. We'd thought she was gone. She ended up making us get on the floor, and we did the whole routine with her," Mohammad says, a shiver running through him.

"You still had a chubby the entire time," Harry howls.

"It was creepy," Noah agrees, looking distraught.

"It was bad," Harry agrees. "We should have watched it in Noah's room. I don't know why we didn't just watch it in your room."

"Mohammad was too excited," Noah says, biting his lip. "No pun intended."

"I was just trying to share my find. Next time I find a pot of gold, I'll make sure to keep it to myself," Mohammad replies, scowling.

"If you find a pot of gold, I *definitely* want to know about it." Harry chuckles.

Mohammad just rolls his eyes again. "Come on," he says, getting up. "I'm ready for my turn."

"Ready to fight?" Harry asks, his blue eyes coming alive.

"Wrestle," Noah corrects.

"Whatever. Let's do this!" Mohammad shouts, running onto the grass.

Harry runs after him, and they get set in position.

"I'd better go make sure they play fair," Noah says to me, sounding like he doesn't want to leave my side.

"Go," I say, nodding toward them. "Or someone will actually get hurt. I think I might call my dad. Check in."

Noah nods. "Say hi for me," he says, getting up.

I watch him walk over to Harry and Mohammad and switch from sweet Noah—at least with me—to very serious Noah.

I pull out my phone and dial my dad's number.

"Hey, Dad," I say when he picks up.

"Hi, sweetie. How are you?"

"Great." I smile, glancing over at Mohammad and Harry, who are now fighting. And I have to admit, Mohammad is doing great. "We're just hanging out. I'm doing yoga."

"That sounds nice. It's your last day there, right?"

"Yeah, last day." And the thought immediately makes me sad. Because I don't want to leave.

"Our flight leaves tomorrow," my dad says, pulling me out of my thoughts.

"Shit."

"Language, Mal."

I shake my head, trying to clear it. "I mean, shoot."

All of a sudden, Mohammad shouts at Harry, completely ignoring the rules and tackling him.

"What's going on over there?" my dad asks, apparently hearing the commotion.

Harry screams back before Noah shouts at them to play by the rules.

"They're wrestling." I frown. "Well, at least, they're supposed to be."

"Interesting," my dad says.

"Yeah … but they look happy," I reply, tugging at a piece of grass.

"So, aside from the wrestling, how have things been?"

I glance up to Noah and think about our weekend.

"Things have been really good. I've had a great weekend."

"That's … nice to hear."

"It is, Dad," I say with a smile. "We watched the sunrise this morning. And then Harry and I have a party we have to go to tonight. Something his family asked us to do. We head back into the city tomorrow."

"That's nice of you to go," my dad says. "How is Harry?"

"He's happy. He loves being out of the city. Away from his family. They don't have the best relationship," I say, wanting to be honest.

"That's a shame. He seems like a great boy."

"He is." I can't help but agree.

"I'm looking forward to meeting your friends," my dad goes on.

"Me too! I can't wait. Oh, I almost forgot. Noah said to say hi for him. He's excited to meet you and Mom."

"Tell him hello for us and Mohammad too. And remind Harry of our drink when he's back from Shanghai," my dad says cheerfully.

"Okay." I nod and try to force a smile on my face.

"Love you, sweetie. Have a good day."

"Love you too. I'll see you and Mom soon," I reply before ending the call. And immediately, my stomach is in knots.

I'm not sure if it's because of their arrival or the fact that my dad clearly has a thing for Harry.

And speaking of Harry, what are his expectations for tonight? Because it suddenly hits me.

We are going to this party alone.

Like, *alone.*

All dressed up.

With me as his date.

I suddenly swallow.

Mohammad runs up to me, apparently done with wrestling.

"Was that your dad?" he asks, sitting down next to me in the grass.

"Yeah. They fly out tomorrow," I reply, suddenly feeling very, very nervous.

"That's great. You'll both be traveling to London then."

I blink. "Yeah, I guess so …"

Mohammad pats my knee and gives me a sympathetic smile. "It will be all right."

I nod, wishing I could believe him.

"All right, Mal," Noah says, walking over to me. "You're up."

"I'm not fighting you," I reply, shaking my head.

"Would you fight me?" Mohammad asks.

I turn to him, sizing him up. "Actually, yeah!"

"What?" Noah laughs.

"I already know with you, I'm going to lose. At least with Mohammad, I might have a chance at winning," I reply.

"Hey!" Mohammad's mouth falls open.

"Damn," Harry says. "That was brutal."

"I've been watching you all fight. Noah is too picky about the rules. At least Mohammad and I could spar around. Have fun," I reply.

"I'm still insulted," Mohammad says.

Noah extends his hand out to me. "Come on. I'll be gentle."

I narrow my eyes at him. "Just like you were gentle, throwing me into the lake?" I question. "I think not."

Noah rolls his eyes, but he keeps his hand out for me to take. "I was gentle. I was also determined, but ..."

I let out a huff. "Fine."

I take his hand and let him pull me to standing.

But before I know what's happening, Harry shouts, "*Go*," and Noah picks me up, and then I'm on my back in the grass.

"You said you'd be gentle!" I growl. "You didn't even give me time to get set up."

"Oh, you've got a fight stance?" Noah asks, amusement flashing across his face.

I get up from the grass, wiping my hands on my pants.

"Maybe I do!" I reply, crouching down like I'm a tiger, ready to pounce.

"Look, I want this to be a fair fight, but I'm not just going to let you win, okay?" Noah says. "You're strong. You've got a lot of energy. You just need to learn to harness it."

"Oh, I know *exactly* who I want to take my energy out on right now," I reply.

And then I attack him. I jump on him, hanging on for dear life as he spins me around.

"What are you, a koala?" Noah laughs, but I know he's struggling to get me off.

"I'm not playing by the rules," I tell him, suddenly letting go.

Then, we come face-to-face, and I charge him. Noah looks at me in shock, and at the last second, I drop onto my knees, crawl between his legs, and press on his back enough to push him over.

"Oh shit!" Mohammad calls out as Noah falls.

"I thought I was going to squash you," Noah says from the grass, shaking his head.

"Not my fault you're *losing*." I laugh.

Noah narrows his eyes at me. "Fine, we will fight dirty."

Noah springs up from the grass and picks me up into the air. I try to wiggle out of his grip, but before I can, he has me back on the ground, pinned below him.

"You're so annoying!" I grumble.

But Noah lets go of me and quickly pulls me back to my feet, and then we're off again.

And again.

I jump on him.

He pins me down.

I run at him, screaming.

He falls over.

I start to tickle him.

He gives up.

The time flies by, but eventually, both Noah and I fall down onto the grass, panting.

"I think we should call it a tie," I say breathlessly.

"I think that's fair," Noah agrees.

I roll my head over to look at him. His chest is rising and falling quickly, and he looks just as out of breath as me.

"That was crazy!" Mohammad says, coming up to us, Harry in tow.

"She really gave it her all," Noah agrees.

I smile, feeling victorious. "I don't like to lose."

"Fucking hell, you really don't." Harry plops down onto the grass beside me, outstretching his legs in front of him. He leans back onto his elbows and crosses one ankle atop the other.

"She really doesn't," Noah replies.

"I'm just glad I wasn't the one getting pounded on," Harry says.

I glance over at him, seeing a playful smirk on his lips.

"I'm not sure she *pounded* on me," Noah says. "She did good. Really good. But honestly, I couldn't very well toss her onto her back."

My mouth falls open at his words.

"Don't try to downplay my skills," I tell him.

"Trust me, Noah can say whatever he wants. But we all saw what we saw." Mohammad laughs out.

Noah rolls his eyes, but he doesn't look too upset.

"You're lucky you had witnesses," Harry agrees.

"All right, all right," Noah says, waving them off. "We get it."

Harry laughs before giving Noah a friendly shove.

"So, you have that party tonight, right?" Mohammad asks, directing his question to Harry.

Harry lets out a deep sigh. "Unfortunately."

"I didn't realize I was such a boring date prospect." I can't help but laugh at Harry's dramatic response.

"I didn't mean that," Harry says, outstretching his hand to take mine. He gives it a quick squeeze. "Of course, it will be nice, having you there. But I'm not thrilled about spending our last night here at the Burtons' estate, just to please my parents."

"It's what got us here, right?" Noah says, picking at a piece of grass.

"That was the deal." Harry nods.

"So, you two are going as ... what?" Mohammad asks, coming right out with it.

"Friends," Harry answers.

"But she's your date?" Mohammad pushes.

I glance at him, trying to figure out what answer he's looking for.

"I'm going to tell my parents once we're in Shanghai that we"—Harry points between me and himself—"decided to be friends. So, yes, technically, tonight, Mallory is my date."

"How do you think your parents will react to that?" Noah

asks.

And his question catches me off guard. If anything, he should be upset that Harry hasn't told his parents we broke up. Or that he sort of fibbed about us still being together when he asked them if we could go away this weekend.

But he doesn't seem to care.

Harry shrugs. "Doubt they'll care. I think they couldn't give two fucks about who I date, if it's of my own choosing. If anything, they'll be pleased. Will probably try to shove some new girl down my throat."

"Hopefully, that's the last thing on their mind with everything else going on," Mohammad says.

"Hopefully," Harry agrees.

I chew on my lip, not sure what to say. Because it sort of bothers me that Harry's parents don't like me. They don't even know me. Even if Harry and I are just friends, I would hope that they would at least respect me. But I guess when his mom invited some girl to try to win him over at the cocktail party, knowing I'd be there, I should have gotten the hint.

"Well, at least it will be sorted soon," Noah says, pulling me out of my thoughts.

"Anyway, speaking of the party, I need to go into town for a haircut," Harry says, running his hands back through his hair.

"Really?" I ask. Because his hair looks great.

"Yeah, I'd rather get it done now, so I'm not getting it cut in Shanghai," Harry explains. "I'll run into town, pick up some more fags while I'm out, and then we can have a big lunch when I'm back."

"Sounds good," Mohammad says, getting up.

"Are we eating dinner there tonight?" I ask, curious about the plan.

"They'll serve dinner." Harry nods.

"I'll come into town with you," Noah says to Harry.

"Yeah?" Harry asks, his face flashing with genuine surprise.

"Yeah," Noah says, standing up.

He grabs on to Harry's hand and pulls him up. Then, he turns to me and extends his other hand. I take it and am standing a moment later.

"Let's change then and get going," Harry says, leading us all into the house.

I bump Mohammad's shoulder.

"Want to sit in the living room?" I ask him.

"Sounds good."

"I'll have Gerald bring out another pot of coffee," Harry says.

"That would be great." I smile at him.

"See you in a bit," Harry says, going to his room.

Noah and Mohammad follow me into the living room.

I plop down onto the couch, grateful to be off my feet.

Mohammad falls down into a low-slung chair. He kicks off his shoes before putting his feet up.

"This feels so good," I say, stretching out my body.

"Think you'll be sore?" Noah asks, sitting down next to me.

"Probably," I admit.

"Me too." He laughs. "You were great."

"I appreciate that." I smile over at him.

Noah leans in toward me and gives me a quick kiss on the cheek.

I'm slightly relieved that he didn't go in for a *full on the lips* one in front of Mohammad.

"I should go change. Stay out of trouble while we're gone," Noah says, getting up from the couch and shooting me a wink.

"No promises!" I call out.

I watch Noah leave the room and can't contain the smile that comes onto my face.

"You two shagged, didn't you?" Mohammad asks when Noah's gone.

"What? No."

"You can tell me," Mohammad says, looking slightly hurt.

"Aw, Mohammad. I know I can. But we haven't had sex."

Mohammad's face flashes with confusion. "Why not?"

"Noah really wants us to take our time," I say, repeating what Noah told me. "It's new."

"But when are you ever going to have a better opportunity? Once you get back and move home, you're done for."

And he makes a fair point.

"I know," I agree. "I keep trying to tell Noah that. But he wants to take it slow."

"How slow?" Mohammad asks, his eyebrows shooting up.

"Well, not *that* slow. I mean, things are progressing between us." I smile, thinking of last night. "But honestly, Noah can be so confusing …"

Mohammad sits up with interest. "Spill."

I glance over my shoulder, wanting to make sure that no one can hear us.

"I'll change the subject if anyone comes in the room," Mohammad says, understanding my hesitation.

"I don't know how I'm feeling. Nothing is making sense! One second, I'm agreeing with Noah, wanting to wait. Then, the next, I'm naked and trying to seduce him." I glance up at Mohammad. "It's wrong. I know."

"There's nothing wrong with that." Mohammad beams.

"Morally, there is. But it's just so intense. I mean, I say one thing, but my body has a mind of its own. I agree with him that we should wait, but then, what are we even waiting

JILLIAN DODD

for? I know Noah cares about me. Granted, it would be a little weird, doing that for the first time in Harry's house …" I say, trying to think through things.

"There is that." Mohammad nods.

"But still," I huff.

"Despite the freak-out, you seem happy."

"I am."

"That's good, isn't it?"

"Really good," I tell him.

Mohammad taps his chin. "Do you think you and Noah are going to be together, or is this just a hot hookup weekend? You know, get it out of the system."

"I'd say, long-term. At least, that's what it feels like. You know Noah; he can be … intense."

"In a good way?" Mohammad asks.

"In an *I'm going to claim your soul as mine forever* kind of way. I mean, I never thought I wanted that with love. I wanted something grounded. Focused," I try to explain.

"That's Noah though. He gives his full attention to a few limited things," he replies.

"It's intimidating sometimes," I admit.

"What do you mean?" Mohammad asks, but quickly, his expression shifts.

He looks to the door, and I follow his gaze to Gerald. He's got a tray filled with coffee and more cups.

"Thanks," Mohammad says when he sets them on the table between us, filling our cups.

I wait until he's out of the room to continue.

"I missed him a lot when we were having trouble as friends. And now that I get him, plus all this other stuff, it's amazing. But what if I lose him? Losing him as a friend, I could barely handle it. And what about once we become more? And to make it worse, Noah thinks I'm going to hurt him," I say, taking a sip of the coffee.

"Why do you think you'll lose him?"

"I just worry about it," I say with a shrug.

"You don't feel safe with him?" Mohammad asks.

"I didn't say that …"

"You did, Miss America. Did Noah tell you he thought you'd hurt him?"

I frown, wishing we didn't have to talk about this.

For one, it's embarrassing. And personal. And I know it should stay between me and Noah.

But I really need someone to talk it through with.

"He thinks that my heart is still split between him and Harry. He knows I … care about him. And that I have chosen him. But he thinks we should wait for sex until I'm *totally sure*—whatever that means." I shake my head, frustrated Noah would think I still have those kinds of feelings for Harry.

"Damn. He's putting down some boundaries," Mohammad says, admiration in his voice.

"Apparently … but I don't think we need them."

"Doesn't matter though. Noah does. And until you can prove to him that you and Harry aren't anything, I don't think he'll give in."

"But we aren't anything," I reply.

"Everyone can see you care for him," Mohammad counters.

"Of course I do. I love him. But I …"

"Love Noah too," Mohammad finishes. He tilts his head. "Why can't you say it?"

"I don't know. It just seems like a lot. I'm scared of losing myself to him. I'm scared of losing him. Noah makes me feel a lot. I don't always know what to do with it."

Mohammad waves off my comment. "I think you should just have fun. If you love Noah, tell him. It will solve your problems, get you laid, and make him feel secure."

I lean back into the couch, wondering if Mohammad's right.

Is it really that simple?

I know I love Noah.

And I know he loves me.

What I can't figure out is, why am I not ready to tell him?

Do I just need more time? Like he said, we aren't in a rush. Maybe Noah and I are the same, but different. He doesn't want to rush into sex. I don't want to rush into love.

In the end, we're both scared of getting hurt.

I just can't figure out … who is going to do the hurting?

What is it, if anything, that is standing in our way?

Simple is nice.
12:30PM

AFTER NOAH AND Harry get back from town, we eat lunch outside with blankets on our laps and the heating lamps on.

I changed into a cream sweater and jeans, knowing that I didn't want to be cold. I also took the time to cut up the coupons I'd made Noah the other day when we were doing our homework. After cutting them, I folded them in half and then put them into a small silk bag I had brought my jewelry in. I stuck the bag in my pocket, knowing that I wanted to give it to Noah today so he'd know how special he was to me.

Especially before I go off tonight as Harry's date.

At lunch, we sip on buttery white wine that's paired with a creamy pasta, fresh bread, and sticky toffee pudding. It's way too much food for lunch, but it's absolutely delicious.

With a full stomach, Harry suggests playing a game of

FIFA. We all move into the living room, taking our usual spots on the couch.

I consider asking them to play, just so I won't be so bored, but I don't really want to play.

Instead, I go get the book that Helen packed for me, and then go back downstairs and start reading.

I'm immediately drawn into it.

Even though it's cheesy and over the top, it's supposed to be. Life and love in books are simple. There's a story arc. They fall in love, something huge happens, and just when you think everything is lost, they find their way back to one another.

Simple.

And sometimes, simple is nice.

"Do you want to go for a walk?" Noah asks me, giving up the controller so Mohammad can play.

I mark the page of the book. "Why not?"

"I think it would be good to stretch our legs, especially after that feast," Noah says, stretching upward.

"Lunch was amazing," I agree, getting up from the couch. I follow Noah outside. "So, where do you want to explore?"

"I'm thinking the bedroom," Noah teases, pinching at my waist.

"I think that's a *great* idea." I laugh and grab on to his hand, trying to turn us around to head back inside.

But Noah keeps his feet planted firmly on the ground.

"I thought you were looking a little bored. Figured you could use some attention, one-on-one." Noah smiles before pulling me into a kiss.

I kiss him back, a grin sliding onto my face.

"I wasn't bored. I was *reading*," I correct.

"That romance book. Anything good?"

"Honestly, it's great. I never thought I'd be one for over-the-top historical romances. But there's something about them that I like."

"Well, you are a romantic." Noah squeezes my hand.

"True. And anyway, I'd happily stop reading to spend time with you," I reply as we walk.

"Are you bored of the video games yet?"

I roll my eyes. "So bored. I can't stare at a screen like that for hours. I have no idea how you three do it."

"You're not just staring at a screen; there's a goal involved. Competition," Noah says.

"But wouldn't you rather be doing this?" I ask, pulling him to my lips for a kiss, "than playing stupid games?"

Noah chuckles, but he kisses me back.

"They're just different kinds of fun," he says against my lips.

"I'll remember that," I reply, shaking my head at him.

"Trust me, I know you will. You never forget anything I say." He takes my hand in his, leading us across the grass and toward the garden.

"Nope."

"Maybe Mohammad was right after all. Women have these powers, don't they?" he asks, flashing me a silly grin.

"Maybe we do," I agree. "You know, Mohammad is pretty useful himself. I had this whole plan to crack into your locker and put something in there last week in the hopes that you'd forgive me sooner. Mohammad was able to get me your locker combo."

"I have no doubt he did." Noah looks at me. "What were you going to put in there?"

"Granola bars." I smile.

"That probably would have helped," Noah admits.

"But then I wanted something more meaningful. And by the time I thought of anything, we'd sort of made up. Anyway, I made you something regardless."

I pull the bag out of my pocket, handing it to him.

Noah looks at me in shock.

"You made me a gift?" he asks, his voice sounding thick.

I nod.

"Thank you," he says, accepting the silk bag. "When did you have time for this?"

"Uh ... when we were working on our homework."

Noah arches an eyebrow at me. "You mean, when I was filling in both of our study guides?"

"You filled mine in too?" I ask, surprised.

"Partially," Noah answers. But then he looks back down at the silk bag.

"Open it. It's nothing big. Nothing of value. But ..."

I bite my lip, watching as he opens the bag, sticks his hand into it, and pulls out one of the folded pieces of paper.

"*A free lunch prepared by me,*" he reads aloud before looking at me.

"It's a coupon bag." I smile at him, hoping that he doesn't find it ridiculous. "Anytime you want a little treat or gift from me, you can pull out one of them and claim what's on it. So, I guess you've just gotten yourself lunch, prepared by yours truly."

Noah looks at me, his cheeks warming. "This is really thoughtful, Mal."

I immediately go red.

"It's silly, I know ..."

"It's not." Noah takes my hand in his. "It's sweet. And I love it."

"Yeah?" I ask, looking up at him.

"Yeah. Thoughtful and practical. It seems I just got a free lunch."

Noah grins at me, and I can't help but smile back at him too.

"Well, I'm glad you like it."

He pulls open the bag, peeking back inside. "So, what are some of the other coupons?" he asks, dipping his hand back in.

"You can only pull out one at a time!" I laugh, swatting at his hand.

But of course, he ignores me.

"*A full body massage*," he reads.

I laugh nervously. "Forgot about that one," I reply, biting my lip.

"Does that mean I have to be fully naked?" Noah asks, cupping my cheek.

"If you want," I reply breathlessly.

Noah brings his lips to mine, giving me a gentle kiss. I quickly deepen it, grabbing on to his sides.

"Speaking of which," I say after a few minutes, "let's talk logistics."

"About what?" Noah asks, taking my hand in his as we continue walking.

"About sex."

"You want to talk logistics about sex?" Noah asks, glancing at me.

"I want to be realistic. What happens if the mood strikes when we get back? How will that work? How are you going to have your big romance with me moving and your parents always home?"

"Logistically, we'll be fine," Noah says.

But it isn't an answer.

"How?"

"Let's say the mood strikes the day we get back, Tuesday," Noah says, causing my eyebrows to shoot up.

"Oh, it struck fast."

"Well, you are demanding. It's a possibility."

"Okay …"

"Then, we have your hotel."

"And if you win out on waiting?" I push.

"My parents go out for date nights pretty regularly," Noah replies, squeezing my hand.

"That's true," I admit.

"Mmhmm."

"And what if your parents decide to never leave the house again and mine are helicoptering with the move?" I ask, wanting to really think through this.

"Helicoptering?" Noah chuckles.

"You know …" I wave my finger in a circle over my head. "What if we never get privacy?"

"We will be fine, Mal. I promise. The right place will present itself at the right time."

"Because you want it to be special." I nod. Because that's such a Noah thing to say.

"Because it *is* special," Noah corrects.

"All right. You win. It will happen when it happens, and I'm sure when it does, it will be perfectly romantic," I say, knowing that's what Noah wants to hear.

"It will be romantic because it's with you," he says, wrapping his arm around me.

"We can do it all up for you. I'll get dressed up. We can share an amazing meal. Have a romantic evening. And then we can finally seal the deal," I say, causing Noah to laugh.

"Mal, I'm not looking for some fairy tale. I'd happily sleep with you … anytime. Anywhere."

"Yeah?" I ask, growing excited.

"Yeah." Noah nods. "Once we've taken that step, I'll want you all the time. I already do."

"That's good to know," I say, unable to control my grin.

"I'm glad you're happy. So, speaking of fancy nights out,

are you looking forward to tonight?"

I shrug. "I think it's just bound to happen. Was sort of a condition for us to come."

"I'm sure you'll have fun," Noah says.

"I don't know about fun … I guess Harry is good company. And if the house is anything like Harry's, it will be gorgeous. But I'd rather be hanging with you tonight."

"Me too," Noah says, his forehead creasing.

"And anyway, it's only a few hours. We will go, have a few drinks, probably eat some dinner, say polite hellos, and then leave."

"Yeah, it's only a few hours," Noah agrees, chewing on his lip.

"You all right?" I ask.

He clears his throat, glancing over at me. "Fine," he says.

But he doesn't look fine.

He doesn't look fine at all.

An ace night.
5:00PM

WE HEAD BACK inside and find Mohammad and Harry right where we left them. In front of the television. I grab my book, curling back up on the couch.

"So, are you two going to be bored tonight?" I ask Mohammad and Noah, causing Harry to look up in interest.

"Nah. I think we're going to make some more pizza and watch a movie."

"Sounds like an ace night," Harry says.

"Any night where I can eat on the couch is a win for me," Mohammad agrees. "Mum always makes us sit at the table.

She insists that we have to eat as a family. If I even tried to order a pizza, she'd have me grounded."

"But you said your parents do takeout sometimes," I counter, clearly remembering when Mohammad brought over some delicious food from one of his parents' restaurants.

"Of course, but it's not takeout from a shop. It's takeout from five-star restaurants. Mum is traditional. Always insists that we have to eat our greens and blah, blah, blah ..." Mohammad rolls his eyes. "She's always going on about how, as the oldest, I have to set an example for my sisters."

I raise my eyebrows at him. "That's actually really smart."

Mohammad glares at me.

"I mean, obviously, the no pizza thing is a little extreme, but it's good she wants you to have a healthy diet. I think it's important families eat together too. You'll appreciate it when you're older."

"Yeah, but until then, the only time I get junk food is when I'm out," Mohammad grumbles.

"Thus, the pizza," I say, then turn toward Noah. "What about you, Mr. Healthy? Are you okay with eating pizza two nights on one trip? I figured you'd think it might kill you," I tease.

Noah lets out a deep, reverberating laugh. "Mohammad's right; we're on holiday. We're allowed to let loose. Plus, we've been exercising, so I'm not worried."

"Exactly. Enjoy yourself, mate," Harry agrees before checking his watch. He pauses the game and turns to me. "We—well, *you* should probably start to get ready."

"What time is it?" I ask.

"Five o'clock," Harry answers. "The car will pick us up at six-thirty, and we'll be there at seven."

"That's plenty of time," I reply. "But, yeah, I need to shower and whatnot. I'd rather take my time than be rushed."

Harry nods and says, "If you want, we can all have a parting drink before we leave."

"Works for me," Noah agrees.

"Same," Mohammad replies.

"I'll change now then," Harry says, getting up.

I get up, too, tucking my book under my arm. I pat Mohammad on the shoulder and run my hands through Noah's hair for a second before leaving the living room. I start off for my room, but something about tonight weighs on my mind.

So, I go to Harry's room and knock on the door.

"Come in."

I find Harry standing at his wardrobe, pulling out his suit for tonight.

"Hey," I say, drawing his eyes away from his clothes to me.

"Hey," Harry says with surprise. He puts the suit back and walks over to me. "Everything all right?"

I press my lips together, hoping that my question isn't going to hurt him.

"I was just wondering, am I supposed to be ... your girlfriend tonight?" I ask.

Harry sucks in a breath. "I'm sure that's what they were told. But obviously, that's strictly in title. I don't expect you to ..." Harry stops himself, worry flashing across his face.

"Okay." I nod.

"I do appreciate you doing this," he says, his eyes finding mine.

"I know you do. And I'm happy to be here for you."

"You just wish it were only as friends," Harry says.

"I'm not sure lying like this is making things easier—for anyone."

"It's not like we're pretending here," Harry says, motioning to the house. "And I don't expect some big, public display there. You're just my plus-one."

"That's true. I just wondered about your expectations tonight."

"I'm sorry to put you in this position," he says, glancing away. "I never would have done it if I had known about you and Noah."

"Noah wants us to tell our families when we get back." I don't know why the words came out of my mouth, but they did.

"Really?" Harry asks.

"I think he wants to make it official. Make everything clear," I explain.

"Shouldn't you be happy about that?" Harry asks, looking at me oddly.

His head is tilted to the side, and I can't read his expression.

"I just mean that if our parents know, then you'll have to tell your parents."

"I already told you I would ..." Harry says, his forehead creasing. "Look, if it's too much, you don't have to come with me tonight. I can tell them you came down with something."

"That's not what I want," I tell him, shaking my head. "We will have a great time. I just wanted to talk first."

Harry puts his hands on my shoulders and says, "I'm glad we talked."

"Me too. And what girl wouldn't want to get dressed up for a night out?" I say, slapping his shoulder. "Besides, we always have a good time together."

Harry smiles broadly. "I promise tonight will be no exception."

"You promise to deliver?" I tease.

"I always do," Harry says with a wink.

I leave his room, feeling better about tonight. I don't

know if I'm worried about anything or if I should be, but I'm glad we cleared the air and that Harry knows my concerns. Because now that he knows, I can enjoy tonight.

We can have fun, like we always do.

I head upstairs and hop in the shower. I wash my body and hair quickly before getting out and toweling dry.

I decide to start on my makeup first.

I run back into the bedroom and pull out my dress to figure out how I should do my makeup. I decide to go light on my skin, focusing on my eyes. After applying foundation and concealer, I add some rosy pink to my cheeks, knowing I'm going to need the lightness to balance my eye makeup.

I start out by dusting over my lids in a gold shimmer, adding in a mixture of warm browns and greens. I line my eyes with a black pencil and apply two coats of mascara. My hair has dried straight, but I want something different. I pull out my straightener, giving the ends a small bend so it doesn't look so straight and blunt.

I brush my teeth, line my lips, and add some lipstick before putting on a few spritzes of perfume. I check the time. It's close to six, so I decide to go ahead and get into my dress now. That way, once we meet downstairs for our drink, I won't have to come back up here.

I pack my clutch and lay my shoes on the bed before stepping into the long, flowing dress I packed for the occasion. It's the one I bought in London. The one I fell in love with instantly.

I didn't have an occasion for it at the time, but I couldn't pass it up.

It's a mixture of metallic earth tones with a deep V in the front that is matched in the back. I zip it up and love the way it feels. How it moves effortlessly around me, metallic gold and gray threads falling in alternating lines down to the floor.

It cinches in at my waist, flowing over my hips delicately.

I sit down on the edge of the bed and put on metallic heels. Before checking myself over in the mirror, I realize there's one thing missing.

The necklace Harry gave me.

I pull it out of the drawer, opening up the box. I secure it around my neck before walking to the mirror.

I look myself over and feel so many things.

The first is that I look beautiful.

No.

I *feel* beautiful.

This dress fits me in all the right places, and the colors make my hair look bright and shiny. The necklace sparkles against my skin, drawing attention to my collarbone.

Movement in the hallway snaps me out of my thoughts. And a second later, I hear Noah's door open and close.

I grab my clutch off the bed before heading to Noah's room.

I know that I should talk to him alone before we go downstairs for drinks.

Before I leave tonight.

I knock on his door.

Noah opens it quicker than I expected. His eyes find mine, but a second later, he's looking me over.

"Hey," I say. "I just wanted to talk before we go down for drinks."

I'm not sure if Noah hears me. He stands rigid, his eyes trailing back up my figure. When he finally works his way back to my face, his eyes have darkened, and he licks his lips.

"You look so beautiful, Mal."

"Thank you," I say, suddenly feeling breathless.

Noah takes my hand and pulls me closer, so our chests are almost touching.

"What did you want to talk about?" he asks, his eyes focused on my lips.

I place my hands on his chest and look up at him. "How are you feeling about tonight?"

Noah's jaw tightens for a brief moment, but he quickly relaxes it. He exhales, his warm breath dancing across my face.

"I'm not thrilled that you are Harry's date," he admits.

"Are you having flashbacks to the cocktail party last week?" I ask, growing nervous. Because I want Noah to trust me. But I also don't blame him for feeling uncomfortable.

"No. I think a lot has changed since then," he says, running his hands up and down my arms.

"Things have changed," I agree. "I'm doing this tonight for Harry. But I won't do it again."

Noah gives me a sad smile that makes my chest ache.

"Don't worry about that. Just have a fun time. I know Harry is looking forward to having you there. It will take some of the pressure off of him. He does well with having a friend as a buffer," Noah says knowingly.

Noah is saying all the right things, things a good friend would say, but I can tell his heart isn't behind his words.

"Noah, you know I'm yours, right?" I ask, lacing my hands around his neck.

"I know."

"And you know that you have nothing to worry about?" I ask again.

Noah presses his lips together and glances away. "I'd rather we didn't talk about that."

"What do you mean?"

Noah steps backward, putting some space between us.

"Do you remember the equation I was talking about in detention last week?" Noah asks.

I follow him into his room, trying to rack my brain for

what he's talking about.

"Sort of … you told me that people couldn't be put into equations or, well, boxes," I say, finally remembering.

"Right. Well, I've been having trouble figuring out the role of one of the variables in the equation."

"Okay …" I say, not sure where he is going with this.

"I thought you might be able to help me," he continues.

"With the variable?"

"Yeah."

"Okay, shoot," I tell him.

"You see a future with Harry, don't you?"

My face immediately drains, turning white at his question, and my body starts to tingle, like I could pass out.

"Noah …" I say, reaching out for him.

"Please don't shy away from the answer," Noah says, not taking my hand.

I drop it to my side. "Of course I see Harry in my future. But that's different from seeing a future *with* him."

"Mal, when we get back, I want to properly date you," Noah says, moving closer and taking both of my hands in his.

"I know."

"I don't want any more confusion. For you. For Harry. Or for me." He looks down at me through dark lashes.

"So …" I say, wondering where he's going with this.

"So, I would ask you to be mine," Noah finishes, stroking my hand.

"You'd ask me to be your girlfriend?" I question.

"Yes."

I look at Noah and instantly feel confused.

"Are you only telling me this because I'm about to go on a date with Harry tonight?"

"I thought it wasn't a date," Noah replies. But then he adds, "I know you've needed some time to adjust, but going forward—"

"You want clarity," I finish. "We would make it official. Tell our parents. The whole thing."

"I know that's scary for you—" he says, but I cut him off.

"Deal," I say. "I'll do it."

Noah immediately looks shocked. And relieved. "Really?"

"Surprised I gave in so quickly?" I laugh, squeezing his hands.

He blinks a few times. "Honestly, yeah. I thought you'd take some convincing."

"What kind of convincing?" I say, flashing him a grin.

"Something that involved showing you how serious I was about this. About you." Noah dips his head, and his lips find my neck. He kisses down it, leaving a trail of warmth. His mouth works its way across my collarbones and my shoulder, and even dips down to the bare skin in the vee of my dress.

"Oh, wow," I mumble, my head falling back.

Noah breaks his lips away from my skin.

"Okay, maybe I *am* slightly jealous." Noah pulls down one of the straps on my dress before sprinkling kisses across my chest. "I just can't believe how beautiful you look. And you smell amazing."

"You're making me flush," I reply, feeling light-headed.

"Good," Noah says, his lips finding mine again.

He kisses me deeply but doesn't push it any further.

"We should probably get downstairs for that drink, huh?" I suggest, knowing that time isn't on our side.

"Right," Noah replies.

And I can see him trying to pull himself together.

He stands up straighter. Pushes his hand back through his hair.

But he looks sad again.

"Don't worry. We'll have plenty of time to continue this

when I get back," I say, giving him my best smile.

"Forever with you won't be nearly long enough, Mal." It's all Noah says.

"Noah … I …" My throat constricts, and I feel myself want to start crying.

I never expected that one day, I'd be cared for in the way that Noah cares for me.

I never expected to find this kind of intense love on a three-week study-abroad trip.

"I know." Noah smiles at me before pulling me back to his lips.

And I try to show him with a kiss how much he means to me.

"Come on," he finally says, taking my hand. "Let's get you downstairs. The sooner you're off, the sooner you'll be back."

WHEN WE GET downstairs, Harry and Mohammad are in the drawing room, drinks in hand. They both turn in our direction, probably hearing my heels clicking on the floor.

Harry instantly smiles and stands up.

I smile back at him.

"You look great!" I say, taking in his look for the evening.

With his fresh haircut and in a three-piece suit, Harry doesn't just look good.

He looks *hot*.

"Thanks," he says, coming over to me and Noah. "Although, next to you, I might as well not exist. You look stunning."

"She does," Noah agrees.

I smile at both of them.

"Thank you. It's fun, getting dressed up."

"I'm even a little jealous now," Mohammad says, looking

me and Harry over. "You two look sharp together."

Harry walks over to the bar cart as Noah leads me to a free chair. I take a seat, expecting him to sit next to me, but he joins Harry in pouring a drink. A moment later, he's handing me a lowball glass of something that's a rich shade of amber. Harry comes back over with two glasses and gives one of them to Noah before sitting down. It feels strange, having both Mohammad and Noah dressed so casually while Harry and I are all dressed up.

I take a sip of the drink, watching as Noah does the same.

It's strong but not bad.

I expect us to joke and talk, but we all sort of sit in silence. I take another sip of the drink, wondering if I should say something.

"Excuse me, sir," Gerald says, stepping into the room. "The driver is ready at your convenience."

"Thank you, Gerald." Harry checks the time on his watch before downing the rest of his drink in one gulp.

I do the same.

"That's us off then," Harry says to me before looking at Noah and Mohammad. "See you two later, yeah?"

"Yeah," Noah says, standing up and slapping him on the back.

"Send photos," Mohammad replies.

"I will," I say, but my gaze instantly falls on Noah.

Harry must notice because he says, "I'll meet you out front, Mallory."

"Okay." I watch him leave before turning to Noah and quickly pulling him into a hug.

He hugs me back, his arms wrapping tightly around my waist.

"Have fun tonight," he whispers into my ear before placing a kiss on my cheek.

"I will. We will be back before you know it."

And then I do something I've never done before.

I kiss him on the lips, right here, in front of Mohammad.

It's a quick kiss, but it doesn't matter.

It is still a kiss with Noah.

I pull away and smile at him, happy to see he's practically radiating.

"See you soon," he says, giving my hand a squeeze before letting me go.

I walk out of the drawing room and through the entryway, meeting Harry just outside the front door. He's already lit up a cigarette and smoking it, casually leaning against the front of the house.

"Ready?" I ask him, moving to his side.

Harry looks up, his blue eyes growing brighter. He flicks the cigarette onto the gravel before putting it out with the bottom of his shoe.

Then, he takes my arm in his and leads me to the car.

I pretend.
7:00PM

WHEN WE ARRIVE at the house, I'm not surprised to find it's just as extraordinary as Harry's. The entire front of the place is lit up, and the Georgian architecture is amazing. It's like something out of a fairy tale. I roll down the window as we wait to get dropped off. Candles glow from every window, and exotic cars line the circular driveway.

"Wow," I breathe out.

"You ready for an evening of delight?" Harry teases, pulling my attention away from the window.

"It's gorgeous, Harry."

He glances out the window, a small smile pulling at his lips. "It is."

When we get to the entrance, the driver comes around, opening the door for us. Harry doesn't bother knocking on the grand front door, instead, he walks right into the foyer.

The first thing I notice is that the house smells amazing.

It reminds me of my apartment at Thanksgiving, when everything smells like butter and sugar and spice. Wreaths filled with fall foliage hang over the doorways and down the banister leading up to the second level.

"This house is incredible," I say, spinning around to take it all in.

"Thank you," a voice says.

I quickly look in front of us, seeing a tall, slender woman approaching us. She's wearing a beautiful burgundy silk jumpsuit, her stylized brown hair falling just below her shoulders. She smiles, looking from me to Harry.

"Lovely to see you, Harry," she says, pulling him into a hug.

"Lovely to see you. Thank you for the invitation," Harry says, giving her a quick kiss on each cheek. "I'd like to introduce you to my date, Mallory. Mallory, this is Mrs. Burton."

She pats Harry lightly on the chest, and then she turns to me and says, "Please, call me Andrea," as she shakes my hand.

"It's nice to meet you. Your home is absolutely stunning."

Andrea smiles widely. "Thank you, dear. It's been a lovely reprieve from the city. I spent too much time and energy on decorating for the evening, but I couldn't help myself."

"I think it was well worth it," I confide.

Andrea laughs and places her hand on my arm delicately.

"Ah, Harry!" a tall, good-looking man says, shaking Harry's hand. "It's great of you to join us tonight. I'm sorry your father couldn't be here, but we were thrilled when you accepted the invitation."

"I was pleased to accept it." Harry smiles at him. "It just so happened that we planned a visit to the country house for the same weekend."

"It was fate," Andrea says, shooting her husband a sly grin.

"Fate indeed," he agrees.

Harry turns to me. "Excuse me for being rude, Mr. Burton. I'd like to introduce you to Mallory."

Mr. Burton extends his hand to me.

"It's nice to meet you," I say, shaking it.

"You as well, Mallory. We hope you enjoy the evening," Mr. Burton says.

He glances over my shoulder and motions to someone. A moment later, a tray filled with flutes of champagne is being offered to us.

"Please," Andrea says, motioning for us to take one.

Harry and I both do, as do Andrea and Mr. Burton.

They raise their glasses to ours before taking a sip.

"We'd better make the rounds, but I'm sure we will get to chat later," Andrea says to me.

I nod at her.

"It was nice to meet you, Mallory," Mr. Burton says, looking distracted as another couple walks through the door.

"You too."

"Harry," he says, clapping his shoulder one more time before moving on to greet their new guests.

"Come on." Harry takes my hand, leading me farther into the house.

"They're really nice," I comment when we get into a grand drawing room.

Candles give the room a wonderful scent. A fire is glowing in the massive stone fireplace. It all makes me want to curl up in the corner with a good book and never leave.

"They are very nice. I'm not sure how they ended up being friends with my parents," Harry says, taking a gulp of his champagne.

"Maybe they knew each other from university or something," I suggest. "Although, now that I think about it, they seem younger than your parents."

"I'm sure our connection is business-related. Would you like to explore the house?"

"Yeah, let's make a round," I agree.

Harry keeps ahold of my hand and leads me through various rooms. When we get to the dining room, I count twenty-four chairs, and I can't help but stare at the table in awe. Silverware sparkles in the candlelight, and there are centerpieces dripping with autumnal leaves and miniature pumpkins along with fall-colored foliage and florals. It suddenly hits me that Halloween is in just over a week.

Harry and I finish our champagne about the time that the announcement is made for us to proceed to the dining room.

Which is good timing, as we are already here. We find our seats right in the center of the table.

All of the food is served family-style, which partially surprises me and partially doesn't. The Burtons seem down-to-earth even though their house is quite extravagant. I glance at Andrea, noticing her smiling at something someone said.

Harry starts out chatting with the man to his right, then to me on his left, but pretty soon, that formality ends, and we wind up talking in a group with those around us.

Harry is charming. And funny.

He's a good time, and everyone knows it.

I think it's because when he smiles at you, you have to

smile back. There isn't any hesitation in Harry's words or his responses. He makes you feel comfortable but excited at the same time.

There isn't any question of his sincerity. It's just there.

No matter who he's talking to, he pulls them in with his laughter and questions and stories. And honestly, it's kind of amazing to witness.

"You having fun?" Harry asks me during dinner.

"Actually, a lot." I smile at him. "For such a fancy occasion, this is laid-back. I love it."

"They've got a good crowd here," Harry agrees, taking a sip of wine.

"They do. Plus, I always have fun when I'm with you."

"Yeah?" Harry asks, his forehead creasing.

"Yeah. I mean, don't you think so?" I ask. Because Harry suddenly seems off.

"We do. It's just a shame that things have to be … weird between us again," Harry admits before taking a bite of roasted potato.

"I don't want them to be," I say sincerely.

"I guess change does that."

"But I thought we said no matter what, we wouldn't let that happen?" I question, suddenly losing my appetite.

"Some things I can't control," Harry replies, his face losing a little of its sparkle. "You and Noah aren't … uh, well, are you?" Harry clears his throat, setting down his knife and fork.

My eyes immediately go wide.

Because is Harry asking if we're … *sleeping* together?

"No," I answer. "But, Harry …"

"Right." Harry nods. "Forget I asked. It's not my place or my business."

I let out a sigh. "It's sort of your business, seeing as we're staying at your house." I take a sip of my own wine, feeling the need for a drink.

"I just ..." Harry starts but immediately stops himself.

"You what?" I ask, grabbing on to his hand.

Because I don't like seeing him struggle like this. I can tell he's having a hard time, saying whatever it is he wants to say. But I want him to be open with me.

Honest.

"I remember the way you reacted to me on Thursday, in the bathroom. It's hard for me because you want this sometimes. I know you do."

I press my lips together, wishing he weren't bringing this up.

Here.

Now.

In the middle of dinner.

"Want what, Harry?"

He looks at me, his blue eyes filling with something I don't understand.

"Me. You've made me think about things the past few days. All your talk of being who I want to be ... it seems to be wearing off on me."

"That was the intended effect," I say, giving him a hint of a smile.

"I love you for that." Harry picks his fork and knife up, moving his attention back to his food.

"I love you too," I say easily.

"Even before you were supposed to leave for New York, I told you that I loved you. That seeing you in New York wouldn't be a problem. You know I still love you. You've shown up for me so many times. Have given me so many chances. Sometimes, I wonder if I hadn't hurt you over and over, if you would be dating Noah right now. I pushed you to him because I wasn't stable. I realize that."

"Oh, Harry." I shake my head at him.

"It's true. I know it is. I also know that I broke up with you because of his feelings. But I instantly regretted it. When he told me that you two were going to date, I understood. I acted like I did at least."

"But it hurt," I say in understanding.

"Of course it did."

"I don't know what to say. How to make it better ..." I stumble over my words, not sure what Harry is looking for. What he wants.

"You don't need to say anything. You've been an angel to me, honestly. And I'm just realizing how terrible I was to you."

"You weren't terrible," I say, nudging his elbow with mine.

Harry tilts his head, not looking convinced. "Regardless, we had our issues. I think being friends might suit us better."

"It seems like it does," I agree.

Even Noah said that.

That Harry and I are closer now than we were when we were dating.

"Yeah. At least for now," Harry says, his blue eyes flicking up to mine.

"For now?" I question.

"We're young," Harry says.

And that's *all* he says.

I glance around the room, letting myself imagine it. Harry and I here as adults. Instead of sitting here as friends, we'd be ... more.

This could be our life.

Hosting dinner parties. Weekends at his country house.

I know Harry would make me happy. It's who he is.

But he's not Noah.

"Regardless, I care about you," I say, not going there with him.

"I know you do," he replies.

"And I don't want you to give up on love."

"You can't have it all," he says, looking distant.

"Yes, you can."

"I can pretend to," he says, letting out a chuckle. "Like I pretend my dad is actually proud of me when we're in public. Like I pretend you're still my girlfriend when we're here, like this. Like I pretend that you and Noah dating doesn't bother me. I can pretend everything is fine. That's what everyone wants anyway."

My mouth falls open, and I don't know what to say.

I thought he was okay with this. I thought he was okay with everything.

Has he been putting on a show this whole time?

In front of me? In front of Noah?

"I never want you to pretend when you're with me," I finally say, catching his gaze. I want him to know I'm being serious about this.

"I don't want to pretend with you either," he admits when Andrea stands up, capturing our attention.

"If you'd like to follow us, we have a little surprise," she says.

Everyone stands, follows her out of the dining room, down a hall that Harry and I haven't explored, and to an elegantly decorated ballroom.

A band starts playing.

There are tables set up on the perimeter, filled with various desserts along with a bar. Mr. and Mrs. Burton start dancing, wide smiles on both of their faces.

"This is unreal," I say to Harry, glancing up at the huge

antique chandeliers, but he doesn't seem surprised.

"Shall we?" he asks, offering me his hand.

And then, suddenly, we're dancing.

It makes me feel like I'm dreaming. Wearing this dress. Being at this party.

Dancing with Harry.

Everything is perfect.

I couldn't have imagined a more beautiful evening.

"You once told me that you wanted to get so lost that you couldn't remember who you were anymore," Harry says to me.

"You remember that?" I ask, thinking back to our date when we talked about traveling.

"It stuck with me," Harry admits.

"Why?"

"Because I feel the same. Sometimes, I wish that I could wake up in a different house. To different parents. To a different life," Harry says, glancing across the room.

"Do you really mean that?"

"Nah." Harry cracks a smile.

I bat at his chest. "You're such a brat."

Harry twirls me around before pulling me back toward him.

"I'm just messing with you. Of course I've felt like that before," Harry says.

"Well … I don't blame you. But my life would be a lot less exciting without you in it." I pull him closer. "I can't believe you leave tomorrow."

"Shanghai will be all right. What Noah said about taking ownership, it stuck with me. Besides, it's a great city."

"When do we have to leave tomorrow?" I ask, thinking about heading back into London.

And that I'm not ready to leave.

"Car will be here at ten o'clock," Harry says.

I frown.

"Not ready to go?"

"Not really," I reply.

"Me neither. This weekend has been …" Harry says, not finding the words.

"Have I changed your memories here?" I ask, looking up into his eyes.

"You have." He nods. "Of course you have."

Harry pulls me closer, his hand staying at my waist, the other connected to mine as we dance.

"Tonight isn't an act for me, you know. Having you as my date. There's a part of me that really likes this, Mallory."

"There's a part of me that really likes this too. But I'm not going to play pretend," I tell him.

"This doesn't have to be pretend," Harry says, his eyes slipping across my face.

"I think, sometimes, this all just feels too real for me," I say, needing air.

"Because you like it too," Harry replies.

"But to what end?" I ask. "Harry … it's not just about us anymore."

"Noah," Harry states. "What is it that you want?"

"I don't want to hurt anyone. I don't want to hurt you any more than I already have. And pretending like we're something when we aren't … Mohammad told me I needed to be careful. He said that sometimes, the fact that I care about you, well, it might make things confusing."

"I think I can figure out the difference," Harry replies flatly.

"I didn't mean it like that," I say, feeling my words get all jumbled in my mouth.

"Tell me what you meant then," Harry insists.

"Harry …" I shake my head.

Because I can't do this here.

We can't talk about this now.

"Come on. I'm in desperate need of a fag, and it's obvious you won't tell me what's bothering you until you've had another drink."

Before I have a chance to disagree, Harry is leading me across the dance floor. He stops at the bar and leans in toward the waiter. I don't hear what he asks for, but I see two crystal glasses, filled with dark liquid, set in front of us.

A second later, one glass is in my hand, and the other is in Harry's. He grabs my free palm, pulling me through the crowd of people toward double doors that lead out to a balcony. He pushes it open with his shoulder and then places his hand on my back, leading me outside.

I follow him in silence, and we end up leaning against a stone railing that looks out onto the grounds. There are lanterns lit outside, causing the whole area to emit a warm glow. A few feet away from us, two men are seated, smoking cigars and drinking. A laugh escapes from the party through an open window.

I look back at Harry. He's leaning back against the stone railing, his legs extended out, one foot crossed over the other. He pulls a cigarette out of the box in his hand and lights it. I watch him suck in a drag, his blue eyes finding mine as he exhales. He swallows and then holds up his crystal glass to me. I smile at him before clinking mine against it.

When the liquid hits my lips, it quickly warms me. It's a chilly night, but after dancing, the cool air feels nice. And with the help of whatever drink Harry gave me in the glass, I probably won't get cold.

I watch Harry empty his drink, his Adam's apple bobbing as he swallows. He licks his lips before inhaling another drag.

"It's beautiful out here," I say as I move closer to Harry. I lean my back against the railing and look toward the party.

"They did the place up nicely," he agrees.

"I've had such a good night with you, Harry. I'm really happy I got to come." I glance toward him, my eyes sliding up his three-piece suit.

"I appreciate you coming," he says, his blue eyes finding mine.

"You should be proud of yourself. You've been great tonight."

"I'm having a good time," he admits, bringing the cigarette back to his lips. "It's different, being here with you. Not having my parents here. Not being plastered."

A laugh escapes my lips. "It's amazing what happens when you're happy and actually yourself," I tease.

I look over at Harry, my heart melting. Harry looks back at me.

"Come here," he says at the same time he pulls me into a side hug.

His arm wraps around my waist, so I'm leaning into his side. I bring my hand up to his chest and let my head rest against him. Harry holds me firmly, his body warm against mine.

I can smell the smoke on Harry's jacket. His cigarette hangs in his fingers, but he doesn't bring it back up to his lips. I take another gulp of my drink, letting it warm me.

"Thank you for coming. For the support," Harry says, his voice breaking the silence. "You told me that you'd be here for me, and you are."

I want to say back, *You never need to thank me. I'll always be here for you*. And I want to. I want to say that. It would be so easy for my mouth to form the words. They'd flow out of my mouth without any effort. But I have to stop myself from

THE COUNTRY HOUSE

uttering them. Because it would be wrong.

Because Mohammad was right. I can't be everything to both of them.

And what I told Noah before I left was true. I can't be here for Harry, in this way, again. I can go to things with him as a friend. I can support him. But pretending we're together. Lying to his parents. Not labeling things to give ourselves time.

It's too hard.

On him. And on me.

Because I love Harry.

But Noah wants my heart. My entire heart. And he was right before, when he said that I haven't given it to him fully.

And it's because of Harry.

"I've had a great time too," I finally say.

I hug Harry tighter, feeling my throat constrict. I don't understand why it feels like I'm losing him. Why I feel my stomach falling through me.

Why is this so hard?

I bring my glass back up to my lips, finishing off the drink. Harry glances down at the empty glass and takes it from my hand. He sets it on the thick railing, dropping his burned-out cigarette into it.

"Every time we're together, it's always fun," Harry finally says, pulling me closer.

I squeeze my eyes shut.

"I know," I reply, my voice gravelly.

Harry must hear it because he looks down at me with concern. His brows are woven together, and his lips are pinched.

He takes my hand, and without saying a word, he leads me across the balcony. We move past the gentlemen smoking their cigars to an empty love seat. Harry sits down, pulling me down next to him.

He drops my hand and leans back, stretching out his legs. I push my back against the pillow behind me, my nerves growing. Because looking at Harry now, I know I'm going to hurt him. I know what I'm going to say is going to hurt our friendship. It's bound to. And I don't want things to change.

I don't want things to be different between us.

"Talk to me." Harry's voice pulls me out of my thoughts.

I bring my gaze to his, pressing my lips together, feeling like I could be sick.

"It's … it's about Noah." I finally get the words out.

Harry visibly frowns. "We covered all that yesterday morning, didn't we?"

"Well, sort of," I reply, clearing my throat.

"Sort of?" Harry cocks his head to the side, confusion flashing across his face. "You're together. Is there anything else to tell?"

"Kind of. He wants to tell our parents that we're …"

"You're what?" Harry asks, his blue eyes piercing mine.

"Together."

Harry glances away, obviously hurt. "You've mentioned that. Is that what you want?" he asks, pulling out another cigarette.

I watch him light it and inhale.

"I … of course I … I just … I just feel so overwhelmed, Harry. Honestly, I want to dance and cry and scream, all at the same time. I'm happy and hurting." I shake my head, frustrated with myself. I press my palms down over my dress, trying to calm down.

Harry moves forward, leaning in toward me. "Why?" he asks.

And it's a simple question.

I flick my gaze over to his, thinking about it.

Why?

Why is this so hard?

"Because when we tell our parents, it'll be real. It'll be serious. Noah ... well, you know, you can't describe him. He's not normal. He goes above and beyond. He loves deeply. He's so serious; it's consuming. But I'm happy, Harry. Really happy. It's just, if we tell everyone, then it'll be real. It'll be real, and I'll have something to lose. It will change things. And what if he stops feeling that way? What if it changes our friendship? Yours and mine. How can I feel so happy and so sad at the same time? It shouldn't be possible ..."

"Hold that thought." Harry holds up his pointer finger to me and then rises up from the couch.

I watch him walk across the balcony and through the door to go inside.

I squeeze my hands into fists, trying to get ahold of myself. But a tear escapes, rolling down my cheek.

I barely notice when Harry comes back.

"Whoa, where are the tears coming from?" he asks, rushing up to me.

"You left," I reply, wiping at my eyes.

"Mallory." Harry sits down and wraps me up in his arms. "I just got you another drink."

He pulls back, showing me that he has a glass of champagne in one hand and what looks like a chocolate truffle in the other.

"You got me a drink?" I ask, blinking.

"I thought you could use it. And obviously, I was right." He hands me the glass, urging me to bring it to my lips. "Why are you crying?"

"Because I'm sorry. Because I ..." My mouth feels wet and dry, all at once. I feel like I have a million things to say but can't say anything at all.

"You're conflicted," Harry states.

"Harry, please."

"I don't want to see you crying tonight. Please don't cry."

I wipe at my eyes.

"What do you suggest then?" I ask, not sure how to get myself out of this funk.

"Let's dance," Harry says.

"Dance?"

"Yeah. There's nothing that will cheer you up like dancing. Think about it. You weren't crying inside."

I give him a pathetic smile. "So, dancing will fix things?"

"Definitely," Harry tells me. "Finish your champagne and eat this."

He holds out the truffle for me.

I raise my eyebrows but decide he's probably right. I take a large gulp before biting into the truffle. It melts in my mouth, and the combination of chocolate and champagne is divine.

"All right, you might know what you're talking about," I say, feeling a little better.

"Good," Harry says with a smile. "Besides, I have something to tell you. Something that I hope will cheer you up."

"What is it?" I ask, finishing off the champagne. I pop the rest of the truffle into my mouth, letting Harry take my hand as he leads me back inside.

We start dancing to a slow song. Harry pulls me close, both of his hands resting at my waist. My palms are holding on to his shoulders.

"So, the news …" Harry says, suddenly looking excited.

"Yeah?" I ask, wondering where this is coming from.

"It's about Shanghai … I told my parents that I wouldn't go unless you could come too."

"You what?" I ask, my heart slamming against the inside

of my chest.

"You want to get into real estate, right? Well, my family owns a lot of it. My dad wants me to grow up? Then, fine, I will."

"What are you saying?"

"I bargained with him. He wants me in Shanghai, then I bring you. If you agree, you can take a meeting with a realty firm there."

"Why would you do that?" I ask him.

"I know it's not backpacking through Asia or anything like that, but it's ... something."

I stop dancing. "Harry, I can't leave."

"Why not?"

"My parents arrive this week. I'm supposed to move in ..." I say, but Harry cuts me off.

"You said it yourself. Your mum will have everything done. I know how serious you are about real estate. I know that moving here messed up your plans. So, come to Shanghai. It's only a few days. Your dad already likes me. I'm sure he'll let you come if he understands the opportunity."

"Harry, it's not about my parents. It's ..."

"It's about Noah," Harry says, his blue eyes on me.

"Yes," I answer.

"Noah will be here when you get back too," Harry says, surprising me. "Look, what you all have been saying, you're right. It's time I determine my path. And there is a part of me that wants this. My family name. The business. Coming to parties like this and feeling appreciated for who I am without my parents' shadow. And then there's you. I owe it to myself to figure out what I want for myself. And it's an opportunity Noah wouldn't want you to miss either. Or your family."

Harry wraps his hands around my waist. "Isn't it time we both take control of things?"

"You want me to go as what ... your girlfriend?" I question, my stomach dropping.

"I want you to go as you. My mate. My ... it ... it doesn't matter what you go as."

"Harry—"

"It would be ... two friends, being there for one another. I know how important your future is to you. And you're making me realize that my future might actually be my own too. We've both been feeling lost. Maybe this will give us some direction. Let's do it together. Come with me."

"You're asking me to go to Shanghai with you?" I ask, not believing the words, even as they come out of my mouth.

"What's stopping you?" Harry asks seriously.

So, I give him the serious answer. "Noah."

"Then, answer me one question."

"Please don't ask ..."

"Why were you so upset to tell me about you and Noah? Why are you scared about telling your parents? Why are you so afraid of it becoming real between you two? Tell me, Mallory."

"Because he could hurt me."

"You're wrong."

"Don't say that," I say, my head spinning again.

"It's because you have feelings for me, and you know that with Noah, if you make that move with him and later regret it, you'll break his heart."

"Harry ..."

"If I'm wrong, then I'm wrong," Harry states. "Look, tell your parents you two are together. Fuck, I'll tell my parents we're just mates. But it won't change anything. I think you should come. Don't come for me though. And don't stay for Noah. Make this choice for *yourself.*"

"Go to Shanghai," I say, trying to wrap my head around

the fact that Harry's even asking me this.

"It will be fun," Harry confirms, spinning me around. "I'll take you to my favorite restaurants. We can visit Yu Garden. I'll even wear a backpack one day and let you lead me around like a bloody tourist."

I look at Harry and roll my eyes. "I'm not sure most tourists walk around with Louis Vuitton backpacks," I point out.

Harry laughs, his blue eyes sparkling. "Fine, I'll leave the backpack. But then you have to agree to let me take you out properly—at least one night. After our meetings," Harry insists.

"You've really thought this through," I say, looking to Harry with real surprise.

"Of course," Harry says, looking down at me, his blond lashes batting against his cheeks.

My heart pounds in my chest.

"So, what do you say, Mallory?" Harry asks, his blue eyes on me. "Will you come to Shanghai?"

ABOUT THE AUTHOR

Jillian Dodd® is a USA Today and Amazon Top 10 best-selling author. She writes fun binge-able romance series with characters her readers fall in love with—from the boy next door in the That Boy series to the daughter of a famous actress in The Keatyn Chronicles® to a spy who might save the world in the Spy Girl® series. Her newest series include London Prep, a prep school series about a drama filled three-week exchange, and the Sex in the City-ish chick lit series, Kitty Valentine.

Jillian is married to her college sweetheart, adores writing big fat happily ever afters, wears a lot of pink, buys way too many shoes, loves to travel, and is distracted by anything covered in glitter.

Made in the USA
Las Vegas, NV
24 August 2022

53937074R00218